For my mother-in-law, Hope Buchan (1917–1997), with love

Against *her* Nature

Elizabeth Buchan lives in London with her husband and two children and worked in publishing for several years. During that time she wrote her first books for children, including *Beatrix Potter: The Story of the Creator of Peter Rabbit*. Her first novel for adults was *Daughters of the Storm*, followed by *Light of the Moon* then *Consider the Lily* — which won the 1994 Romantic Novel of the Year Award — *Perfect Love*, *Against Her Nature*, *Secrets of the Heart* and *Revenge of the Middle-Aged Woman*. Her most recent novel is *The Good Wife*. Elizabeth Buchan has sat on the committee of the Society of Authors and was a judge for the 1997 Whitbread Awards and Chairman of the Judges for the 1997 Betty Trask Award. Her short stories have been published in various magazines and broadcast on BBC Radio 4.

For further information go to www.elizabethbuchan.com

Against
her
Nature

ELIZABETH
BUCHAN

PAN BOOKS

First published 1997 by Macmillan

This edition published 1998 by Pan Books
an imprint of Pan Macmillan Ltd
Pan Macmillan, 20 New Wharf Road, London N1 9RR
Basingstoke and Oxford
Associated companies throughout the world
www.panmacmillan.com

ISBN 978-0-330-34685-6

7 9 10 8

A CIP catalogue record for this book is available from
the British Library.

Typeset by SetSystems Ltd, Saffron Waldon, Essex
Printed and bound in Great Britain by
Mackays of Chatham plc, Chatham, Kent

Acknowledgements

Very many people are owed thanks. To David Forcey who showed me round Lloyd's, answered my questions with the utmost patience and read the manuscript. To Anthony Townsend and Natalie Rizzi of Rea Brothers who read the manuscript. Both gave freely of their time and allowed me to sit in on their work. To Andy MacNab who kindly gave me permission to make use of material from his book *Immediate Action* (Bantam Press). To Isabelle Anscombe, Carole Golder, Mike Morgan, Jennifer Pantling, Suzie Procter, Lance Poynter, Tim Stephenson and Ingrid Tress who offered their help and allowed me to bombard them with questions. My debt is unquantifiable. Any mistakes are entirely mine.

Two books in particular proved useful: *Ultimate Risk* by Adam Raphael (Bantam Press, 1994) and *For Whom the Bell Tolls: The Scandalous Inside Story of the Lloyd's Crisis* by Jonathan Mantle (Sinclair Stevenson, 1992). I took factual information and drew on ideas from both these works.

Finally, I would like to thank the Macmillan team for their faith and patience, in particular my editor Suzanne Baboneau, and Hazel Orme, Philippa McEwan and Morven Knowles. Also my agent, Caroline Sheldon who, as always, proved a rock and Peta Nightingale, who helped to nurture the book along. Friends too are beyond price and my love and thanks go to Anthony Mair and Julia Peyton Jones, for making France so easy, and to Marika Cobbold, for listening.

Once again my family took the brunt. I cannot thank them enough.

Chaos Theory: The branch of mathematics used to deal with chaotic systems, for example, an engineered structure, such as an oil platform which is subjected to irregular, unpredictable stress

From the *Hutchinson Encyclopaedia*

Prologue

Perhaps it was something to do with their height: tall women are treated differently from their small sisters. Being tall means that you must work hard to blend.

Perhaps it was their differences: one from a gentle, unthreatened upbringing in Hampshire, the other from the tough outreaches of a council flat in Streatham, and they recognized in each other the polarity essential to balance.

Perhaps it was the era, which promised that all things were possible. It was not so surprising that a girl nurtured in the city's anarchy should be drawn to one to whom it had always been suggested that the world was ordered for her comfort. They were not to know that a decade of excess was closing and, with the arrival of the modern imperialists and pirates blowing in from Europe and the unleashing of natural disasters, that a furious battle would be waged between the ghosts of the past and the spectres of the future. In the bitter clash would die the belief that we had wrapped up life, with antibiotics, insurance and social security.

Whatever, the two girls met at a reception given by Women in the City (WIC) a new and, of necessity, rather poorly subscribed association. For ten seconds or so, they scrutinized each other. Long seconds. Instantly, and to her immense surprise, a love, both deep and loyal, destined to outlive feelings for lovers, perhaps husbands, trembled on the edges of Becky Vitali's uninhabited and sceptical heart but drove a spear through Tess Frant's. And that was that.

'Let me draw sustenance from life,' wrote Tess in her childish five-year diary. 'I must not fail.'

Chapter One

It is written, somewhere, that if a butterfly flaps its wings – a delicate flash of orange, blue or white – over the grasses of an English meadow, the result can be an earthquake in China. Such are the connections between events that are, to begin with, considered random.

The first letter arrived on 25 June 1987, the day of the Frants' annual cocktail party. Like most letters, it looked innocuous: in a rectangular white envelope with a typed address.

> I am writing to inform you [it said] that the Quattro
> Marine Syndicate 317/634 will produce a substantial loss
> in respect of the 1985 Underwriting Account.
>
> You will see from the enclosed letter, which Mr Quattro
> has sent to his direct Names, that the overall loss is approxi-
> mately 200 per cent of allocated premium income . . .
>
> A schedule summarizing your underwriting position as
> of 31 December 1987 is enclosed from which you will note
> that your cash call will be approximately £6,400 . . .

Colonel Frant read it in the privacy of his study at the High House. Conscious that his heart-beat had raised a little, he frowned, laid the letter to one side and rejoined his family in the kitchen.

Of its contents he said nothing.

*

Summer had applied its colours over the shires and the day was filled with bright hot sun, and with the sound of skylarks swooping over the crops in the fields that lapped the village of Appleford. By six thirty the heat had distilled and rested heavily over the land. Clearly, the sun was going to take its time to set.

As this was England, the topic of the weather was on everyone's lips.

Mrs Frant moved or, rather, sailed through the drawing room and the coveys of guests. Recognizing a superior might, steam victorious over wind-power, as it were, they gave way and many followed in little dribs into the dry, manicured garden. From time to time, her snorting, slightly anarchic laugh, so at variance with her appearance, could be heard above the murmur of conversation.

'Margery, my dear,' she said, halting beside two women on the York stone patio, and kissing the powdered cheek that had been proffered. 'How lovely.'

'Lovely,' echoed Margery Wittingstall, middle-aged, divorced and depressed, but the sentiment did not seem to register with her hostess, who turned to the second woman.

'And Jilly. How lovely too.'

Jilly Cadogan smiled, safe in the knowledge that she was a beautiful woman who donated energy and attention to the maintenance of that beauty. 'With time and money, *any* woman can be good-looking,' she was heard frequently to say to her friends, and Jilly had plenty of both.

Jilly also proffered a cheek. 'How good of you to invite us.'

On a hot summer evening, Jilly would have preferred to have been sitting in her own garden, a careful – and fashionable – concoction of scent and colour, but she seldom allowed her preferences to override her social ambitions or duties. In Jilly's case, these were routed mainly through her husband, Louis, and it was for his sake that she had donned a black linen shift and lipstick, and stood making conversation with the abandoned Margery.

'That's just what that guru chappie said. "Think the unthink-able, question the unquestioned, say the unsayable . . ."'

Mrs Frant caught the tail end of a conversation, and a somewhat tired cliché she considered, between a young Turk in the City and the local Tory grandee who resided, with a lot of fake ancestral clutter, in the manor house to the north of Appleford. Both were endeavouring to impress the other.

She beckoned to her son, Jack, who abandoned the group that contained her daughter, Tess, and Tess's friend Rebecca, or Becky as she preferred to be called.

'Hand round the drinks, darling,' she ordered fondly, never ceasing to admire her tall, rangy, unusual son who, during the twenty-five years she had known him, had never given her any worry at all. Until now. 'Your father's being a bit slow.'

A toddler in an expensive and useless blue romper-suit, of the type favoured by well-off Parisians, clung to his mother's leg while a second, older one wove between the legs of the guests unfortunate enough to be in its vicinity. Mrs Frant's invitation had specifically excluded children, and it was with mild amuse-ment that she saw that the mother, clamped, hobbled and flushed, was paying for her sanction-busting.

Satisfied, Mrs Frant moved on. A big woman, who had once been as slender as a dream, she was given in late middle age to wearing tweed skirts, floral blouses and pale stockings, none of which suited her. Today, however, in honour of her annual showcase party, which was designed to make the point – very subtly, of course – that families like the Frants were the real heart of the village, she was wearing an old-fashioned shirt-waister and flat sandals that revealed unpainted toenails. Yet, in contrast to the gaudy assembly of her guests, well-to-do and smart, there was something magnificent in Mrs Frant's refusal to submit to the tyranny of appearance: a spirit and indepen-dence that, if it had been recognized, might have been admired.

In fact, Mrs Frant was admirable in many ways, not least for her secret life. Like many people who are burdened domestically and tied to one bit of earth, a part of her had cut free, gone undercover, to explore the strange and awful regions of the spirit. Her epic journeys, she called them, secret voyages to match those of the Greek heroes, herself an Odysseus. In reality, Mrs Frant rarely ventured further than the south coast.

'Becky,' Tess Frant grabbed her friend, 'you must meet Louis Cadogan. He's rich and wicked and he's lived in Appleford for ages.' She turned to Louis. 'And this is Becky, who's also wicked but poor and wants to make lots of money.' Unfortunately, this was the sort of comment Tess made when she was nervous and struggling to be interesting and witty. Occasionally, she hit the mark. She finished the introduction in a rush. 'Becky and I met at a City do last year.'

Height, looks, energy: with his usual quickness, Louis summed up the girls. He judged Becky to be the same age as Tess. Twenty-two? Possibly twenty-three. Of course, he already knew Tess. Tall, fair, slightly plump and dressed to attract attention away from that condition, she combined innate, hopeless romanticism with innocence; Becky, tall, pencil thin and huge-eyed, hid, he saw with a clarity that startled him, an orphaned spirit under glossy hair and skin (and cheap clothes). Her face was dominated by those doe-like eyes above which were drawn, as if by a thick black pencil, a pair of eyebrows. Once seen, few would forget the curious combination of brow and eye. In that careless arrangement of features was cast her future.

And what would be the changes and transformations, wondered Louis, to dent those tender, unformed spirits and write on the untouched faces?

A significant proportion of the men she encountered were smaller than Becky. Louis Cadogan was not. He was big, but narrow, loose-limbed, well dressed and, she calculated, approximately twenty years older than she was. Instinctively she knew it was the moment to use her smile – a seductive smile that, along with her eyes and eyebrows, was the sole inheritance of any use bequeathed by the parents who had been so careless of her procreation and subsequent nurture.

'Let me guess,' said Louis, who even if he was dazzled recognized a wile. He studied the face in front of him. 'Fund management?'

'No,' said Becky. 'I've just started at Landes.'

Louis's interest quickened. Landes was one of the biggest managing agencies working at Lloyd's and, as one of Lloyd's noted underwriters (El Medici, said his friends and enemies), he knew it well. 'As?'

'A secretary. But I'm hoping to get a job as a reinsurance claims clerk.' She shrugged. 'Apprenticeship. It has to be got through.'

'And?'

'Well, I'll have to see,' said Becky. 'I don't intend to stay there long.'

Louis turned to Tess. 'How are things with you?'

After university (BA Hons, English and psychology), Tess had taken time off while she considered teaching as a career. After a year of reading through textbooks on semiotics and deconstructionism, and temping – a hideous combination – she had decided to flee the shores of literature. An active pursuit of money had been frowned on by the more intellectual undergraduates, the type with whom Tess had mixed. They had felt that Art and Culture were so much more important. At any rate, this was what they said, although Tess noted that the two who had been the most vociferous (and who had produced the plays with the most nudity and violence) had subsequently got themselves extremely well-paid jobs in advertising and the civil service. Tess was more honest and it was, after all, the eighties when, thank goodness, there was no nonsense about getting on and it was not unfashionable to be interested in making money. The upshot was that Colonel Frant made a telephone call to Louis and the job at Metrobank had materialized.

Lucky Tess. There was always some contact to fall back on. Some prop to hold her up. At least, that's what Becky had said once or twice when they'd talked over their past and their future (which did not appear to include marriage or children). It was not a bitter or envious remark, merely one that summed up the situation.

Lucky Tess.

While Tess talked to Louis, Becky was making a covert study of his English features, fashioned into good looks by generations of prudent marriage plus a fortunate deployment of genes. Those looks were lent extra interest by a pair of knowing, clever, slightly weary eyes and a mouth that suggested this was a man capable of feeling.

Then Louis made the mistake of turning his head towards Becky. Mutually startled, she by the honesty of his gaze, which told her that he wanted her, and he by the hunger in hers, they exchanged a look. This time, it was Louis who smiled at Becky.

'Hallo,' said Jack. Fed up with doing bottle duty and, wishing to chat up Becky, he pushed his way into the group.

Colonel Frant was dispensing drinks on the shaded part of the patio by the house. To the onlooker, he seemed entirely absorbed in his guests. In reality, he was mulling over his business affairs, to wit his run of profits (that is, until this morning), resulting from being a Name at Lloyd's.

Features set in a smile poised exactly between bonhomie and slight reserve, for he was a little shy at these affairs, he pressed a glass of iced champagne onto a latecomer who was in fact the chairman of the district council and a golfing companion. The glass was positively snatched from Colonel Frant's hand and the chairman, having exchanged only the briefest of greetings, hightailed it over to the group under the apple tree, which contained his mistress. Colonel Frant poured out another glass.

A man who, after leaving the Army at the age of forty-five,

had reinvented himself as a businessman and latterly as the chairman of a small fruit-importing company, he was both shrewd and cautious. But the eye contains a blind spot and it was possible that Colonel Frant did not see the whole picture with respect to his connection with Lloyd's.

Yet 1983 had seen profits of around six thousand, 1984 had jumped a little to over seven and, gloriously, in 1985 to more than nine. Nothing excessive but very nice, all the same. Colonel Frant's linen jacket was new, his shirt hailed from Jermyn Street and a gleaming set of golf clubs reposed in the hall of the High House.

'Over twenty-five thousand Names,' Nigel had said as he wooed. 'Capital base? No problem. Means requirement? Say two hundred and fifty thousand. The risk–reward ratio? Best ever. A hundred thousand underwrites three hundred and fifty and we'll split it up among some darling little syndicates.

'Covering yourself? Take out stop-loss. You know about that sort of thing. Must do.

'Good or what?'

'Tell me,' said Nigel Pavorde, members' agent, materializing at the side of Colonel Frant, 'who's the chap who's just moved into Threfall Grange?'

'Farleigh,' replied Colonel Frant. 'Made a killing with an estate agent chain in the West. His wife, though, has made him move back here.'

Nigel looked as though he had been fed a bone. 'Good or what, John? Introduce me.'

But Colonel Frant had caught his wife's gaze and picked up a champagne bottle. In its blanket of ice, the glass had sprung a delicate bloom and he wrapped it carefully in a napkin. 'Duty,' he said. 'Talk to you later.'

Nigel had a taste for outrageous waistcoats and possessed a great many. Some, the unkind, suggested that it was the only way he would ever appear interesting. Certainly, those who on first meeting him had been agreeably taken by his expansive figure and gestures found they were less so on the second encounter. Tonight, despite the heat, he was wearing a waistcoat striped in gold under a beige linen jacket, from the pocket of which he pulled a notebook.

'8 p.m. discomfort in lower stomach, 4 glasses champagne,' he wrote, on a page filled with similar notations.

He looked up to find Becky watching him. 'I like to keep a record,' he explained.

'Quite,' said Becky. 'So useful.'

'I'm Nigel Pavorde.'

Becky introduced herself, and set about finding out exactly what Nigel Pavorde did for a living.

They walked down the garden towards Eeyore's Paddock, where Tess had once kept a pony, beyond which was a meadow that Colonel Frant had bought years ago from a farmer who went bankrupt too early to be saved and subsided by the EU.

Becky had no interest in gardens but she could, and did, appreciate the sight of the meadow dotted with poppies and cornflowers, a lush, old-fashioned sight. Colonel and Mrs Frant were great conservationists and last year had been delighted to find that the tiny harvest mouse could be tempted to nest in a strategically placed tennis ball. To the south lay a flattish plain and the market town of Granton. To the west was the cricket pitch: a tended strip of emerald that managed to be both plutocratic and democratic at the same time. Jimmy Plover was hard at work mowing and the sound of his machine reverberated, vague and soothing, through bursts of the guests' conversation.

Appleford was a village in imminent danger of growing out of itself. Its centre was composed of old brick and timbered houses and of gardens awash with peonies, roses, sweet peas and verbascum. Two plaques for best-tended village were screwed into the wall above the local shop, which had recently metamorphosed into a mini-supermarket, and profits of the eighties bonanza were discernible to interested passers-by in the flashes of blue swimming pools and glimpses of conservatories to be had on the way to buy bread and milk.

At the north-east end of the village, and situated in a dip, which those who lived there swore was damp and those who did not swore was the opposite, was a housing estate, built in harsh, unforgiving red brick. Fortunately, for the aesthetically conscious, the estate did not intrude on Appleford's charm – although, now and then, some of its boys made it their business to smash windows and tear up fences fronting the listed houses.

'It's pretty here,' said Becky, who had no intention of moving into a period dwelling or of remaining in a council flat. Her full red skirt twined around her long legs and acted as a beacon to quite a few of the men present.

'Hallo again,' said Louis, bearing a bottle. 'Would either you or Nigel like a refill?'

'No, thank you,' said Becky, who was generally indifferent to food and drink.

With his free hand, Louis prised away her glass. 'You know, life is too precarious to pass up opportunities and you don't seem to me to be a natural puritan. You should never say no to champagne and you should drink the best, which this is. I advised John on the choice.'

A newcomer to the village, a widow anxious to be merry and to gain a niche, and who had made the mistake of moving away from the scene of her previous life, was circulating with a plate of rye-bread circles. 'Hallo,' she said to Louis and Nigel. 'This is my way of introducing myself.' The plate, held out to them with an obvious effort, shook slightly for Jennifer Gauntlet tended to tremble at the slightest hint of nerves.

Louis took a slippery circle and placed it in his mouth. 'How kind,' he said. 'Thank you. Now, do let me take the plate from you.'

'No, thank you,' said the Widow, who had gained control of the plate by holding it with both hands. 'It's my little duty to the kind hostess.'

11

'Louis,' said Jilly, gliding towards them, 'I think it's time we left.' She ignored both the plate held out to her and the Widow. 'Hallo, Nigel.'

'Meet Tess's friend, Becky.'

The two women assessed each other, neither drawing flattering conclusions. And, yet, they had several aspects in common.

'How very nice,' said Jilly, and turned to her husband. 'Louis, really, we should . . .'

'If,' said Louis, 'you would like to change your job, get Tess to give you my phone number.'

The Cadogans moved off, leaving Becky with Nigel, who shot his cuffs and said, 'Time for the old dins, I think.'

Tess slipped her hand into the crook of Becky's elbow and murmured, 'Thank God they're going.' But Becky's attention was fixed elsewhere.

Accompanied by a setting sun, the Frants' guests said their goodbyes and made their way home through Appleford's quiet, pretty streets, luxuriantly fringed with willow and beech, which had once witnessed Bad King John's hunting party and a progress of Good Queen Bess.

Suddenly, shockingly, the peace was shredded by three ambulances racing up the ridge, sirens blaring, towards the motorway.

Later that night, Tess lay awake in her bedroom. She thought – for she was rather interested in space and all that – of the world whirling on through the darkness and, in their eyries, of the men and women patrolling the furthest outreaches of the universe with their instruments.

Why, she thought, visualizing the winking screens and rows of mathematical calculations, if the watchers in the laboratories and observatories are slipping through time they must be encountering the future as well as the past; the conflict and cruelty to come, as chilling and devastating as that which has been.

As a child, her life had been one of sensation: ice cream dripping stickily down fingers; the whiff of new hay in Eeyore's Paddock; a scrape of leather against her thighs; stomach-aches like stones; bubbles of excitement held in her body like the first mouthful of Tizer; the strange, heart-stopping moments when she learnt something frightening, embarrassing, ominous, and wished she had not.

Now it was different. Lying there in the High House, Tess felt overwhelmed by the challenge of living, the sheer business of feeling, for her feelings ran deep and were often tempestuous and she despaired of mastering them. Above all, she longed to find God and was failing to do so, sometimes, even, berated Him for not being there. She also told herself it was bad luck to have been born into an age where there was no longer room for a Deity and where any mystery was given a scientific, rational explanation. Either that, or a documentary on television.

Longing for God was akin to feeling hunger. You could be plump, as Tess undoubtedly was, and still be a hungry person. As hungry as the thin, restless Becky. Starved. Famished. At least they had that in common. Sharing something with Becky mattered to Tess and it thrilled her to know that the need was returned.

Perhaps, if she relaxed her mind would be free to roam the highways and byways of knowledge and emotion and to make the connections that would fill her with power, energy and love.

Chapter Two

Round about the cheese course, Nigel had become a little drunk which, while not unpleasant, loosened his tongue. 'Bloody Americans!' He strove, as always, to impress his peers. 'I reckon all these court settlements will be disastrous.'

Nigel had been permanently allocated the role of buffoon (the waistcoats and notebook helped). However, it did not necessarily cancel the correctness of his observation. The willingness of American courts to settle in favour of plaintiffs – Shell was currently facing a bill for £200 million to clean up the toxic waters leaching into the water table in the Rocky Mountain Arsenal in Colorado – was affecting the insurance market.

The cheese, Cheddar and Wensleydale, was excellent, and its spicy, tangy taste was commented on knowledgeably and with affection, almost love.

'Bloody Americans,' repeated Nigel, to no one in particular, and ate his cheese. 'I wonder if this was made with pasteurized milk?'

The Bollys had met at Luc's restaurant in Leadenhall Market. A group of ten colleagues, they had been so dubbed because of their fondness for champagne by Chris Beame, who fancied himself a wit. They met to exchange gossip, because they liked one another and because it was both useful and agreeable to mull over the business. As an informal gathering, it counted two active underwriters, a managing agent, a members' agent, an investment expert and an accountant among the ten. With his beaked nose and hooded eyes, Matt Barker, an underwriter with a Midas touch and a member of Lloyd's council, gave it a welcome touch of gravitas, and Louis its glamour. Except that they all enjoyed healthy earnings, nothing of significance united them, neither taste nor lifestyle – apart from Louis's and Matt's mutual fondness for roses.

Yet once absorbed into the Lloyd's sphere something odd tended to take place. Much as patients given new hearts have been found to develop the tastes and craving of the dead donors, so recruits into the world of Lloyd's could be said to step inside the skins of the seniors.

Insiders, including the active underwriter, have by custom to demonstrate faith in their own judgement by investing their own money in their own syndicates. It was thought to be sufficient, and soothing, demonstration of good faith to the external Names. If the insiders were putting money where their mouths were, then the external Names – those like Colonel Frant, who knew nothing of the market only that they wished to make money for little effort – could rest easy.

Strangely, not one of the ten here at Luc's, neither the seniors nor the juniors eating their cheese and drinking their claret, had ever been tempted to place their personal business on the syndicates specializing in reinsurance, known as the LMX, which was reputedly flourishing. Or on those known to have long-tail liabilities. (For example, claims were coming in to some syndicates for cases of cancer caused by asbestosis as long ago as twenty years). Yet a percentage of Colonel Frant's underwriting liability had been placed in precisely these dubious areas by at least one of the men sitting round the table.

'The Far East . . .' Chris Beame had the sheen of excitement on his face. His syndicate was a relatively modest one, having around five hundred Names and an underwriting capacity of twenty million or so. Unlike some of the stuffier underwriters, he did not care – well, not *much* – if the Names on his syndicate did not include the royal and the titled. No, Chris argued that the aristocratic pot was empty and that it was better to concen-

trate on culling a new harvest of politicians, lawyers, account-
ants, businessmen, sports stars and – even – women. It was, he
had been heard to say with only a trace of complacency, a
remarkably progressive, democratic set-up.

'Self-regulation at Lloyd's,' Matt Barker had a trick of
drawing his listener into a conspiracy, whose secrets promised
to be intoxicating, 'will have to be seen to be better managed.'

Louis nodded and moved his glass around his knives.
'Tricky.'

Well back in the past, both men had been aware of, indeed
had dabbled in, activities that were not criminal – no, nothing
like that – but were open to criticism. Activities such as the
creation of baby syndicates and, when taxes had been high, a
little bond-washing.

Louis's position, which he shared with Matt, was simple: if
the opportunity was there, take it. They knew how to operate
the market, and operate it they would. There was, particularly
with regard to the younger men, a lot of sabre-rattling and
declarations of 'Let him who dares, dare.' Louis had reached
the age when he simply did it.

As a result, Louis's personal wealth could now finance rose
gardens from Arctic to Antarctic, and Matt, if he wished, could
have bought up a couple of factories specializing in the production of his favourite bright-coloured ties.

Neither man was dishonest.

Sometimes Louis asked himself why the business fascinated
him so much. Then he would recollect the childhood where
each step had been proscribed, each thought tagged with
potential damnation, each impulse questioned. A childhood in
which the Virgin Mary's dreaming face and rose-bordered
shimmering blue cloak suggested all manner of tenderness, but
the cold, hard discipline exacted by her and her Son was
anything but. A childhood where a sense of possibility had been
whittled to nothing – and from which Louis had escaped.

In part, only in part.

After a satisfactory lunch the Bollys broke up and, in the gents' afterwards, Nigel examined his reflection in the mirror. Was he imagining things or was a touch of yellow painting his eyeball? He felt for the portion of his torso containing his liver and prodded it. Nothing.

It was tiring being a hypochondriac, tiring and burdensome, and it was an effort to stave off the terrors that threatened each corner he rounded.

'What a good party it was.' The Widow cornered Angela Frant in Appleford's mini-supermarket. 'Wasn't it? It was *so* nice of you to invite me.'

She looked for further affirmation to Jilly, who was buying *Tatler* at the counter on her way to her monthly appointment with her astrologer and then on up to London for a little lunch.

Jilly smiled but with not too much warmth, for the Widow had been marked down in her mental social register as a non-runner. She waited while Jennifer coaxed forth the coins in her plastic purse for a tin of soup, a small loaf, a half tin of baked beans, and then paid for her magazine.

She drove to Granton – once a solid market town, specializing in candles and cattle, now a vision of white paint and shop windows selling the *World of Interiors* magazine, artificial flowers and coloured bathroom fittings – more than ready for an expensive dose of reassurance.

Mercury is making a good aspect to Uranus, Jilly was told. Be prepared for changes. She must also take care not to overstretch herself. Jilly made an immediate resolution to cut down on her charity work.

Money, pronounced the astrologer, who did her homework, is there. Plenty of it. But beware the tricky aspects of Pluto in your House.

*

17

On the way home, Mrs Frant asked the Widow if she would mind signing up to help with the annual fête. 'Then,' she added, 'there are the cricket teas. I think Mrs Thrive would appreciate some help.' The gist of Mrs Frant's meaning was that Eleanor Thrive, who could not organize the contents of a lavender bag, was as usual making a hash of her rota. The implication was also that, being alone, the Widow would have plenty of time to give. But, Jennifer bravely concluded, it was infinitely more comforting and less bitter to be included on a dubious basis than not at all.

Mrs Frant walked slowly back to the High House, so-called because it had been built by a Regency remittance man on the top of the only rise in a flat swathe of rolling Hampshire land. The rise did not immediately strike the onlooker as very high but she liked to think of the house as occupying a rarefied stratum with purer air; it was a home that worked to make her better.

At present, she required the reassurance: Jack, her good and wonderful son, was becoming a source of worry.

If he had given her no trouble during his childhood, Jack had, nevertheless, been difficult to understand. Or, at least, his mother found his motives and ambitions, and the marked puritan streak, mystifying and, lately, a source of pain. Certainly, his progress since leaving Oxford with a degree in philosophy had not conformed – if taking a series of temporary jobs in reputable charities was not conforming. He had been lined up for a position at a merchant bank, and all would have been well. But he had had other ideas and held out stubbornly to work in Africa for a charity. It was Tess who had gone into the merchant bank.

'Jack is a missionary *manqué*,' Tess informed Becky as they waited at Waterloo for the train down to Appleford, the weekend following the party. 'He sort of burns with fervour to do good, or at least to flagellate himself.'

'Why?'

Tess raised her shoulders and stepped back to allow a flock of girls to scuttle down the platform. 'Some strange tic in his make-up. Maybe we have a saint in our past.'

Becky, who that week had been telephoned twice by Jack, had her own views. He had already declared his love for her (it took him five seconds, he had said) and when she protested that he did not know her, Jack asked why that mattered.

He was waiting for them at the station and drove them back to Appleford. Prowling and preoccupied, Mrs Frant fed them soup and roast chicken and watched her children – a maternal computer recording heart-beats, skin tone, mental fitness. Both the quality and intensity of her gaze, Becky felt, were disconcerting but, then, she possessed no knowledge, no memory of maternal love.

Like his sister, Jack was fair, but unlike her lush, moisturized-by-rain looks, his seemed bleached in anticipation of the sun.

'Tess was quite right,' he said, in a clever way, as he bore Becky off for a drink at the Plume of Feathers.

'About what?' Becky matched his pace and her red skirt swirled in a way that made Jack feel quite dizzy.

'You're a red colour. Vivid and scarlet. Like a poppy.'

Becky was amused. 'And Tess?'

Jack halted at the entrance to the pub. 'Let's sit in the garden. What colour do *you* think she is?'

'Powder blue. Soft and full of depth.' Becky tested a bench with her finger. 'This one's damp.'

'Come here, then.' As Jack sat down beside her, she felt his energy and fervour trap her in a magnetic field. They talked about his future and Becky's work and, every so often, Jack turned his gaze on the English countryside around them, bathed in the milky light of a high summer evening.

For Jack, the vista was bred into his blood and bone, as familiar as the skin on his palm, and it barely registered as he contemplated the idea of another landscape: lunar, unyielding, irradiated with intense light. One, moreover, where he would be needed.

'It's a wounded world,' he announced.

Becky stared at him. 'Really?' Endeavouring to understand what he meant, she said, 'The world has always been wounded, as you put it.'

Later Jack got up to fetch a second round and, a little hazy with wine, Becky watched his progress with an uncharacteristic mix of emotions. Desire, a worship of his beauty and strength, a yearning to be part of them.

'Where do you come from?' Jack put the refilled glasses on the table, spotted with mould.

'It's very peculiar.' Becky watched his expression. 'Everyone always wants to know where I've come *from*.'

'It's your surname.'

Becky's eyebrows rose. 'My father was Italian. Or so I'm told.'

'Your mother,' Aunt Jean informed her niece, 'sinned and she didn't stand a chance.'

'Why, Aunt Jean?'

'Because, because ...' Aunt Jean had been washing up during this conversation and up to her wrists in clumpy suds '... your silly mother listened to the first man who came along. Or rather, if she had stuck to listening and not laid on her back, it would have been a different story. And then she lumbers me with you.'

Aunt Jean had been lumbered with many things. Her heart complaint. Her religion. Her job cleaning offices in the evening. And, if I'm anything like my mother, Becky concluded, I know she was not taken in. She merely took what she wanted and made a mistake.

That's all.

'Your aunt Jean brought you up, then.' Jack's expression was tender as his blue eyes sought and engaged Becky's huge, deceptively soft ones. His compassion, not yet outweighed by middle-aged sternness or zeal, was a huge, slippery emotion that often gushed out of control. From suffering Africa to the damaged spider in the garden shed, his pity flowed indiscriminately. It flowed now, wrapping Becky in the downiest of coverings.

'My mother abandoned me when I was a couple of months old,' said Becky, whose reservoir of pity was, by comparison, limited. Especially, to be fair, in relation to herself . . . 'Which was hard for my aunt Jean who did not, does not, like children.'

'Poor baby . . .' Jack's gaze was now firmly anchored on new details: Becky's skin lustre, the sharp slash of her collar bone and, despite her height, her air of fragility.

A modern woman: clever, sensuous, knowing. Lover, siren, . . . achiever?

Jack found himself thinking foolish thoughts . . . that Becky had a flame burning inside her. A bright, leaping flame that would cast warmth over, that would be shared with, the right person.

'Sentimentality,' she was saying, 'is a weakness. I gather my mother is living up north somewhere. That's all I know.'

Jack took her home the long way, via the footpath that ran trenchant, across a cornfield. At its edge, he stopped abruptly, took her in his arms and kissed her. Unguarded and disarmed by the unfamiliar harmonies of earth and sky, Becky submitted, her busy mind for once still and quiet.

Heat rose from the baked perimeter of the field, the smells of chalky earth and ripening grain, and the chorus from the swifts high up accompanied the desire running through Jack and Becky.

I don't like her.

In her garden, Mrs Frant was marching her routes, which

she did every day. This one took her past the rose bed – too much orange, she decided – and along the herbaceous border. She stopped and bent over.

Where was the cosmos? Ah, there, almost hidden by the selfish, springy growth of a garnet penstemon. The cosmos was special – its deep blackish-purplish colour and chocolate scent promising all manner of revelations – and autumn without the cosmos (she liked the name, too) was not autumn.

Satisfied, Mrs Frant marched on.

Marching the routes stilled and soothed her. It imported structure and rhythm into her day, into her spirit, *on which she could rely*. And, provided she followed the exact path of the chosen route, things would be well.

'I don't like her, John,' she had told her husband. 'She means trouble.'

Angela Frant was a traditional matron, much concerned with parish matters, the WI and WRVS, but one with unexpected reserves. While Colonel Frant's daytime musings might focus on the pound's climb or fall against the dollar (the $1.55 during the dreadful 1976 providing a benchmark) or, latterly, *that* letter, Mrs Frant found time to ponder the implications of world famine, France's political configurations and the Russian nuclear disaster at Chernobyl. The broad sweep was Mrs Frant's territory, the minutiae her husband's. It was a standing joke between them that she never read the small print.

Yet when it came to her children, Mrs Frant was as parochial as it was possible to be; living proof that maternal love is an anvil on which the sharpest of swords are forged.

'Rebecca is not suitable for Jack.'

'Aren't you jumping the gun? Jack's enjoying himself, that's all. Becky is very taking.'

Mrs Frant had noted the 'Becky'. She walked on down the garden towards the paddock on her now thickened ankles. Rebecca, she concluded correctly, is on the make. With his job prospects, Jack would make a good catch and, clearly, there was a bit of money in the family. All the things she wants.

When she put this point of view to her husband, he surprised her.

'Don't be silly, darling.' Lately, Colonel Frant had only used 'darling' when he was irritated. 'Girls don't think like that, these days. Anyway, how do you know what she wants?'

'I know.'

The image of Becky buried itself in Mrs Frant's mind, and she carried it carefully and self-consciously, exhuming it from time to time for examination.

In fact, Jack was in a bind for he could think of little other than Becky. Quite apart from his African ambitions warring with the merchant bank, there was the thorny problem of Penelope (an earnest BA Hons in agriculture, and putative co-worker in Ethiopia), who was standing by at her home in Reading, waiting for the telephone call.

Instead of phoning and embarking on the Reading pilgrimage, which he had faithfully promised the faithful Penelope he would do, Jack tracked down Becky at Paradise Flats in Streatham.

Becky had just got back from work. She let him into the ground-floor flat in the block and ushered him into the main room, off which opened two bedrooms and a kitchen. The smell from yesterday's supper of tinned steak and kidney pie lingered in the air and a pile of clean washing roosted in one corner. In the flat upstairs, someone was trying to flush a lavatory.

Becky apologized for the state of the room. 'Aunt Jean's out cleaning and her work with the Holy Spirit during the day generally leaves her too tired to do her own housework. *Ergo*, God must be a man,' she explained for Jack's benefit, adding, 'the God Squad was over here last night. Tea, ginger biscuits and sing along with the Lord.'

But he was too full of other ideas to sympathize. 'I've been talking to my contact in HAT.'

'In what?'

'Help for Africa Today. It's partly funded by UNESCO, partly by a government aid agency. They need workers for a limited period in Ethiopia and it might be possible to get taken on. It would be perfect.'

A mental picture spread out before Becky. Of negotiating with officials and civil servants under a hot sun. Of walking between children with outstretched hands. Of being congratulated on her skills . . .

'Good God,' she said and, for an awful second or two, Jack thought she was laughing at him. 'What about the magnificent Penelope?'

'Penny? Well, I've confessed to her. She's . . . um sad, but she's going out to Africa whatever happens.'

I could, thought Becky, rummaging in the dark areas of her heart, allow Paradise Flats to rule my life. They could be the template for the way I am. For ever. I could allow myself never to move on.

Deep-seated melancholy induced by a deprived background was a state of mind she had often mulled over and rejected. Not for Becky was the depression induced by unsatisfactory vitamin levels, high-rise vertigo or the tyranny of no hope. Nevertheless, she darted a look of dislike at her aunt's flowered overall hanging behind the door.

'Poor Penelope,' she said. 'I do understand her feelings.'

A large smile spread over Jack's thin face, and his expression grew tender at this evidence of his loved one's generosity. 'I knew you would.'

He yearned so to cherish her, much as he would cherish his starving charges in the camp. Becky stretched out a hand and Jack seized it.

'I've got a job,' she said. 'And I don't want to leave it.'

Jack's face fell. The script he had written during the long sleepless nights portrayed him as resourceful and irresistible. He studied his shoes. They required polishing and, clearly, so did he. Before he knew what he was doing, he had slid to his knees in front of Becky's chair and recaptured her hand. The upkeep of the floor had defeated Aunt Jean and an upsurge of dust accompanied the movement. Outside, a summer storm was lashing south London into a frenzy, a thrilling shuddering backdrop that Romantics demanded for the significant encounter. (Think Beethoven. Think Goethe. Think Brontë.)

'Oh, Becky,' he murmured, thus exposed and yearning. 'What have you done to me?'

Becky's eyes were enormous as she ticked off the consequences of being weakened by love. There knelt her would-be lover: a big, golden, nervous example of its power, stripped by it to the bone. She bent over and touched his mouth with a finger, letting it slide, light and uncommitted, around the contours of his mouth, and relishing the slight harshness of his shaved skin.

Somehow, for the moment at any rate, Jack had dodged through the entrenchments dug into her stoutly defended heart. Why Becky Vitali, she thought, dazzled, you've been missing out.

She noticed a tiny tremor in his hands and smelt the sharp aphrodisiacal tang of male sweat. 'What do you want, Jack?'

Afterwards, Jack gathered Becky in his arms. 'Why don't we forget all this?' He meant jobs, family, London. 'We'll do worthwhile things, you and I.'

He sounded energized and directed. A tangle of hair and limbs, Becky stared past his shoulder at the ceiling. (NB A web of mould appeared to have taken root at the junction of the two big cracks. Reason? Neighbour's overflowing bath? Decaying joists? The council had promised a makeover.) She was limp and deliciously drowsy.

'Why not?' she murmured.

*

'*Drive* to Africa! Drive there?' Mrs Frant was horribly aware that she sounded like a parrot. She was wearing rubber gloves and had a duster in one hand.

Jabbing her finger down on a pink oblong, Becky looked up from a map of the Sahara that she and Jack had unrolled over the dining-room table at the High House. She had pulled back her hair and was wearing khaki shorts and a T-shirt.

Jack ignored his mother. 'Which route do you think, Bec?'

'Tamanrassat would be the main stop. Presumably they'd have supplies out there.'

Mrs Frant sank down on a chair opposite them and listened. Phrases such as 'dry season' and 'wind factor' were being bandied about. 'Listen to me,' she lunged at the table with the duster, 'this is not on, Jack. You have your job to think about. So do you, Rebecca. They won't make allowances while you jaunt off to Africa.' She rubbed savagely at the table top: it could have been Becky's face that she was endeavouring to obliterate.

Her son looked up, and Mrs Frant's heart squeezed with fear. 'Don't worry, Mum,' he said. 'This is the final fling before we settle down. One glorious expedition and then I'll come home and be as good as gold.'

Mrs Frant's dusting movement continued. Does she dust in her sleep, wondered Becky.

'Promise,' said Jack.

Chapter Three

Colonel Frant's career had been distinguished by a certain sort of courage, the kind that did not question too much and got on with it. He was not used to asking favours or advice and was surprisingly diffident – at least, with regard to himself. It was with reluctance that he sat down in his study to write a letter to the managing agent.

'I am sorry to be bothering you on such a subject,' he wrote, 'but I wonder if you could clarify my position a little more precisely? Am I likely to incur more cash calls?'

The letter that came back suggested that the Colonel was worrying unnecessarily, and that his exposure was such that any cash calls would, in the event, be paid for by profits in other areas.

Looking back, Louis was aware that his meeting with John Frant in the Bluebell Wood had been of significance. That it was accidental, and incidental, did not alter or diminish its importance.

Both men were walking the dog and, as they approached each other from opposite directions through the greenish light filtered by the trees, the dogs wheeling and circling, they had time to make choices.

'I wonder, old chap,' said Colonel Frant, 'if you would give me some advice? I'm a little concerned about my exposure. Do you think I should resign from Lloyd's?'

Louis clicked his fingers and Brazen came to heel, bringing with him the odour of hot dog and saliva. The rankness curled under the noses of the men.

'No. I don't think so.' Louis was as aware as any working Name of the dangers of under-capacity. That is, of Names such as Colonel Frant not possessing enough liquid capital to pay for the cash calls in bad years. 'You should be fine. But if you like I'll have a word with Nigel, who should look into it for you.' He spoke with the advantage of possessing knowledge that he did not impart. Colonel Frant listened with the disadvantage of ignorance, which he should have sought to alleviate. Neither questioned further.

They parted. One to walk home, reasonably reassured. The other to pursue his way through the wood, dry and brittle with drought, up onto the ridge where Caesar and his men once camped. From this vantage point Appleford appeared untouched, for the road and housing estate were hidden. Only the grey stone spire of the church and a cluster of houses could be seen, drowsy and complete.

Becky and Tess were comparatively new friends and, as is the case with older friendships, areas had not yet emerged that were unwise to examine. They discussed everything, obsessively and at length. It was extraordinary, Tess exclaimed, how every detail, every nuance that they aired of their feelings drew them closer together, and how well they understood each other.

Becky was less sure of the last point but willing, for the time being at any rate, to go along with it.

'You really don't mind about me and Jack?' she asked Tess, for the fourth time. She seemed uneasy.

It was Friday night and the two girls had been to a French film in Notting Hill Gate and had emerged blinking into the night.

Tess did not stop to reflect. 'Of *course* not. I love the idea. Why should I mind?'

The certainty returned to Becky's expression. 'As long as you don't object.'

Her best friend. Her loved brother. Tess admired the neatness and symmetry of the affair and, since it did not occur to her that things did not always happen for the best, she sat firmly on the occasional stab of jealousy. Becky had been hers first and, sometimes, it pained her a little to see Jack claim her.

Funnily enough, for she did not often waste energy on such sensitivities, Becky understood. 'But I love you too,' she said, and gave Tess a quick kiss before running to catch her bus home. After a few paces, she turned to look back. 'Mind you go to that party,' she called.

Tess had been invited to a party by a colleague and Becky had had to work hard to persuade her to go. Tess had declared that she was too fat and the women would be beautiful. Becky replied that Tess was in danger of living too much inside herself and it was making her lazy.

'It's too easy to turn inwards,' she scolded. 'And, given half a chance, that's what you'd do. You'll end up holding parties in your head and becoming a recluse.'

Tess was so pleased and flattered that Becky had bothered to think about her in such depth and with such a degree of insight that she found herself agreeing to go.

London was swathed in late summer dust, whirling pollens and pollution, and the following evening Tess sneezed several times as she walked down the Chelsea street. So fresh and inviting earlier in the year, gardens were now filled with ochre and yellow, their city soil exhausted by the demands made on it.

The party was being held in a house owned by the portfolio administrator at Metrobank. By nine o'clock it was in full swing and Tess had been hating it for the last half-hour.

'Hallo,' said a square-jawed, square-shouldered man, with a

lock of dark hair falling over his forehead. 'I'm George Mason and I've been watching you.' (Watching Tess's treacherous, glowing skin with its frequent blushes.)

'Hi.' Tess hated herself when she said hi. She searched in her handbag for her cigarettes.

'And this is Iain MacKenzie,' said George, pointing at the older man who stood beside him. 'Fellow officer and friend who hauls me out of trouble. Frequently. I give you fair warning that where I go Iain comes too. Providing Flora, the wife – his wife, I mean – lets him.'

'Will you shut up?' Iain smiled at Tess. 'One glass and he reverts.'

'How do you do?' said Tess.

Iain took her hand. His was warm and large. 'It's nice to meet you but I can see Flora signalling, so . . .'

George watched his friend's retreating back. 'Ruled by his wife,' he said.

A youth lurched past them, pupils boiled-looking and drugged.

'This is the sort of party,' Tess said, 'where if anyone looks deep into your eyes, it's to see their own reflection.'

George bent over and looked deep into hers. 'In yours I see a maiden who needs rescuing.'

It is not often in a life that its course is determined within a second, but when it does happen, it is worth recording. Tess always remembered the exact scent of the tobacco plants in the terracotta pot on the patio, the colours of the women's clothes, the strange, whitish quality of the sky.

'You look interesting,' he told her, still looking into . . . What *was* he looking into? Her soul? 'I know you're interesting.'

Cigarette in hand, and bothered by his actorish quality, she looked back at him, her lower lip caught, in her confusion, between her teeth. Her silky, youthful bloom caught George on the raw.

'George!' shrieked a voice. 'Darling, darling! Where've you been with not a squeak out of naughty you?' In a Lycra dress that barely covered her rump, a girl wrapped thin arms around George's neck and kissed him over and over again.

Women, Tess had once been lectured by a feminist, should make the running. Consider for how long the chains have been round our necks. *Break 'em.* She considered what the running might be in this sort of situation and concluded, not for the first time, that theory and practice were not related.

George and the girl appeared to be wriggling about satisfactorily and Tess was awed to see that she was not wearing any knickers. Behind the girl's back, George raised one finger and pointed it at Tess. 'Wait,' he mouthed.

Tess slid away from him and the entwined nymph and went to admire the small, smart London garden. On balance, she did not rate being young, a condition that left her frequently depressed and underlined her inexperience and sense of powerlessness.

It was not a fashionable view, but bugger that, she thought.

She lit another cigarette. Nicotine, wonderful nicotine, burned its way into her system and the smoke hit the back of her throat with its customary thud. Glorious, unselfish cigarettes, little pencils of comfort and courage. Tess smoked hers down to the stub then buried it in the flowerbed.

'Dinner.' George Mason had detached himself from Miss Lycra. He did not seem to think that she might say no.

Nor could she.

Over dinner in a restaurant poised equidistant between the very smart and the avoidable, George spoke on the subject in which he appeared to excel: himself. Charming and persuasive, he threw disconcerting flashes of modesty and humour into the sparkle, much as dun-coloured feathers among fancy plumage soothe the eye. Yet Tess was not entirely convinced for she gained the impression that this display was an effort for him,

31

even distasteful. She suspected, too, that he did not like himself very much, just as she did not always like herself either, and her romantic instincts stirred.

'The Army sent me to university. Edinburgh. I was lucky and got an early captaincy.'

'How old are you?'

'Twenty-eight.'

'And then?'

George's attitude suggested that what he was going to say did not matter at all. 'Northern Ireland. I had a good tour and my platoon found a cache of explosives.' Tess had an impression that she was looking at a file marked 'Top Secret'. George paused, his unmilitary hair falling across his forehead, and decided to close the file, leaving her tantalized. 'Success is always useful.'

For the life of her, Tess could think of nothing interesting to say. Her tongue was tied, her waistband was tight and never, ever again would she eat dessert. How else could she ever be naked in front of this man? She dropped her head between her hands and pushed back her heavy fair hair. When her face emerged, the skin was stained a pure rose.

'I wonder,' she said at last, 'how we would be, how we would think, if we did not have the Northern Ireland problem. Like the Empire, it shapes us.'

'Ah,' said George, eyes narrowed. 'The psychology of politics.'

He was teasing her, perhaps even patronizing her. Tess's flush deepened but she ploughed on. 'We have a dark edge running along one of our perimeters.'

After an awful moment, when Tess could have died for the banality of her remark, George said, 'Yes, I suppose you're right . . .'

On leaving the restaurant, George asked, 'Where do you live?'

'In Pimlico. I have a flat there. Or, rather, it's my father's and he lets me rent it.'

'Ah,' said George. 'That's nice.'

'Hurry up, petal,' said Freddie Ahern. 'Bill's been asking for you.'

Tess opened her drawer – a horrible sight – and stuffed her handbag into it. Then she remembered her pen, opened the drawer again and extracted it with her reading glasses. 'What does he want?'

'There's a dowager, rich, rich, rich, who he wants netting in and thought you should sit in on the meeting. Then he'll want you to set up the new portfolio.'

'Right.' Tess's hair had worked loose from its velvet scrunchy and she adjusted it before grabbing her things. As she passed him, she tapped Freddie on the head with her pen. 'Don't you look so smug, Frederick. Your turn next.'

Considering that he was sitting down, Freddie did a remarkable imitation of a flounce.

When she came back to her desk, feeling quite pleased with her performance, the office was an organized frenzy. The previous day there had been one of the biggest rights issues of the decade and the price had gone through the roof. Today, at 9.01 a.m., something had gone wrong and it was falling.

'What the devil . . . ?' Tess's director, Bill – thirty-fiveish, wearing a blue striped shirt, red braces and a red tie – stared at the screen where the Strip revealed a large wobble. 'You'd better offload the smaller holdings and top-slice the larger.'

Women, Bill had mentioned to Tess in passing when she had been hired, are not just good on the eye. Had she got it?

Tess had got it.

'OK. OK . . .' Kit, the assistant director – thirtyish, wearing a red-striped shirt and blue tie – swivelled round to face Tess. 'Beam up my holdings,' he said. 'Give me the numbers.'

She sprang into activity. Since the stock had only been acquired the day before, the print-out was no help and she used the screen. 'OK, Kit,' she said. 'Here we go.'

She heard him get on the phone to the sales trader, who would get on the phone to market-makers, and sat back.

Freddie winked at her. 'Go and get me some coffee,' he said naughtily.

She looked at him, formulating something witty and stinging with which to reply, and froze. 'Oh, my God, Freddie. I've done something terrible. I've given Kit the total holdings. Not just his.'

'Christ,' said Freddie, and turned pale for her. After a moment or two, he said, 'I'll send a large bouquet to the funeral.'

Tess got up. Everything about her was shaking. 'Make it large and lilies,' she said, and made her way across to Kit's desk.

'You *what?*' Kit stared at Tess. 'You . . .' Words failed him. 'You know how much money we could lose? Well, you get on the phone and explain and now. Make good.'

By the end of a morning's frantic work, the situation was mostly retrieved, but not entirely. Bill had hauled Tess over the coals in front of the whole office, back room and all. 'Here is an example,' he had said, voice pitched exactly to take in everyone, 'of someone who has not got the little mind back into gear after a weekend of excess. Yes?'

Yes and no. Tess had spent most of Sunday in a daze, going over and over her meeting with George who had deposited her back at the flat in the small hours with the promise: 'See you sometime.'

Her punishment could have been worse, far worse. After all, she had made a mistake. Initially Tess had felt that she would die, but now detected a little iron creep into her soul. That was how it was. You made a mistake. You got on with it.

George waited a week then rang to suggest they had dinner. She came home weak with laughter for he turned out to be an expert mimic. After that, they met frequently but the affair did not progress. At least, not as Tess wished it to. Fuelled by laughter and an instinct that there was more to him than he was permitting her to see, she fell headlong in love ... arms whirling above her dazzled head, her heart pulsing with the electricity of passion, her mind filled with images of glory.

'I can't work it out,' she confided to Becky, over an evening drink in a crowded bar in Broadgate. 'I'm not sure what he's playing at. He's taken me out several times, dinner, walks, that sort of thing. But he's being a gentleman.'

Becky ran over several possibilities in her mind as to why George was failing to come up to scratch.

Non-gentlemen, Tess had been taught by the careful Mrs Frant, ravished females with lustiness and the lack of considera-tion of William the Conqueror's knights. Gentlemen took their time. Tess had queried whether, since the ends appeared to be the same, the means mattered. 'Without a doubt,' Mrs Frant had replied firmly.

'What do I do, Bec? Is it because I'm too fat?'

'For the last time, Tess, you're *not* fat.'

'I feel it, and that's the same thing.' Tess helped herself to more crisps. '*What do I do?*'

But Becky seemed far away, preoccupied with matters of her own.

'Come back,' said Tess. 'I need you.'

'Sorry.' Becky pushed her mineral water round in a circle.

'How's Jack?'

'Fine,' said Becky, but her tone suggested the opposite.

'Everything's all right?'

Eyes veiled, Becky smiled at her. 'Everything's fine. I'm just tired, that's all, and Aunt Jean is driving me potty. I can't wait to get out.'

'You will soon.' Tess was thinking of the African expedition.

'Yes, I suppose so,' said Becky.

Tess returned to her own agenda. 'Well, what do I do, Becky?'

'Ask him, for God's sake. It's easy.'

Women, break your chains.

On the tube back to Pimlico, Tess analysed the battle-cry. What did it mean exactly? When hormones, passion and biology fused, it was impossible *not* to feel imprisoned. She raged at her stupidity at being felled by love just when she was required to be free.

She wanted to concentrate on her work, but instead she was mugging up topics such as 'Arms and the Modern World', 'Does the Army Have a Role in the Post-Nuclear Theatre?', 'The Ethics of Killing', in a jumble of will-he-won't-he? and does-he-doesn't-he?.

Love, it seemed, stole your wits, your conversation, your sleep and your muscle tone. What a thief it was. Mrs Frant had done her duty in lecturing her daughter on rape and rapine, but she had neglected to inform her how physical love was, how uncomfortable its effects.

Tess looked down at her handbag, bulging on her knee, and asked herself: What if this distracting condition is long-term?

'Surf the market,' said a naughty, malicious Freddie in her ear. 'Easy go . . . that's how the boys do it.'

That night, after a pasta dinner in Chelsea, Tess, exhausted as she was, looked George in the eye and said, 'Would you like to go to bed with me?'

George's attention was brought back to the flushed, yearning, tenderly disposed Tess, for he had been thinking of something else not to be shared and not to be spoken about. And it was that remoteness that nagged and galvanized Tess.

He is, she thought, observing every detail, beautiful. He was made of fine material: brocade, velvet and silk from the Emperor's garden.

George would have been mad not to have accepted the

invitation, and if George was many things about which Tess had no idea, mad was not one of them.

Latterly, the instructions from God to Aunt Jean had taken a more specific turn and Aunt Jean had been told to Involve Herself More With the Homeless. The result was confusion. While the Mission flourished, the flat and her niece were neglected.

God had caught her, Aunt Jean once confessed to Becky, not on the road to Damascus but on the bus for Streatham High Road, which was as good a place as any. He had caught her at the bit where Etam and Dorothy Perkins battle it out for customers by the traffic lights. At that vital intersection, he had arrived, scooped her up and irradiated her life with purpose and love.

As far as it was in her nature to be so, Becky was glad for her aunt. Sometimes she questioned why the aforementioned Love, which apparently brimmed over in her aunt for others, never flowed towards her, for Aunt Jean only tolerated her niece.

'Why does it have to be God?' Becky was driven to ask one evening, after Aunt Jean had come home stinking of a drug addict's vomit. 'Why couldn't you have fallen in love with Mammon? Or a pools winner so we could have a new bathroom?'

Small and, despite the heart condition, pickled in tobacco, Aunt Jean favoured Becky with a look that certainly did not contain Love but, rather, combined the ruthlessness of the righteous with pity for one who was so bereft of spiritual resources as to ask the question in the first place.

She peeled off her bright pink cardigan, dropped it into the sink and ran cold water over it. Becky shuddered.

'Why not God?' replied her aunt, as if that wrapped up most of the great questions posed by humanity. 'Why not Him?'

'Because He's selfish and He hasn't got His head round

plumbing,' answered Becky. 'I must introduce you to Tess. The two of you would get on.'

Her aunt whirled round: an ageing messenger on earth. 'If you say anything more, then you'll have to go.'

'Don't make it too easy.' Becky's eyebrows snapped together. 'Just say the word.'

'Huh,' said Aunt Jean, and added, with a dignity that tore at Becky's heart, 'What about the free rent I grant you?'

Even her language is Biblical, thought Becky savagely, and that damn rent.

Swaying a little, the two women faced each other, the older struggling not to give in to temper and sinful thoughts about the younger.

If Aunt Jean had made one move to touch Becky, to offer affection, then Becky might have been different, might have made different decisions. But none came.

Becky leant back against the cheap wallpaper, felt the uneven texture between her splayed fingers and laughed at the sight of the two of them squared up like gladiators.

Aunt Jean finished washing out the pink cardigan and laid it flat on the *Streatham Advertiser*. A series of drops plopped steadily off the end of the sleeves. 'There's a tin of chilli on the shelf,' she said. 'Heat it up.'

Becky peered into the courtyard of the flats. An iron pulse beat in her, pushing life around her body. Out there, framed by the council's plate-glass window, another life gushed and swirled with dust, pollution and effluent. With an almost righteous anger, she tallied up the peeling paint, the grimy net curtains, the broken glass lapping the dustbins.

'I love you, Becky,' Jack had said, when he phoned earlier, and she had looked out of the window facing the road where a huge advertising hoarding was plastered with promises and glossy lies. She had stared at it hungrily.

'Aren't you going to say anything, Becky?' Jack was jumpy.

'Love you too.'

Running alongside the crackle of static from the nylon carpet, the persistent drip of the tap, the smell of damp that made her nose prick, the billboard dreams were seductive and siren-like.

Becky made a second phone call.

We are used to plagues, concluded Tess pacing the sitting room of the flat, the Black Death, Spanish influenza, Aids, and we understand them. As humans we like to pay for our sins and, the link between oestrogen and guilt being apparently solid, women are good at exploiting the highways and byways of guilt's octopoid properties.

Actually, money is less easy to quantify and love is hardest of all. A connection between love and work is, indeed, being spun together in our minds, a linkage that has not been traditionally feminine. But this is what happens in human history. The myths change.

Becky and I are thoroughly modern women, for we considered *eros* to be only a part of our lives – or that is what we *want* to believe. Our work is important, our men are important but neither is of greater importance than the other.

'I am so happy, so happy,' wrote Tess in her diary. 'And yet so unhappy.'

Chapter Four

Before she met Louis for coffee Becky had already made a reconnaissance of Mawby Brothers. Close to the Lloyd's building, its offices were built with a similar flamboyance and arrogance. Yet it worked. Light refracted through plate glass, illuminating a temple filled with exotic plants and a tree whose importation costs had had to be fudged by the architect.

Water ran from a feature in the centre of the atrium, voices issued from offices built off the central area and a large board, around which clustered a permanent group, flashed up figures in neon red and yellow. Clad in post-modernist steel and glass, Delphi had apparently abandoned the scented hills and enamelled skies of Greece, whirled through the centuries and alighted near Lime Street. Becky liked what she saw. It made her feel alive, important, and told her that she was now in the sight of the right horizon.

Louis had suggested that they meet before the interview at Mawby's which, at her request, he had set up for her. It was, she supposed, a favoured method of seduction.

They met in an up-market coffee bar of the kind invading the City – cappuccinos and fresh, good sandwiches. Becky refused the latter and only sipped the former. Louis smiled and made no effort to conceal that he was observing her closely. However coolly she had determined to handle this encounter, his effect on Becky was precisely as he would have wished.

'I suspect you don't eat much.'

His acuteness touched her, for it confirmed that he had considered *her* not just her body. 'I don't.'

'Tell me what you know.'

'The crucial requirement of insurance, any insurance, is the need to spread the risk. The market is divided into two. The primary insurer, who does the deal with the broker placing the insurance, and the reinsurers, who reduce the risk of the primary insurer. The brokers place the business.'

She was pleased at her prowess and, infected by her pleasure, Louis said, 'Obviously you were a child who mastered the tongue-twister. Peter Piper picked, et cetera.'

Becky laughed. 'How did you guess?'

He picked up his cup and she smelt an expensive aftershave, and heard the soft little sound of his costly shirt moving beneath the material of his Savile Row suit. In his turn, Louis allowed Becky to scrutinize him. As yet, she was too young to have learnt to conceal her thoughts and he was more than a little stirred by her ambition and energy. A pilgrim, he thought. At the beginning . . .

He reached across the table and placed a finger under her chin – a gesture that he had no right to make. Very gently, she removed it. 'You mustn't do that.'

'Why not?'

'Because I haven't given you permission.'

'True . . .'

Louis felt a little ashamed when he saw her visibly relax.

'Sorry,' she said, worried suddenly that she had blown her opportunity.

'It's all right.'

Lloyd's dealt in money's mythical properties, or so Louis had once written in his younger days in a university newsletter, an article which he now disowned. In it he had waxed lyrical and drawn on the classics, as post-graduates often do before they grow up or transfer their romanticism elsewhere.

He wrote of money's capacity for parthenogenesis, its chimera promises, its zephyr breezes, its slaughterous revenge. His business as the underwriter, he wrote, was to chase money, unleash it, run its projections through his fingers. In doing so, he was continuing in the tradition of Britain's mercantile and imperial past, spinning a web (how could he have employed such overworked metaphor?) of insurance and reinsurance, which links a staggering 40 per cent of the world's merchant ships, its aeroplanes, mines, cars and its political risks. A great, glittering procession winding through the centuries of trireme (he should have said tea clipper) and dirty salt stack, of giant tanker and spice ship billowing with white sails. Myrrh. Oil. Bananas. Gold. The soft, tingling smell of cinnamon and coriander, nutmeg and dried curry plant.

'You must always layer your risks,' Louis instructed Becky, over the second cup of coffee, 'vertically and . . . horizontally.'

'Of course.' Eager to learn, she pulled out a piece of paper from her handbag and scribbled something down.

'Don't do that,' said Louis. 'Listen instead. Otherwise you look amateur.'

Carefully, Becky laid down the biro.

Louis continued, 'No one should ever expose themselves to intolerable losses. That is the first rule.'

She was breathing faster than normal, and felt a pull of desire deep in her body (for what, she was not clear) and an exhilarating charge, like electricity.

'Always pass a layer of risk onto others.'

Clearly she was a fast learner, for he could not read her expression any longer and she sat quite still.

'What percentage of risk should I take, Louis?'

He spread out his thin, well-tended hands. 'The received wisdom runs that the insurer should never retain more than ten per cent of a risk.'

'So,' said Becky, her eyes soft and shining, 'how many levels of risk are there?'

'Are we talking business?'

Becky looked at her watch and adjusted the strap of her fake Chanel handbag. 'I'm so sorry, I'd better go. They'll kill me if I'm late.'

As Jack had once been, Louis found himself transfixed by the courage with which she carried herself and wore her evidently cheap clothes – and by her slightness which, being Louis, he translated as defencelessness and fragility. Perhaps he was right. Certainly his heart, a much deeper and more complicated place than either his wife or his colleagues suspected, was softened by pity, but a pity sharpened by lust.

'They'll like you at Mawby's,' he said. 'They've set out to be progressive.'

Her eyebrows climbed upwards. 'Oh, God,' she said. 'Tokenism.'

'Don't knock it.' He went off to pay for the coffee.

He walked with her down the street to Mawby's entrance and stopped. A girl carrying a large flower arrangement edged past them through a revolving door. Becky clutched the strap of her shoulder bag, and the knuckles turned a revealing white. The girl placed the flower arrangement on a pedestal near the door and began cleaning each leaf with a rag.

'Louis. Something tells me that your help is more than philanthropy.'

The awkwardness with which she said it made him pause, a little repelled. 'It's too early to say. You've met my wife. I have two sons, more or less grown-up, the upkeep of an expensive house, two cars, a gardener and a Vietnamese maid called Thuk.'

'And?'

'A lot of money.'

'And?'

'I stay married. I'm a Catholic without a God.'

Becky's knuckles returned to a normal colour. 'How inconvenient. All of the trouble and none of the benefits.' She laughed.

'True.'

'I live in a flat, on a council estate in Streatham, which has one toilet, one basin, a priceless collection of glass on the stairs and I'm working on the maid.'

He bent over her. 'You can make money, you know, from the broking. Even more, perhaps, than from underwriting, for the capacity is unlimited providing you can deal with the business. I suspect you're a quick learner.'

It flashed through her mind that he loved her already and she looked down at her feet. 'Yes, I think I am.' Then she raised her eyes to his, and both she and Louis imagined that they understood very well what each wanted from the other. 'You'll have to watch and tell me.'

'I will.'

The revolving door performed another circuit and Becky shivered. Exasperated by her starveling quality, Louis produced from his pocket a paper bag containing a doughnut. 'Here,' he said. 'I bought this for you.'

She cradled the bag between her fingers, as the fat stain colonized the paper. 'Thank you.'

She watched him walk down the street. Lust, it seemed, came tempered with kindness, seduction with rough-and-ready practicality, selfishness with an odd humanity – for that Louis was selfish she did not doubt. Then, so was she.

When he was safely out of sight, she threw away the bag with its sweet, sugary offering.

Once upon a time, Mrs Frant had been young. Now, she was not. She was getting old. Therein lies a paradox and, for some, tragedy: possessing a size forty bust and swollen ankles does not mean that you *are* old. Unlike some of her contemporaries, Mrs Frant could remember, for instance, the wild surges of feeling when, urged on by her mother, she had netted Colonel Frant.

And quite a business that had been. She could also remember, to the exact timbre, the wilder, infinitely savage grief of giving birth to a still-born baby, her first, and in the aftermath the drawn-out agony of piecing herself back together.

Then, as now, she fell back on the bit of herself hidden beneath her twinsetted, permed carapace, its existence private and unsuspected.

In Mrs Frant's secret self, a door was set between this world and the next. Every so often, she would give it a nudge open with her foot, look through at the unimaginable beyond and shut it again. It was her insurance and provided a strange and neccessary kind of freedom.

The clock in the drawing room of the High House was ticking away and the curtains – chrysanthemums on an ox-blood background – were drawn right back to let in the evening sun, now shining directly onto Great-aunt Alice's prints, which had been hung a little too high.

In the armchair opposite, Jack was studying lists. Settled in hers, Mrs Frant was stitching hellebores on a tapestry. Rubies, pinks, peaches and primrose yellows. The dark and exquisite Lenten rose. A white Christmas rose – 'Christ's Herb'.

Hellebores also have a secret life, a murky, hidden, poisonous existence. That was one of the reasons why she liked them.

'Jack.' He looked up, fair hair caught in the light. 'Don't get too involved with Rebecca.'

There, it had been said. Mrs Frant had gone into battle with resolution, if not exactly cunning. Why not? A taste for petit-point and tweed skirts does not mean your cause is unworthy or your fighting strategy limited. In went her needle, and out.

Jack went through the motions of tidily folding the lists, but she knew he had become wary. 'We're going to Africa together,' he said. 'You know that. We've discussed it often enough.'

'I don't want you to go, but if you have to, Jack, go alone.'

He made a movement to get up from the chair and, once

again, she was struck by the ascetic quality of her son's features. He could be a saint, she thought, half thrilled, half chilled at the idea.

'Don't interfere, Mum.'

Mrs Frant sewed two more stitches and the black hellebore was almost finished. 'Please. Don't make the mistake.'

'I want to marry her.'

During her life, Mrs Frant had been hurt several times in a variety of ways. The terrible episode when Colonel Frant had fallen in love with the blonde divorcée ... and, of course, the baby. The tapestry fell onto her lap. She clasped her hands together and sat up very straight, for she had learned that good posture, plus her cherished inner reserves, helped her to cope. 'You will regret it, Jack. She's not of your type. No,' she saw his raised eyebrows, 'I don't mean socially. What I'm trying to say is that she's not made the same way as you, Jack. She's different.'

'You don't regret the things you do do, only those you don't.'

'Hold me, hold me, Becky darling,' he had whispered, utterly vanquished by the brilliant and captivating shooting star that he had captured.

'I will. I am, Jack.'

Carelessly, we underestimate the power of maternal love, which rests on its ability to exact self-sacrifice: to suffer, to feel deep in the bones, to tear flesh. How often does it work secretly, through the judiciary, through business empires and through politics? (There is a famous photograph of President Kennedy at a state banquet leaning towards his mother, the two figures bound together for ever.) How many decisions taken in the board room, on the shop floor, in the bank have at their root the spectral figure of an older woman?

Mrs Frant picked up her tapestry and set the last stitch for the evening. Ripe and silky, the hellebore under her hands swelled and bloomed with life. 'She will hurt you badly, Jack. You must listen to me.'

46

He got up, came over to his mother and slipped an arm around her shoulder. Mrs Frant was suddenly dizzy from happiness. 'Don't worry, Mum. Everything will be fine.'

The day after the interview at Mawby's, Louis sent a bunch of red roses to Paradise Flats. Aunt Jean took the delivery and dumped it in the basin. There they sat, slightly artificial and incongruous, until Becky retrieved them and placed them in the window so that Mary Biggs opposite would be set to speculating.

Louis underwrote mainly political risk. Too wide an area to be specific, he had informed Becky. Too secret to provide any details. It was an area to which many rules were attached. Becky liked the idea of secrets, for secrets suggested power and the notion that their keeper was close to the centre.

The next day she rang Louis at his box at Lloyd's. 'Thank you so much.' Then she added, 'That was a cliché, you know.' She remembered touching one of the blooms with the tip of her finger, and how soft and insubstantial it had felt.

With his free hand, Louis rearranged some documents on his desk while keeping an eye on his junior, who had a habit of eavesdropping on his conversations. 'Possibly. But does that make them unpleasant to receive?'

'Not at all. Isn't it the sort of thing that an old Etonian with a soul to match would do?'

'Being?'

'Very clever, informed and prey to emotional surges at the sight of old buildings.'

'Enjoy,' said Louis, smiling, 'and let me know the Mawby's outcome.' He put the phone down and his junior turned away, with the quick movement of the listening animal.

Becky sat at her desk and pictured Louis at the box while a queue of brokers formed to do business with him. The image pleased her, and she wondered how corrupt he was. A little? More than a little?

Becky did well to ask. Observation had taught her that money has a habit of rubbing away at goodness, rather as practitioners of politics and teaching find that their good intentions are eroded. Not that she objected.

Money. Those without it counted the pounds on their fingers. The careful middle classes totted totals on their pocket calculators of those joyously pregnant deposit accounts and portfolios, offspring of a swaggering market, bullish profits and confidence.

At heart, though, he would be malleable and soft . . .

Becky was partly correct, mostly not. Louis, like his colleagues, dealt in results. The percentages netted in swiftly, stacking one upon the other, a mirror image of the layers of insurance, a *mille-feuille* of profit.

And what would she do?

She began to type with bad grace but, as with anything she did, efficiently.

The rubbish by the bins at Paradise Flats now included a decaying fridge and, with the arrival of the autumn rains, the brushstrokes of moss up the grimy brickwork had taken on new, vivid colouring. It was a geography of deprivation and, as she picked her way down the corridor, Becky vowed it would not be hers.

She let herself into the flat and waited.

The minute Jack walked in, Becky told him that she had taken a job as a trainee broker at Mawby's, starting in two weeks' time.

He sat down hard in the tacky armchair and, visibly, energy drained out of him.

Becky looked at the roses on the table. 'I'm sorry, Jack.'

At last he asked, 'Is it someone else?'

'I've got a job, Jack. A good one.'

'Can't it wait?'

She went over to the chair, picked up one of his hands and

held it to her cheek. '*I* can't wait, Jack, and I should have known.'

He turned his head away from her. Already he was retreating and, suddenly, she regretted what she was doing. Jack was young, directed, innocent and uncorrupt.

'So you never cared.' He made it sound like a statement. 'Why on earth did you bother?'

Trust, his mother had pointed out to him, and Rebecca are foreigners.

'You have your work. I have mine. That's all.'

'Work! Don't make me laugh.'

She put her hand on her hip. 'Yes, work, and don't be patronizing.'

'Oh, God,' he said, and ran his hands dramatically through his hair.

He raked the room, searching for answers among the few possessions: a couple of mugs on the shelf, a print of a pink Redouté rose on the wall, an old-fashioned clothes-horse. Bare of photographs, with no icing of china and knick-knacks, no clues as to how the two lives were conducted between the walls, it was as different as it was possible to be from the High House.

He gripped her hand. 'Becky. Please think again. You won't get another chance to do this. To do something proper and worthwhile. Don't give it up.'

She stared down at him. Without knowing it, he had assumed the pose that she had seen in a photograph at the High House, one taken with his grandparents. She had examined it carefully, identifying the links between the generations: the shape of a chin, the set of a head. Available and obvious, the links were there to read and she had been struck by the poverty of hers. But, if she had no patterns in which to fit her life, she was free.

'You're wrong, Jack. I'm taking up. Not giving up.' She flushed suddenly, a bright, unlovely red. 'It was all a pipedream. Africa.'

'I thought we would get married.' A cold, shocked Jack

49

watched her pleat the hem of her T-shirt between her fingers. Her fingers stilled and a storm of agonized desire was unleashed in Jack, his coldness melted by the burning wish to make her understand. He pushed himself to his feet, grabbed Becky tight and buried his head in the white flesh that he so desired, and for which he hungered, much as he hungered to walk over cracked, heated plains. 'Marry me.'

She lifted clenched fists to her chest, as if, he thought bitterly, she was defending herself against him and what he represented. 'No, Jack, I don't think so.'

'*Please.*'

Gently, she pushed at him and moved away, flaunting her delicacy and grace in contrast to his hot, heavy disappointment. Again she touched the roses with a fingertip. Then she swivelled and leant back against the table.

'Come here.'

He did so reluctantly. Becky reached up and slid her hands down his back.

'You . . .'

Helpless, and shackled to the spot, Jack watched as Becky pulled her T-shirt over her head and undid her bra, which she allowed to drop to the floor. The change in temperature turned her skin to gooseflesh.

'Jack . . . ?'

To his angry, grieving eyes, she seemed the epitome of willingness, trembling with abandon.

'You're a liar,' he said. 'You were never going to come with me.'

She undid his shirt. Her curves brushed against his bare flesh and he shivered. 'Listen, foolish Jack,' she pressed close to him, 'it's unwise to get to the bottom of things. You never know what you might find.'

She was so warm, so silky, so very alive.

'See?' she said later. 'There was no need for all that fuss.'

*

Afterwards, Jack wept in her arms and she soothed him as she might have done a baby. After a while, he got up and dressed and left the flat without saying goodbye.

While they had been making love that Friday evening, 16 October 1987, the American stock market crashed.

On Monday the nineteenth, Becky was hard at work at Landes typing with half an ear to the huddle of men by the door, who were discussing the situation, when the phone buzzed. It was Tess.

'Is anything happening with you, Bec? It's all hell here. The Dow-Jones and Tokyo have gone bananas and now we're crashing.' Tess was urgent, breathy and excited. 'The computers are throwing everything into chaos. The programme trading can't cope and it's bucking the system and selling everything.'

'Financial melt-down is the word here.'

'Oh, God. I'll speak to you later.'

'Tess, I've left your brother. Will you forgive me?'

'Oh, *Becky.*' Tess hesitated. 'For goodness sake, this isn't the moment. Ring me tonight.'

Becky returned to her work.

It was easy to lose a fear of sex and of being exposed by its intimacies. Perhaps it was as easy to lose a fear of love and its capacity to change a person? Becky could not come to a conclusion for she had not loved, but if you lose a healthy fear of money, treat it with the familiarity of lukewarm spouses, then you can become careless.

Was that what had happened? she wondered.

By the end of the day, fifty billion pounds had been wiped off the value of publicly quoted companies, the Dow-Jones had fallen by 508 points and, in the dealing rooms, the slaughter had turned the computer screens (red for down, blue for up) into a bloody and unforgettable crimson.

Chapter Five

'Follow me,' ordered Charles Hayter, Becky's new boss, unnecessarily.

It was unnecessary because she was already following him through Mawby's showy atrium but Charles, who had an endless fund of good nature but was worried by it, had a habit of issuing commands as an antidote.

'I want you to be my shadow, my tail . . .' he had said, rather dramatically, when Becky had first presented herself in October. 'You must watch and listen.'

She had offered no comment. Today she had watched and listened through the nine-thirty forthcoming-business meeting, watched and listened as Charles briefed the backroom staff and listed his appointments with his secretary. She had also watched and listened during the past eight weeks as she helped to prepare policy documents and slips, dealt with American corre-spondence and – once – delivered a cover note to an under-writer. Currently she was preparing to watch and listen for three months in the claims department.

'You will need to sit the Lloyd's Test as fast as you can. It's only set once a year and without it you can't work at Lloyd's. And I expect you to be sitting the ACII exam within four years. Without *that* you won't get promoted.' Charles had rattled out the objectives as if he was at target practice.

At least they were clear.

'Where are we going?' she asked, having a pretty good idea.

'Lloyd's, the Room,' he said. 'Where else? Where you are to watch me.'

'Ah,' said Becky. 'Of course.' She suspected that his more than usually rapid speech this morning hid a mind occupied elsewhere. (She was right. Charles was worrying about Martha, his wife.)

The street was full of men: men in a hurry holding sheaves of paper, men grouped confidentially, tall men, short men, fat men and, circling, lean and hungry prowlers. The tarmac was slicked with winter rain and the cold was of the damp, depressing variety.

Oblivious, Charles strode on, a little loud-looking, certainly confident-looking, but not stupid. Already Becky had come to appreciate his sharp, hustling, sniffing-out brain and his good nature, but failed to see the integrity he brought to his work, which, in a world of the sharp and the cutting, made him successful.

Brokers are the marketing arm of the insurance business, he had confided over their first lunch. We bring in the business. Someone like you will do it easily. She had been pleased that he did not once refer to her sex.

But now, as he ushered her through the entrance to the Lloyd's building, Charles peered at Becky, doubting her reception, unsure how to handle her. She sent him a look that suggested admiration, submission and the non-confrontational, and tried to convey that she had donned the white robe of the neophyte. He seemed reassured.

'Hi, Charley boy.'

Someone slapped him on the shoulder and Charles responded by grabbing the greeter's tie and continuing a conversation that had been started elsewhere. Then he beckoned to Becky.

She had been in the Room several times and was acquainted with the hum of light and activity that, after the first impact on the eye and ear, muttered subversively. It was a noisy, gleaming,

53

arched marketplace but it was the trading that interested Becky, not its architectural swagger or spectacle.

Marine. Non-marine. Aviation. Motor. Charles made a stab at being a guide. Becky remained silent, contemplative even, and allowed his rhetoric to rush past her, staccato and urgent.

The active underwriter accepts the risk, at an agreed premium, and reinsures it; the underwriting agent handles the affairs of the syndicate's members, accountancy and related matters.

'Yes, I know,' Becky gently reminded him.

'There are over twenty-five thousand external Names.' And he added, a stranger to irony, 'Seventeen per cent are foreigners. Twenty-two per cent are women.

'Names,' he pronounced, with the emphasis that she was beginning to recognize as a feature of Charles, 'are warned that they are liable to their last waistcoat button.'

'I thought it was cufflinks.'

'Oh,' said Charles, annoyed. 'Yes. You're right. Cufflinks.'

'How simple,' she said later. They had ascended to the top of the building and were looking down through the well sliced out by the escalators. Below them the underwriters' boxes clustered in ants' cells. A vision, Louis had told Becky, that an Old Master might have borrowed for his version of Usury, even Hell.

Becky could not quite see it. 'How beautifully clear,' she remarked instead. The space, the subdued hum, its dedication to a single activity, its sense of purpose, spoke to her as powerfully, perhaps as God spoke to Aunt Jean.

Charles's expression was that of the baffled male.

They retraced their steps and he led her towards a box. 'You must always start to get your project underwritten by a leading underwriter,' he explained, 'otherwise you won't get the followers.'

'Bit like one's life,' flashed Becky, and then realized that whatever other advantages Charles possessed, a quick wit was not among them. 'Should you always try for a specialist in the area?'

'Yes.'

'As a matter of interest, do you have to have a formal training to be an underwriter?'

He took the trouble to consider the question carefully. 'Yes. But listening is important. Theory is only useful up to a point. Having said that, the number-crunchers are becoming more influential than they used to be. But nothing beats the feel, the hunch, the seat of the pants.'

They stopped in front of a box where a small queue had formed. While they waited, Charles tapped his papers and fiddled with his tie.

'He does nuclear business.' He conveyed the information in a hushed voice. 'And oil and energy.'

Becky looked again at Matt Barker, a man who dealt in the biggest risk of all. Did he really believe that a piece of paper could bottle up the nuclear whirlwind? Pick up the pieces when it had ripped, shrieking and murderous, across a Russian steppe or an American plain? Probably not, for Matt Barker looked shrewd and experienced. Perhaps, Becky thought, having taken into account humanity's frail defences, Matt Barker reckoned that a piece of paper was as good as anything. You made money on it.

Eventually they reached the head of the queue.

'Becky, meet Matt Barker. Matt, this is our newest and brightest trainee.'

Matt got to his feet and they shook hands. His junior, a clone of the older man, did not. He ran an indifferent pair of eyes over Becky and returned to his calculations.

The formalities over, Matt stretched out his right hand. His knuckles cracked audibly. 'What have you got?' he asked.

Charles changed into the appropriate gear and Becky listened – primary policy, rate on line, catastrophe layers – and learned. As they made to leave, Charles turned back with a final

thought. 'We think we've got a big sweetie coming up, Matt.
FEROC are building a new rig. Two billion or so. All the latest
equipment and suchlike. I'll be back.'

'Sure,' said Matt Barker, inscrutable and conspiratorial.
Crack, crack went his knuckles.

'A big sweetie,' Charles repeated.

'How much is he likely to take on a new rig?' Becky enquired,
when she and Charles were drinking coffee and debriefing
themselves in the canteen.

'A ten per cent line. Once that's done the rest will follow.'
Charles ran a hand over his chin.

He had a nice, healthy-looking neck, Becky decided. She
asked, 'Will all the business on the FEROC rig – should it come
Mawby's way – be done in here?'

Earnest and, in his anxiety to teach, a touch patronizing,
Charles leant forward. 'Probably not. It's too big. We'll go to
Europe.'

'And will Matt Barker reinsure the ten per cent he
underwrites?'

'Yup.'

'I'm not sure he was very impressed.' Becky pushed her half-
drunk coffee to one side.

That bothered Charles. 'Really. Why?'

Becky shrugged. 'Instinct.'

'He's one of the most successful underwriters in the business.' Charles, a little uneasy, wiped the foam off his upper lip.
'He keeps very cool.'

The coffee finished, Charles suggested that Becky wandered
around the building while he did some business. She smiled at
his obvious wish to be shot of her and picked her way through
the aisles to Matt Barker's box where she waited.

Matt looked up. 'Have we forgotten something?'

Becky towered above him and widened her eyes. 'I'm told you're one of the most successful underwriters in the business and your syndicate one of the most profitable. I wanted to know why.'

Several phones were ringing in the box and the junior was fielding them all. Matt ignored them and considered the girl in front of him. 'Since you ask, you must invest the syndicate's funds well for the bad times. That is the key. That, and finding out exactly the risk you're underwriting. Keep asking questions, down to the tiniest detail.'

It was so obvious and Becky was disappointed. Again Matt stretched out a hand and cracked his knuckles. 'Come to me if you ever want any help,' he said, and his junior glared.

Half-way down the escalator, Becky passed Louis going up. She looked across to the dark, weary gaze and he looked back at her. He knew all about her, he told her silently. He understood the baggage of ambition, insecurity and appetite of which she was made. He understood that an orphan is orphaned many times throughout a life. Not just once.

No more powerful an aphrodisiac was required than that silent, generous comprehension.

Abruptly, she turned away. Louis continued up, she continued down and, around them, the making of money went on.

Back in Appleford that summer, Jack had accused Becky of making him feel like Gulliver in Lilliput, pegged out and helpless on the sands. He had confessed such to her in the wood: a vivid, fragrant, vigorous backdrop. Sun had exploded across her vision and, aghast at his vulnerability, she had allowed Jack to draw her deeper into the undergrowth. He had begged her to tell him that she loved him.

She had done so, cupping her hand around the contour of

his chin, for Becky truly believed that the world functioned on lies. Otherwise, civilization was impossible.

To his mother's grief and his father's despair, Jack continued with plans for Africa, merely discarding the plan to drive across the Sahara and changing the destination to Ethiopia. There, in exchange for Becky, patient Penelope – who wished to work in the Fistula Hospital in Addis Ababa – would join him.

Loyally the Frants gathered at Heathrow to see him off.

In the car Colonel Frant fought his way up the approach road to the terminal and unloaded a very small amount of luggage. Jack had insisted on keeping everything to a minimum. He had gone through his bedroom at the High House, discarding, discarding, until the room was bare and cold. As if, his mother thought with a catch in her throat, it had never been inhabited. It frightened her, this cleansing of a past.

Even so, Mrs Frant could claim victory over Becky but it tasted bitter.

Face rigid with the effort of not displaying her feelings, she dug her hands into the pockets of her camel coat, felt the warmth of her body through the lining and wondered where she had gone wrong. To lose a baby was grief enough, to lose a son, for she did not doubt that she had lost Jack ... well, could she survive?

What you do is get your head down and march. One day at a time. One day at a time.

Oh, Becky, thought Jack.

The departure lounge throbbed and bulged with people and their possessions. Eyes underlined with fatigue and midriffs slackened, businessmen drank coffee and read papers. Whole families, clearly relocating elsewhere, stood guard over piles of hand luggage.

Oh, Becky.

Yet even as the pain drove its now accustomed dart through his body, the image of Becky was growing a little faint, and Jack was moving on to contemplate heat, physical discomfort and the satisfactions of dispensing charity.

He swallowed. Was it worse to remember or to forget?

Mrs Frant touched his arm, more alive and sympathetic to his unhappiness than he had supposed. Tess hugged her brother, embarrassed by her connection with Becky. 'She's my friend,' she had told him. 'I can't give her up.'

Now she said, 'Take care. Don't get kidnapped.'

'Jealous, Tess?'

'No way.'

'Have you got enough money?' asked his father for the third time, at a loss for what else to say. It was noticeable that Colonel Frant had lost weight and his colour was not as healthy-looking as usual.

They were being very good, his parents, despite their feelings. (Goaded, Mrs Frant had cried out, 'Why Africa? Why not somewhere we understand?') A rush of affection for them suffused him and he put his arms around his mother.

'Jack!'

Jack released his mother, so abruptly that she staggered slightly. He swivelled, heart pounding like a battery gun.

'Jack?'

Mrs Frant stiffened and Tess went pale as Becky carved a passage towards them, clutching a carrier bag. Tess hoped, she did so hope, that there was not going to be a scene.

'The tube was terrible, and there was miles to walk. But I couldn't let you go without these.'

'What on earth are you doing here?' Jack's yearning returned in a floodtide. But he was angry too. Becky and he had had their farewell scene. Why go through it again?

Becky ignored the question and the other three Frants who were apparently struck dumb. 'Sun-tan cream. Thrillers for the long, dark nights. An outsize box of plasters. Glucose tablets. I thought you'd need them. At least, to begin with.'

'Oh, Becky,' said Tess, wishing that Becky had had the sense not to come, 'how sweet of you.'

I hate her. Mrs Frant's face was set in granite. (If motherhood is influential, it is not always soft.)

Massaging her fingers, which were numb from the handles of the heavy bag, Becky turned, at last, to greet the Frants. Her hair drawn back into a fashionable French plait, skin porcelain clear and glowing, Becky was clearly embarking on a transformation. At that moment, Jack wanted her more than anything else on earth.

But he could not have her. Or, at least, not in the way he wanted and he was still too young to make do with spoilt dreams.

'Good luck,' she said, impervious to the Frant parents' frigid aspect. 'See you in a year.'

Dropping the bag, Jack captured Becky's hands. An aircraft screamed in the sky outside. There was an eddy of passengers towards the departure lounge. The Tannoy issued instructions. The world was in a hurry and on the move and it was time for Jack to leave.

She reached up to kiss him on the cheek. 'Good luck, and I'm sorry.'

'But you came to say goodbye.'

'Of course.' Her smile both mocked him and told him not to take her too seriously.

Mrs Frant positioned herself by her son. Go away, she was implying. Leave us in peace to say goodbye.

Between them, they were consigning Jack to the African sun and to its tawny landscape, which would seize and mould him. There Jack would encounter the strangeness, terror and violence that ringed the edges of existence, cancelling the strangeness, terror and violence of the feelings he had experienced at home.

Becky turned to Tess. 'Tessy,' she said, placing a hand on Tess's arm, 'can you lend me a fiver to get back with? I'll reimburse you later.'

Becky's office at Mawby's barely justified the name: it was a corner, cut off from a general space crammed with VDUs, print-outs, research literature and bodies. Somehow, she had created a space that was recognizably hers and bore her tidy stamp.

The possibility of the FEROC deal was whipping up general excitement, and Becky had spent some time thinking over the details of such a project. At the nine-thirty meeting on the Monday after Jack's departure, she took a deep breath and, when the topic was reached on the agenda, asked the exact composition of the personnel on a rig.

Tom Pritchard, the older partner, stared across the table at her as if she had raised a question concerning unspeakable practices. Becky did not flinch.

'The usual,' Tom said. 'As it happens, FEROC has not supplied that level of detail yet but you're welcome to look back at previous records.'

'Thank you,' said Becky and, for the rest of the meeting, confined herself to taking notes.

She spent the next week amassing data on oil rigs: personnel (what type?), turnover of said, ratio of accidents to claims, risk to accident.

Charles was intrigued and found himself increasingly drawn to this part of the office. He wanted to know why she wanted to know. He eyed up the coils of computer print-out on Becky's desk. 'Are you going through everything?'

'Why not? It's the business.'

Becky leant back in her chair, tipping it gently, a habit she had quickly adopted. The contrast between the relaxed, almost dreamy suggestion of sensuality and her obvious cleverness made Charles's blood quicken a fraction. He liked what he saw: the feminine casing folded over a quick mind; the reddened lips and the sharp, foxy quality of the bones in her wrists.

Hurrying along the career and marriage paths, Charles had forgotten about the chase. About scented flesh. The fullness of satiation. Now, he found himself remembering.

'Do you really want to know?' She looked up at him and he felt extraordinarily alive.

'Of course.'

'I was at the airport the other day,' said Becky.

'So?'

'More people work in an airline than the crews. Cleaners. Waitresses. Messengers. I wondered if they were all insured against the 747 crashing down. And would it be the same on the oil rig? What about the cleaners?'

'So what do you propose to do about it?'

Becky's chair returned to its normal position and she gathered up her print-out. 'I'll tell you when I've found out.'

'Look.' Charles leant over the desk a little further than was necessary. He held up his hand, revealing shirtsleeves that had been hitched up with a pair of elastic bands. 'I think your energy and interest are wonderful.' It was true. He found the intensity of her focus almost erotic. 'I mean it. But don't imagine you'll get a new take on the business overnight. There are people here who've worked at it for decades, and there's not much they don't know.'

Becky handed back to Charles the end of his yellow tie, which was hanging over her cup of coffee. 'Sure.'

To his amazement, Charles found himself walking round the desk where he pulled Becky to her feet and . . . let her go.

'Don't be too cocky,' he said, and left the room.

If Jack was all golden, young and idealistic and she had sent him packing, an indulgence, and Louis was the opposite, then Charles . . . ?

What was Charles?
Charles was a conduit for useful information.

Lavish, wine-drenched and civilized, the 1987 Christmas meeting of the Bollys at the Savoy Grill was no different from previous Christmas meetings. But the mood had changed.

Louis and Matt found time to hold a lengthy and serious conversation about the 1983 underwriting year for which, unusually, two sets of results had been published. The first, announcing an underwriting profit of £28 million, had not taken into account the disastrous results of a syndicate accused not only of carelessness but of fraud. The second figure added these to the bottom line and announced an underwriting loss of £115 million.

They talked about damage limitation, press involvement, their own profits and – again – the long-tail problems coming in from North America.

'American lawyers,' reiterated Matt thoughtfully, 'are not on our side.'

Louis sensed they were talking about the finale to the old days. The mood was changing, forces governing circumstances were changing. An optimism, or was it complacency?, had become pessimism. He did not care to question what was happening to himself, or to the others. For Colonel Frant he did not spare a second thought. (But for Becky and their as yet unconsummated affair, he spared many.)

'We must take care,' he said to Matt. 'Guard our castles. And someone clever should be put on the damage-limitation programme.'

'To the defence of our castles,' said Matt, and passed the port to Louis.

Chapter Six

Tess spent the weekend before Christmas with her parents at the High House.

People came and went, bringing presents of potted plants and mince pies or presented themselves for a regulation sherry. Chit-chatting and *Merry* Christmasing. Several times the postman toiled up the gravel drive, raising beneath his feet a sodden spume of pebbles. The house smelt of a combination of citrus fruits and mud. Its windows, recently cleaned by Jimmy Plover, reflected a merger between the neon street lamps and the Christmas lights.

One Christmas. Two Christmas. Three Christmas. Four . . .

The old rhyme that she and Jack used to chant echoed in her mind, a childhood reprise from the time when it mattered very much how well the day went. Children do not like change or, at least, they like to be warned of it. Quite quickly, Tess had learnt that adults can turn nasty at Christmas, or change out of all recognition. But she felt the expectation laid on Christmas was unfair. How could it live up to its promise? Much as chocolate, cinnamon and brandy are so seductive to the nose on first encounter, so elusive or cloying a second or two later.

It would have been lovely if George could have come, at least for some of the time. Plucking up courage, she had invited him to spend Boxing Day at the High House but he had told her he was busy. His refusal had caused her to waste a whole day as she probed minutely for its significance.

She had wanted very much to see him in her home, being normal, talking to her parents. Thinking about it, which she did incessantly, there were points of likeness between her father and George, the same set of shoulder, a corresponding manner of speech.

'I wish Jack was here,' said her mother, when Tess discovered her in the kitchen staring into a saucepan of boiled chestnuts.

Tess slipped an arm around her shoulders. 'It's only one Christmas. He'll be back.'

'Will he?' Mrs Frant seemed unconvinced. 'I think your friend broke his heart and he'll stay out there.'

Mrs Frant's melodrama irritated Tess, partly because she, too, was angry with Becky but had lost courage when she should have had it out with her, partly because she suspected that her mother was right. That was the trouble with Becky: it was impossible to pin her down.

'Yes, of course Jack was upset. But we all have love affairs that come to nothing and it's a very good thing,' she lied, thinking, *I'll die if it doesn't work out with George.* 'Just give him time to get over it.'

Early on Sunday evening she returned to London with an idea of doing some tidying up, and surveyed the prospect. Piles of newspapers had taken up permanent squatters' rights on the furniture and there was a lot of unhoovered carpet. With a sigh, she picked up the phone.

Becky was fizzing with frustration. 'I don't think I can bear it any longer. Aunt Jean is completely doolally and, if I hear one more prayer or hymn, I'll kill her. The whole bloody world's gone fundamental.' She added darkly, 'Fundamentalism will be the scourge of the age.'

'Becky,' said Tess, 'I've been meaning to ask you to come and live here. Why don't you?'

There was a pause at the other end of the line and Tess, impetuous, generous Tess, plunged onwards. 'Don't worry about rent, Bec, if that's a problem. This is Dad's flat, a little invest-

ment he made after a good year. You don't have to pay anything.
Just the bills.'

The reply came within a second. 'I'll move in tomorrow.'

And she did.

'But I don't like Becky,' said George, who had come round
for supper during the week. He was folded into the small sofa,
which was waiting for a cover, his highly polished Chelsea boots
propped on the arm. 'Does she have to come here? It'll be a
bottleneck.'

'Here' meant two bedrooms, one cramped sitting room and
a cupboard that masqueraded as a kitchen. George had a point.
Becky was out, entertaining clients, but although she had
brought little with her, the flat had shrunk.

'Yes, she does have to be here.'

Tess had been swift to pick up George's real objection,
which was about sex. She lit a cigarette and focused on the
contrast between the white paper and the dark, angry red of the
burn.

'George ...' she attempted. Everyone she could think of
enjoyed frank and fearless discussions about it – pundits, agony
aunts, friends. Adverts reeked of it, television was stuffed with it.
Et cetera. Sex and everyone else were on excellent terms with
each other. But, when it came to airing the topic, it and she
were nodding acquaintances, polite, awkward and wishing to get
to know each other better.

'George ... ?'

'Oh, come here,' he ordered, and proceeded to demonstrate
his predilection for the noisy, cavemanish variety and to feast on
Tess's honey-coloured, satiny body. Drowning in love and desire,
Tess's doubts about George and the progress of their affair
loosened their grip and sank.

Afterwards, she lay still, tender and quivering, and reflected
on the confusion existing between her mind and her body.
Once, she had pictured a future in which she would exercise
her mind, so painfully toned at university, flexing and contract-

ing its muscles. She had wished to build into it capacious rooms for storage. To become a mental athlete. Instead, she was reduced to intense contemplation of – obsession with, even – the flesh. Her own flesh: yielding, weeping, longing and desirous. And other people's flesh: so desirable, so cruel, so on display. She dwelt on the contrasts, and the discoveries, to be made: the exact shades and tints of George's arm, the blue vein searching through his groin, the silk down on his chest.

'Kiss me again,' she demanded of George, and he obeyed with a mouth from which passion was already retreating. Tess tasted him, savoured him and demanded more. She had what she wanted and yet ... And yet it was not enough. She craved further, more tangible and absolute proof that she possessed and was possessed.

It was impossible to have too much love.

When it was quite over, George sighed and said, 'We'll have to watch it from now on, if Becky's around.'

He got up and went in search of a drink. 'Don't you have anything more serious than sherry?' he asked, naked but impervious to the chill.

'Only wine.' Tess was lying on the floor where they had ended up. Too lazy to move, she pulled her clothes over her and shivered. 'Why don't you like Becky?'

'She's on the make.'

'What's wrong with that? So am I.'

'She's too obvious. Women shouldn't be so obvious. Not with money anyway.'

She knew enough about George by now to know that he did not necessarily admire money-making. No, he talked appreciatively of Darwin's voyages, Watson and Crick's discovery of DNA, the making of the Challenger spacecraft and of the astronomers who patrolled the night skies. He also admired, believe it or not, the peace-makers.

'Women,' George was warming to the theme, 'should be careful.'

She did not quite believe him, knowing that he liked to stir things.

He shot her a look. 'I mean it,' he said.

While he dressed, Tess digested the implications. In his jeans and boots, George looked the part of an off-duty Army officer. Was he what he showed the world? She supposed he was. Not for the first time, she questioned how it was possible to be so in love with someone with whom she so profoundly disagreed.

Fortunately, these pinpricks, so significant when two people have almost reached the end of a road, so insignificant in an infant love affair, did not spoil the evening. When Becky returned in the small hours, she discovered a dreamy Tess on the sofa, smoking. She had twisted up her heavy hair, anchored it with a pencil, and was studying the varnish on her toenails, which needed attention.

'Disgusting,' pronounced the immaculate Becky.

'You are addressing the spirit of enquiry.' Tess stubbed out her cigarette. 'Pure science. I wanted to see how long it took to grow the varnish out.'

Becky had a glass of water in her hand, and pointed at the ashtray. 'You should choose your addictions more carefully.'

'Yours, I take it,' said Tess, 'will leave you wiser and richer.'

Becky drank the water in one go. 'Smoking ruins your skin.'

'Don't you know we're a dependent culture?' said Tess flippantly. 'I'm a child of it.'

'Perhaps you are,' said Becky, bored. In the pursuit of the perfect skin, Becky drank a second glass of water and went to bed after using up all the hot water.

'My darling,' Mrs Frant came stamping in from a Christmas Day march around the garden and caught Tess idling over breakfast, 'don't leave it too long to find someone nice to marry. I'm worried about your future.'

Was George nice? And had Tess left it too long?

Until George, the future had not concerned Tess overmuch, for she felt it to be manageable. The politics of feminine inactivity – all that sitting about on sofas by Jane Austen heroines while they waited and prayed for their lives to be completed, and suffered and loved in silence – had changed. The blackboard had been scrubbed clean. The chains had been snapped. Until George. Whereupon Tess had been made uneasily aware that the chains had not disappeared. They had merely been buried out of sight.

Her conclusions had shocked her. Along with the eighties children, Tess was too accustomed to assuming that the world could be put right. After all, there were antibiotics and welfare benefits, and it was inconceivable that either would run out. If Tess had been less of her time, for instance, she might have noticed that, during the unusually peaceful, fragrant Christmas of 1987, her father had been very quiet.

'Talking of antibiotics . . .' Dressed in a dull navy blue suit and navy blue tights designed to depress the remotest suggestion of sex, Tess buttonholed Freddie when she got back to work.

'Were we?' Freddie had a hangover and post-Christmas seemed more post than usual.

'Yes, we were. Their future needs looking into, don't you think?'

'I don't think anything,' said Freddie. He looked up at the air-conditioning duct, which blew straight onto his desk. 'Except that I'm in line for Legionnaire's disease.'

'The body count's high, I'm told.'

Kit wandered over and began to chat, thumbs tucked into his braces which he snapped from time to time. 'Are we settled?' he asked, kindly, which was touching in one who was only five years or so older.

'More or less.'

'Would you two like to join the rest of us for a lunchtime

drink?' The invitation was the first such issued to the two graduate trainees and marked an advance. Freddie's eyes were twin pools of *faux* eagerness and innocence. 'Of course,' he said, for both of them. 'We thought you'd never ask.'

Freddie's braces were patterned in black and white, Kit's were bright red and Bill's were navy. What dressers-up men were. Tess smoothed the dull skirt over her navy blue knees and prepared to slog away at the print-out.

Lunch was raucous, and she made the mistake of drinking two glasses of wine.

'Right,' said Kit, on their return. 'Time to make contact with one or two clients. On your tods. No more sitting in on meetings and looking pretty. You've got to do some work.'

As luck would have it, the first client Tess rang to introduce herself was a professional Northerner.

'Why should I trust you, Miss Frant?'

His objection was reasonable and logical, and Tess told him so. This elicited a laugh, and Tess was encouraged. Unwise. From there on the conversation took a downhill plunge.

'Look, Miss Frint or Frant or whatever your name is. I don't want some fanny in a tight skirt muddling about with my money.'

'I agree about the muddling, Mr Fitch.'

'Get your boss to ring me, not some wet-behind-the-ears bit of fluff.'

'You beast,' said Tess, after she had put down the phone and regarded her blank client sheet on which she had neither defended nor proved herself, and set about considering how to circumnavigate eleven centuries of North–South antagonism and an eternity of male chauvinism.

It took a bit of doing, but she won her point and a couple of days later Tess found herself on the Intercity 125 travelling north to Leeds. She had rung Fitch and asked him to clear space in his diary. She took as consent the silence at the other end of the line.

Balding, stomach nudging open the fastenings of his shirt, a man opposite Tess talked non-stop into his mobile phone, which rang repeatedly.

'Darling,' he said finally, sneaking a look at the passengers close enough to be impressed, 'it won't be long.'

The jottings on Tess's notepad grew increasingly wild. At the last 'darling', she struggled to her feet and leant over the table.

'I wonder if "darling" would mind shutting up.'

Surprised at and impressed with herself, she moved down the carriage towards the blessed peace of rattling crisp bags and the automatic door.

In his cluttered, down-at-heel offices with steel window frames and a dying potted plant, Ted Fitch looked at Tess. 'I knew you'd have a tight skirt.'

Tess looked briefly out of the window, at a narrow, claustrophobic valley bisected by streams that had cut through the fern-patterned rock. Here, for five generations, Ted Fitch's family had struggled to make a living. She could almost swear, but not quite, that their dark presences were there too, and the air was charged with the memory of their sweat and tears. Suddenly she understood. She was not up against regionalism or sexism, or any of the isms that were flung around, merely a man who wished to make the most of his hard-earned money.

'If you're out of your depth, swim, Tess. You know how.'

As she searched for the right opening, she could recollect the exact nuance in her father's voice. She picked up her briefcase, extracted the projections she had made and handed them over. 'Shall we begin?'

'I don't want any risk, mind.'

'No, Mr Fitch, that's why I've built sterling debentures into the portfolio, which are index-linked, and suggested a good spread between the sectors with a bias towards blue-chip FTSE 100 stocks. But, Mr Fitch, I must warn you, there's always some risk.'

Five minutes later, Ted Fitch had thawed sufficiently to switch his attention from Tess and her skirt to the outrageous cost of administering a portfolio and, from there, it was only a step to castigating bankers and their outrageous salaries. That subject having been beaten to death, Mr Fitch was ready to listen.

'You tamed the old boy.' Bill was approving on Tess's next showing in the office. 'He's like a little lamb and quite a chunk is coming our way.'

'Good,' said Tess.

'You were *very* lucky,' said Bill.

'So it seems,' said Tess drily.

Tess had learnt that institutions borrowing large amounts of money must not over-expose their flanks to interest-rate movements. They had to strike a balance – the golden mean, on which the ancient Greeks had been so keen.

Balance . . . agreed Tess, mulling over her love affair. Yes, balance.

Money was complicated and capricious, a shining stream running through our minds. From the goat or bushel of wheat used for barter to the rudimentary coin was one step in its history. From the coin (first seen in 800 BC) to the modern-day gradations and categories of M1, M2 and M3 was quite another.

Falling in love was equally complicated and required a similar balancing act – between the upward-sloping yield curve and the plunge into chaos and debt. And the emotional dividend? What would that be?

'Don't expect too much, Tess.'

In the flat in Pimlico, Becky and Tess were eating an evening meal of pizza.

'Why not?'

'I don't know,' said Becky, and Tess had an uneasy feeling

that she knew more than she was prepared to say. 'I don't want to see you hurt.'

'Don't be silly,' said Tess. 'Everyone gets hurt.'

'Yes, but you don't have to be. Manage the risk.'

Tess thought for a second or two, but the subject was too fraught so she steered onto another path. 'Risk management,' she licked tomato off her fingers, 'is really housekeeping. Women are good at housekeeping. They like to keep tins in the larder.'

Becky had also moved on. 'Do you know what Louis Cadogan's nickname is?' She sounded unusually dreamy. 'El Medici.'

Jack would have recognized Becky's delicate shudder of anticipation. A movement of lips ready to sample the ripe blackcurrant of the vintage wine.

'And Jilly?' asked Tess, after a moment. 'How does she fit in?'

Becky sat back, and crossed her endless legs. 'Apparently, Jilly's stars have warned her there'll be changes but no shortage of money.'

'Did Louis tell you all this? Bec, have you . . . ?'

'Not yet. But I will. Probably.'

'*You* be careful, Bec.' Tess leant over and helped herself to the rest of Becky's pizza. 'He's married.'

'They all are, Tess.'

'Jack wasn't.'

'No, no, he wasn't.'

After supper Tess, on impulse, took a taxi to George's flat in Battersea, which he was sharing with Iain MacKenzie who lived there during the week and returned to Flora in the country at weekends. She had cleaned her teeth, hoping that the mint would cancel the tobacco but knowing the tobacco would beat the mint.

She decided to give up smoking.

George had presented her with a key and she let herself in.

Nothing. Silence. Yet she knew someone was there. Knocking gently on George's bedroom door, she pushed it open.

'It's only me,' she said.

How many times had the same phrase been uttered by the dupe in the film: the betrayed wife, the vicar stumbling over discarded knickers? By the foolish, the cuckolded, the trusting?

'It's only me.' Each word a stone: bruising and hurtful. And a naked George rolled lazily away from the girl last seen clad in Lycra at the Chelsea party.

A curious buzzing invaded Tess's head.

'Oh, Lord,' said the girl, 'she's going to faint.'

Rather than seeing him, Tess sensed George's naked figure come towards her, felt his legs and the warm jumble of his genitals press against her arm as he helped her upright. The pain hit her a physical blow, and she gave a little gasping sob.

Wrapping herself in the sheet, Miss Lycra said in a light, indifferent tone, 'Have some water.'

Tess observed the pattern in the rug on the floor assemble and reassemble, much as patterns form and dissolve under water, and concluded that life without the burden of innocence was much, much easier. Nothing need be expected in the way of good behaviour.

Now that that was settled she must flee from George and the slippery, slender body wrapped so carelessly in the sheet.

It came as a relief, really, truly, that it was no longer necessary to pretend that dark areas did not exist. They did. They did.

Never quite sure how she arrived back in Pimlico, Tess bore for a week red marks on her leg where her shaking hands had caused the tea, made by Becky, to slop. During that time, when she travelled from grief, to anger, through the arc of revenge and back to misery, the world had changed in an unexpected and peculiar manner. Her room looked different, she looked different and there were cracks in the ceiling.

She told herself that, way up in the stratosphere, astral winds were howling and screaming. Astral dust was being blown into feathers and the fierce light of many suns was cutting through infinity. Down below on earth, trapped by a ring of pollution, the Odden Feature in the Greenland Sea was behaving strangely. According to the papers, it looked as though, for the first time, it would fail to form its tongue of ice, which powered the currents around the world's seas. The delicate ecological balance of the world was being threatened. That was more important than her darkened life.

Oh, where was God? If He was what He was, surely he would help her.

In the silence and indifference that surrounded Tess, it was clear that He was not there.

Balance, Tess.

'Grow up.' After witnessing a second week of Tess's weeping, sleeplessness and furious smoking, Becky was moved to speak her mind. 'It's stupid to get so upset. It means so little.'

'Does it?' Tess stared at the television.

Becky threw a packet of aspirin at her. 'Take these and stop crying.'

Canned laughter filtered into the room. A couple on the screen held hands and Tess was gripped by a fear of being left alone. 'Don't go out, Becky,' she pleaded. 'Stay here.'

But Becky was mascaraed and ready for an evening of entertaining clients.

'Sorry, Tess,' she said, in her cruel, charming way, and stroked Tess's disordered hair. 'In your present state, I wouldn't be any use anyway. And the clients are big ones.'

'Bugger the clients.'

'Well, I don't think I'll do that exactly . . .' Becky fetched a glass of water. 'Take the aspirins.' She looked down at Tess. 'Have you talked to George at all?'

'No.'

'Well, you'll never get him back that way, will you?'

Longing for animal comfort and warmth, Tess was left to

stare at the space in the wall where a fireplace should have been.

OK, Jack, what would you do?

From however many thousand miles away, he told her.

Not surprisingly, Jack's telepathic message was an exact reflection of Tess's own wishes and the following evening it resulted in Iain MacKenzie letting her into the flat. He was kind and concerned, and retreated tactfully to his bedroom.

Tess faced George and demanded to know where she stood in the line-up of females. 'Don't I mean anything to you?' she raged.

'Of course you do. And if you hadn't come butting in, then you wouldn't have known.'

'Why give me a key, then?'

George raised his eyes to the ceiling, and Tess saw that he had accepted her on a different basis from the one she had conjectured. Neither had understood the other.

'I thought we . . .'

'We are. But . . . Sophie and I are old friends. That's how it is.'

'I don't think I want that kind of arrangement.'

'Grow up, darling.'

Everyone was telling her to grow up. Clearly, negotiations over fidelity and loyalty, which she had considered absolutes, had only just begun.

'People only tell others to grow up when they're on shaky ground,' she countered.

George poured himself a drink. 'I don't think this conversation is getting us anywhere,' he said.

Tess had always thought of pain as akin to walking over a chessboard, moving from square to square, with respites in between. But pain was being wrapped in tarred roofing felt, a sticky, squeezing material whose adhesive properties burnt strips off her spirit.

'Half the world is starving,' Mrs Frant said, quite frequently when faced with a crisis.

Tess looked hard at the faithless, swaggering, unfathomable George, and committed the sin of wishing that she *was* starving for it would take her mind off her famished heart.

In the end, Iain MacKenzie drove Tess home. He stopped the car outside the Pimlico flat and took her hand gently in his own. 'You will get over it,' he said, searching obviously for the right words.

> *I want to understand* [Tess wrote in her diary]. *I want to understand what has happened. Why I react as I do. Why betrayal matters so much. If I knew it was likely that he would go off with someone else, and I suppose I did, why wasn't I better prepared for it happening? But I should also question myself closely as to why I bother with George.*
>
> *Fiduciary law teaches that greater risk requires a greater reward. I have decided to concentrate on that. If I agree with it, surely I feel that George is worth the risk.*
>
> *Today, despite all my resolutions, I've eaten a Mars bar and a bag of Maltesers. My attempts to give up smoking are also hopeless.*

Chapter Seven

In the kitchen, Thuk moved daintily from oven to table, juggling the production of roast beef, glossy vegetables and a trifle swathed in whipped cream.

Jilly and Louis were entertaining weekend guests over on a business trip from the South of France. Jilly knew the form and, like everything else she did, the Sunday lunch was well organized.

Permanently bronzed and plumped with expensive creams, Sonia Lambert stuffed canapés into her mouth. 'Delicious. How do you manage it, Jilly?'

'I have the wonderful Thuk.' Jilly offered the plate to Richard Lambert. 'A treasure without price.'

'Thuk?' Richard seemed puzzled.

'The maid, darling,' his wife explained, flapping her hand on which reposed a large emerald ring. 'She's Thai or Vietnamese or something like that.'

'Ah.'

'Lovely ring, Sonia.' Jilly eyed the emerald, which was surrounded by fine diamonds.

'Oh, darling. I can't tell you. André, my jeweller in Bond Street, says all sorts of wonderful stuff is suddenly flooding the market. People are selling. Strange, isn't it? Anyway, as soon as he saw this he knew it was for me.'

'Will you be staying in the French house this year?' Richard Lambert asked Louis.

Louis glanced at his wife. 'I don't think so,' he said. 'Jilly doesn't like it much.'

True. Jilly found France unsympathetic and the elegant villa with its grey-blue shutters on the hill above Vence a headache too far. Or, perhaps, she felt she could not compete with the smart crowd down there. Whatever the reason, they never went and the villa remained, a poised, expectant folly. Jilly sipped her champagne and smiled, and sipped, and it took Sonia two or three seconds to realize that the smile on her hostess's face had a frozen quality.

'Anything wrong, Jilly?'

Under the expensive foundation, Jilly was a fiery red. 'My tooth,' she said piteously. 'I think I've swallowed it.'

'Darling . . .' Sonia swooped like the Assyrian. '*Let*'s see.'

'No.' Jilly clamped her mouth shut and avoided the sight of Louis's raised eyebrows. *He*, of all people, could not help her. 'It's fine. False alarm.'

Untrue. Jilly could feel the large – achingly large – space where the false façade of a tooth had been gummed onto the real one. Where the façade was going to finish up, Jilly was not going to consider.

'Are you sure?' Sonia was persistent. Jilly nodded, she hoped convincingly.

That bloody dentist. He swore the technique was infallible and that he'd been to America to learn about it. He had *promised* that resurfacing the teeth, at great expense, in a shade up from their natural colour would make Jilly look younger, but the camouflage ripped away, what remained was a filed-down yellow stump.

Oh, how she hated ageing. It was a bloody awful business. She sat through the lunch, barely opening her mouth.

Becky was passing the weekend in working for her exam and in reading a copy of a samizdat report, slipped to her by the co-operative Charles. 'Many members of Lloyd's in senior positions,' it ran, 'were not even vaguely aware of the legal obligation on agents to act at all times in the best interests of their clients . . .'

'Tess,' Becky looked over to where Tess was slumped over the Sunday newspapers, 'have you ever talked to your father about Lloyd's?'

Tess sighed. 'No, I haven't.'

'Well, you should. Do you know if his syndicates are OK?'

Tess adjusted her waistband.

'Are you listening? It might be important. I hear a lot of gossip these days.' Becky got up and papers subsided in a fan on the floor. She bent over Tess, assessed her state, saw it had not progressed and her expression hardened. 'How often do I have to tell you? *George isn't worth it.*'

'He is, he was, to me.'

'It's lucky I'm prepared to put up with you,' said Becky.

Tess grabbed her hand and held it for a second to her cheek. 'Sure.'

Becky snapped the paper fan together. 'Don't forget to talk to your father.'

But Tess did forget.

If Louis was the sure-footed hunter, Charles Cadogan was the prairie dog: attractive, busy, honest. According to office gossip, picked up and pieced together, he was kind in his dealings with women, perhaps something of a chat-up man but devoted to his wife.

Nevertheless, cornering her by her desk and up against the noise of the photocopying machine, Charles shuffled, without *really* meaning to, over a line between sense and recklessness and asked Becky out to dinner – to discuss corporate strategy, of course.

'Just to go over things.'

Carole, the secretary Becky shared with four others, looked up from her battle with the latest software and raised her eyebrows. Do you wish to be rescued? she signalled, a willing member of the helpful sisterhood.

If Charles was not really aware of what he was doing and its implications, Becky was. At first assessment, he was not a patch on Jack but that was too bad. She ignored Carole's lifebuoy and directed her smile at him.

'Look,' said stirred-up, muddled Charles that evening to Martha, his wife, about whom he worried incessantly – more from habit than necessity. After the third baby, Martha had suffered some kind of temporary breakdown and had refused to leave the house, but she was better now. 'I'm taking the trainee out to dinner to discuss strategy. Just so you know.'

Martha moved with regained confidence between the kitchen table and the worktop. She reached for the correct knife and began to peel and chop an onion, which she did in a way that suggested she was probing and analysing its texture.

A thin, seemingly fragile figure, with a slackened stomach from childbirth and curious orange-coloured hair (quite natural), she had been watched by Charles a hundred thousand times. He was proud of her dexterity, her cool application achieved through will-power. Martha had battled with her illness and won.

'Do you mind about the dinner?'

Martha wiped her cheeks with the back of her hand, so white-skinned it was almost transparent. 'Of course not.' She reached for the frying pan and switched on the hob. Then she opened the cupboard above it and located a tin of tomatoes. 'Should I mind?'

'No.'

'Well, then.'

She listened to his feelings, applying the secret, additional sense that she had developed through her marriage. Charles was agitated.

'How are the girls?'

'Anthea fell over and cut her knee, Pammy had a tantrum and Tiny was sick.'

'Oh, Lord,' said Charles, deeply thankful that he had not had to deal with any of it.

There was an eruption of flushed, clean-smelling girls into the kitchen, followed by a weary au pair, and a general wail went up for biscuits, stories, comfort ... Instantly, Martha stopped what she was doing and scooped up Tiny who fell, stone-like, with an expression of utter thankfulness onto her mother's chest. The smile that curved Martha's lips was tender and sure in the knowledge that she was wanted.

Charles drank his wine. The confining walls and domestic focus were as welcome to Martha as they were unwelcome to a woman like Becky. This was Martha's domain: fiercely guarded and given additional sweetness and contentment by three daughters.

I am the spirit of maternity. That is my business.

No ifs, no buts. The knocks and intensity of motherhood insulated Martha from the things she did not wish to hear.

'Have you thought any more ...' Charles settled a billowing napkin onto his lap in an expensive London-playing-at-being-in-France restaurant '. . . about personnel on the oil rig?'

Before Becky could reply Charles was diverted by the wine list, over which he fussed and dithered. Finally, he ordered a Macon Lugny and looked up at Becky, transparent and boyish in his pleasure at having done so. 'I've a mind to go into wine importing.'

'Really.' There are some people, and I suspect he is one of them, Becky reflected, who are clothed in adult trappings: marriage, children, cheque books and sharp little pension plans. And yet, like the pantomime horse, they do not convince the audience.

'Back to the oil rig,' said Charles eventually, over the coffee.

'Like I said, I wonder, when rigs are insured, if it takes account of all personnel and their life assurance policies?'

'Well . . .'

'If every cook and cleaner has taken out a policy and the rig goes down or there's an accident, that must add hugely to the liability.'

'Plenty.' Charles was aware that he should give the idea attention, but Becky's large eyes were disconcerting.

Becky switched the subject. 'Tell me about your family.'

'Three daughters ...' Charles plunged into an account of scenes from domestic life. The impression that Becky gained was of an overweening femininity into which Charles, shell-shocked from producing so many girls, had been sucked. Bubblebath and leotards. Floral wallpaper, a huge assortment of nightdresses in the daily wash and pet hamsters that gyrated all night in perspex balls.

'Does Martha work?'

'Martha? No, she's a mother.'

There was a long pause while Becky absorbed the infor-mation. Did it add to Charles's interest or detract from it? 'Presumably motherhood doesn't affect the brain,' she said.

'Martha decided she was needed at home. I agreed with her ...' Charles faltered, realizing that Becky might be one of those terrifying, nose-ringed, man-eating feminists circling the increas-ingly infertile male.

'Of course,' said Becky, and Charles relaxed.

Martha! Home-loving Martha. Becky pictured her in detail: a big-boned, big-hipped matron in an A-line skirt with little pads of fat beginning to attach themselves to the jawline. Women like that always conveyed an impression of a straining zip. Their body language flaunted the tally of sacrifices made for their children: peaceful baths, ambition, looks and a serviced mind.

In a practised gesture, Becky curved her shoulder above the scoop of her silk camisole. Look at me, it signalled. I am lithe, fatless and free.

'Right,' said Charles, his judgement and good nature diluted with lust. 'I think you're ready to do a little broking on your own. Supervised by me in the background.'

'Of course.'

'That Nigerian project requires five per cent to complete. See if you can get it tomorrow. But keep checking back with me.'

The following day, Becky went straight to Louis and queued for three-quarters of an hour at his box. Every so often he looked up at her.

'How much?' he asked at last. 'And what?'

Becky told him, itemizing the facts smoothly but flushing a little with tension. Behind them screens blinked, pasting information subliminally onto retinas.

Louis checked Becky's papers. The project was not his normal area and Nigeria was always tricky. Facts had a habit of turning turtle there, of being magicked into mist by the witch doctors. Had the right man, the right tribe been approached? he asked. And was she aware that the question of good faith meant separate things to separate cultures?

'Is everything here that I need to know?' he repeated. Underwriters had to be sure that they had been told all the facts, and non-disclosure by the broker was the greatest sin.

Becky knew the form and did not hesitate. 'Sure.' She gave the word as much emphasis as possible.

'OK.'

She reached out to take back the slip. Louis gave it to her and his fingers brushed her sensitized palm. 'Tomorrow,' he said. 'Twelve thirty. Outside the main entrance.'

In the taxi with Louis, Becky shivered, whether from danger or anticipation she did not know. Silently, he took her hand and placed it on his thigh. The driver navigated his way eastwards through the city. Louis turned the hand over so that Becky's wrist was exposed. Then he bent and kissed the thin skin at the point where the pulse beat.

'I'm taking you to Harvey Nichols,' he said. 'After that . . .'

They lunched in the restaurant on ceps and turbot, Becky leaving most of hers.

Louis raised his eyebrows. 'Let me see if I can't give you something that really pleases you.' He led her down to the first floor and said, 'Go ahead, I've got plenty of money.'

Becky did not bother to say anything conventional. Surrounding her were expensive women, experts in the demands made by beauty. They chatted, they conferred, they swirled in front of one another in a rich, oestrogen-steeped parade of dresses, skirts and suits, their jewellery flashing a Morse code of the exclusive.

Silenced, Becky paced along the rails of softly draped cashmere and silk. Once she stopped, allowed her hand to trail over a black chiffon evening dress, tracing its encrustation of jet beads: an archaeologist discovering the outlines of a new fossil. These expensive clothes had been made for tiny women with bird bones and skinny hips, which screamed for pelvic space in childbirth. They were not intended for housewives, big women who toiled and moiled, but for those small enough to be placed in gilded designer houses.

In the changing room Becky stripped to her underclothes and examined the triptych of her in the long mirrors. In the confined space, there was no place to hide, no protection from herself. She was what she saw: bone, flesh and ambition. Here, despite her meticulous grooming, was the slightly grubby skin under the armpit. There was the stray hair in the plucked eyebrow and, there, the suggestion of slack in the muscles.

No wonder a woman demanded her Armani, her Catherine Walker, her Yves – her hard-won, hard-pressed badges of confidence. Becky picked up the trouser suit that Louis would pay for and walked out of the booth.

'You've led me a dance,' Louis told her later, in the hotel room, satiated and almost tender.

She sighed, impatient and dismissive of his call on her

emotions yet powerless to deny his attraction. 'You know,' she murmured, 'you could be my father.'

'Not *quite*.' He shifted to put his arm under her and pull her closer.

'You'll have to pay.'

'I already have,' said Louis, thinking of the huge bill Becky had run up.

She smiled at him across the pillows, then laughed. He felt her thin, greedy hands dig deep into his emotions. It spelt danger, possibly change, and he knew it.

The hotel, situated on the south bank, was cheap. The bed was uncomfortable and the small amount of fruit in the bowl on the table must have been picked from a plastic tree.

'Yes,' Becky said thoughtfully. 'You've paid for me. But I've kept my side of the transaction.'

Louis frowned, and she knew in future that she would have to be more subtle. She hesitated while she worked out how best to deal with the change of mood and then, with one of her soft laughs, leant over him and brushed his lips with her own. Louis drew her closer.

'You're a witch, Becky.'

It was not the moment to ask him for information or gossip that she would have liked. That would come later. She relaxed against him and raised her hands into the air, twisting them this way and that.

Her blood-red nail varnish flashed memories to Louis.

It was the colour of Father Jerome's red morocco prayer book, which had faded in the exact places where his finger and thumb used to rest.

'Shall I tell you something, Louis?' Becky's arms fell back to the bed. 'I've discovered a conspiracy to make things seem difficult. You can see why, of course.' She turned towards him and, light as thistledown, Louis traced the contours of her eyes. 'To make money seem difficult, I mean. They like to make its language inaccessible.'

'Yes,' said Louis, his finger now making a second journey, a wicked, seeking traveller.

'Women in particular aren't supposed to understand it.'

'Stuff, Becky.'

A little later, Becky laid her hand on his bare shoulder and said, 'I must warn you, Louis, that I intend to seduce Charles, my boss.'

In reply, Louis bent over and kissed her. Underneath his, Becky's mouth opened and yielded. 'Why bother?' he whispered. 'Is this not enough?'

She struggled to resist him and to ignore the curious sexual bargain that, between them, they had constructed. 'Because . . . because you won't be leaving your wife,' she said with a rush, vulnerable and curiously exposed. Touched and guilty, Louis again took her into his arms and rocked the slender body until they could begin all over again.

In the taxi back to work, they were silent. Then, in the street ahead, the sky appeared to transform itself in a flash of light, turn white and explode. A moment of suspended silence gripped the shuddering taxi and released it. As Becky watched, a glinting flight of glass arched its way up to the leaden sky, hesitated and speared lazily back to earth, sprinkling a diamond dust over the black bonnet. In the background there was a sudden noise of gushing water and of burglar alarms.

'Jesus,' said the taxi driver. 'It's a bomb at the end of the street.'

He and Louis were out of the taxi and sprinting towards two blood-shrouded figures lying in the road. Beyond them were the smoking remains of a car and an office block with most of its windows blown out except, curiously, the ones on the ground floor, which remained shinily intact.

Several seconds behind the two men, Becky had hung back. 'Don't!' she tried to call after him. 'There might be a second bomb.'

87

Now, the silence was replaced by screeching brakes, shouts, pounding feet, orders, and the terrible cries of the injured. Becky ran after the men.

The taxi driver was endeavouring to calm a group of hysterical tourists. Louis had dropped to his knees in the road by one of the victims and Becky did likewise by the second. A young, red-haired man, who looked up and through her. He moved his head from side to side. Just like the wooden tortoise I used to have with the waggling head, she thought, appalled at the randomness of the recollection.

The man began to emit hideous choking noises, and Becky fumbled in her handbag, among hoarded bits of string and sachets of shampoo which she had filched from the hotel, for something to mop up the blood. In the end, fearing she might vomit, she pressed her hand against her mouth, pulled her scarf from her neck and wadded it over the biggest wound. The man's right hand was horribly mutilated, but his left seemed untouched, a dirt-engrained hand with nicotine stains.

It was not so much an innate sense of humanity that made her take it in her own, rather the sense that it was expected of her and she must perform. The man's flesh was cold with shock and heavy in her equally cold palm and she continued to hold it, not knowing what else to do. When she looked up for a second or two, it was to see one of the tourists, a man, calmly taking photographs.

So Becky sat in the blood-spattered road holding a stranger's hand until help arrived, feeling curiously detached and remote from the scene. Neither was she surprised. Sometimes the truce made between violence and non-violence held. Sometimes it did not and the results spilled over into the streets. Life in Paradise Flats, Streatham, had taught Becky that lesson. You made love in a ditzy hotel. A bomb went off in the London streets. That was how it was.

After a long, long time, but in fact only a few seconds, Becky began to stroke the man's hand. If he registered a human touch, she was not aware of it.

'It won't be long,' she told him, but it was apparent that he was too dazed to understand.

The paramedics took over and Becky and Louis left the scene separately. In her taxi, Becky examined her blood-stained skirt and cried with shock and the driver refused to accept a fare.

That evening as she watched the news, she learnt that, in all probability, the men she and Louis had attempted to comfort had been the terrorists themselves, their smallish bomb intended for a bank in the City. Instead, they had blown themselves up and killed a tour guide shepherding visitors to the Tower of London.

'If you had known they were terrorists,' asked a shaken Tess, supplying Becky with cups of tea, 'would you have comforted them?'

Becky concentrated on holding her cup of tea. 'I don't know.'

Tess bit her lip and said, 'You were so brave, and it could have been you.'

'Rubbish,' said Becky, who would never confess her lack of feeling even to Tess, and began to shiver uncontrollably. 'I didn't think. If I had, I would have run away.'

Tess put her arms round her friend and drew her close. 'So brave,' she repeated lovingly.

Which were, more or less, the same words that Jilly addressed to Louis at breakfast the following morning, adding, 'Still, Jupiter is on your ascendant, it was unlikely you would have come to harm.'

'Thank you,' said Louis.

The planets having been assigned their place, Jilly stretched out for the marmalade with a hand that was showing the tiniest symptoms of age.

'Don't be late this evening,' she said. 'The Coopers are coming.'

'Oh, God,' said Louis, and threw down his napkin. 'Why?'

Jilly was puzzled. 'You know why. Bridge.'

Louis got to his feet and placed his hands on the table. He leant towards his wife. 'No. Not tonight. Cancel them.'

Jilly searched her husband's face for a clue to his behaviour and concluded that he was more upset by the bombing incident than he had let on. 'Bridge will settle you,' she said soothingly. 'You'll see.'

'No,' said Louis, and left the room.

In the pretty green and white breakfast area with a watery March sunshine filtering through freshly curtained windows, Jilly sat and assessed the physical condition of her hands with a thoroughness that she never applied to her soul. Clever Sonia Lambert had told her about hand lifts and she really must enquire further.

She was due to have coffee with the Widow – Jennifer had earned the outing with a skilled application of flattery. And since Jilly categorized her meetings with the latter as charity, both parties were happy. In her customary organized way, Jilly began to make a list of Things To Do.

The aqueous light turned the room and its glossy arrangements into an aquarium, through which Jilly – not normally given to flights of fancy – imagined herself swimming, sure in the flip of her strong, lazy tail. Whatever else she may have been, Jilly appreciated her buttered bread and never whined. She understood the terms of her existence. If Benisson fabrics, trips to Henley and Wimbledon and an account at Harrods could be said to constitute life, then life had been good to her.

Chapter Eight

'Thank you for your communication,' went the letter of 21 March 1988 to John Frant. 'We have noted its contents. We regret to inform you that it is not possible for you to resign as a Name while the year 1985 remains open.

'Meanwhile, you might find it helpful to have the enclosed summary of your financial position.'

The letter suggested that a third cash call, to the tune of £10,000, would be coming his way.

During their marriage, the Frants had learned, if not to understand, at least to read each other. While it was true that Mrs Frant was more adept and fluent, it was also true that the Colonel was no mean pupil.

He knew that his wife knew that he was worried, to the degree that he was almost sick with it, and that in the mutual collusion that made their life possible, she was turning over his worry in the part of her that she held back from him. That spring he watched, with a heavy heart, her progress around the garden, clipping the clematis, targeting infant tendrils of bind-weed for extinction, inspecting the compost or marching along the beds and round to the paddock. Fighting cold and damp, she was out there. Most days.

Business life was full of reverses. Importing apples and bananas was a positive drama of bad weather, deficient cold storage and unpredictable transport and he had waged war against them. And yet, Colonel Frant was not sure that he could fight this last battle. He had neither the men, the weapons nor knowledge of the terrain.

Lead weighed down his spirits, and he sensed that his body was struggling to maintain its customary patterns.

The wind, whistling down the valley, held the sharp, cold notes of March and, as she moved down the border, checking the position of the plants against the diagram in her notebook, Mrs Frant was glad of her thermal vest and thick herringbone stockings. She noted the temperature, lower than last year, and wrote a summary of the weather in the section at the back of the notebook. Later, she would enter it up in the leather book in the kitchen.

Weather was important and she had always been fascinated by it. Jack had written to her of the heat in Ethiopia, and the freezing nights, of rock cracked by the extremes of temperature, and dry, scrubby vegetation. Faithfully, she pictured what he described.

He also described death, as it made free with the starving and the depleted, and she pondered over his version – death, the cruel thief. For Mrs Frant, death was the tease with whom she flirted when the life outside her secret life seemed especially worthy of contempt or unreal. Like her daughter, she had also searched for God. Unlike Tess, she had found him, but he was a smaller, less compassionate, more wayward figure than she had hoped. It pained her to admit it, but try as she might, Mrs Frant could not admire the Deity.

She got down on her sponge garden kneeler, pulled off her glove and cupped her favourite hellebore in her hand: dark and fascinatingly freckled, contained, strong and faithful like the best of friends. Hellebores enjoy a remarkable longevity, some living for fifty years or so, and there is something comforting about growing old with a plant.

Such beauty, she thought, such joyous beauty.

The Widow, who happened to be passing the High House, was treated to the sight of Mrs Frant on her hands and knees under the lilac trees. Quite, quite strange, she confided to Jilly Cadogan over biscuits and coffee, Angela was talking aloud but no one was there.

'What do we do?' asked Mrs Frant of her husband, over a lunch of cold meat and salad.

Her husband shuffled the unappetizing slices of lamb around his plate. He loved his wife but, by Jove, she was no cook. 'I've had a word with Nigel who says there's nothing to worry about.'

'How can one believe the reassurances of someone who is no more than a dating agency?'

She had a point but Colonel Frant wanted to believe Nigel, and that made a difference. 'You can't make an omelette without breaking eggs. And we've had a straight run for several years. I'm sure the syndicates have proper reserves, invested in the best way, and we won't get any more calls.'

'Yes,' agreed Mrs Frant, for there was no point in doing anything else.

Naturally, both spoke from a position of ignorance.

The phone went on Tess's desk at Metrobank and, one eye on the screen, she picked it up.

'You win,' said George. 'I was a naughty boy. Spend the weekend with me.'

'No,' said Tess, and the screen in front of her blurred.

'Yes, you will.'

'Stop behaving like an ape. Anyway I'm going down to my parents.'

He spotted the opening in her flank. 'I'll drive you.'

After a long crawl out of London on the Friday evening, they nosed onto the A3 and began to pick up speed.

Tess sat with clenched hands: she was finding conversation a little difficult. She had discovered before that it was easier to say things on the phone and the silence in the stuffy, dark car seemed pregnant with disappointment that neither had come up to scratch for the other.

Guildford flashed by, a paradise of business parks and heavy traffic, the angel on top of the city's cathedral gamely illuminated by its spotlight. Tess's nails made little red crescents on her skin.

George cleared his throat. 'I want to get sorted.'

He usually ducked out of making personal statements and the directness took Tess by surprise.

'What sort of sorted?'

He swung off the road and onto the Hogs Back. 'Have you ever thought about Northern Ireland?'

'You know I have.'

'I'm going back to Belfast. Soon.' George flipped back his hair with his free hand. 'Difficult. The whole place is crazy and everyone is busy convincing the other side that their prejudices are correct.'

She sneaked a look at George. He was difficult to see in the dark, but his outline suggested a frightening remoteness and Tess was too much in love to realize that this quality only added to his attraction but did not, necessarily, add substance.

'I think you'd better marry me,' he said, pressing the accelerator.

It was as if, she reflected at three a.m. the following morning, she was an appointment in his diary that had to be ratified. *Sorted.* If she married George, they would be sorted. Into what? Paper bags? Piles of china?

But she wanted to marry him, oh, how she did. She wanted for herself George's handsomeness, his air of mystery and his challenge.

Yet she had imagined events differently. The private, female part of her had craved, expected even, the sweetness and excitement of being pursued and captured. She had imagined gazing down on George's glossy, bent head and allowing a little time to elapse before she consented.

In the event, she said yes before one second had ticked away and, for the rest of the drive, they conducted an adult conversation about Army quarters, children, her work, his work. Nothing about fidelity, which she very much wished to get straight. Nothing about craving or needing each other. Tess had wanted, too, to be told that she was loved.

I'll make it work, the romantic Tess avowed, lying in linen sheets in her white cotton nightdress. Accommodation is part of love; the bending and flexing. Corn in a rainstorm. The object: to survive.

In the spare bedroom across the landing, George was also staring into the darkness. Tess was lovely. She was good. Maybe, just maybe, she would bring order into a rackety existence.

George also considered the comfortable home in Appleford, the flat in London and Tess's expectations. The equation appeared to satisfy him for he fell asleep, suddenly and deeply.

Like Tess, Mrs Frant remained awake, praying for the future happiness of her daughter. George Mason was exactly the clean, salaried, well-mannered type of man that she would wish for her. Unfortunately Mrs Frant was not sure that she liked him.

She leant over and shook Colonel Frant awake. 'What are we going to do about the wedding, John? We always promised that we'd give her the best we could manage.'

For the first time, a spurt of anger fuelled Mrs Frant's feelings towards the husband who, after all, had got them into a financial mess and her maternal anvil was emitting sparks.

'Of course we'll give her the wedding,' he said, from the isolation of his side of the bed. 'If it's the last thing I do.'

Outside in the garden, Mrs Frant's hellebores shook their heads in the night wind: secret, beautiful and poisonous.

*

George deposited Tess back at the flat on Sunday evening and a radiant Tess burst through the front door with her news.

On hearing it, Becky sat down hard on the sofa. 'You'll want me out of the flat.'

Her reaction took Tess aback. 'Yes. I mean no. Sometime.'

Becky did not smile. 'That'll be the end of us, Tess.'

She was right. Tess had a vision of Becky not being in her life. Not being in the bathroom, on the phone, in the everyday housekeeping calculations. 'Don't be silly.'

'Well, congratulations.' Becky sounded as flat as Tess had ever heard.

It was with a curious sense of disappointment, even anger, that Tess went to bed. She wished that she dared to ring George just to say goodnight but, feeling she did not know him quite well enough yet, had not done so.

She was stuffing papers into her briefcase early the next morning when Becky emerged from her room into the hall. 'I want to apologize.'

Tess said nothing.

'I should be happy for you. I should have said so.'

'That's all right.'

'I don't like the idea of change, that's all. You'll disappear behind a front door, children, all that sort of thing.' Tess listened, scarcely breathing. 'We'll lose touch. In the *real* sense, I mean.'

'Don't,' said Tess. '*Don't.*'

The Good Fairy ... Tess swung through the doors of Metrobank ... never points out in the stories that getting married involves death. Granted, only little ones of friendship and habit, but deaths all the same.

'Where've you been?' Bill was irritable. 'You're late.' Tess glanced at her watch: eight fifteen. 'Fitch has been on the phone. Wants you to go up there again.'

'Oh, Lord.'

Tess retreated to her desk.

'Dollar's up,' said Kit. 'And the word is Brewsters Bank will be fined for not declaring its overdraft.'

'*Naughty!*' Tess was beginning to feel better.

The room was filling up. Freddie lounged over his desk drinking cappuccino, looking raddled and blown. Computer screens winked and the printer emitted sighing noises.

'Why are you late?' Clearly, Bill was in a ferreting mood.

'Well,' said the flushed Tess, pushing back her hair, 'I'm getting married.'

Bill regarded her. 'I didn't think women got married any more. I mean, women like you.' He called over to Freddie. 'This mad woman's getting married.'

Sharp and louche, Freddie looked up. 'What the hell for?' He seemed genuinely puzzled.

Tess beamed at him. '*You* don't have to worry, Freddie. Not your neck of the woods.'

'Touché.' Freddie struggled to his feet. 'Listen, you lot. Tess is getting married.'

'Fuck me . . .'

'Champagne's on you!'

'Will you warm *my* slippers?'

'*Don't.*'

'You'll turn into your mother.'

'Watch it,' called a voice from the back. 'A big wave's building on the FTSE futures.'

There was a dash back to the screens, Tess among it.

All morning she watched: tracking and cross-tracking numbers that slipped, dodged and ran. Behind their configurations lay a story: nervousness, fashion, good management and the struggle to maintain a positive relationship between the return on an investment and its costs.

I'm more at home here, Tess reflected, threading her way through the figures, with this work and this language, than with anything else. I understand better what to do when a yield curve inverts than how to handle the man I'm going to marry.

'You talk of self-regulation at Lloyd's,' said Becky, 'but surely, at best, it's an idea with elastic tendencies. No one, not even the saints, self-regulates themselves.'

She was sitting at Louis's box, having persuaded him to take another 5 per cent on a second Nigerian project. They were discussing a reinsurance scandal that was emerging from a syndicate that had run into trouble – fortunately, still only a mutter in the press.

'You realize that Nigeria and this project are not my area,' Louis had commented, after examining Becky's slip, but scribbled his signature all the same.

He opened a drawer, took out a packet of paracetamol and swallowed a couple.

'You take a lot of those,' Becky pointed out.

'I get headaches.'

Risk identification demands a clear head and Louis's was aching. Whether social or financial, it requires skill to isolate, finance, reduce and manage risk. Greed fuels risk. The trick, in the language of the insurance game, Louis and Becky's game, was to avoid the trap of unplanned risk assumption. (Definition in *Dictionary of Insurance*: that which results from ignorance and inertia. Colonel Frant might have done well to ask whether ignorance and inertia had been the cause of his financial predicament or whether his risk had been well managed on his syndicates.)

A steady file of underwriters and brokers in suits walked up and down the aisles. Up and down. Round and back, in a pattern that can be observed in insect colonies.

Louis looked at Becky. 'It's all very well to criticize but the economy depends on the invisible earnings, the business here, otherwise the level of exports is affected. You must understand that the insurance market ensures that we remain the money market of the west so we can't rock the boat too hard,' he said. 'By and large, we manage. Someone like you just fixes on the things that go wrong.'

'Funny,' said Becky gently, 'so do the press.' She smiled at her lover. 'You mustn't be so sensitive, I'm not accusing you,' she said. 'I'm greedy too.'

As always, she exuded the suggestion, irresistible and marked, of intense life. She was, he thought, all slenderness and tender flesh tints. In a shortish skirt and tiny-waisted jacket ('Dress to kill,' Charles had advised), he knew that she knew she was a focus in the male-dominated Room.

A battle was being conducted in Louis between his customary assurance and a new disequilibrium. As the expert in risk analysis, Louis understood perfectly that, if permitted, Becky was a bully. He also understood that he was attracted by this.

Stacked behind him was intelligence data on Syria and Iraq, which had been beamed, via CNN satellite, onto his desk. A client was requesting cover for a trade delegation to this area and Louis was conducting an assessment of the probabilities.

Becky got gracefully to her feet. 'Louis . . . which syndicates is Tess's father on? Do you know?'

Louis reeled off the names.

There was a moment of profound silence. 'Oh, God,' said Becky. 'Isn't he the run-off man who's in big trouble?'

Louis shuffled his papers and, again, resisted picking up this problem. He asked quietly, 'How's the seduction of Charles progressing?'

'Fine,' said Becky. 'He's nice.'

'Why lumber yourself with him? There are others.'

'True. But the point is . . .' Becky turned away her face. 'The point is, I haven't met them so the question is irrelevant.' Papers folded to her chest, she looked up at Louis.

Father Jerome's thumb had not only pressed an imprint, whorled and grained, on the red morocco of his prayer book. It pressed also on Louis.

Becky slotted her papers into her briefcase.

'Hallo ...' A curious Nigel Pavorde broke into the conversation. 'I was passing and since we're all lunching ...'

'Hallo, Nigel.' Becky twitched at her jacket cuffs. 'I was just going.'

'Good business?'

'This and that in Nigeria,' said Louis.

'Oh.' Nigel's expression adjusted up a notch. 'Not your line, really, Louis.'

Becky waved her fingers as a goodbye and moved off. Nigel observed the retreating back. The muted rings of telephones gave the impression that the building was covered by a large blanket. Black was the dominant colour, overflowing in the boxes, moving along the aisles, sprayed in dots up and down the escalator. Among that subfusc, Becky's long legs, sheathed in opaque black tights, and the hair, caught back in the French plait she favoured, were startlingly noticeable.

'Ambitious, isn't she?' commented Nigel.

'Very.'

'Good thing she's not ugly.'

They walked out of the building together.

Two hundred thousand asbestosis-related deaths are predicted by the Yale School of Organization and Management over the next twenty-five years. Cost $50 billion.

Where did I read that? Louis searched his memory. Where? In the stack of documents on his desk?

'I wonder,' said Nigel, blinking in the daylight, 'if things aren't on the turn. There's a lot of talk about Names kicking up stink.'

American actuaries are predicting that the cost of cleaning up polluted America will be in the order of $1000 billion.

100

'There is,' Louis replied. 'But we sit tight. We make provision.'

'For ourselves?'

'As much as anyone.'

The silence of men, such as an underwriter and a members' agent, contemplating financial crisis, even melt-down, is akin to the silence of women contemplating childbirth. The impending event is too big for mere words.

Becky finally told Charles about the bomb over dinner, the third to which he had lured her in a fortnight. He surprised her by turning pale and shaking.

'Oh, Becky, Becky, I could kill the bastards.'

A little surprised but touched by his concern, she endeavoured to shrug it off.

'It was pure chance,' she said, deceptively cool, for her sleep had not been entirely untroubled since the incident. 'That's life and we shouldn't bother about it too much. I won't allow myself to bother about it. It's someone else's war.'

Throughout the meal, Charles worried at the subject until it had been beaten thoroughly. 'I can't believe how near to death you came. How I might have lost you.'

'Look,' said Becky, who had noted the personal pronoun. Her smile was calculated to remove the sting from her words. 'We can overdo this. Let's forget it.'

After coffee, Charles insisted on escorting her back to Pimlico and on coming inside with her. 'I want to tell you something,' he said, looking mysterious and important.

'What?' But she had a good idea as she led him through the vestibule and into the lift. The doors closed and Charles put his hands either side of Becky, trapping her. 'I love you, Becky. I can't eat. I can't work. I can't think of anything else.'

She had been expecting a request to enter her bed not a

declaration of love and it rocked her equilibrium. Perhaps this transaction would be conducted on a different basis from the one she had originally envisaged.

Charles was gazing at her with moist, loving eyes, and it was clear that he had meant every word. Becky closed hers for a second. So had Jack and Louis ... Well? Who knew? Charles was more insistent than Jack, more experienced, and that told in his favour.

The lift jerked upwards and Becky and Charles's stomachs were left behind, adding to Charles's sense of euphoria. He waited for Becky's reply.

She did not give one verbally but, once inside the flat, she took him by the hand and led him into her bedroom.

Chapter Nine

'*To wed*: To wager or stake (now obsolescent). To bind.' *The Dictionary of Historical Slang* also defines it as 'emptying the necessary house'.

Tess hoped that 'to bind' and 'to empty' were not linked.

Weddings are exercises in irony. They are occasions that demand and are granted the broad brushstroke: the exchange of big promises, the public passage from one state to another, the marshalling of individuals into unity before the centre breaks and the congregation disperses.

That's the theory, Tess thought, in some exasperation, having discovered that a wedding is an accumulation of small details. Or, at least, the wedding that Tess was having.

Flowers. What colour in the hall? In the guests' lavatory? Where should the umbrellas be sited? Iain and Flora MacKenzie required a taxi at five fifteen. Jenny Parsons's mother was coeliac – could the caterer oblige? Who would give the caterers their lunch?

Sometimes Tess looked up from the lists, the piles of presents, the smoothed-out stack of tissue paper, and talked to St Jude the patron saint of lost causes.

'I hope you don't mind,' she said, 'but I don't want you taking an interest in the wedding. *It is not a lost cause.* I may look at the end of my tether, but I'm perfectly well aware that in order to arrive I must journey hard through the politics of tetchy relations, my mother's wishes – a hard one that – and George's lack of co-operation. In good time, I will also deal with a superabundance of pickle spoons, decanters and three toast racks, and George's hostility to the pile of knick-knackery that sits in the corner.'

St Jude remained silent.

I don't really know George . . . Tess found her nights restless. I don't know him at all. There's no point of reference with someone whose parents are dead and whose only brother works on the other side of the world.

What if George had the Aids virus? A secret life? Perhaps a child somewhere?

During this period, Tess returned to the poets she had abandoned after university and searched out the ones that, once, had meant something or given pleasure. She yearned to read about the tap of chestnut blossoms on the bedroom window, of a sun rising in fierce splendour over misty fields, or descriptions of satin and silk whispering against skin and of the blood rising hotly through the body.

Each morning, Mrs Frant telephoned her daughter at the bank and dictated the tasks for the day. Thank-you letters. Queries. Dress fittings. And Tess obeyed.

A week before the wedding Colonel Frant caught her reading one of the poets after Sunday lunch.

'Oh dear,' he said. 'It's got to that stage, has it? Who is it?'

'Francis Thompson.'

'Don't know him. Should I?'

'He was a Catholic poet.'

Colonel Frant's feet were planted so solidly in the Anglican tradition and his grasp on its doctrinal tenets was so unwavering that it would never occur to him that Tess might look for comfort elsewhere. He laid a hand on her hair.

'I hope you'll enjoy your big day. Your mother and I have done our best.'

'Oh, Dad.'

'By the way,' he nodded at the book, 'be careful. I was young once and I remember well the temptation of extremes.'

He succeeded in astonishing his subdued and rather troubled daughter, who had presumed that her father's ruminations did not extend much past the theory and practice of well-placed capital and that his youth had been long forgotten.

Her presumption was misplaced. Yet, entrenched in the habits of years, neither was prepared to explore further.

'We are not,' Tess wrote in her diary, 'in the habit of talking to each other.'

Jack was flying over a couple of days before the wedding, adding mysteriously at the end of the letter that he had his own news to tell them. (Oh dear, said Mrs Frant, placing a hand over her eyes. Oh dear.) Becky was to be bridesmaid. She and Mrs Frant had almost, but not quite, come to blows over the subject of the dress, Mrs Frant favouring a floral pink, Becky white with a coloured sash. Becky suspected that Mrs Frant only favoured the pink because she could see that it did not suit Becky.

Perhaps Becky was right. Mrs Frant was not a woman who neglected her vendettas or forgot her wounds – and an image of Becky forced into a dress she did not like would offer a tiny recompense for the exile of her son.

The colleagues at Metrobank clubbed together and bought a very large silver photo frame onto which Freddie had stuck a packet of condoms in Day-glo colours. He was in agonies over which waistcoat to wear: too elaborate a one, he felt, would be at war with the marquee's décor.

In the peaceful green paddock, the marquee went up. A stretched white canvas temple, lined with pale blue and white stripes, dotted with clusters of white roses, lilies and scented stocks. Stippled with graceful summer flowers and rippling with grasses, the meadow beyond gave an impression of lapping gently at the edges of the busy activity. A sea running with wild beauty, at peace with its own nature.

*

On 6 July, the day before the wedding, there was a scream of escaping gas in the North Sea, followed by two explosions ten minutes apart. The sea boiled, the metal platform buckled and twisted and men leapt, human torches, into blazing salt water. The oil rig, Piper Alpha, self-destructed.

The newspapers were full of images: stark representations of unimaginable pain and anguish. Gagging from nerves, Tess stared at them in the kitchen of the High House on her wedding morning and tried to eat a bowl of muesli. At first, they made no impact, and she thought, instead, of sheer white tights, of silk and pearls.

'Give me those,' said her mother. 'It's bad luck to look at things like that.' She dumped the papers on the window-seat and stood over Tess. 'Eat up, darling. You'll need your strength.'

Tess looked round the familiar room, at the clutter of the well-to-do: china, flowers, shopping lists and notices of charity events. Nothing was ostentatious, nothing there that did not have a purpose – her careful mother saw to that. Obediently, she bent her head over the cereal bowl.

In front of the mirror, she felt differently. She felt, suddenly, that the world she knew had been too small and she was too inexperienced to have any understanding at all. Violence was reflected in the silver mirror – Becky's bomb pulling apart healthy flesh, a bullet carving a tunnel through bone, men twisted by an oil-lit fire – and the gleaming whiteness of the dress hanging on the wardrobe appeared to turn crimson.

These were the things with which George was involved and about which they never talked. But she had not asked.

Needing to hear him, she left the bedroom and, in search of a phone, went into her parents' room. Her mother's outfit, blue shantung, lay on the bed, her father's morning coat arranged neatly beside it. The windows had been flung wide open and high summer streamed through. There was the smell of sensible talcum powder and a light drift on the carpet where her mother had shaken the tin too vigorously.

While she waited to speak to George, she crossed and uncrossed her legs, already sheathed in white gossamer.

'George.'

'Tess. Everything all right?'

'I just wanted to say hallo.'

'Well, hallo.'

'Are you happy?'

'Of course.'

She felt a slight chill stroke her skin under her new underclothes. 'I love you, George.'

'Ditto,' he said, in his impersonal way.

After Becky, also in white silk but with an apricot sash (she had won), and Mrs Frant had departed, Tess made her way cautiously downstairs. At the door of her father's study, she halted and looked in.

Colonel Frant was reading a letter which he put down on the desk when he saw Tess, but not before she had caught sight of the name of his managing agency and tabulations of figures.

'All right?' she asked, alarmed.

Colonel Frant was struggling to cope with his losses, his daughter and his money and, in contemplating their significance, he felt lessened.

'All right, Daddy?'

He gave himself a few seconds, then stepped forward and took Tess in his arms. 'Absolutely dandy,' he said. 'Don't I have a beautiful daughter?'

Oh, God, she thought, alerted by the letter and the strain on his face, Becky did try to warn me.

But she swirled round on the spot to show off the dress, her veil floating out around her. 'Thank you for all this.'

Thus Tess went to her wedding, dressed in a virgin's white and shrouded in a veil, carrying lilies, her heart thudding, not to the music of the organ or to high emotion, but in response to jumbled images of death and pieces of paper with Lloyd's written on them.

As she stood by the church door with her father, she waited to be seized by an enormous sensation of feeling, by God, but felt, instead, a detachment as if the veil had spun a membrane between her and the rest of the world. Then she felt a touch on her elbow. It was Iain MacKenzie and his wife, Flora, late and out of breath.

'Good luck,' he said, and entered the church. Flora sent her a little smile with a mouth that puckered at the corners.

George's regiment formed a colourful guard-of-honour outside Appleford's ancient church. George seized Tess's hand and pulled her through. And then, only then, did she quicken with excitement, and go gladly with him.

Waiting in the receiving line with the bride and groom, Colonel and Mrs Frant exchanged a long look and the Colonel gave a tiny smile.

'My goodness,' said Nigel, in an aside to the Widow as they waited in the line, 'there's been some money spent here.'

He spoke in a speculative and, the Widow felt, rather unpleasant tone.

'Well, of course. She's their only daughter.' The Widow shuffled out of Nigel's proximity. He was eyeing the champagne. A glass or not? Champagne was hell on the veins in the legs. Better to wait for the Puligny-Montrachet he had spotted on the menu for lunch.

The Widow edged towards Jilly. 'Save me,' hissed Jilly to Margery Whittingstall. 'I can't take another dose of Jennifer just yet.' However much Jilly might pander to the Widow in private, she was not prepared to take her on at public functions.

'Cost you a lunch,' said Margery, and surged forward.

Jilly turned away and bumped into Jack who, if she was truthful, looked yellow rather than brown.

'Hally, Jilly. You look wonderful, as always.'

There was, she decided, ignoring the puritan set of his nose and chin, a fascinating suggestion of the exotic and erotic about him. 'So do you, Jack.' She pecked him on the cheek. 'Tess looks nice, very nice. Of course, you won't have had time to get to know George yet.'

It was a second or two before Jack replied and, following the line of his gaze, Jilly realized that it rested on Becky. All flushed skin and gleaming hair, Becky was dancing Ring a' Ring a' Roses with two toddlers, white skirts swirling and whirling and her sash tossing lazily behind her.

Aha, thought Jilly.

'Do you know that I got married?' said Jack. 'Last month. At the camp. I thought I might as well.'

'Oh, how lovely, Jack. Congratulations. Um. Is your wife here?'

'Penelope? No, she felt she was needed in Addis as there's a crisis brewing. I'm going back at the end of the week.'

After lunch, things became noisy.

'Ra, ra . . .' A chorus went up from the regimental contingent, who were doing an impromptu hokey-cokey in the middle of the marquee. Standing at the centre, Freddie whirled his cravat above his head and was drinking glasses of champagne as fast as he could from a tray held unsteadily by the best man.

Nigel watched them. 'This must have cost a packet,' he repeated to no one in particular, and shook his head.

By midnight, the flowers in the long-deserted marquee had drooped and the specially laid floor was encrusted with food. Remains of the cake were crumbled onto plates and flakes of salmon oozed between stacked ones. Still clad in the shantung suit, now spotted with champagne stains, but in her bedroom slippers because her feet had swollen, Mrs Frant surveyed the scene. A smell of cigarettes, damp lawn, old drink, food and a residue of expensive perfume hung over the debris.

All was quiet.

Inside the house, Colonel Frant sat in his study.

Beyond the marquee, the paddock and the meadow, with its corncockles and poppies, slept under a black summer sky. Mrs Frant switched off the electricity supply into the marquee and stood, quite still, for a long time in the dark. Then, in an odd gesture, she raised her hands palm up to the black sky, and walked back to the house.

On the second day of their honeymoon in Crete, which he had organized, George disappeared into a nightclub and failed to return until four o'clock in the morning. He found Tess sitting up in the bed, hands clasped over her knees, watching the first harsh fingers of sun reach across the horizon. In the hill above the village, several donkeys were braying.

'Why aren't you asleep?'

She favoured him with a look that he had not seen before. 'Why do you think?'

He gave a snort of laughter. 'I'm sorry I kept you awake.'

She wanted to show how angry she was but did not dare for she was not yet sufficiently sure of her husband to allow herself to be angry with him. Instead, she looked out of the window at a balding landscape with its patches of scrub and rocky outcrops. George sat down on her bed, hair flopping, stinking of drink.

'Why don't you tell me I'm a beast? Go on.'

Uneasy, she fingered the bedspread made of cheap cotton. Once or twice before she had noticed that George seemed to like – need – confrontation.

'Go on. Say it.'

Sick with misery and disappointment, she was silent.

'*Go on, Tess.*'

Abruptly, she pulled the sheets around her. 'Go to sleep, George.' She lay, burning with the anger she had not expressed, and listened to him moving around the room, his bare feet making a soft sucking noise on the stone.

Having breakfasted alone on yoghurt and coffee, Tess picked her way to the beach across scrub and lumps of concrete abandoned from the building programme further up the hill and settled herself on the only unoccupied and clean bit of sand she could find.

The heat was colossal and the beach was full. Hot stones stuck into her bottom, the sand was a burning cradle, there was no shade and the sea looked like warm soup.

So there she sat, alone and unhappy, under a blue sky and yellow sun, on a beach fringed by aromatic marjoram and thyme, bullied by the heat into releasing their aromas.

She lit a cigarette and inhaled deeply.

Suddenly, it was whipped out of her hand. 'No, you don't,' said George, grinning like a boy. 'No more smoking but plenty of swimming.'

He half lifted, half dragged Tess down to a sea the colour of pulpy black grapes. She gasped as her feet were burnt as they ran, and gasped again when the water hit her body and George pushed her under. When she came up for air, hair streaming down her back, he caught her round her waist and kissed her salty mouth.

'I love you really, Tessy. Darling Tessy.'

She kissed him back. They were to be a normal honeymoon couple after all and, weak with relief, she clung to him.

'You know, I'm not so stupid,' said Becky, on the phone to Charles.

'Did I ever suggest you were?'

'Matt Barker told me that the pay-out costs on Piper Alpha are going to be bigger than originally calculated. Why do you think that is?'

'You're going to tell me, I know.'

Becky gave one of her soft laughs. 'Apparently, the insurers hadn't taken into account all the life assurances of the catering and cleaning staff.'

She was clever, his Becky, so good on detail (in bed too), and that cleverness was the most erotic of aphrodisiacs. Pricking and stirring him until he was driven mad with desire.

Sometimes, Charles reasoned, if you put your head down and don't look up, a problem goes away. He knew this to be true from his experience at work. Skilled prevarication was an art and, from time to time, he had proved he was a master at it.

But he had reached a juncture where he felt desperate. Desperate to have Becky, and equally desperate not to hurt his family. He owed Martha much; he owed his daughters an unclouded, straightforward future. Security. Structure. Good parenting.

So, he had got his head down during that spring and summer, but what he felt for Becky would not go away. It was, it seemed, indelible. Charles's awakened passion accompanied him to the office and wound hot, sticky tendrils around each thought. It returned with him each night to the meticulously maintained house in Clapham. Sometimes Charles (who was not an imaginative man) imagined that it took a physical form and he was walking in through the door with it clinging to his back.

He was aware that the last thing on earth he should do was to hurt his troubled Martha. He also suspected that that was precisely what he was going to do.

'Leave him alone,' Louis had warned Becky.

She had thrown back at him, 'Don't be a dog in the manger.'

'And you,' he said, 'mustn't be a bitch.'

'Well,' said Becky, 'that wraps up the canine imagery.'

'Why do you want him?'

'He's kind. He's well off.'

'And what about the children?'

Becky did not hesitate. 'Children survive.'

One evening after supper Martha tackled Charles. 'What's going on? I think something is.'

She waited for his reply, every sense strung taut, listening to his mood while she twisted a lock of orange-coloured hair around her white fingers. Charles took a surprised breath. He had never imagined discussing the subject over pork chops and boiled potatoes. 'I've fallen in love with someone else.'

Martha's hand made a journey back to her lap. 'So?'

Charles, who had been prepared to act deeply sorrowful and guilt-ridden, sat up. 'What do you mean "*so*"?'

'So, my poor Charles, you've fallen in love with someone else. It happens. It happens quite a lot.'

Dynasty, the cat, wandered by and Charles concentrated on the tortoise-shell fur. 'I'm so sorry, Martha.'

Martha's mouth was twisted with distress. 'It doesn't surprise me. I'm not the most glamorous creature in the world. But I'm prepared to help you.'

He could not bear the flash of bitter hurt that she revealed in the remark she had made about herself. Could not bear it.

'I don't think you understand,' he said, and suddenly his decision was made. 'I want to leave you.'

'Yes, I know,' she said, listening frantically to what he was feeling. 'You think that at the moment, but you can't. Because of the children.'

'Can't I?' He ran impatient fingers through his hair. Just like a boy.

'No. Be patient and the feeling will pass.'

A net had been thrown over Charles, and instead of striking out into open sea he was thrashing in the circle made by the fishermen's boats. But he fully intended to swim out.

Martha's questioning had released the torrent of feeling damned up in her husband, and he made the additional mistake of imagining that no further hurt would be inflicted by talking. He got to his feet and paced the kitchen.

ELIZABETH BUCHAN

'I've never felt like this, Martha. Never before. Never so strong. It's quite extraordinary.'

He fiddled with postcards stuck on the noticeboard, snapped the lid of the breadbin shut, and seized an unopened bottle of wine and proceeded to uncork it.

'I didn't see,' cried Martha. '*I didn't see.* The wife never sees.'

There was a clatter of plate pushed against glass and the harsh grind of a chair pushed back. Hands on stomach, Martha was bent double as if she had been punched. Charles let go of the wine and a glass fell to the floor where it bounced on the cork tiles with a dull sound. He leapt towards his wife and crouched down beside her. Gasping and breathless, she pushed him away.

Wincing, Charles squatted on his heels. 'You mustn't worry, Martha. I'll make sure you and the girls have enough money.'

The view of the run-off insurer is this: having covered the first layer of possible loss with a time and distance policy up to a certain figure, any claims arising would, statistically speaking, occur only over a long period. This long period allows for profits to be made from investing the insurance premium, which should make enough money to cover any subsequent loss. Providing, of course, that the premiums charged by the one underwriting the risk had been adequately pitched for the risk being carried.

In some respects, this practice provides an excellent blueprint for the conduct of our personal lives.

That night Charles lay awake in the double bed, shifting with the greatest care away from Martha, who was also sleepless. It had not occurred to him that the first loss in a dissolving marriage was the freedom to move around in a double bed. Frozen into their respective sides, the Hayters resembled effigies under the duvet, mourning the death of a partnership.

Whereas Louis, clad in pyjamas from Simpsons, lay in his

114

bed and considered the architecture of disaster. Asbestosis, pollution, earthquake and, yes, marital breakdown.

The rules are written in stone, Father Jerome had taught him. Big immovable blocks against which you may battle all you wish and end up only with bleeding fingers.

Had he, the sharp and successful underwriter, investigated the risk sufficiently? With a combination of lust and gentleness, Louis lay and thought of Becky.

And Becky? What did she think?

Certainly she was not contemplating rain dripping off freshly washed trees, or the smell of earth invigorated by summer. She did not, like Mrs Frant, dream of the hellebore, or, like Tess, fall asleep with a heart soft and palpitating with love. Reining in the more slippery of her longings, Becky totted up the advantages of her position and set her face, metaphorically, towards the dawn.

Chapter Ten

Some acts are embedded in the memory for ever, so shameful and so sharp that the skin that grows over them has to be doubly thick. After a while, a second skin is formed. Then a third. But it cannot hide the true nature of what it conceals.

These days, lots of people leave their wives and get divorced.

At the moment of walking down the stairs with his luggage, after two unspeakable days of argument and bitterness, Charles was assaulted by violent doubt. What on earth was he doing? Was this the action of a civilized man? He dropped the suitcase at the top of the stairs and looked down at Martha in the hall below.

'You should have tried harder to stop me,' he said.

'*I* should have stopped *you*!' Martha made the gesture, now almost habitual, of pressing her hands into her stomach, as if to press it out of existence.

Charles picked up his suitcase. 'What am I saying? I didn't mean that.'

Martha had cried so hard that the skin on her face had sprouted reddened patches. 'You have a nerve,' she said. Anthea, who was clinging to her knee, whimpered, and Martha placed her hand on the child's head. 'And I imagined, Charles, that you would never do anything to hurt the children.'

Charles felt his mouth grow dry. 'It's better this way.'

'Better! Have you learnt *nothing*? Except clichés? What possible reason do you have for this to be better?' Martha raised her arm, and her patterned jumper fell back along it to her thin elbow. She seemed all skin and bone, a rattling witch, he thought, and was instantly ashamed.

Upstairs on the top landing, the Swedish au pair leant over the banisters and watched.

'You're wrong to do this, Charles. Wrong. Wrong. Wrong.' Martha spoke in a low tone.

Once again, Charles paused.

'Remember what we wanted, Charles. It wasn't that ambitious. The house. The children.'

'Daddy? Where are you going?' Anthea watched her father finally descend. At the bottom, he hesitated and his wife caught her breath. Then he moved towards the front door.

'Daddee?'

He continued out into the Clapham street and away from his home. At the end of the road were two men, drugged and ravaged. One propped himself against the wall, shaking. The second, defiantly filthy, was talking to him quietly. As Charles passed, the comforter lit a cigarette and guided it into his friend's mouth.

He walked on towards the car parked a street away, ricocheting between his infatuation and a deepening astonishment at his newly discovered capacity for ruthlessness. The man who quibbled over stealing a paper-clip from the office was to ask himself over and over again: How did I do it?

After camping in various friends' flats for a couple of weeks, and in order to celebrate, Charles bore Becky off for a ten-day holiday in Thailand.

Charles did not enjoy himself in the way he had anticipated. More than once he had been forced to acknowledge that, for a new lover, Becky paid him little attention. The air had been seductive with scent: jasmine, cardamom and hot human life. The hotel was a triumph of discreet service, the food magical. But Charles had spent a lot of time sitting beside a brilliant turquoise pool watching Becky chat up a merchant banker, whom he suspected of being deeply into recreational cocaine, and the blonde he had introduced as his wife.

It niggled him that Becky was blind ... no, he should not use that word ... *oblivious* to his aching wish to be alone with her and to his desperate guilt.

Had it been during that first dinner? Or the talks over the coffee? The times when, a Ruth to his Boaz, Becky followed him into the Room and he would glance over his shoulder and know that she was there.

During those lonely moments under the tropical sun, he had found himself searching to locate the point where he had really decided to make changes. He found no illumination, no intersection on the graph between the intent and the action, just an all-consuming hunger and need for Becky.

On the plane back home, Charles played a game. At the airport, he would kiss Becky goodbye and leave her. Waiting in the concourse would be Martha and the girls, flushed and sticky and smelling of babyness. 'So glad you've had a nice break,' his wife would say. 'Now let's go home.'

'I'll see you have enough money,' he had promised, in an agony of guilt that later turned to rage that Martha was not taking the business quietly, which would have allowed him to feel better. Scenting plunder, Martha's lawyers already looked set fair to making sure that he kept his word.

He turned to Becky, who was reading a book on oil politics. She had recently sat and passed the Lloyd's test and was going hell for leather for the ACII. 'Do you love me?'

She looked over the edge of the book and thought of Louis who had been so unreasonably angry when she announced her decision to live with Charles. 'Of course,' she said, her eyebrows drawn together, and went back to the text.

'Really?'

She did not look up but patted his thigh. 'Really, really.'

I'm like a dog, he reflected savagely, who has been flung a bone.

To her credit, Becky (who was far too smart to do so) made no comment whatsoever about Charles's financial arrangements. She had set, she informed Tess, her own agenda. For her part, Tess was not at all sure about this latest development in Becky's life.

'Why Charles?'

'You sound like Louis. Why not Charles? He wants me. He's nice and he's got stacks. And . . .'

'And what?'

'Nothing,' said Becky. 'Nothing at all.'

'Listen,' said Tess, with the authority of the new bride, 'if Charles leaves one wife, he'll leave a second.'

'Perhaps it won't matter by then,' said Becky enigmatically.

Once Charles had declared his intention of living with Becky, she had set about flat-hunting and within days she had pounced on a riverside development in Battersea. The three-bedroom flat was over-priced, although not quite as over-priced as it might have been a year ago. Property, the estate agent informed them, was iffy, a bit volatile. The complex included a gym, a swimming pool, a fresh-fruit juice bar, and its flashy atrium was the size of a small aircraft hangar. Facing north, the flat was not exactly sunny but it had a vista of the river which, on the best days, could be described as dazzling.

At first, Charles declared they could not afford it. Becky, whose business vocabulary was continually being added to – words such as upbeat and combative – spent some time extolling the attractions of the flat as an investment. When he pointed out the estate agent's misgivings, Becky kissed him and brushed her mouth against the exact spot below his ear, a tactic that always sent him wild.

The next day she got on the telephone, and by the evening she had negotiated herself another job and better pay at the rival Coates Brokers (who had woken up from the sleep of centuries to the value of the token female, especially one with Becky's potential profile), handed in her notice at Mawby's and committed herself and Charles to a hefty mortgage.

As he signed the relevant papers, Charles knew he had been outmanoeuvred.

Becky set about filling the flat with Ralph Lauren linen, glass coffee tables, huge sofas and a chandelier from Murano in Venice. There was also talk of a housewarming party.

They moved in two days after returning from Thailand, Becky bidding goodbye to the Pimlico flat that Tess had insisted she share with her and George, and Charles to his depressing *pieds-à-terre.*

'Becky . . .' Charles eased his sunburnt shoulders into a shirt on the morning of their first weekend in the flat. 'We have to cool it a little. Expense-wise. Do a bit of down-trading.'

Becky picked up his hairbrush and handed it to him. He looked at it. 'What's this for?'

'They were over on my bit of the dressing table. You must keep your things in your bit.'

'Good God.'

Becky's loosened hair swung from side to side. 'You don't mind, do you, darling? I do like my things to be just so.'

Charles threw the hairbrush onto the bed where it made a soft indent. 'I suppose I don't.'

She flicked him a look from under lashes that, to his dazzled eyes, had grown even longer during the night. 'How about the party?'

'We can't afford it.'

In a trice, Becky was beside him, twining her arms around his neck and Charles was inhaling her scent, jasmine mixed with tuberose.

'Think credit,' she said. 'Think of the freedom that credit gives. Freedom to give a party.'

'Stop it,' said a helpless, uneasy Charles, never sure whether Becky was joking or not.

'Have now. Pay later.' Becky undid the shirt that Charles had just put on.

He had *nothing* to complain about, Charles concluded, drowning in physical sensations that had long since faded with Martha. Rediscovering the itch of the flesh was magic: the exhaustion after a night's passion, the taste of feminine skin on the tongue, the surprising fullness of a slight breast under his hand and the terrible desire to lose himself in another.

Becky liked the walk from Coates to Lloyd's. It allowed time for reflection. Anyway, she liked the City. The big buildings, and the wind that whipped around them.

Today, however, the sky was plum-coloured with incipient rain and the air tasted nitrous. It seemed colder than it really was. Darkness was gathering in corners, but in buildings glaring with light dealers and pundits strove to hold steady a queasy market.

How would Tess describe it, Becky wondered, and decided that Tess, romantic Tess, would see the market free-fall in relative – and poetic – terms. She would say that when a star falls in a burning arc through space, and asteroids whirl around the solar system, formulae are shaped and put on paper to provide an explanation. We *need* explanations, she always insisted. It doesn't matter that we don't know if they're correct or not. Ah, thought Becky in her turn, but the confidence that seals together a network of shares, bonds and investment has to be explicable. Otherwise, a huff and a puff, and away it goes. Just like that.

Inside the Room there was a cluster of men round the rostrum and the talk was all, still, of the disaster on Piper Alpha.

'Yup. The investors were Texaco, International Thomson,

Union Texas Petroleum, Occidental Petroleum . . .' one broker was saying into his mobile phone. He paused. 'Spread throughout the world, of course, but mostly reinsured here.' He stamped his foot lightly on the word 'reinsured'. 'No. Not good.'

A huff and a puff, thought Becky, then made her way to Matt Barker's box and waited for fifteen minutes in the queue before handing him a prepared slip.

'Talk me through the clause four here,' said Matt, after a second's perusal. 'And twenty-one.'

Becky gritted her teeth for she was fluent in neither, a mistake she would not make again. 'Ask me about clause ten.' She smiled at Matt. 'I'm an expert on that one.'

'Go away,' said Matt, letting her off lightly, which made his junior, who was used to watching scenes of carnage between Matt and brokers, gasp. 'By the way, why did you leave Mawby's?'

Becky took another risk. 'That would cost you a coffee.'

The previous night, Charles had knelt in front of Becky, who sat on the impractical, primrose-coloured sofa. 'Becky, I miss my daughters.' He had bitten his lip. 'I miss them very much. You must help me.'

'I can't,' she had said. 'I wish I could.'

'As soon as we're married we'll have a baby.'

'Sweetie, I have a job to think about.'

'Think about it, won't you? Please, Becky.'

'Done.' Matt cracked a knuckle, and Becky laughed with delight. 'Coffee it is. Then we'll do business.' After she had left, Matt turned to his junior. 'That girl's got character, which I prefer to the prat who number-crunches.'

The junior did not comment.

The Frants regarded each other silently over the breakfast table, neither wishing to broach the subject. In the end, it was Mrs Frant who took the initiative.

'There's the Regency side table, John, and the Lalique vase.

We could sell those.' She paused to gather strength. 'And the silver.'

Colonel Frant's toast had gone cold. 'Yes.'

'We could do bed and breakfast. Lots do.'

'Yes.'

Mrs Frant's irritation again rose to the surface. 'Well, we must do *something*, John.' His quietude bothered her. 'Unless you're not telling me everything.'

Colonel Frant did not feel well and had not for some time. The worry was one thing, the effort at concealment was another, for he had confided in his wife neither the whole extent of his debt nor what he was planning to do.

'What went wrong, John?'

His shoulders lifted briefly then sagged. 'I've found out a bit more about it all. It seems that Nigel was linked in with an agency that was not so keen on the old kind of syndicate. Like the marine ones, for example. The managing agency he was pally with specialized in reinsurance. They thought it was copper-bottomed. Anyway, they probably paid him a lot in introduction fees.'

'Is it too late?'

There was a silence.

'Look, I'm going up to London to meet someone who might be able to help.'

Mrs Frant looked out of the kitchen window to the paddock. 'It seems a long autumn,' she said. 'And I expect it will be a long winter. Christmas will not be the same this year.'

Colonel Frant looked over towards the dog basket. 'I think . . . I think we should have Sage put down.'

His wife's coffee cup crashed back onto the saucer. '*No*, John. Not that.' She dropped her head into her hands. 'Surely not that. Give him away. Don't kill him.'

'I couldn't bear anyone else to have him,' said her husband. 'I just couldn't bear it.'

*

When Louis woke, which he did in a blink, he always sneezed, and Jilly groaned.

'I can't understand why you do that.' Smelling of sleep and yesterday's bath essence, she rolled over.

'I know why you sneeze,' Becky had teased him. 'You sneeze because you don't want to wake up. Your subconscious doesn't want to take second place.'

'So?' he had replied.

'So,' asked Becky, 'what is it, Louis, that your subconscious can't bear to let go?'

It was quiet in the bedroom, silent with carefully assembled luxury: deep-pile carpet, interlined curtains, *en suite* bathroom. Louis lay still.

He thought of grey stone walls, dotted with invasive ferns. The suck-suck of the river winding through the ˙swold village where he had grown up. Of his boyish self   ured in the church – aching knees and incomprehension. I... thought, too, of the frame imposed on his mind by a faith that prided itself on its grip. Stubborn and adhesive, it had stayed with Louis. An old companion. An unwanted companion, at times a clamorous companion, but as much part of him as his blood.

He looked at the clock on the bedside table and braced himself. Jilly slid her legs out of bed and inspected them carefully. He heard her give a tsk before reaching for her dressing gown.

'Up, Louis,' she said.

Over breakfast she became business-like and asked if he had any plans for the weekend.

'Are either of the boys coming?'

'No. Are you going to mass?'

'Probably.'

Jilly opened a letter. 'Why do you keep going?'

'Why do you go to church?'

'To be part of the village, of course.' The subject dealt with, Jilly now cleared her mind of inessentials. 'Would you object if I bought some furniture for the conservatory?'

'Not at all.'

Louis finished his breakfast and went to catch the train. Because he was running late, he was forced to park the number two car (Jilly used the Jaguar) at the furthest end of the car park.

The breeze blew specks of wood ash from a fire on the embankment into Louis's eyes, which made them water and he did not recognize John Frant until he had virtually bumped into him. Sometimes, in a rare moment of empathy, it is possible to penetrate through the surface of skin and bone to a truth undercutting the exterior. Underneath John Frant's neat, dapper exterior – check shirt, Army greatcoat – Louis sensed inner sickness and fear.

'How are Angela and Tess?' he asked.

'Fine. Thank you. And Jilly?'

'Fine also.'

The moment when Louis could have acted, said something, offered help, came and went. Nothing too substantial, for that was not possible, but a gesture of support *was*, even morally imperative. Yet what was Louis to say? John Frant had been placed on syndicates that were now in deep trouble, of which two remained open for 1985. Piper Alpha was going to make matters worse.

One of the defining factors of a morality is its absoluteness, to which one should cling in the teeth of the wildest gales, the hottest holocaust.

The moment came and went, and both men retreated into their newspapers.

Later, installed in his box, Louis knew he was guilty and was diminished by the knowledge.

Oh God of the grey stone church walls, I am guilty of silence.

The Mafia have the tradition of *omerta*. We are all silent about the inevitability of death otherwise it overwhelms us. But John Frant had been owed, at the very least, a sentence. A word.

I am guilty of not helping.

*

125

Fortunately, the word was with Aunt Jean, who opened her mouth and sang louder than normal in the Chapel of the Pentecost in Streatham. She found her singing satisfactory (and presumably God did, too), even if it was a little hard on the big black lady sitting next to her who shifted further down the bench. Despite her air of fragility, Aunt Jean was capable of a great noise: something to do with air resonating, perhaps, in an entirely fat-free body.

A woman, or so she liked to think, in whom pride and desire had been whittled to a minimum, thus making her powerful indeed, Aunt Jean was strong in her faith. This was fortunate for her heart, whose daily heavings for oxygen and blood caused it to knock against the thin shell of her ribcage, was failing.

'You want to be free for God,' Aunt Jean whispered to it as it banged about in her chest. 'Be patient. You'll be there soon.'

Her neighbour decided to issue a challenge, opened her mouth, let forth and the chapel was filled with ebullient sound. After all, even if inflation was running at 6.4 per cent, Christmas was coming.

Back home in Paradise Flats, Aunt Jean filled a kettle and sat down with a thump in the armchair. Flashing shapes and whirling lights danced across her vision. The kettle was boiling, but she was distinctly disinclined to get up. Pity that Becky wasn't there any longer.

Becky. Aunt Jean placed a weary, shaky hand on the arm of the chair. For as much as I have sown, so will I reap. I did not love her. I never loved her.

When she was next aware, it was to experience the sensation of a straitjacket. Both arms were pulled tight and needles had been drilled into them. There was an unfamiliar hiss of machinery. On turning her head, a fold of green curtain with an unfamiliar pattern presented itself. Someone spoke.

'She's conscious.'

'Of course I am,' she said crossly, and discovered that her throat had turned into builder's sandpaper.

'Aunt Jean?'

Becky swam across the horizon, a blow-dried, lip-glossed Becky who looked as though she should be somewhere else.

Somewhere else – a major client meeting intended to bring in major business, the first she had attended for Coates – was precisely where Becky should have been. 'Your aunt,' the exhausted-sounding registrar had reported on the phone, 'has only a slim chance. She was discovered late last night by a neighbour who did not know where to find you.'

'But,' said Becky, 'I have a meeting.'

'Don't we all?' replied the registrar. 'Don't we all?'

Becky had dressed, thinking perhaps she could juggle locations. Pop into a deathbed scene then pop into a meeting. Charles seemed appalled when she outlined her strategy.

'It doesn't matter about the damn meeting.'

Becky frowned. 'It does to me.' The past was never safe, and she had ducked and woven, hoping to find a place of safety and of affection. And never had. 'Aunt Jean never loved me,' she said.

'That doesn't matter,' said a shocked Charles.

Whatever, her aunt lingered long enough to scupper any chances of Becky attending the meeting, or the one the following day where the deal was negotiated. Instead of drinking champagne, she forced down cups of hospital coffee.

Towards the end, Aunt Jean opened her eyes and smiled happily. 'I'm very near,' she said, meaning to God.

Not unnaturally, Becky misunderstood. 'No, you're not,' she said sharply. 'The hospital's at the other end of London and I'm thinking of moving you.'

'Don't bother.' Aunt Jean closed her eyes. Her thin, transparent hand crept with infinite effort over the bedclothes towards her niece. Becky watched it knowing that Aunt Jean was asking her forgiveness.

A hot, choking feeling gathered in her chest. To pick up that hand or not? To make peace, to acknowledge forgiveness.

With an uncharacteristically rapid and graceless movement, Becky got up from her chair and left the room.

Aunt Jean's eyes remained closed, the mask lying over her features gradually congealing. Half an hour later, she whispered, as if surprised, 'It's come,' and died, leaving the hiss of machinery to fill the denuded room.

Chapter Eleven

'Becky wanted a quiet funeral but, apparently, her aunt left instructions for a rousing, happy-clappy send-off. Her friends at the chapel are organizing it. Becky's terrified at what they might come up with.'

'Really?' George was lounging, naked, in bed and not listening. He was concentrating on a memory that bothered him a lot and had changed his thinking. It was of Rainey O'Shaughan, her grief and the shooting in Belfast that had turned her modest dwelling into a slaughterhouse, and her husband and two sons into butcher's meat.

When George and his men had raced to the scene, Rainey had let herself out into the back garden and there, on her knees by the small patch in which she cultivated flowers in Republican colours, she said, 'At least my men died in front of me who loved them. Not in front of strangers.' She added, 'They won't be on the run any more. They were homesick in the south, you know. My boys.'

Tess stepped into the skirt of a black suit and struggled with the waistband. Then she brushed out her tangled fair hair.

The bedroom in the Pimlico flat was not a scene of order. Added to Tess's natural chaos there was an additional layer of wedding presents not yet stowed, some still in the packaging in which they had arrived. It was the kind of jumble of a person who had most things. Or, perhaps, the kind of jumble to remind someone that they were newly married.

She added a black velvet hairband to the ensemble. 'How do I look?'

'Very Army wife.'

'Very promising banker, you mean.'

There was a tiny, but significant, chilling of the air. The lowering of temperature between two people who are not understanding one another very well.

Oh, God, thought Tess. Not again.

George flung back the bedclothes and got up. Tess sat down at the stool in front of the tiny mirror allotted for her dressing table and made up her face with quick slashes and dabs. She had to say something to break the silence that had descended.

'Have you heard from Iain and Flora? Are they well?'

'They're fine. They've asked us to go and stay for a weekend.'

'How lovely,' said Tess, aghast at how uninterested she sounded. 'Do let's.' She picked up her handbag and threw her brush and lipstick into it. 'I've got to go and support Becky.'

Will we ever beat it? George asked himself, as he got dressed. Or will it take the end of the world to scrub the martyr complex out of the Republican heart?

Of Tess he did not think at all.

Among the congregation, composed of friends from the Mission, bingo cronies and neighbours, was Aunt Jean's solicitor. He was a bright-eyed, bobbing young man with a taste for thick-soled rubber shoes and evidently smitten with Becky. As Tess slid into a pew, Becky pointed him out and hissed, 'He's just told me that Aunt Jean left virtually nothing except two hundred pounds to my mother.'

'Your mother! I thought she was dead.'

'She is. To me.'

'Jesus loves me,' sang the congregation, at the urging of the minister, and swayed and swooped to the music in their pews.

The women sported an amazing array of hats. *Loves me . . . loves me . . .*

Standing beside Becky, Charles stuck his head forward in the manner of the embarrassed English male. Becky allowed her eyes to wander around the large, bare room with fake green marble set into the floor and plastic flowers.

'Jesus loves me,' she sang and it was then that the implications of a remark made by Charles in the car struck her. What Charles, stupidly, had let slip was: Mawby's had not yet signed with FEROC because it was insisting on more detailed figures.

Becky reckoned that, if she was clever, she could work on a few figures in the loo with her pocket calculator and make the call to Coates during the funeral tea. Then she thought better of that. Once released, information is hard to control and she wanted to manage this deal.

The funeral and the tea afterwards were as Becky had feared. There was much hugging, sistering and brothering and curiously dignified sorrow directed as much to the smart outsider that Becky had become as to the dead woman.

You fools, she wanted to tell them. I was never an insider. That was the trouble.

Afterwards, Becky insisted on taking Charles out to an expensive restaurant, as a reward for being so good and understanding and, after he had drunk a bottle of white burgundy, she grilled him gently about the FEROC deal.

Divine Nights, alias Art and Hal, the party planners, had short dyed white-blond hair and leather aprons. They also possessed visions of grandeur and excitement whose scope was not necessarily limited by space or finance unless they were dealt with firmly. But they knew what was what. They definitely did. Buck's Fizz was out. So was *nouvelle cuisine*.

'The things you learn,' said Becky.

'Can't beat a gooey roulade,' said Art, on the night of Becky and Charles's party, bearing one in each hand towards the draped table in the drawing room.

'Quail's eggs.' Hal was right behind Art, holding a plate of beautifully speckled ones in their shells arranged around a pile of peeled ones and a saucer of brown and white salt. 'And lots of *Boy's Own* puddings.'

His tone held a hint of acid for the boys had wished to art-direct the party as either a Japanese forest or a Winter Wonderland. Charles had put his foot down and they had had to be satisfied with eau de framboise champagne and spraying the room with scent and artificial cigar 'for that rich and opulent feeling, darling'.

'Where did you pick them up?' asked Tess, sprucing up her hair in front of Becky's bedroom mirror.

In the bathroom – French tiles, his and hers basins – Becky was applying make-up.

'Oh, the grapevine, you know. Amelia next door recommended them.' She drew a wisp of violet under her lids. 'It's a good thing Aunt Jean didn't pop off two weeks later than she did otherwise it would have interfered with the party.' Becky now lowered her lids and applied mascara.

'Do you miss her?'

'Not really. I don't have anyone to worry about now.'

Tess regarded her neatened hair in the mirror. 'There is Charles,' she said drily.

'He doesn't count. Not in that way, I mean.'

Tess shifted on the stool, perturbed and not a little unhappy. 'Something smells wonderful.'

'Joy.' Becky sprayed a mist of it around her, and felt the pinpricks of moisture descend onto her skin.

'I could do with some joy, Becky.' Tess wanted Becky to stop preening, to sit down beside her, to take her hands and say: Tell me. Let me help.

Of course George loves you.

Becky recognized the plea. 'Darling,' she said. 'Not now.'

They entered the sitting room whose curtains had been swept back to reflect the river, and which had tiny white fairy lights scattered throughout and over a huge orange tree in a pot. Becky turned to Tess. 'I rely on you,' she said. 'You know the worst of me.'

Jangled and unsure, in love with love and with George, yet sick at heart with its roller-coaster rides and also prone to the feminine propensity to self-sacrifice, Tess replied, 'Of course. Rely on me.'

Composing a guest list has points in common with acquiring a new lover. Pored over, admired, contemplated at night, relegated to the wastepaperbasket the following morning, it can be milked for drama. Baffled by its theatre, Charles had enquired of Becky if their party was meant to be an endurance test. By that time, Becky had netted two lords, whose aristocratic blood had been thoroughly diluted, an MP, involved in a cash scandal and, thus, delighted to be invited anywhere, and an actress, recently sacked from a West End role for reasons not specified.

Yet . . . Charles admitted to himself . . . Becky had a gift for this sort of thing, and it did not matter that he felt a stranger in his own sitting room and that the guests were quite different from those he would have invited to the house in Clapham.

Dressed in Armani, the bill for which ticked on Charles's credit card, Becky moved gracefully from one group to another, dispensing Divine Nights' canapés and caviar.

'I shall think of you, sitting on the balcony on summer evenings,' Louis murmured into Becky's ear.

She smiled up at him. 'Do I detect a wistful note?'

Charles was dispensing drinks, a little eagerly perhaps. 'Yes,' he replied, to an enquiry, 'Becky and I will be getting married when the divorce comes through.'

'I'm on my third,' stated his interlocutor. 'Imagine.'

'You look tired, Nigel.' Becky paused on her way back from the kitchen. 'You need to get out and play a bit.'

Nigel's hand found its way to his midriff, which he prodded. 'A touch of gallstone trouble,' he said.

'How's it doing?' Hal, marooned in the kitchen, asked a cruising Art.

'Riff-raff,' replied Art, with dignity. 'Only riff-raff.'

When Lily let herself into the flat through the front door, which had been propped open, the party was well into its stride. Short, not above five foot four, and fat, balanced on a pair of white leather high heels, she was wearing an expensive dress whose colours could only be termed recklessly bold, and a raft of thick gold bracelets which jangled on her arm. She was out of breath from the exertion of negotiating the lift.

She stood in the doorway surveying the scene, a flamboyantly coloured insect, and since it was not what she had quite expected, her shoulders sagged for a second or two.

She pushed her way into the sitting room. Nigel was closest to the door.

'Do you know what?' he was saying. 'Some regulatory prat has decreed that members' agents should go on courses to bone up on the law of agency—' Noticing the apparition, he broke off. 'You must be lost,' he said.

She bristled at the implication. 'Rebecca,' she said, in a tone that was an enlivening combination of South London larded with Manchester, 'I'm looking for Rebecca Vitali.'

'Are you sure?' asked Nigel.

'Just point her out, will you, sonny?'

'There . . .' Nigel's finger traced Becky's progress.

Lily stared hard, features creased into little sausages of fat.

'Oh,' she said, and seemed disappointed. 'Not bad. But looks a bit of a tricksy mare.'

Nigel was not sure that he had heard correctly. 'Would you like me to call you a taxi or something?' he asked. Lily favoured him with a look and he amended his words. 'Or, rather, would you like a drink?'

'First bit of good sense I've heard from you.'

Nigel grabbed a glass from an extremely blond, extremely slender young man with a tray and looked, for a moment, into his eyes. Then he refocused on Lily. 'Could I ask who you are?'

Lily accepted the drink. 'Who are *you*?' She was not to know that Nigel often considered that question and the answers gave him some unease. Lily addressed the slender tray-bearer. 'I've left a suitcase with the porter downstairs. Could you get it? On second thoughts, you don't look strong enough.' She turned to Nigel. 'Perhaps you could.'

The tray-bearer tittered.

Lily took a swig of champagne and, holding the glass to her bosom, barrelled her way through the pin-striped suits and minimally dressed women towards Becky.

'Rebecca,' she said, in her loud and unmistakably alien voice. 'Is that Rebecca?'

Glass in one hand, a plate of caviar on pumpernickel in the other, Becky was radiant with the success of her evening and innocent of what was about to unfold. She swivelled towards Lily. She was, she had told herself many times, a free spirit now, unimpeded by superstition, religion or ties and she watched, puzzled, as Lily teetered towards her.

'Rebecca?'

'Yes.'

'I'm Lily.'

'Yes ...' Becky's down inflection held, just, a note of apprehension.

'I'm your mother.'

The reply was instantaneous. 'I don't have a mother.'

The insect was seen to wince. 'True, but that which is lost shall be found.'

Becky swivelled. 'Oh,' she said. 'Oh.' The syllable cracked and splintered with her shock. As Louis stepped forward to help, Charles remained frozen to the grey Wilton, and Becky whispered, 'That's just the sort of thing Aunt Jean would say.'

'How extraordinary, how bizarre . . .' The girl to whom Louis had been talking was a professional mistress, and her over-made-up eyes were bright with malice.

Louis said nothing but turned, once, to look at Becky and did not look at her again.

Outside the flat, the river continued to wash its dirty water over the mud-flats, the last aircraft of the night stacked around Heathrow and the tramps were being let into the doss-houses in Vauxhall.

Still bustling, Art lit a Manova-scented candle, which he always reserved for the end of an evening. A light, flowered scent stole through the gathering.

'Darling,' whispered a riveted Nigel in Becky's ear, slipping his hand under her elbow, 'do you want me to get rid of her?'

At the other end of the room, Tess tried to move through the crush but George put out an arm and restrained her. 'Leave it alone,' he said. 'It's not your business.'

'But it is,' she hissed at him. 'Becky *is* my business.'

'No,' said her husband. 'I'm your business.'

Shuddering inwardly for, like Tess, he hated scenes, Charles knew it was incumbent upon him to direct proceedings. He held out his hand, his good-natured features wreathed in a polite and welcoming smile. 'How do you do?'

Louis beckoned to Art and exchanged the professional mistress's empty glass for a full one. Then he proceeded to tell a story that made her shriek with laughter. At a stroke, the scene reanimated and attention was switched away from the two women.

Without a doubt, Lily's entrance had made Becky's party in a manner Becky had not calculated.

Fifteen or so minutes later, Louis shepherded a group towards the door. 'Thank you so much,' he said to Charles, but did not hold out his hand. Neither did Charles hold out his.

When Louis kissed Becky, their faces brushed together for a second longer than was necessary. She looked at him and, once again, he told her silently that he understood.

Then he was gone.

'So delightful,' said a departing guest. 'How exciting.'

'Yes, wasn't it fun?'

The room was being drained of noise and warmth, the overflow washing down the stairs and into the street.

Tess retreated into the kitchen and put on the kettle. George poked his head in. 'Come on. We're going home.'

'Not quite yet. I must help.'

George watched her bustle around with the tea-pot. 'Right,' he said. 'I'll take a taxi.' And he tossed her the car keys.

Tess whirled round. 'Please wait.' But George had gone.

When the last guest had departed, Tess brought in a tray of tea to find Becky sitting at one end of the smart sofa with hands folded in her lap and Lily at the other, hers likewise, looking as if she was in training to be royal.

'Do you plan to go to sea in this thing?' Lily was asking, and her bracelets clinked as she moved.

Becky ignored her. She was exploring the sensations that accompanied profound surprise. First nothing much. Then a feeling that her skin had been lifted from the flesh underneath by an electric shock.

I don't want a mother.

Outrageously dressed, slashed with lipstick, with small fat feet, Lily was an incarnation of a future that Becky had not dreamt of.

Lily ignored Tess's tea and nursed yet another glass of

champagne. 'I'm not sure,' she said, 'that you're quite what I had in mind. But the lawyers had contacted me so I thought I ought to have a look.'

With a visible effort that made Tess ache for her, Becky pulled herself together. 'What have you been doing all these years?'

A sliver of tongue appeared between Lily's scarlet lips. 'I've made money and don't be asking me how.' She shot a look at Becky. 'That'll interest you, won't it?'

'Yes, it does actually.' Becky noted this strange woman's liver-spotted hands and papery skin, an older version of hers.

'What a noisy, dirty, hard world it is.' Lily looked pointedly around the luxurious room. 'Motherhood's a responsibility, you know.'

Quick as a flash, her daughter suppressed, as she always had, memories of anguish and loss that writhed through her past. She said, 'How would you know?'

'Here,' said Tess. 'Drink this.'

Becky sipped it gratefully and looked up at Charles. 'It would seem,' she reflected, 'that you won't be getting out of a second mother-in-law, after all.'

Charles was consumed by the need for a whisky, made for the drinks tray and poured himself a large one. On cue, Hal and Art emerged from the kitchen and began to rip down the fairy lights. Little eddies of plaster dust drifted to the floor, which they brushed away frantically. When they had finished they stowed the lights in a bag that had 'Lunch is for Wimps' stamped on it.

'We're off,' they chorused.

'Cheerio,' added Art.

'Do you bear me a grudge?' Lily was inspecting the plate on the kitchen table at breakfast the following morning. She shot Becky a naughty look. 'What are these?'

Becky returned the look fairly and squarely. 'You've seen a croissant before.'

'True.' Lily helped herself to a large one. 'We're quite civilized up north.' She took a bite. '*Do* you?'

'Bear you a grudge? Not really.' Which was not the sentiment she had expressed to Charles in the privacy of the bedroom.

You did not want me. You left me.

In daylight, it was possible to see that Lily's eyes and brows had once been as remarkable as Becky's but the eyebrows had surrendered to harsh black eye pencil. 'And Jean,' she was asking. 'What did you make of her?'

'She did her best.' At this point, Charles dragged himself into the kitchen in his dressing gown and Becky shoved a cup of tea towards him. 'But she didn't like me much.'

Lily assessed the fashionable, if not entirely functional, kitchen: the French oven, the *batterie de cuisine*, the twin sink. 'You haven't done too badly out of it. And it doesn't do to be liked. It softens you up.'

'What do you want from me?'

Lily's bracelets almost played a tune as she helped herself to another croissant.

'Well?' said Becky.

'I'm getting old,' said Lily unnecessarily. 'I thought I might see if I could live with you. The clever solicitor who traced me gave me your address.'

For once, Becky's hair was loose and flowing around her face and she ran her fingers through it thoughtfully. The effect was of extreme, untried youth. 'Why?'

'I was curious.'

'You must have been curious before this.'

'I need looking after.'

'You didn't,' Becky found herself saying, 'look after me.'

Painted in frosted pink, Lily's nails tapped against her plate as her fingers scuttled between pieces of croissant. 'Is it conducted like that?' She sounded surprised. 'If you do this, I do that.'

'In general, yes.'

Courtesy of the eye pencil, Lily's raised eyebrows seemed much fiercer than her daughter's. 'You don't know anything, my girl. And you probably did better without me.'

'It killed Aunt Jean.'

'Jean spent her life searching for martyrdom,' said her surviving sister. 'I gave it to her.'

'Yes.' Becky felt a rare tug of loyalty to her aunt. 'You certainly did that.'

At this point, Charles woke up. 'How do we know you're not a fraud? I think we'll need some proof. Some assurance that you are who you say you are.'

'I haven't any,' said Lily. 'You have to take me on trust.'

'Trust!'

Then Becky succeeded in truly astounding him. 'Oh, I wouldn't worry, Charles. I don't think there's any doubt at all that this is my mother.'

Lily looked from one to the other and saw the differences between them. 'I could tell she was difficult from the moment I saw her,' she informed Charles. 'Too tricksy by half but smart.'

Becky stirred as if from a dream. 'Takes one to know one.'

'Why aren't you more surprised?' Charles asked Becky later. 'That's what surprises *me*. This woman bursts in on us out of the blue.'

'She's been waiting to happen,' said Becky. 'I just knew it.'

Chapter Twelve

Tess came home from the party to an empty flat, which did not surprise her. She removed the little Lycra dress, which was really too tight but showed off her long legs, and stowed it on a padded coat-hanger. After that, she brushed and cleansed and, gradually, her face lost its glittery public look and emerged from the flannel dimmed into weariness and disappointment.

'Prince Charming has turned into a frog,' she wrote in the diary, 'the Princess into an overweight nag, the hearth is piled with ashes and Cinderella's contract looks a bit dodgy. I did not realize that conflict is the basis of marriage, not harmony.'

She lay in bed, waiting for sleep, and planned the diet that she was *definitely* beginning in the morning.

Tess phoned Becky early the next day. 'Do you need any help and how's your mother?'

While she waited for Becky's reply, she cradled the telephone with one shoulder and practised her nose exercises in the mirror. Unlike other extremities, your nose, she had been told, continues to grow throughout life, a reliable indicator of age. If length of nose tallied the years – Tess squinted at hers – then she was a hundred.

In the bedroom, George was sleeping the sleep of the drunken and guilty.

'Lily's fine,' said Becky, 'and I've got a firm to come in and do the cleaning.'

'Where does she live?'

'Outside Manchester. She was married once but left him a couple of months later.'

Tess recollected the terrible but expensive dress and gold jewellery. 'She looks reasonably well off.'

'Don't ask me where she got that.'

'Tell.'

'She informed us that she's been quite a party-giver too, in her time.' Becky sounded genuinely admiring. 'I reckon she's been a madam, and must have survived the pimps and the fuzz. Anyway, she also tells me she's made quite a lot of money.'

Tess's professional instincts rose to the challenge. 'I hope she's not letting it sit around. Tell her if she wants any advice . . .'

'I will,' said Becky, 'especially if I benefit.'

During the unpredicted and strange encounter between Becky and her mother, Tess imagined that Becky had died a thousand deaths, as she would have done, and she quivered with loyal anger. One minute, Becky was living her life, discreet and, but for Charles, solo. The next she was being presented with a woman in a dreadful frock.

'It was cruel to turn up just like that.'

'Oh, I don't know,' said Becky, carelessly. 'No time is a good time.'

Tess concluded that Becky was tougher than she had given her credit for. Either that or she was pleased. 'How's Charles taking it?'

'Charles?' Becky seemed genuinely startled at the question. 'He's all right.'

'Be kind to him, Bec. He's vulnerable, you know.'

'Tess, you've got to stop saving the world. Charles is a big boy now.'

'And Louis?'

'I haven't a clue.'

Tess heard Becky's intake of breath and probed further. 'How do *you* feel?'

'I feel fine,' said Becky, and followed it with a silence that alerted Tess to the probability that this, despite Becky's insouciance, was a delicate area. 'Oh, Tess,' Becky sounded choked, 'I was doing fine without her.'

Tess took a deep breath while she searched for something to say. Courtesy of Freud, she decided to interpret events in terms of the psychological rather than the obvious. 'You might have been searching for her, Becky.' She added knowledgeably, 'Many do.'

'Well, I wasn't.'

Tess tried another tack. 'Didn't you say she's going back up north?'

'I don't think she likes me,' said Becky.

'So? She didn't like you when you were born. You can cope.'

When Tess put down the phone, George had surfaced. There was a silence as they faced each other and Tess made nervous remarks to the effect that Becky's father must have been very tall.

George scratched his head and Tess softened at the spectacle of his handsomeness and assurance, trophies that, as a wife, she wore with pride. 'Or,' he said, 'some marauding Viking got in on the ancestry.'

That was good: he was talking to Tess normally and reasonably. Sometimes their conversations were like walking on bits of glass. Then, inadequate and fearful, Tess darted hither and thither to avoid the slice into her flesh. Desperate love was all very well for Shakespeare and other writers, but in real life it paralysed. Imperceptibly, she was fumbling towards the idea that, perhaps, love and marriage were not a good combination either. Or, at least, the two put together constituted the highest risk.

In the tiny galley kitchen, she ran hot water for the washing up. Question: Is quivering passion the best or worst basis for negotiation?

'Any chance of some breakfast?' George had put up his feet on the sofa and was reading the paper.

'Sure.'

Fool, Tess told herself, needing to realign the balance of power. She examined the prone figure of her husband. One day, I'll earn more than you, she thought. And she entertained a delightful playlet of George marooned behind a pile of washing up while she floated out of the door clutching a Vuitton briefcase. She was changing. These days there was less of an urge to search for meanings. To find God. Or to find the energy and grace she had once been so anxious to locate. From those deductions, the syllogism looked a little bleak for, it appeared, neither love nor modern life had either room or time for God.

London water is hard and unyielding and Tess had allowed her hands to get into a bad state. 'It is never too late to take steps,' *Vogue* instructed. Tess searched among the muddle of dusters and polish for rubber gloves, failed to locate them and gave up. As she fried bacon and eggs for George, she tried to concentrate an analysing the Zen of investment but every nerve was straining to see what George was doing.

Had he looked at her as she prepared his breakfast? A couple of times? Once? Not at all?

'Here.' She placed a tray in front of her lounging husband and looked at him with a combination of passion and need which, if she but knew it, always made George irritable.

She dried up the knives and put them away in the drawer and then retrieved them for she had put them in the wrong way round.

'Tess ...' George cut into his wife's ruminations. He had draped himself over the doorpost, loose-limbed but curiously watchful. 'Listen, Tessy, I'm being sent on a course, training and things, and then it's Northern Ireland again. You won't be coming.'

The skin on her fingers had gone prune-like and she picked at a cuticle. 'Oh, no pay, pack and follow?'

''Fraid not. This is a sort of special assignment.'

'Can you say what?'

'Not really.'

'Oh. Oh, well, then.'

'You wouldn't have wanted to leave your job, Tess. Be honest.'

'How dangerous will it be?'

George straightened up and Rainey O'Shaughan's wild weeping sounded in his ears. He was being seconded to the 14th Intelligence Unit, which was run by the Army, as opposed to the secret services, devoted to intelligence gathering and surveillance. Long-term surveillance. 'Well, Tessy. It is Northern Ireland. And the players are clever. Worse, fanatics.'

He was as serious as Tess had ever seen him and, suddenly, the intimacy that she so craved was there between them, and she ached with a rush of love. Then George spoilt it.

'You have my permission to take old boyfriends out to dinner.'

She pushed past him with more violence than she had intended, sat down in the sitting room and lit up. The absence in her infant marriage of an element, mysterious, glowing and perhaps as dangerous as the radium that Marie Curie had searched for over the years through the piles of pitchblende, was the one that Tess also sought. It hurt and offended her that he should make such a suggestion.

Marriage did not make for wholeness, that was for sure.

George opened the post and glanced at a letter. 'Good Lord,' he said, 'did you know about this?'

Tess stubbed out the cigarette and read the letter, which was from her father. 'That's a bore, him wanting us to sell the flat.'

'When?'

'In the spring.'

'Why do you think he wants to do that?' George looked a little uneasy. 'Well, I suppose there's Army quarters. But . . .' He did not add that, in marrying Tess, he had hoped never to inhabit them.

'I'll talk to Dad. He'll sort something out.'

As the words left her lips, it occurred to Tess that *they* should sort something out. Together. George should be offering.

He bent over Tess, ignored the generosity and tenderness in her expression and saw only her misery and bewilderment. Tipping up her chin with a finger, he said, 'You mustn't get so het up. You're a big girl now.'

Sensibly, they gazed into each other's eyes and the chemistry of desire was activated. George made the first move. 'Four months is not a long time,' he murmured, as he kissed her. 'Now will you shut up?'

Since what followed possesses a remarkable facility for blotting out the short term, all was well and George made up for his differences with a fine, sweaty show of lust.

The following day, he rang Tess at the office and announced that the two of them, plus the MacKenzies, were going to Berlin for a quickie pre-Christmas weekend, where they were borrowing an Army quarter.

'Nice?' He seemed to want her approval, and Tess felt small and mean that the prospect of two days in a military camp in Berlin, rather than a hotel in the West Indies, did not excite her.

'Nice,' she echoed. 'But why?'

'It's a cheap weekend and I thought you and I could have some time sightseeing or something together.'

'Are you going to say anything to me at all?' George asked on the plane over. He was on his second mini-bottle of wine.

'Sorry.'

The plane cut through the air corridor, and circled over the divided city, doubly divided now that it was evening by glowing electric light shining wastefully on the capitalist side, by dark on the Communist.

Tess considered the geographical division below. Single, you carried your own burdens of disappointment and your expectations were mercifully private. Being married, it seemed, had the effect of taking a tin opener to the lid kept on them. That was the point of it. Wasn't it?

'How long have you known Iain?'

'Ages.'

Their friendship was puzzling, inexplicable, really. George so swaggering, Iain so contained and watchful. 'He's a good sort,' she said carefully.

George tapped the window of the aircraft to indicate Berlin below. 'I love Iain,' he said. 'He's my anchor. My lifebelt.'

'Oh,' said Tess, and swallowed painfully.

Iain met them at Tiegal and whisked them off in a borrowed Mercedes. 'I know the city well,' he said. 'We were posted here four or five years ago. Flora's making some supper. She's looking forward to seeing you.'

If Flora was pleased to see them she managed to hide it, and Tess got the impression that she would have preferred the weekend alone with her husband. Inclined to mousiness, emphasized by a brown skirt and cream blouse, she led them round the house, exclaiming, in her soft, reedless voice, at the efficiency with which it had been built.

'See?' she said, leading them to the basement. 'A dedicated washing and drying room. Only the Germans would be so clever and so organized.'

Tess gazed at this palace of housewifery and felt, unaccountably, depressed.

In the morning, the men disappeared for a couple of hours. Tess looked at Flora and her heart sank. Her vision of feasting on a froth of white and gold rococo palaces retreated. Flora suggested coffee and then a nice walk in the woods.

'It's quite tricky out here,' she said, giving Tess her coffee and pouring hot water for herself. 'The wives get restless and homesick, especially if hubby is away. There're drug problems, beatings-up, and when I was here a quartet of wives set themselves up as tarts and earned quite a lot of money.'

'Did the husbands know?'

'No, thank goodness. They'd have killed the women.'

Tess had an idea that she was being rehearsed and briefed.

'Mess nights . . .' Flora was saying, with the air of someone who had been born to shoulder burdens. 'Playgroups, lunches for the wives . . . You've got all this coming.'

'Have I?' Tess was startled. 'I suppose I have. But, of course, I have my job.'

'But you'll give that up?'

'No, I don't think so.'

If disapproval could be measured in colour, Flora's expression would have been black. 'So the Army can't count on you.'

'Not in that way.'

'Goodness me,' said Flora, in a soft voice. 'How things are changing. Of course in the past . . .'

What past? A great deal of past. Consider the network, the huge web spun by women's work stretching across continents. Soothing, caring, child-rearing, underpinning welfare states with voluntary work, being unselfish and receptive and loving. Entirely unpaid.

Flora recollected herself. 'You're in investment.' The subject brought a faint colour to her cheeks. 'Terribly grand.' She leant forward. 'Do you have any tips? The Army pay, you know . . . and there's talk of cuts, which we're *terribly* worried about. Everything is so unpredictable and depressing, don't you think? I was even thinking of buying one of those Amstrad thingies and having a go at a children's book.'

Tess did a good job of looking interested.

Flora's breathy little punctuations continued. 'I was terribly against buying shares in British Gas and those sort of utilities. I didn't agree with selling off the family silver.' She sipped her hot water. 'On the other hand, it's silly to ignore an opportunity.'

'Quite,' said Tess.

On a diet of disapproval Flora's pallor improved steadily during the day, and she confided privately to Iain that she rather thought Tess would have to learn a thing or two. Iain annoyed her greatly by replying that, these days, women were entitled to their own lives. This had the effect, Flora concluded, of downgrading her own sacrifice of a career as a successful hospital administrator. In a very soft voice indeed, Flora asked him just where he thought he would be if she had pursued her life rather than his.

If she had reservations about Tess, Flora would have hated Becky. Sometimes Tess disapproved of Becky, but only in relation to Louis. A newish bride struggling with the intricacies and silences of living together, Tess felt that Becky's liaison was not supporting the institution.

'How do you know I'm not propping it up?' was Becky's invariable response.

During the Berlin weekend Tess thought about Becky in little flashes, much as the stone in the stream is sometimes visible, sometimes not.

Becky would not have cared for Berlin. Too decayed. Too much ancient history and suffering. When the party set out for some serious sightseeing, Flora confided to Tess that when she had been here, among the empty spaces and pocked buildings, she had found herself longing for the ordinariness and reassurance of a congested M4, of marigolds and polythene-covered Cheddar.

Tess longed to ask George what Iain had seen in Flora but thought better of it. If women had a loyalty to each other, so did men. George remained silent on the subject of his best friend's wife, which she was beginning to see held its own significance.

On the Saturday night, they went to the opera in the eastern sector. Passports held up to the window of the coach, the security camera winking, they drove through the checkpoint through a cityscape of cold winds and concrete tower blocks to the old opera house.

Fresh, fit-looking and smiling, Iain had touched Tess's elbow and pointed out the more exquisite features. Suddenly, Tess scented danger. Or, rather, disturbance.

The opera was *Così fan tutte*. Mozart had also scented danger and skirted around it with delicacy and tease, to which the cast responded with passion.

'I was warned once by a mad English professor that disguises are more dangerous for those who put them on,' Tess remarked to Iain, in the interval. 'They end up seeing things they didn't bargain for. You wait, it's the men who are going to suffer in the end for testing the women.'

'What rubbish you talk sometimes, Tessy.' George smiled at Flora.

In soft blue, with large gold earrings, Flora looked at the floor and murmured, 'Well.'

'And the women?' asked Iain.

'They're tougher. They get away with it. Their toughness surprises the men.'

To Tess's amazement, Flora nodded in agreement with more vigour than Tess had imagined she possessed.

On the way to the western sector, Tess watched the lights of the restless, stricken city.

What chance did one small marriage have of working when it was framed by such fractures, such dangerous movements in the world? Such betrayals. And such slippages of faith and flesh.

Other than in sleep, Tess and George had not spent one moment alone.

'Right . . .' George called from the bedroom, closing his suitcase. 'That's it.'

Tess was on the phone. It was early February and post-Christmas malaise hung over the flat. She had not got round to removing sprigs of holly from the pictures or to folding up Christmas wrapping paper and only that morning her lack of housekeeping had been a source of marital sniping.

'Lodgers, Daddy? Are you quite sure?' She listened to her father. 'How will Mum cope with the extra work?' There was another pause. 'Of course we'll get out of the flat. It's about time George and I stood on our own feet.'

At the other end of the phone, her father signed off gratefully and said her mother wanted a word.

'Mum,' she said, 'I know things are bad but have you really got to do this – what's it called? – yes, this Wolsey Lodge business?'

Angela Frant had spent some time trying to decide whether her heart was breaking from anger, grief or routed pride. 'Well,' she said in her practical tones, 'we could sign up with Amway. We have to eat and it doesn't make sense to sell the house. Or, at least, I don't want to sell the house.'

'I see.' Tess was ashamed. 'Bed and breakfast it is.'

George had dragged his suitcase into the hall and was checking through his pockets. Tess finished her conversation. 'Listen, Mum, I promise to come down and help you.'

She traced a pattern on the plastic casing of the phone with a finger and did not look up. 'If the flat is sold while you're away, I'll find somewhere to rent.' She sighed heavily. 'Mum and Dad are in big trouble.' Tess could tell that George was not pleased. 'You might at least say you're sorry or something,' she burst out.

'I've told you how sorry I am.' George stuffed his wallet into his jacket pocket. 'I can't keep on saying it. We had a flat, now we don't. It's a bore and a pity, but there we are.'

He smiled as he spoke and Tess, looking up swiftly, caught the smile, and her suspicion that George was not focused on her was swept away by a familiar surge of excitement.

'When shall I phone you?'

'I'll phone you,' he said. 'When I've got a moment. So don't worry if you don't hear immediately.'

So much had gone into George and so *little* was coming back, however hard Tess tried, however hard she hoped. With a shocked gasp, she ran at him, grabbed him by the shoulders and shook him hard.

It was the first time in her life that she had ever done such a thing, the first time control was impossible. 'I *can't* think why you bothered to marry me. You're so ... so ... bloody detached. I seem to be nothing but an encumbrance. Or a free lunch or a free flat.'

'Hardly the last any more.' Calmly, George prised off her hands. Tess resisted and he brought to bear his considerable strength. With a moan she gave up. 'Now you stop this,' he said. 'You've got to grow up.'

She dropped her hands and averted her wet face. 'I thought you'd make me whole,' she said miserably, realizing, finally, that George would not understand.

He shoved his hands into his pockets. 'I think you think you married your father, someone who'd baby you and look after you,' he said. 'But you haven't, you know. And the sooner we agree on that, the better.'

She stared at George, at the fit, handsome body that she loved and desired so passionately. 'Oh, go away,' she whispered. 'Go away and play at soldiers, if that keeps you happy.'

'That,' said George, and again he smiled, 'is the silliest thing I've ever heard you say.'

He picked up the suitcase, let himself out of the door and banged it behind him.

I was wrong, wrote Tess. Marriage is a power struggle. A bitter, bloody power struggle between what we expect and what we get.

Chapter Thirteen

Becky's fact-finding trip to a rig on the North Sea was put off because of wild and angry weather from late February until milder mid-April. This made it possible for her to combine the expedition with the trip to America to attend a conference on oil pollution.

Anxious to demonstrate its lead in technology and safety, the oil-rig trip had been organized by FEROC, and its guest list was a painstakingly composed mixture of brokers, financial analysts, underwriters and a couple of hand-picked journalists who could be relied on to file the right report. Becky was the only woman.

'Why you?' asked Charles suspiciously, when she told him her plans. 'It should be us at Mawby's.'

'My legs, darling. What else?' If Charles had been in an observant mood, he might have spotted a suspicious light in Becky's eye. 'Why not me? FEROC has put a big budget towards training and public relations. It needs friends and it's making sure it has some. Anyway Dick, the corporate-relations chap, has become a friend, we must have him to dinner, and he promised me a peek at the real thing.'

It may have been spring, but in the North Sea, off Aberdeen, subtleties of seasonal change were irrelevant. Swooping in from the air, the rig metamorphosed from a toy castle on a grey sheet into a vast, airy cathedral, and Becky experienced a fleeting moment of fear. Piper Alpha was only recent history.

As they struggled out of the helicopter onto the landing pad, the wind lashed savagely at the members of the group and flayed a layer of salt onto their skins. A month here, thought Becky, and I would be as dried and brittle as salt fish.

They filed into the reception area. The door closed behind them and, miraculously, the weather was shut out.

'You'll be wishing you were back in a cosy office.' One of the party, a rugger-playing type called Jim, turned to Becky.

'Will I?' said Becky sweetly.

They were inhaling an odour peculiar to extra insulated and heated buildings. Becky wrinkled her nose and the smells and enforced intimacy of living in close confinement were borne in on her. Tact in bucketfuls would be necessary to survive. Or, maybe, one learned to put up with the worst. Or went mad.

She looked out of the window. The rig was a monument to endeavour. To profit. It was poised on the edge of the world, and she did not underestimate its rapacious nature.

Harnessed, hatted and carefully marshalled, the group were shown around. They watched the oil flare, listened to the ceaseless rattle of machinery in the wind, and felt the prickle of nerves in response to their exposure. At times, as they clambered down steps, they appeared only just to be hovering above the sea's bluster. As they clambered up, they grew remote from its roar, gathered up instead by the astringent wind.

After the first futile attempts, no one took notes.

At lunch, they were served with soup, fish (of course) and a good fruit tart. Unusually, Becky was hungry and ate all the courses, a serene-looking female among the men.

'How about a drink this evening?' The rugger player was trying his luck.

'I think not,' said Becky politely. He flushed and turned away.

Back in an over-furnished hotel room in Aberdeen, Becky ignored the message from Charles: please ring. Instead, she sat down to write up her report on the new, state-of-the-art laptop she had wheedled out of Coates.

Only then did she permit herself to pick up the telephone and to ring Louis. 'What are you doing?' she asked.

'Can't tell you.'

Becky examined her reflection in the mirror. 'Louis. I wish you were here.'

'I've got to go home. Jilly's expecting me.'

'Yes, of course.' She lay back on the bed. Her skin felt tight and wind-lashed. At some point, age would get to work. Mottling and dulling skin. Thinning bones, sculpting flesh into folds. What then?

'Becky,' said Louis, 'I love you.'

Becky was so astonished that she put down the phone.

She rang Tess's home number and left a message on the answerphone. 'Tessy. Can you have Charles over or something? He needs cheering up and he's useless on his own.'

Finally she rang Charles, who sounded a little drunk. 'Bec,' he said eagerly, 'had you forgotten you were supposed to be ringing me?'

'I'm ringing now,' she pointed out.

'How did it go?'

She gave Charles an edited account. 'Good,' he said, sounding like the decisive Charles to whom Becky best responded. 'We're working night and day to get the figures sorted for the FEROC deal.'

'Charles,' said Becky, then thought better of it. She looked down at her expensively shod feet (Aunt Jean had never in her life bought a pair costing more than twenty pounds) and reflected on the flat by the river, filled with objects that she had desired and bought. She thought, too, of her old life and her new one and of money, the commodity that made perfect sense.

'So nothing's been signed up?' she asked.

'No. The boss has been away. He's back tomorrow.'

'Listen,' said Becky, 'Tess will be ringing and asking you over for a meal.'

She realized Charles had drunk more than a few glasses of

wine when he confessed that Martha had also rung and wanted him to go over to Clapham because Anthea had been bed-wetting.

'Fine,' said Becky. 'But take a Resolve first. You'll find it in the bathroom.'

'Hang on.' Charles abandoned the phone and returned. 'Got one,' he said, a boy discovering treasure after the adventure. 'Thanks, Bec. You are good to me. Love you.'

The telephone receiver was warm and slightly damp. As she dialled Coates's number, Becky tapped a martial rhythm on her knee with her free hand. She got through to her boss at once.

'Mawby's still reckon they're in on the FEROC act,' she said quickly.

'Don't worry, it's more or less wrapped up. We'll announce it in the next day or two.'

'That's good.'

Her boss seemed puzzled. 'Doesn't your chap work at Mawby's?'

'Yes,' Becky replied. 'Does it matter?'

'Not to us ... unless there's a conflict of interest, as we discussed originally.' His tone was unsure, even sounding a little repelled. 'But maybe to you.'

'No,' said Becky. 'Not at all.'

Before dinner, she went out for some air. The hotel was situated on the outskirts of Aberdeen, and behind the city's formal Georgian composition, which had been so rudely thrust into the twentieth century by the discovery of the oilfields, was the Scottish countryside.

She stretched up her face to the flat cold expanse of sky and breathed in deeply.

If she was truthful, the burden of Charles was beginning to press on Becky. The little boy, the troubled lover, the guilty man. To a degree, she had been the architect of the last. She had taken him on because he had money, he was willing, he was good at his job and, yes, he was nice.

How quickly reasons turn dull and lose their urgency.

The sky was empty, a grey and unyielding expanse. Courtesy of God, Aunt Jean had been sure of what she was doing. Like aunt, like niece. Becky was sure too. She knew where she had come from, and precisely because she was clear on that, she knew where she was going. And what lay at the end.

Clutching the collar of her expensive coat around her neck, and in her expensive shoes, she trod back towards the hotel, which smelt of pot-pourri and gussied-up food. If doubt and disappointment ever speared through the cunningly contrived armour in which Becky had clad herself, she did not acknowledge it.

It was after eleven o'clock when Becky left the hotel dining room. Fatigued and a little bored, for the men at play were tedious, she stopped in the foyer to examine one of the glass cases containing jewellery and china.

The intense, and idiosyncratic, manner in which she looked at the objects, the waterfall of hair caught up in a pair of combs, the long, long legs impressed the interested onlooker on the nearby sofa with a curious combination of familiarity and rediscovery.

'Becky . . .'

She whirled, for once unguarded and wordless. At last she said, with a little gasp, 'Louis.'

'As you see.'

'Good heavens. You took a risk.'

'Who better?'

He picked up his briefcase and together they moved towards the lift. Outside her room, Becky slotted the plastic card into the lock, let them in and leant against the door. 'How did you do it?'

'Easy. Got the last flight.'

'Tell me.'

Her insistence on the details amused Louis and he spun out the story of last-minute dashes, taxis and booking details. Then she asked about his work and he replied that he was dealing with business in Northern Ireland.

'George is there.' Becky wore her teasing, witchy smile.

Louis had had enough. He pulled her towards the bed, flung her down and unzipped the tight skirt. 'Will you shut up?'

She did nothing to help him, but after a minute she was naked.

Half-way through, Becky said, 'I've betrayed Charles.' She did not need to add 'again'.

'How?'

Becky told him about the FEROC deal. Above her, Louis smiled and she smiled back.

They rang for room service and ordered champagne. Louis got up and took a couple of aspirin. When he came back to bed Becky lay as close to him as she could manage and filled him in with the details.

'All's fair in business. I believe that.'

Louis recollected the cool grey stone church and, conducted inside it, his halting confessions and the absolutions. Shamefully, both his desire and the degree of his complicity increased. 'All is fair,' he said, 'but not necessarily right. Let's be straight about that.'

With a quick movement, Becky buried her face in his shoulder and ran her hand up his body. 'Who are you to talk?'

'I can't.'

She was alerted by a heaviness in his voice. 'It's all we've got,' she said, meaning work. 'Otherwise there's nothing. You're greedy and I'm greedy.'

He rolled towards Becky and gathered her up in his arms. 'You're wrong, Becky. And you're wrong because you've been wronged.' He began to kiss her eyes, then her cheeks, then her neck. 'You mustn't make the mistake of imagining I understand or I don't know.'

'Know what precisely?' She seemed puzzled.

Louis checked himself for he saw no point in continuing the conversation and raking up Becky's origins. Instead he kissed her again. 'It doesn't matter,' he said. 'Enough. It's all too short to worry about.'

It crossed Becky's mind that Louis was the only person who ever made her feel safe. At least for a minute or two.

'Talking of which ...' Louis continued, 'who knows about us?'

'Only Tess,' replied Becky. 'She knows most things about me.'

Both were silent, for a dim but unmistakable intimation of their mortality had crept through them, a cold contrast to the sensations of their warm, naked bodies. It drew them even closer. For as they had shared their bodies, they also shared the knowledge that both had a dark and restless spirit.

If he loved her ... then. If she loved him ... then. Breathing him in, his flesh against her face, Becky found herself crying helplessly.

Out of the blue, Louis said, ' "I will not leave you orphans." '

'What's that?' she asked, and wiped away the tears on her cheeks.

'A promise I heard as a child. So you must be quiet now.'

'Sometimes,' she said, through fresh tears, 'you talk rubbish.'

Louis held her against his heart until she stopped and murmured over and over again that he loved her.

The following day, Louis flew back to London, without having noticed that he had been in Scotland.

'Surely ...' Tess gave Charles a hefty gin and tonic then poured a strong one for herself, 'you don't regret being with Becky. Do you?'

Charles had come over to the Pimlico flat for supper, a depressed-looking, half-packed-up flat in which Tess was uneasily anchored, not knowing whether she was to be here or there. It was proving difficult to sell and the property market was showing signs of a serious slump.

'I *can't* understand it,' her father kept repeating, each time with a degree more desperation.

Charles sucked eagerly at his drink. 'I don't regret it at all. But Becky is a bracing person. Martha was . . . is not. It takes time to adjust.' He added in a low voice, 'One makes one's bed.'

This did not sound the song of a happy man.

It takes one to know one.

Surveying him over the rim of her glass, she concluded that he *did* have a depressed air and that troubled her. She had grown fond of Charles in a safe, platonic way, perceiving that he had two sides, often at war with each other. Anyway, her own unhappiness made her sensitive to his.

The lightest of fingers stroked across her tender heart.

'Becky's the best person I know,' she said. 'You won't go wrong with her.'

'I know.' Charles thought it over. 'Of course, she's quite brilliant.' He gave a self-deprecating laugh. 'Too good for me, really.'

'Charles . . .' Tess stood over him with the gin bottle. 'Stop it. Another one?'

He held out his glass and, for the first time, she noticed the bright blue eyes. So English, and hiding confusion and doubt. 'I sometimes wonder . . .'

'Let's have supper.'

Over fresh spaghetti and tomato sauce, they got through two bottles of burgundy. They touched briefly on holidays, where and how expensive, a film they had both seen on which they disagreed. After that, the conversation, which was a little sticky, faltered. Only those who know each other well can indulge in the luxury of silence. Eventually, after another pause, Tess made an inspired guess and mentioned an investment she was evaluating. Immediately Charles brightened up and responded with an anecdote about insuring bicycles in Holland, which made Tess laugh.

Over the cheese, they talked money, assessing its waywardness, its black magic and the cloud that had folded over the eighties economy.

During this conversation, Tess was aware of big, boiling emotions below the surface.

After the ice cream, she brought up the subject of her parents and the mood changed. Taking the wine, they moved to the sofa.

'I don't know what to do about them,' she confided, and her eyes grew wet. She rubbed them impatiently. 'The last demand was for fifty thousand pounds. I feel Dad was misled or, at least, not properly advised. In fact, I know he wasn't.'

Whatever failings he had, Charles was excellent on tears. Feeling strong but, of course, detached, he slipped an arm around Tess's shoulders.

'What does George think?'

'I haven't *really* talked about it with him.'

So sympathetic and, somehow, so buoying up, Charles's arm tightened and Tess found herself in one of those situations where what she thought was happening probably was not. Yet indubitably it was.

At that precise moment, her reasoning was not brilliant but good manners suggested that it was bad manners to imply to someone that they were seducing you when they were merely offering comfort. Equally, it was very bad manners to allow your best friend's lover to seduce you as part of the comforting process.

'Poor Tess. Your poor parents . . .' Charles poured more wine for them both. 'And . . .'

'Yes?'

'Poor Martha.'

Pity is an excellent aphrodisiac with a facility for demolishing barriers. Pity shared can achieve all manner of results.

Why, thought Tess, I have been too conformist all my life. Too restricted in my behaviour. Ungenerous, too, with my body. I should share it.

I've stepped over the line once, thought Charles, and it's impossible to go back. So what does it matter? I need help. Reassurance, not reinsurance. Some way of assessing what I'm worth. Otherwise, I'm lost.

Help me, Tess.

Tender-hearted Tess, so anxious to give, responded and when Charles leant over and kissed her, she did not move away. Then he buried his face in her hair, letting it drape between his fingers. Five minutes later, Charles was kissing her and pushing her into the pillows.

In Belfast, George was asleep, worn out and over-full from a late supper of fried bacon and sausages, which had been left to stew on a hotplate. He had eaten it doggedly and resolutely because his body required fuel. The night had been difficult, but he would sort out the implications after he had slept.

It had been tiring, bloody tiring, and he hated the clothes. A pair of grimy jeans, with a 9mm Browning tucked into them, and a donkey jacket that had seen better days.

While Tess was otherwise engaged, George had been staking out a bomb factory on a housing estate to the north of the city.

Eyes slow. Keep walking. Look the part. On the target. Squeeze pressal button on radio to tell Alpha on the net where he was.

Who was that talking to the tall man in the anorak? George dropped his eyes and lit a cigarette. That was Kelly 'all-British-are-fascist-pigs' senior. And if Kelly senior was around, the likelihood was that Kelly junior was too.

It was time to move. From the staked-out house came the

sound of grinding. A bomb was being made in a large coffee grinder. Alpha whispered in his ear to get out.

George made his way along the street up to the Shamrock pub and eased his way through the crowd to the bar. He ordered a whiskey.

The Kellys came in after him. He could feel them. He could hear them. Last time George had seen them close up was after they had been brought in for questioning. He hadn't liked them then and he didn't like them now.

Around him, the talk went on and on. He caught at snippets. So much hatred lurking in hearts. And it didn't matter how capital was poured by the government into shopping malls and supermarkets, it didn't buy out hatred.

Who knew? This pub was probably crammed with more undercover agents than *bona fide* rebels.

Someone was singing, rather beautifully, and the man next to George joined in. George lifted his glass and drank and, as he did so, his eyes collided with those of Kelly senior.

Understanding flickered over the older man's face, and a strange out-of-place compassion. Why, thought George, you're as trapped as I will be.

He was burnt.

Tess woke with a start and a headache. I went to bed with this man because, in the end, I did not want to seem bad-mannered, she thought.

'Look,' said Charles, from beneath the sheets, 'I'm very sorry about this.'

She searched to recapture the sense of liberation and wild mood of the previous evening. 'So am I. So am I. But I understand.'

Blue-eyed and tousle-haired, he reared up from the pillows and questioned her eagerly, 'Do you really?'

'I think so.'

'Thank God.' He shot a look sideways at Tess's peachy skin and the mass of hair. 'I didn't mean it to happen,' he said thickly, and reached over to touch her.

Tess clutched the sheets around every bit of her bare body and shut it off from him. 'Would you mind closing your eyes, Charles? I want to get dressed.'

Obediently, he did as he had been bidden and Tess put on her clothes, shivering and a little queasy. Then she sat down on the edge of the bed.

'Charles. You must go.'

'But what are we going to do?' His eyes were round.

'Do? Nothing. George comes back for the weekend tomorrow and Becky will be back in a week's time. We do nothing. No, that's not quite right. We forget.'

'We forget,' said Charles, and sat up. Tess softened for he was, without question, handsome. 'This is our secret. We'll never talk about it again.'

'No,' said Tess, 'no. That's agreed.' And with that undertaking, she was changed, utterly and for ever.

Chapter Fourteen

Lunch at the Lloyd's Club was a mixed affair. The beef was voted not quite up to scratch but the mood veered between the sombre, because warrants for the arrest of two underwriters had been issued by the Serious Fraud Squad, and guarded optimism, because the American court had ruled against Shell and in favour of insurers over the question of the pollution of the Rocky Mountain Arsenal (from which the company derived profits of between $12 million and $20 million a year, using open-air evaporation basins for its toxic wastes).

The Bollys made up for the beef with some excellent claret. It was not quite enough to square the future favourably but it helped to make the atmosphere a little more congenial. The pollution crisis was not, Matt and Louis agreed, going to go away.

'Met someone the other day,' Nigel announced.

'Really?' Matt's knuckles cracked.

'Told me about this new expert emerging in the States, the insurance archaeologist. They trawl the archives digging out old policies with loosely worded general-liability clauses.' Nigel had no need to add that many of the clauses would be thrown back at Lloyd's.

'Hate the buggers,' said Chris Beame.

'We've survived worse,' said Nigel, searching in his pocket for an antacid pill. 'The chatter in court of moral responsibility,' he was referring to the Shell case, 'doesn't end in us having to pay.' He paused. He chewed another pill. 'It isn't our fault.'

'No,' said Chris Beame.

'Nigel,' interjected Louis, 'I think you'll find there are approximately four hundred thousand hazardous waste sites in the United States, all requiring to be cleaned up.'

After that, the lunch seemed to lose its point and the Bollys dispersed.

Colonel Frant was of the school who believed that personal calls should not be taken in the office so Tess was surprised when he rang her at Metrobank.

'This is just to let you know, darling, that since we haven't sold the flat I've had to make other plans and I want you to come home at the weekend and discuss them, if you would.'

'Of course,' said Tess, who had one eye on the screen and a rather important stock that was not behaving as she wished. 'How's Mum?'

'Worried sick about Jack. But we think he's better.'

Jack was in hospital in Addis Ababa with a dysentery bug; according to Penelope, he was taking his time to get better.

'How was George?'

'Oh, Dad, it was only two days and then he was off again. Not long enough, really. We just lazed around and went out to dinner. You know, that sort of thing. Dad, I must go. I'll see you on Saturday.'

On arriving back for the weekend, George had said, 'Let's not think of our differences, Tess. Let's think of our similarities.' And Tess had rejoiced, for it was the first such sentiment George had voiced. It made her feel, in a curious way, that she was seeing him properly at last, and she felt anticipation and optimism stir strongly inside her.

Then she remembered what she had done, and her feelings became muddled with pain and anxiety, and she grieved for her own shortcomings. What's the point? she thought. What *is* the point?

George had been loving to Tess but quiet. He spent much of the time either sleeping or watching television, but before he left he pulled her close and said, 'We'll make it, Tess. You'll see.'

The letter was waiting for Becky when she arrived back from her ten-day trip to the States.

> I hope you've recovered from the shock [wrote Lily]. I should, I suppose, say sorry. But I don't feel sorry. I always say that you should never be sorry for things you do, only what you don't do. I wanted to see you and now I have. You seem to have done all right and I respect you for that. Perhaps it runs in the blood.
>
> As you will have gathered, I'm not one for mothering. For all her God-ing, Jean was a much better bet. If you feel hard-done-by and resentful, think about that.
>
> I don't expect we'll meet very often. I refuse to be robbed by British Rail and my feet swell on the coach. But if you want to telephone me at any time, I'm here.

Becky read it in the hall, surrounded by her luggage, and found herself smiling.

Charles was also waiting for Becky, on the primrose sofa, anticipating the sound of the taxi and the opening door. Becky's palm tree, which he considered hideous, threw spiky shadows on the wall. A huge drinks tray sat under a lit Provençal landscape that she had also insisted on buying.

These were visible appurtenances of a particular life. Bought at cost, maintained at cost. The showy familiars of an economy whose murmurings and eruptions, egged on by the boys in striped coats, the brokers, the insurers, the punters, the plodders and, of course, the vultures, were Charles's daily fare. Not that he thought of his affluence in those terms, if he considered it at all.

The habit of introspection had come only recently to Charles and it tended to concentrate on one subject: a slow, awkwardly conducted investigation into emotions that threatened to become too painful. 'I love her, I *love* her,' he repeated often to himself, aware that tiny seepages of distrust and disappointment were draining his reserves.

He sat quietly, legs crossed in a manner reminiscent of the days when he had been in control. When the front door opened he did not get up but waited until the sound of a heavy suitcase being manipulated into the hall ceased.

'Charles? Are you there?'

He remained silent and Becky put her head round the door, a tired-looking, travel-smudged Becky.

'You *are* here. Why didn't you answer?'

'Hallo, Becky.'

Puzzled, she advanced into the room, and threw a new Chanel bag onto the chair. 'Not even a kiss?'

'Since when,' Charles heard himself saying, 'have you minded whether I kissed you or not?'

'Oh dear, it's that bad.' She bent over him, trapping him with her arms and he caught the waft of her perfume, the jasminy one that she loved and he loved because she loved it . . . 'Are you going to tell me?'

He fended her off, knowing that his strength and resolution were less clear cut than he wished. There were no buttons he could press. No figures from which he could form a conclusion. He had imagined that by leaving his wife, loved with the depth of a long association, for a new passion that snared him in wild and haunting dreams, he would be empowered, as other men had appeared to be. Too late, Charles had discovered that he was not a dreamer, would never be a dreamer. He had tumbled at the wrong time to a secret: he did not match the models he had chosen. In that discrepancy, however small, can be hidden a tragedy – in this case, the tragedy of Charles's betrayal.

'Mawby's,' he said heavily, 'were informed yesterday that FEROC would be giving the business to Coates.'

Becky straightened up. 'Ah.'

'Did you do it deliberately, Becky?'

If possible, Becky's eyes seemed larger than normal but that, Charles decided, was the effect of blurred mascara. 'Do what?'

'Tell them we hadn't signed. There was a delay on our side. Whatever. Apparently your big guns were sent in and wrapped it up in twenty-four hours.' He sighed. 'Funny how they got hold of the figures so quickly.'

'Don't ask me.' Becky folded her arms and looked down at Charles.

'You must have done it, Becky. There's no other explanation. You set out to do me down.'

She sighed. 'Don't be so stupid, Charles. Lots of people had the information, all of them with their own agendas. Of course I didn't set out to do you down. You mustn't be so self-centred.'

Charles gave a snort.

Becky's expression was reassuringly untroubled. 'It's possible that I said something and, if so, I'm sorry. But there's business to be done. Good business. That's how it works.'

'You *did* say something.'

She shrugged. 'If I did, not deliberately.'

'What were you thinking of?'

'Money, business, profit,' said Becky. 'What else?' She seemed bewildered by his question.

'Becky, let me ask you something. Have you one shred of loyalty in that body of yours?'

'Charles. Do you *have* to talk in clichés?'

Where had he heard that before?

'All right. If you didn't care enough to be careful about me you should have cared about your own reputation.'

There was a tiny silence. Becky sighed. 'Don't give me that

nonsense about honour. If you can't accept how the business works, that leaks happen, whether knowingly or not, you shouldn't be in it. There's no great drama. Coates moved quicker than Mawby's, that's all.'

Stung, he raised his voice. 'Don't tell me about the business. I was in it before you were out of nappies.'

'Well, then,' she said, quietly and reasonably.

Charles lifted his hands and let them drop. The prairie dog, so delightful and brisk when busy and purposeful, so miserable when not. 'I'm now out of a job.'

Becky sat down on her handbag and put her hand up to her head. 'I think I'm jet-lagged.'

'Did you hear what I said?' Charles sprang to his feet and flung himself over to the window. 'I've bloody lost my job. They had me out of there before I could say P.45 because they reckoned we'd enjoyed some pillow talk. Do you know what that means to me? Do you know how I'm being laughed at? Do you know how long I took to build my reputation?'

Yet another silence punctuated the conversation.

'Come here, Charles.' He remained where he was. 'Please.' Treading heavily over the deep-pile carpet, he did as she asked. She took his hand and stroked it gently. 'Don't look like that, darling. Are the lawyers handling this?' He nodded. 'Listen to me,' she said. 'I've been thinking it's about time you upgraded. You need to be more innovative and use your expertise. Mawby's were holding you back. I know. I saw when I was there. They reckoned they had you tamed. But you're better than that.'

'Oh,' said Charles nastily. 'I haven't come up to scratch, then, in your expectations? Backed the wrong horse, have you, darling?'

Then he remembered Tess and what had happened.

But what had happened there was not the same. It hadn't meant anything.

Becky sat very still, every line proclaiming patience. 'Charles, you're a big boy now. The FEROC deal was common knowledge. Mawby's was dragging its feet. It could have happened at any time.'

Frantic to have things back on course, he searched her face. She was so tired that the skin had turned a chalk colour, but her expression seemed genuine. Honest – loving, even. In the old days, when moral relativism was a term for a party game, life had been uncomplicated and Charles was swamped by a rush of longing to have it back.

'If you have a mind for it, Becky, you can make black look white,' he said dully, and she knew she had won.

Her fatigue was so intense that she felt sick. She rummaged in her handbag and tossed a package to Charles. The wrapping paper said Cartier.

Charles held up a pair of enamel cufflinks. 'Not quite thirty pieces of silver,' he said, 'but they'll do.'

The enamel was blue and vivid. Becky was right. He needed a new job. He had been undervalued and, with things as they were, he could do with earning a bit more loot.

Tess was coming to terms with her new self and she hoped that no one had rumbled the process, certainly not Becky.

Her outer layer worked and played and adapted to the shapes of her life. But at her centre, reverberating with energy and anger, was her secret, and she was astonished that she, Tess Frant, well-mannered and well-intentioned, had done what she had done.

She was astonished that, out of the airy ambitions she had set herself to achieve in her life, she had finished with this lead-like disappointment and deceit.

'Been overdoing it, duckie?' Freddie passed her on the stairs. 'Do we look a tad used? Old liver curling at the edges?'

Tess managed a smile and the nausea that had plagued her for the last few days returned. 'I think I've got a bug.'

'Money bug, dearest. It gets us all in the end. The antidote is champagne. Gets a boy into proportion.'

He vanished into the foyer.

She sat at her desk and flicked through the pages on her screen. What a sticky and neurotic market it was. Naturally the clients were in a fair way to being the same. She began to take notes and then made some phone calls. Bill came over and told her off for not taking enough trouble with a potential client. 'The dear little clients don't want someone whose eye has wandered from the ball,' he informed her. 'Lots of love and undivided attention. OK?'

Tess took herself off to the ladies' and hung over the basin while her stomach settled. Then she applied a bright red lipstick and brushed pink onto her cheeks. She looked into the mirror.

'How do you do?' she said. And in that encounter Tess was formally introduced to her new self.

The six thirty train drew into Appleford station dead on time on Friday evening and disgorged a load of white-faced, sweet-eating commuters.

At the ticket barrier, Tess bumped into Louis. 'Hallo,' she said, never quite sure, these days, how to treat him.

'Hallo, Tess.'

'How's the family?'

'Jilly's fine,' answered Louis. 'Andrew has a job at Warburg's, and David's still working at Sotheby's and very happy.' He stepped aside to let her through the ticket barrier. 'I'm glad I've met you, Tess. I presume you've been talking to your father about his plans but I should warn you there's a great deal of feeling running against him in the village.'

She stopped abruptly, forcing Louis to follow suit. Bodies brushed against them and she swayed.

Louis drew her aside. 'Did you know that he's gone into partnership with an organization and applied for planning permission for a showground stretching over your paddock and field?'

'Eeyore's Paddock,' said Tess involuntarily. 'A showground? My father?'

'Eeyore's?'

She shook her head. 'It's a nickname. As a child, I thought Eeyore lived there.' She stared at Louis, so assured and expensive-looking, and hated him. 'Thank you,' she said. 'For all your help.'

It gave her pleasure that Louis flushed.

Formerly, Friday nights at the High House used to be rather sedate, rounded off by the *Nine o'Clock News*. Today, Tess was greeted by strange cars in the gravel drive and her mother in an apron, face dusted with flour. She was making bread for the guests' breakfasts, she explained.

'It's cheaper.' Mrs Frant forestalled her daughter's protest. 'Look, darling, you'll have to make your own supper tonight and please stay in the kitchen.'

Tess was conscious that something was missing in the kitchen. She looked over to the niche under the cupboards normally occupied by Sage, along with her smelly tumble of rug and rubber toys. It was empty.

'Mum,' her voice rose, 'where's Sage?'

Her mother did not look at Tess. 'Darling, I think your father wanted to talk to you about Sage.'

I'll think about Sage later, thought Tess, riven by the foreboding that, these days, was a frequent companion.

She took her bag upstairs, pausing to look into the drawing room in which sat four strangers, neatly dressed and drinking sherry. With a shock, she saw that the Lalique vase, which had stood for ever on the table between the windows, had been removed.

'From the north,' said Mrs Frant, slamming the oven shut with one foot while balancing a tray filled with chicken wrapped in filo pastry. 'They want to do the south.'

She looked tired. Tess got up to help but the smell of the food made her feel so sick that she sat down again with a thump.

'Easter's coming,' said Mrs Frant, 'and we're full for the next two weeks.'

Tess ate a supper of scrambled eggs and a sliced tomato and went up to bed.

Over breakfast in the kitchen – 'Don't go into the dining room, darling' – she tackled her father. Her mother was hanging up sheets in the back garden.

'What's this showground, Dad?'

Her father appeared guilty, defiant and determined all in the same second, none of which she recognized in him. 'I've never made use of them before, but the Eeyore's P. and the meadow are a source of potential income, which I need.'

'So? I'm in the business. Tell me.'

'Well ...' Of the generation where women in a family did not handle financial affairs, Colonel Frant was not expansive. 'It's bad,' he said reluctantly. 'Bad.'

'And?'

'There's an organization called the Countrymen who special-ize in setting up big events in the countryside. They hunt out sites, contact the owners and draw up programmes. Um ... Clay-pigeon shoots, athletic events, motocross, that sort of thing and um ... part of the organization deals with rock festivals. These rock things being held at the moment are illegal and they want somewhere permanent, which is all above board. The Countrymen handle all the legal work and the planning per-mission. In return, I lease them the fields and receive a royalty on ticket revenue.'

'*Rock* festivals,' said Tess. 'Am I hearing you right, Daddy?'

'They would have two, possibly three, a year. A maximum of a hundred thousand or so is estimated as an attendance figure.'

174

Tess abandoned her breakfast and went over to the kitchen window. Bright with new growth and tussocky, hiding secret caches of insect life, the meadow rolled like an enchanted sea; riding on it were ghostly ships carrying her childhood and Eeyore and Pooh and the rest of her companions into the past.

'I'm surprised you haven't been lynched, Daddy,' she said, deadly quiet. 'A hundred thousand people in Appleford.'

He made a little sound, half-way between a cough and a sneeze.

'Have you thought what this will do? You, the conservationist who gets upset if a litter bin is put outside the shop? The cars, the buildings. It will need loos and that sort of thing. Then the land will go down in value. The clever and well-off will move out. Those who can't will remain and suffer.'

'There is money to be made.' Her father bowed his head.

Tess retreated from the window and picked up a piece of paper lying on the sideboard.

SAVE OUR VILLAGE

Dear Appleford Resident, I am writing to you because you may be aware of the proposed plan for a showground to the east of the village at the High House, plans which have already been considered by the District Council.

They include provision for five toilet blocks, three service buildings, and several structures for formal shooting in the field. These will be visible from the highway, the main street and some public footpaths. In addition, there will be marquees and other temporary structures present on the site for up to 161 days in the year . . .

'Where did you get this?'

With a shade of his old self, he replied, 'It came through the letterbox.'

She shoved it into the open file lying beside it, which she banged shut with a clenched fist. Then, without looking at her father, she went to find her mother.

Mrs Frant was folding sheets. 'What do you think, Mum?'

The latter dumped a pile into Tess's arms. 'Hold those.'

'Mum. This is serious. You've got to stop it.'

'Tess, your father and I are in trouble. I don't like it any more than you do.'

'But the village . . .'

Mrs Frant piled more sheets into her daughter's arms. Good linen sheets, well worn and well cared for but hell to iron. These days she stayed up late at nights to get them done. Tess smelt their sweet-hot smell from the airing cupboard and saw the care with which they had been folded, order from disorder, and was silent.

'Help me make the beds, will you?'

Obediently, she followed her mother into the spare room. Curtained in faded glazed cotton, with sprigged wallpaper, it had always been a warm, successful room, but never over-indulgent, a place into which she and Jack had ventured at their peril.

It had lost some of its charm. Yet another picture, the one of Edinburgh from Arthur's Seat, had vanished from the wall leaving a mark. A litter of cotton-wool balls and tissues on the dressing table proclaimed recent occupation. A pair of tights was stuffed into the wastepaper basket and there was an unfamiliar smell. Lavender? Face powder? Tess was not sure.

Her mother stripped the beds deftly and, together, they remade them. Stretching. Patting. Smoothing. Out of such actions a life was made, a woman's life in particular, and Tess was out of practice.

'In the end,' said Mrs Frant, arranging a pillow, 'survival is the most important thing. Other considerations have to go.' She spoke with some bitterness.

'Surely not. Not the things that *really* matter?'

Mrs Frant looked at her fair and lovely daughter. 'I hope you never have to find out.'

'Why didn't Dad ask me for some help? There's probably some sort of package we could have put together.' But Tess knew that the odds were low on such things being possible. She tugged a bedspread straight. 'How will you live with the hostility?'

Her mother took time to rearrange the pots on the dressing table and to pull straight a lace mat. 'Very easily,' she lied. 'As you will appreciate, it's a question of living . . . or not.'

Mrs Frant's loyalty was a fine and perfect thing to behold.

Dimly, Tess heard a scrunching in the gravel outside and voices growing louder as they approached the house. At the front door, they ceased.

Guests, she thought.

The bell pealed through the house. She heard her father's tread through the hall, a questioning murmur after he had opened the door, the answering counterpoint of his deeper voice. The door closing.

After a minute, Colonel Frant came into the spare bedroom. He trod heavily and with care. 'Tess, darling, you're wanted downstairs.'

'Me?'

One step. Two steps . . . The childish game tugged at her memory as she came down the stairs, each foot planted carefully below the other. Then, across the hall and into the drawing room that was no longer their own.

Two men waited by the window. One she did not recognize. The other, face creased with distress, was Iain MacKenzie.

'Tess . . .' He walked forward and took her by the arms. 'I'm sorry. I'm sorry.'

She was bewildered. 'Why?'

His grasp intensified and she winced. She looked up into his kind eyes and grave face, and the nausea rose from her stomach into her throat. 'No,' she said, uncertainly. 'No.'

'George was killed in the early hours of this morning,' said Iain. 'An ambush.'

'Ambush.' Tess was puzzled. 'George would never let himself be caught in an ambush.'

'It happens to the best,' said Iain, and pulled her towards him so that she could lay her head thankfully on his shoulder.

Chapter Fifteen

Somehow, within twenty-four hours, the Widow found her way up to the High House, slipping through the front door, a small, nervous but ruthless rodent.

'I'm so sorry, I'm so sorry, I know what you're going through.'

Trapped in the kitchen – the drawing room was full of guests, which added a farcical quality to the events – Tess observed Jennifer Gauntlet through unfamiliar sensations of nausea and sleeplessness. It crossed her mind to ask how the Widow had heard the news, but the question became muddled with another thought that slipped in and then out of her mind.

Jennifer patted Tess's arm with her trembling hand. 'You think me intrusive ...' She nipped out the words through her small yellowish teeth (no American facings for the Widow). 'But I know. We widows must stick together.'

Yes, thought Tess. Fat, thin, old, young. A net of black-clad, sharp-chinned women cast over the world.

Mrs Frant swooped. 'Jennifer, how sweet of you to come but I think my daughter's in shock and really can't see anybody.'

Tess remembered her mother's face seen over Iain's shoulder. Underneath the coral lipstick Mrs Frant favoured, her mouth had appeared bleached of colour, and it had seemed to Tess that two colours, red and white, were stacked, like sheets of tissue, one on top of the other.

Iain had gone now, taking the other man (who was he?) with him. Apparently, Mrs Frant said, Iain had made huge efforts to be the one to break the news (why?) and the Regiment had done their best to make it possible. The Army was good on death.

The High House was echoing with noise and a bustle that was continually shushed for her benefit. Its life was being suppressed so that hers might be given breathing space. As if Tess minded. The drive was parked with unfamiliar cars and every lavatory in the place was in constant use. Her mother served coffee ceaselessly to strangers, and the vicar had rung to say that he was in the intensive care unit at the hospital but he would come as soon as possible.

'As soon as he's dispatched whoever it is,' said Tess.

'Now, darling.' Mrs Frant was remarkably calm. 'Now, darling.'

Tess fled into the garden and found herself pacing one of her mother's routes. First to the rose bed, down to the wild patch under the tree and back to the mixed border.

'I like my routes,' she could hear her mother say. '*I need them.*'

The early spring flowers had come and gone. Patient and watchful but their time over for this year, the hellebore blossoms were running with sticky sap as their death throes began. But, in the border, great leafy coronets were unfolding: the lupins, peonies and poppies that Mrs Frant also favoured, planted so precisely.

Actually, thought Tess, I don't think I like the way Mum does the garden. I would do it differently.

Beyond Tess was a green and tender countryside, old and dragooned into obedience. Peaceful and uninvaded, marred only by the pylons scything through it.

Actually George is dead.

Later, after the guests had been served lunch and a pitiful attempt had been made by Tess and her parents to swallow what had been left over from the beef casserole and apricot mousse, Tess asked, 'Dad, *where* is Sage?'

Having no option but to tell her, Colonel Frant said, 'Darling, I had her put down.'

Tess digested this latest piece of news. 'What you mean is you've murdered her. Just like George has been murdered,' she said, in a light conversational tone. Then, and only then, she began to weep.

She looked *very* odd, poor thing, reported the Widow, popping into the Cadogans' on her way home. *Very* pale. Wearing an expensive Escada suit, Jilly tsked, a gesture that she judged could be interpreted as neither too heartless nor too sympathetic.

Jilly got on the phone to Louis. 'Tess Frant's husband was murdered yesterday in Belfast. Jennifer told me. God knows how she knew.'

Louis took a moment or two before he said, 'Yes. I was aware there'd been trouble.'

'Why didn't you tell me?'

'Jilly,' said Louis, 'I didn't know the exact details, nor whom it involved, and, besides, the family had a right to know first.'

'The question is,' speculated his wife, 'can we bring ourselves to write? Given we're now sworn enemies.'

'Of course we'll write.'

'No of course about it . . .' Jilly brushed aside Louis's implied criticism. You could always rely on him for a conventional answer. 'You feel as strongly as I do. John Frant is doing terrible harm to Appleford. Worse than death.'

Jilly had never been a woman to reflect on, or even appreciate, ironies. In that, Louis conceded, as he terminated the conversation with an 'I won't be late', lay her strength.

He rang Becky and was informed that she was in a meeting. 'Get her out of it,' he ordered the flustered secretary.

After a minute or two, Becky came on the line. 'Louis? You mustn't do that.'

'Listen,' he said. 'Tess is in trouble. George has been killed. It's on the news now.'

'Oh, my God . . .'

'Can you go?'

Becky cast around while she tried to get a grip on the situation, to stabilize her position in the picture. 'I don't think the old bat will have me in the house. Anyway, I'm in the middle of this huge meeting. The final details . . . FEROC.' Becky ground to a halt, all manner of images crowding through her mind, so strong and so vivid that she screwed up her eyes.

'Becky . . .'

'All right,' she said. 'I'll go tonight.'

'Good girl.'

Becky gripped the telephone. 'Louis. How did he die?'

'He was spotted in a pub car park getting into his car. They kidnapped him and took him into the country.'

'And . . . ?' Becky's knuckles were white.

'I can't bear to tell you any more.'

'I don't understand tribalism,' Becky cried. 'I just don't understand what makes people do it.'

He was not quite sure what she meant, but let it pass.

After work Becky drove down to Appleford. Due to road-works, the A3 was blocked and, at the best of times, she was a bad driver who attacked a route with gritted teeth and damp hands.

'Why did you have to go and die?' she addressed George, and narrowly missed a collision at the junction of the A3 and the Hogs Back. 'Think what you've done. You've turned into a statistic, to be worked into future probabilities, and introduced violence and interruption into the conveniently sanitized.'

That's twice now that I've been engaged with spilt blood, she thought, gripping the wheel extra hard, for her life seemed full and very sweet. Is that an average? Is that the total actuarial risk that Mr and Mrs Bloggs should expect as their years dwindle in Acacia Avenue? Two encounters with spilt blood?

The drive at the High House was choked, and Becky was forced to park in the street. She got out of the car and stood for a moment, gathering strength.

Mrs Frant answered the doorbell. 'Oh,' she said, on seeing the tall, smart figure on the doorstep. 'What do you want?'

Becky was hoping to be invited inside but Mrs Frant did not move. 'Mrs Frant, I'm sorry to arrive so unexpectedly but can I see Tess, please?'

Mrs Frant considered. A daughter lay upstairs, widowed and sick with grief. A son sweltered under an African sun, his health and looks and, more important, his prospects draining away. How and why she made a connection between the two situations and the girl on the doorstep, Mrs Frant was not capable of explaining. But of the limits of maternal authority and her right to exercise jurisdiction, she was absolutely sure.

'I don't think so,' she said coldly. 'Tess isn't well enough to see anyone.'

The two women assessed each other.

Becky's black eyebrows climbed up her forehead, a fighter acknowledging a fellow fighter. 'She'll see me, Mrs Frant, I know she will.'

It was unlike Becky to misread the script but she happened to choose the words most calculated to inflame Mrs Frant, who did not consider that anyone except herself knew what her daughter wished. Yet however much she wanted to hustle Becky down the drive, Mrs Frant's cast-iron training in good behaviour propelled her to step aside and allow Becky into the hallway.

A pile of post lay on the table and two bouquets, still in their Cellophane, had been stacked – and forgotten – beside the letters.

'Wait here.'

Becky watched as Mrs Frant, not bothering to quicken her pace, trod upstairs. As she did so, Becky's mobile phone shrilled. Mrs Frant froze and, her back still to Becky, said, before continuing magisterially up the stairs, 'I would rather you did not use that thing in the house.'

The idea that Tess might need Becky did not enter her head; otherwise she might have stopped to reconsider her objective, which was to drive Becky out of the house. As it was, she went into her daughter's bedroom and asked only if she wished for a cup of tea.

She returned downstairs and waited for Becky to finish her telephone conversation, her face composed into distaste.

'Couldn't you finish? As a favour?' Becky was saying. 'The master rig line slip? That's under control. Look ... I'll talk to you later. I'm a little tied up.'

The unfamiliar vocabulary only underlined Mrs Frant's determination to exorcize Becky. 'She's sleeping, I'm afraid.' The lie tripped neatly off her tongue. 'The doctor gave her a pill and she probably won't wake until tomorrow. I would offer you a bed but we're full.' Her tone grew regal. 'I'm so sorry, but I'm sure you can't help. No one can.'

Before she could calculate a riposte, Becky found herself out of the door and trudging back down the drive. Half-way to the gate, she stopped, returned to the house and stood under Tess's window.

Upstairs, Tess was curled up like a child on her bed in an effort to ballast herself against the sensation, impossible to describe, that had taken possession of her body. Somewhere, in the distortions that were wrecking her sense of time and place, she wondered why Becky had not come.

A week later, after the funeral, Tess returned by herself to the flat in Pimlico.

She stood by the sitting-room window, looking out at the window-box she had placed on the sill.

'If that damn thing falls off,' George had said, 'we'll be done for insurance.'

He had not reckoned – or, at least, she did not think he had – on bits of himself being scattered over a country lane in Northern Ireland. Then, again, perhaps he had. During the past few days, Tess had relearnt the lesson that, in the urgency of living, she had forgotten. No assumption should be cast in iron.

The variegated ivy in the box straggled over the edges and drooped. Tess decided to look at something else. What? What could she possibly look at?

She knew what she did not want to look at. George's side of the bed. Or the jumper thrown over the chair where he had left it that last weekend. Where next? She certainly did not want to look inside the wardrobe where his suits hung on their hangers. Or on the shelves where his socks slumped in a badly constructed pyramid.

No, none of these things justified her scrutiny – for they induced a pain so serious that, if she relaxed her guard for one second, it made her gasp.

George's things.

She wandered back and forth from the sitting room to the bedroom, from the bedroom to the kitchen. A silence had folded over the flat. Dust had been added to the accumulation from Tess's desultory housekeeping and a smell peculiar to unlived-in buildings had crept in too – infiltrating under the door, through the window, up the lobby stairs.

The experience of grief is to encounter yourself, she had concluded. In funny ways, too. I didn't know I possessed nerve ends in unexpected areas of my body and heavy, oh, so heavy, bones. Grieving is to sink into a deep, inner selfishness. I want to say: Thank God it's not me that's dead, but I daren't. Instead, I listen to my own speech scrambled by fatigue into nonsense and I watch my performance on the centre stage.

How I shock myself.

The previous day Jack had phoned on an appalling line. 'Tess, oh, Tessy, what can I say?'

185

'Tell me about Africa,' she had replied. 'Just talk to me about something normal.'

'Nothing is normal in Africa,' Jack shouted through the static. 'Famine, plague, drought, fundamentalism, fatalism.'

'What do you mean?'

But the line was so bad that Tess had given up.

She tried to think about codes, structures, strictures. So far, she had failed to make sense of any of them, except to conclude that she had failed. She had failed to husband her resources sufficiently to see her through . . . *this*.

George had not been interested in the subject of death. Now that she considered, Tess realized there had been many subjects in which George had not been interested, or that he did not wish to discuss. She sank down on the sofa and lit a cigarette. It tasted disgusting and she stubbed it out.

'George,' Tess addressed the empty room, 'we had only just begun.'

Out of a weary spirit and the emptiness, she must remake herself.

When Becky let herself into the flat with the key that she had kept, she found Tess sitting so still and quiet that, for a second or two, her heart went into freefall. Then she scolded her for giving her such a fright and asked the question that others were asking over and over again.

Have you eaten? Have you slept? Have you looked at the will? Have you signed papers? Which, what, where?

'Have you eaten anything, Tessy?'

Tess looked up. 'Not you, too.'

Becky sat down beside her and took her hands. 'All right, then,' she said, chafing them gently. 'I'll lay off.'

Tess's mouth was set in the wryest of lines. 'My baggage of grief is private,' she said. 'I don't want it opened up for public display.'

'No,' agreed Becky, continuing to stroke Tess's trembling fingers. 'But what's that to do with eating?'

186

'You do see, though?'

'I do see.'

'What's the time, Becky?'

'Drinks time.'

'I don't think I can face alcohol.'

'Funny, nor can I.'

For a long time they sat in silence while the sun slid to the west and disappeared. Eventually Becky sighed. 'I've done something stupid.'

This succeeded in producing a reaction from Tess, who turned her wet face to Becky. 'You never do anything stupid.'

Becky looked unusually thoughtful. 'This time I have. I've just come from the doctor. I've gone and got myself pregnant.'

Tess absorbed this news. 'Is it Louis's?' Then it struck her that the question should have been formulated in the opposite way. *Is it Charles's?*

That's what's wrong, she thought. Everything is the wrong way round.

Becky's face was contorted with passion and feeling that sat oddly on its beguiling features.

'It's Charles's, of course. There is some honour among thieves. Not much, but enough. It was after I got back from America. After a disagreement about the FEROC contract. I came home with a stomach upset and the pill didn't work.'

Tess's second question was not much better. 'Will you keep it?'

Becky punched the dusty sofa cushions. 'Charles caught me heaving the other morning. And that's that, really.' She looked appalled at the prospect, trapped, angry. 'Tessy . . .' She lowered her voice. 'I look to you to set me right, hold my hand and all that. I don't know . . . I don't know how to behave well.'

Fatigue was again scrambling Tess's speech and lack of interest – grief was insatiable. 'When?'

'Mid January. Ish.'

Charles had been a warm body, warmer than George who was – had been – chilly-skinned. Charles had been needy, hurt and passionate. 'I love her,' he had told Tess, again and again while he made free with Tess's body. 'I love her.'

There are worse violations than seeking comfort.

Tess looked at Becky and, with a whimper, dropped her head into her hands and wept.

'Tessy . . .' Becky dropped on her knees beside her. 'I'm sorry. I shouldn't have told you. I thought it might introduce a lighter note, a bit of black comedy into the awfulness. You know my views on children.'

But Tess only wept the harder.

Becky wanted to take Tess back to the flat on the river but Tess refused, saying that she needed to be on her own.

She was the bereaved, the widow, two stages on from the child and the bride. Becky was not, and from that fundamental division of experience would flow their different courses.

'Well . . .' Freddie was in good fettle. He watched Tess slide back into the seat at her desk. 'Are we managing?' He peered at her. 'I'm afraid we're not looking as glam as the Scottish widows in the adverts. Here. I got you a cappuccino.'

He pushed the cup towards Tess but the sight of it made her nausea return. She put up a hand to hide a retch and Freddie's eyes narrowed.

'You got through?'

Tess's recollection of the funeral was of George's cousins crowding into church, of piles of sandwiches and flowers, piles of letters and not much else. 'It was like one of those television plays, all camera-tracking and no script,' she said. 'Yes, I got through.'

'Bill's been fidgety without you. Fitch has been on the line several times and there's a big cheese that Kit wants you to chat up. Apparently your legs have something to do with it. Lunch in the boardroom, best suit and muzzles. And there's a couple of divorcées with fat settlements.'

'Oh.' Tess opened and shut her drawer without purpose.

Freddie tossed his head. 'Are we working through the numb and angry stage? No? Are we merely patrolling the perimeter of grief? Tut, tut. My shrinky friends, such bully boys, tell me that you must positively throw yourself into the centre. Go for grief's core, darling. Otherwise, it won't be a meaningful experience.'

Tess felt unwilling laughter claim her. 'Freddie, you're always spot on. All sorts of people have been telling me what to feel. Anger, bewilderment. I don't feel any of those things. Just sad and bitterly, bitterly sad. That's all.'

'You be as numb as you like, darling. I can take it.'

'Sweet Freddie.'

'No, not sweet,' said Freddie. 'Not sweet at all.'

What had George been doing?

'He was killed,' wrote the commanding officer to Tess, 'while doing his duty. He was a good officer, popular and efficient, and he will be missed by his Regiment.'

No details. No catalogue of events. Neither of the scene, nor of what was said by whom. Merely the phrase 'killed while doing his duty'.

What had George seen in the course of doing his duty?

Loitering in the shadows, he had observed a section of the city in detail, a shadow-play of dense blocks and moving shapes, none of which or whom had offered him refuge.

He was angry. Earlier in the day one of the men, Ginger from Newcastle, had been blown up while removing a Republican tricolour from the top of a telegraph pole. The men had picked the bits up from the road and the hedge, and the locals had leaked out of their houses and clapped and cheered.

News of violent death always spread like marsh gas, flickering as fast as light and leaping out of control. George had heard about it sooner than Louis, for all his technology and watchfulness. George had known and liked Ginger.

Money had been poured into this country, a bloody and

obstinate place. Money that was intended to mend and build. But it did neither of those things.

From the pub opposite, George heard the strains of the same Republican song filtering out into the night. Briefly, he fingered his new moustache. Lives here were hard. But these stone people were also expert in enriching themselves with the gaudiness of martyrdom, and with the comforts of being a rebel.

Ah, yes, thought George, minutes before he was bundled into the car that prowled out of the shadows at the top of the street. There must be comfort to be had for the Republican in behaving precisely as your enemy, the British pig, expected.

In the situation in which he found himself, neither the pressal button nor the Browning were any help.

Half an hour later, he knew there was no hope. The car had been driving too far and too fast. The men were too nervous. He could smell it. He could also smell country through the gap in the window: a rain-washed, innocent mix of smoke and silage. Then one of the men leant over George and sweat and cigarette smoke drove away the other smells.

This was the end of his life. Blood trickled down from a cut above his eye and he darted out his tongue to taste it for he did not imagine that many sensations were left to him. Would he manage what was coming without talking? The question pressed down on his bladder and squeezed his heart.

George doubted it. But he had to try.

The car swooped and bucked to a halt, and George was thrown out of it onto mud-slicked tarmac.

'You pig,' said a thick, Irish voice.

And that was all.

As he died, George thought, I've managed well enough.

My business, wrote Tess, is not to think.

I'm angry with you, God, for not being here. You could have saved him.

That was all.

Yet in the respite granted between the bouts of wild and frantic grief crept a quite different sensation, one of relief.

Tess was aware that she had been given space. However she chose to reinvent herself, it would be in her own time and at her own pace.

Chapter Sixteen

On Midsummer's Day, the first lorries drove into Appleford and successfully clogged the road outside the village stores. A man in jeans with a pony-tail hopped out of the largest and went into the shop to ask where he would find the High House.

The Widow, who was buying the cheapest baked beans and margarine, craned her head to see what was going on. Within minutes of paying for her purchase she was back in her cottage and on the phone.

Edging down the narrow road, the lorries ground past the verges, harvesting bits as they did so, and manoeuvred round the back of the High House and into Eeyore's Paddock. In turn, they were followed by a flotilla of cars out of which emerged several bare-chested young men in shorts.

During the morning, the bones of two marquees had been constructed, rising high above the summer grass.

'Vandals,' cried the Widow, from her vantage point over the fence where she and a group of equally irate supporters were standing. 'You should not be here.'

One of the pony-tails heard the cry and looked up. He was young, muscled and glistening with sweat. 'Get a life, lady.'

But the Widow had a life, and it was raging inside her depleted body, giving it extraordinary strength. With a shout that might not have disgraced a football fan, she broke free from the group and propelled herself into the field. Running so hard that her modest dress flapped up over her thighs, she panted around the paddock, feet lifted like those of an old-fashioned sprinter, and waved a branch broken off by the lorries.

'Go away. You will destroy us,' she shrieked, blind to the picture that she made.

The foreman had a hasty word with one of his lads and stepped up to the back door of the High House. Almost immediately he returned with Colonel Frant, who managed to grab Jennifer Gauntlet by the arm and end her strange progress.

'Jennifer. Please.'

The Widow turned her hot gaze on the Colonel. 'How dare you?' she panted with contempt. 'How dare you destroy the village?'

Colonel Frant removed his hand. Years of chairing committees had taught him a few things about human nature and he did not ask why she alone was shouldering the village's defence given that she had only lived in it for a short time. Yet, indisputably, she was, and he was diminished by her gasping breath and wild gestures.

'You must not allow it, Colonel.' The Widow struggled for control. 'Once it starts, it's unstoppable.'

He knew that she spoke the truth. But debt performs conjuring tricks, and it had done so on the Colonel, turning an absolute belief into a relative one, overshadowing regret and guilt with something far stronger.

Peter had to pay Paul.

Sending out waves of lavender soap, the Widow swung round to confront the half-assembled marquees, which now resembled jagged teeth, eating up grass, space, light and peace. 'I curse you,' she said, a witch from the black haunts – and for a second Colonel Frant admired her. 'And I curse them.'

Colonel Frant opened his mouth and lied. 'My dear Jennifer. It's only this once. And, if I may say so, you know nothing of the matter.'

The Widow may have been on a state pension, plus a meagre contribution from her late husband's employer. She may have been nosy and neglected, and have lived in a house with a fake portico (commented on by purists), but she knew untruth when she heard it. Furthermore, sacrificing without a pang her social ambitions for Appleford, she was going to make her feelings clear. 'You know it isn't,' she said. 'You know you won't stop there. You have been greedy and wicked. And I am afraid I will not be able to bring myself to speak to you in future.'

The Colonel did not reply. The foreman and his lads had downed tools and were watching the drama without much interest. In the course of their work, they had seen and heard this sort of exchange before.

Silently, Colonel Frant led Jennifer Gauntlet towards the gate where her supporters, which included two mums from the council estate and the chairman of the local conservation society in a bright green dress with strawberries on it, waited and exchanged urgently delivered opinions on the scene unfolding in front of them. Jennifer was ushered out of the field.

'You have not won,' she said defiantly. 'Whatever happens, Colonel, you have lost.' The little group closed around her and moved off without anything further being said.

Above them, the blue sky was irradiated with summer sun.

John Frant returned to the High House where the sound of hammering filled every room. Having reached a state of mind where nothing but his terror and anxiety held any validity, he did not waste a second in reflecting as to whether, as the Widow had put it, he had won or not.

During the afternoon, Mrs Frant made a check on her provisions and, noting that she required coffee and sugar, set out for the shop. It was hot and the shop interior was stuffy. In its efforts to maintain a correct temperature, the deep freeze emitted a fractious note.

Tilda, Molly Preston's daughter, was serving behind the till. She smiled at Mrs Frant. 'I'm thrilled with my free tickets, Mrs Frant. It's very generous.'

'Free tickets?'

'Tickets to the tribal gathering at your place, this weekend. It's our perk if we live here. The company gives them out. I don't know what all the fuss is about and why people are so against it. It'll be fun.'

Molly Preston was rearranging bottles of Fanta and Coca-Cola and overheard the conversation. She frowned at her daughter.

Jilly Cadogan came in to pick up *Tatler* and *House and Garden*. Mrs Frant was counting her change and looked up. 'Hallo, Jilly. How are you?'

If men make war with weapons, women do so with a gesture. Jilly sent Angela Frant a look that declared hostilities and turned her back.

'Oh,' exclaimed Molly Preston, helplessly. 'Oh dear.'

'Thank you, Molly,' said Mrs Frant, and handed over the correct money.

Trapped between her natural instincts and taste – that is, an aversion to a rock concert in her own back garden – and her loyalties, which decreed that she should support her husband in sorting out his financial nightmare, Angela Frant was to be pitied. On the way home, the string bag containing a jar of coffee and a bag of sugar banging against her legs, she struggled with her pride and to staunch her wounds. The wounds of a woman who had spent her life endeavouring to live in the correct manner, only to discover that the formula did not run true. In return for her good behaviour, she had expected, indeed been taught, that a home, husband, children and, of course, a degree of material comfort would be hers.

But to rail against her false indoctrination was not in Mrs Frant's nature. She had married John for better or worse, and stick it out she would. She must.

That she considered his financial decisions imprudent, greedy even, would not pass her lips.

No one watching the tall, competent-looking figure continue on her way down the village street would have guessed that underneath the floral blouse raged many battles to keep the ship on course. Or that a door in Mrs Frant's mind was being pushed ever more open.

Remaking – reinventing – was more painful than Tess had anticipated. Her father had done it, in his transition from Army officer to businessman. Becky had done it. To a degree, Charles had done it. Even Jack had done it. Her mother was doing it. Recasting, recomposing. It was, Tess told herself, the spirit of the age. Its self-consciousness.

And what was she doing? Struggling to be a widow. Struggling to be the investment expert. Struggling to make sense of what was happening to her parents. Struggling with money – or, to be more precise, with debt whose reach appeared to run through everything she surveyed.

But, yes, Tess was also beginning to understand that she did not know herself and, until recently, she had been ignorant and fearful of her capabilities.

She fought on.

'My goodness,' commented Nigel Pavorde, on meeting Becky in the Room. 'You don't look very well.'

'Nor do you.' A white, somewhat frail-looking Becky raked huge eyes over Nigel's compact figure. 'You look dissipated.'

'Yes, well. One or two parties.'

'And Ascot. And Henley. And the little weekends in Normandy.'

'It's a nice life.'

Becky was amused. 'Yes, it is, isn't it?' She beckoned him closer. 'How're the gallstones?' she whispered.

'Bad.' He was grave.

Becky spotted Louis talking to Matt Barker by the huddle

that had gathered at the Rostrum. She allowed her eyes to rest on him briefly. 'And how's business, Nigel?'

His expression was not happy and he seemed overly nervous. Bad publicity had driven away potential Names and the commissions gained on the introductions to the Lime Street agencies were no longer so easy to obtain. If you are dependent on a river source, it is a matter of panic when it dries up. Nigel was not made of the stuff that enabled him to pack up the tent in a hurry and move on.

'Bad business, Piper Alpha,' he said. 'And the hurricane.'

By chance, Nigel used the same words of the disaster as Charles had. Becky was forced to conclude that these men had been taken by surprise that, in the end, insurance was in place to deal with emergency. In the glut of easy business, they had lost sight of the end. They, she, all of them had grown used to dealing with the form, not the substance.

'Keep off the cream, Nigel,' she advised, and moved on.

In fact, Charles had been strangely affected by Piper Alpha. He confessed to Becky of dreams filled with images of that awful death, and of other terrors. Wild winds, dying animals, stunted children whose blood flowed white not red.

Becky's response was to tell him to cut down on the wine and to lay off whisky altogether.

'It's part and parcel, my duck,' said Lily, during one of the phone calls that were beginning to be a regular event, 'of the all-talk-no-bottom brigade with a conscience.'

Becky had laughed. 'He's a nice man,' she replied, at her lightest and most charming. 'He cares about things.'

'You should know,' said her mother.

'Whatever,' said Becky. 'He's very trying at the moment. Still, when he starts his new job at Viscount's he'll calm down.'

'Didn't take long, then?' Lily was properly admiring. 'Lots of readies on offer, I take it?'

'Lots. They wanted Mawby's secrets.'

'Will they get them?'

'With *Charles*? Never. But they don't know that yet.'

Rebuffed by Becky's indifference, Charles found himself – on the pretext of sorting out child-care schedules – treading inside the front door of his ex-home and discussing his nightmares with his estranged wife.

'Those poor men.' Martha gazed angrily at Charles. 'I hope the families are being looked after.'

'Normally,' Charles looked down at his tea and wished it was whisky, 'one doesn't care too much about these things. We just move on.' He replaced the cup on the saucer. 'Martha, do you have any . . . ?'

'It's too early.' Martha anticipated his request.

He sighed. The kitchen was much the same: shabby, overloaded with toys and children's equipment, albeit stacked with precision. Tell-tale money-off coupons were stuck to the fridge door with magnets.

'Martha?' She leapt with alacrity to her feet. 'Have I given you enough money?'

She stopped dead in her tracks and ran her fingers through her orange hair: fatigued and wearing a T-shirt splattered with the tomato sauce she had been making, she was as far removed from Becky as it was possible to be.

'Money,' she said quietly, 'is not the problem.'

Sighing, Charles noticed, was becoming a habit with him. 'Tell me about the children.'

Martha explored her T-shirt, reconnoitring the tiny encrusted patches of red. 'What can I say? Once upon a time you were here, then you weren't. You can't expect them to be settled.'

'Don't say that.'

Martha had planned no scenes, had promised herself guile and patience. But now she quivered with anger. 'What do you expect, Charles? What *did* you *expect*?'

He remained hunched over the tea-cup. Martha had turned

into an avenging angel, the essence of the mother defending her children, of the authority he had discarded. 'Becky and I . . .' he said.

'Yes, Charles?'

'Becky and I are having a baby.'

Silence.

'Get out,' said Martha. 'Get out. Go.'

Feeling as if his anchor-line to safety and coherence had been cut, Charles did as she asked. On the front doorstep, he turned back to look at the house where he had spent ten years of his life, and encountered only strangeness and hostility.

Two days later, he received a letter from Martha.

I don't want to see you again but we must think of the children. You must have a divorce for the sake of the child and you must see our children as often as possible.

I will behave as best as I can manage. Whatever else you do Charles, whatever we do to each other, they must suffer as little as possible.

For most of her early and middle pregnancy Becky felt ill, exhausted and worn to the bone. Dark eyes and brows set in startling contrast in a bone-pale face, she seemed low and lustreless. Fortunately, her tall, narrow body only swelled a fraction, which meant that she could conceal the lump from colleagues until she judged it an appropriate time to reveal it.

She said nothing to Louis.

When her colleagues were informed, they were properly admiring to her face of her ability to carry on. They thought the pregnancy's lack of evidence simply *amazing*. Indeed, the general conspiracy to ignore it conspired to make the impending birth something of a miracle.

But, behind Becky's back, the same colleagues had marked her down, finished. She would, they agreed, be gone before the birth.

Becky hated, oh, how she hated, the whole business. The discomfort, the slowing down, the sensation that something inside her flounced and fluttered with the abandon of the truly at home.

April, May, June, July, August. Still she said nothing to Louis.

'Now you know why I packed my bags and fled,' said Lily, yet again on the phone. 'Packed my bags and went. It's a bloody awful business.'

Becky always had difficulty with the word father. 'Did *he* know about me?'

Up north, comfily installed in her favourite chair and surrounded by cushions adorned with lilac tassels, Lily wrinkled her forehead.

'He didn't stick around long enough.' There was just a trace of something in her voice that might have been called regret. 'But he was gorgeous and sort of hungry, if you see what I mean. I enjoyed being on my back with him.'

'You make it sound easy.'

Lily's lips were the product of smoking, criss-crossed with fine lines. 'But it wasn't, chuck. Not at all. In those days we were supposed to be good girls.'

Becky made a valiant effort to attach shame to sex, and failed.

'I thought,' Louis remarked, when he met Becky for lunch in one of the city's duller, but discreet, restaurants and she reported her conversation with Lily, 'that you wanted nothing to do with your mother. And there's you holding regular conversations.'

It was true. The garish insect had turned into something much more comfortable. A friend? A mother, possibly?

Louis had just returned from three weeks in Tuscany and looked brown and oiled. Becky drank some expensive mineral water, poured from a blue-frosted bottle. 'There's a lot of things I thought would go one way and have gone the other.'

'Why don't you go and visit her?'

'That old bird,' said Becky sweetly, 'abandoned me when I was a month old. Is there not justice, not to say self-preservation, in keeping my distance in her old age? She might dump me for a second time.'

But he was not listening. She leant forward, quivering with the love she habitually ignored. 'What's wrong, my Louis?'

But he was distracted and she was forced to ask the question for a second time. 'What's wrong?'

He smiled at her, and she was conscious of relief that she was not the cause of his evident distraction. 'Disasters all round,' he said. 'I think . . .' His hand circled above the breadsticks in a parody of a blessing. 'I think things . . . the LMX spiral may be out of control.'

'No,' she said. 'You're taking fright at the press reports. You just have to sit it out.'

'Not this time, Becky. I don't think.'

'You mean,' she was extra tart, 'that shunting excess-of-loss policies around the market each time for ten per cent commission has made some of you a lot of money and you don't want anybody else to get to know about it.'

He smiled and she sensed she had lost him. 'Something like that.'

'Listen.' In a bid to get his attention back, Becky circled his wrist with her fingers in a hungry movement, noting how the hairs had turned gold with the sun. 'You're not on any of the LMX syndicates?' He shook his head. 'Then what are you worrying about?'

'Lloyd's will get it in the neck. It will be seen as working for the benefit of insiders while the external Names are squeezed.'

'So what? So does the Bank of England. Or Parliament. Just sit tight.' Her fingers clamped down on his. 'Do you have anything to cover up?'

'Not really. And if things go wrong I have back-up.'

Becky refrained from asking what the back-up might be but her eyes narrowed a little. She removed her hand and sat back. 'Is Jilly very expensive?'

Becky rarely referred to his wife. Louis knew he was on dangerous ground and that he was, perhaps, missing a clue to what Becky was driving at. 'Yes, she is. You know that.'

At his answer it was Becky's turn to retreat. After a moment, Louis said, 'You're right. Sit tight.'

'After all, isn't that what generals do?'

After Louis had paid the bill, they went out into the street. Traffic dammed the road and a cache of litter rustled in the gutter as a wind whipped round the high-rise buildings.

I love this place, thought Becky.

At the traffic lights, Becky touched Louis's arm, a gesture not normally permitted in public.

'Louis, I'm pregnant.'

That evening, when he came home from work, Charles discovered Becky weeping in the bathroom.

'Darling ...' He tried to gather her up in his arms. 'What on earth ...'

'Don't touch me, please. Go away.'

This was unlike Becky and he grew alarmed. 'It's not the baby?'

She swivelled round to face him, her face reflecting into infinity in the three-sided mirror. 'No, Charles. It's not the baby.'

But it was the baby. The baby that was Charles's and not Louis's. 'I can't bear it,' he had said despairingly, jabbing the button repeatedly at the pedestrian crossing. 'Why isn't it mine?' The woman beside him, clutching a plastic mac, had looked at him with unconcealed curiosity.

'I can't have your baby,' Becky had flashed. 'Anyway, I don't *want* anyone's baby. It's a mistake.'

Louis had run his eyes up and down her body, and Becky had been overwhelmed by panic for she knew instinctively that he was saying goodbye.

They crossed the road and he turned to face her.

'But you took me,' she cried. 'It was you who led me, seduced me, taught me and I followed. Willingly. You can't abandon me now.' Without knowing it, she echoed Tess's words to George. 'It's unfinished. Our business together.'

A deep tan often has the effect of making faces appear good-natured and untroubled. Louis seemed unperturbed as he said, 'There's a child to consider,' but his voice had darkened.

'Why these antiquated notions all of a sudden?' Becky demanded. You don't care normally. You're a buccaneer not a vicar.'

'Even I,' said Louis bitterly, 'have limits.'

'What about your children? Did they come into it when you had me?'

'They had gone.'

'You want to get rid of me.'

He was very gentle. 'Do you really believe that?'

She looked up at the features she knew almost as well as her own. 'This is nothing to do with the good of a child,' she said, gathering together her shrewdness and courage. 'This is to do with your jealousy.'

He knew her inside out. Her passions. Her ambitions. Her careful control. Her wounds. And if Louis loved Becky against his will, he loved her too well to lie. 'Maybe,' he said, 'but it doesn't change my mind. And it does not invalidate your baby's need for a secure home.'

'I'll get rid of it.'

She spoke in a furious whisper, and the woman with the plastic mac who had stayed to watch this street theatre was thrilled by the tender gesture that Louis made in cupping one hand around Becky's face and stroking her hair with the other.

'No, you won't,' he said. 'You know you won't. You like to

think you're capable of anything, but it would be killing yourself.'

She shook free of him. 'All right.' She gave in. 'That's it, then.'

'Goodbye, Becky.'

'If you think, Louis,' she said, with the first real despair he had ever seen on her face, 'that this guarantees my baby's future security, then you are far, far more stupid than I had ever imagined.'

'Take care, Becky, won't you?'

We like to think that we are shaped by our surroundings, our families, our climate, our jobs, our lovers. Yet there is a point where the process is arrested and the remainder of the business of fashioning a life remains with us and only us. In the end we shape our own lives, assume responsibility for our thoughts, are endowed with a power to choose.

Becky understood the point very well.

'Listen,' Charles coaxed a still sobbing Becky, 'you'll hurt the baby, if you don't stop. Please stop.'

She allowed him to draw her out of the bathroom into the sitting room where he sat her down. 'How can I help?' he asked.

Becky looked past him through the window. 'You can't.'

'Yes, I can. You see, I've done it before.'

'Go away. Please.'

Charles made for the kitchen and paused by the drawing-room door. 'I'm looking forward to a son.'

How strange, ran her thoughts between the dying sobs, how strange. In the end, it was not death separating her from Louis, as it had intervened between Tess and George, but the prospect of a new life.

Charles bustled out of the kitchen, carrying a tray with neatly arranged cups and saucers on it which he put down on the table. He spread a napkin over Becky's knees and placed in front of her a plate of exquisitely cut bread and butter.

'Eat up,' he said.

With a startled look, Becky obeyed. Watching her force down the food, Charles was reminded of the time he had looked after Martha. The memory gave him pleasure.

Chapter Seventeen

Temporarily, the Bollys had lost heart. A couple of its members were abroad, one was ill and the rest were submerged by work. The autumn lunch was put off until the late autumn.

Matt and Louis met for a drink in a wine bar which was already occupied by Boulderwood, one of the more flamboyant and hugely successful brokers in excess-of-loss policies. Louis drank his wine and watched Boulderwood, who had a party of younger men, with cleverness and ambition written all over them, clustered around him.

'I gather he's just bought a third Ferrari.' One of Matt's more likeable qualities, and for which Louis admired him, was his lack of personal cupidity, and he spoke without envy.

Louis smiled. 'So?'

Matt returned the smile. 'So?'

For a moment both reflected on the differing styles of being rich. At the bar Boulderwood oozed and dripped with the stuff. Matt and Louis had money built, like the calcium deposits, into their bones. But it was not to be denied that they were brothers under the skin, just that Louis and Matt went about their business more subtly.

They talked in low voices about the scandal that now looked inevitable. Their conversation made references to various terms – 'excess-of-loss', 'under-reserved', 'asbestosis', 'computer leasing' – and, with a note of incredulity, to the name of a syndicate that had agreed to reinsure the run-off of a second syndicate with a large exposure to asbestosis and pollution. The two men

206

agreed that, in normal times, these problems were containable. Placed in the context of a market that had been sent reeling by a series of disasters, beginning with Piper Alpha, and add to it a nosy press and a band of ruined Names who, if reports were correct, were fighting back, the picture was less reassuring. But they also talked of unease in Korea, the rise of China, and terrorism, the areas of turbulence in which Louis, the expert in political risk, was interested.

'If I was dealing with all that,' said Matt at last (who, it must be remembered, underwrote nuclear matters), 'I would have ended up very pessimistic indeed.'

'Nonsense,' said Louis. 'It's the same as betting on the horses.'

Yet the immediate outlook, they agreed, was somewhat rocky, a prospect that, strangely enough, Louis rather relished. Not that he would mention it to Matt. Why he should feel so, he was not sure. Bloody-mindedness? An idea that it was impossible to wrap up matters securely? Approval that nature hit back? Father Jerome had held strong views on retribution and perhaps . . . perhaps, he had been right.

He recollected Nigel's declaration: 'We haven't done anything wrong.'

The inverse logic, however, was not to conclude that anything had been done correctly. Louis put this point to Matt.

Matt and Louis were men from the same mould. As was usual with any problems, they resorted to figures. Yet, having mulled them over, these did not offer much comfort to Matt, sharper on the immediate. But Louis, whose mind was strategic, was more robust.

'Don't lose your nerve,' he said.

'No indeed.' Matt seemed more conspiratorial than ever.

More champagne was being consumed at the bar and when Matt and Louis left Boulderwood was in full flight.

*

207

During the spring and summer a small battle had been waged among the by-laws and regulations concerning the English countryside. The District Council had refused permission to hold the first rock gathering at the High House. The magistrates' court had decreed an unequivocal no but the Crown Courts had wavered.

'Par for the course,' a representative of the Countrymen debriefed Colonel Frant. 'It's just a question of sitting it out. We tend to win in the end. We have the funds, the time, the expertise. Locals don't. Look at the bypasses.'

A petition signed by two thousand people was handed in. Advertisements for the gathering were heard on Radio One. The anti-rock gathering brigade in Appleford held its breath, and many bitter opinions were aired about the Frants. The pro party felt a blow was being struck for liberty: the liberty to enjoy themselves in their own chosen fashion.

The party of the indifferents was too small to make its voice felt. What happens, asked one of its members, if the gathering is cancelled and all these people turn up anyway?

Colonel Frant's necessary journeys through Appleford, once such pleasant excursions, were painful reminders of his fall. As he performed his errands, it was borne in on him that a life that had been conducted so moderately – and moderately successfully – was in its latter part proving quite the reverse.

At the beginning of September, the magistrates' court ruled that it was permissible for the rock gathering to take place.

'How many back-handers did that take?' demanded Jilly Cadogan of Louis.

As promised, the Countrymen paid any bills that were owing, and the District Council retired, smarting, to consider the second application for a permanent showground at the High House.

'I can't understand it,' was the most frequently heard refrain in conservationist quarters – from whose ranks Colonel Frant had been banished for ever. 'How could he?'

A financially secure position was, as always, a comfortable place from which to criticize.

On 21 September fifty thousand people converged on Appleford.

Their vehicles, which included a couple of clapped-out London buses, clogged the roads and rendered the lanes impassable. Their occupants were noisy, mostly good-humoured and young. Some were drunk, some drugged, some neither. Within hours, the village had been turned into a vast car park.

From mid-morning to midnight, the music beat, a pulsing accompaniment to the fleshly delights being pursued in the marquee and the fields beyond. At Riley's Farm, the music affected the pigs, who ran in wild circles and refused their feed. A skim of litter settled on the roads and in the gutters, and blew over Appleford.

Meanwhile, at the east end of the village, the Appleford Beekeepers Association set up their annual stall. Molly Preston stacked the pots and set out her till with a ten-pound float in it.

She stood for a long time but, in the end, her varicose veins played her up and she sat down. After a four-hour vigil, the tally of honey-buyers amounted to three.

In the afternoon, the *pétanque* club, for which the village was noted, began a much-debated match with a rival team. After an hour, the match was abandoned for the noise was too great for concentration.

In the church rooms, the jumble sale to raise money for the playgroup was a fiasco: it was invaded by strangers, who picked over and plundered the knick-knacks and old clothes and left without paying.

Throughout the long day, protesters and supporters went about their business and, eventually, to their unquiet beds.

During the night the Widow was woken by a pounding on her door. A little dizzy with apprehension, she padded downstairs and opened the door on the chain. In the porch light, a figure with large staring eyes stood swaying. 'They're coming,' he announced. 'Hide me.'

'Go away.'

'HIDE ME.'

The Widow slammed the door and fumbled her way towards a telephone. Later, peering out from her bedroom window through the curtains, she watched the man being led towards a car by a policeman.

I fought the fight, she congratulated herself, and returned to her abandoned, and now cold, bed.

I'll never get used to living alone, she thought, and climbed into it.

The telephone rang in the Pimlico flat at two-thirty on 22 September. Woken by its first ring, Tess waited until her head had cleared before she picked it up.

It was her mother. She spoke fluently and clearly and issued instructions. 'Your father has collapsed and has been taken to Blackwater Hospital.'

'Oh, Mum.'

'Ask for intensive care. It's serious.'

It was only after she had put the phone down that Tess realized that the car was in the garage being repaired after her unfortunate collision with the lime tree outside the flat. After a second or two of panic, she acted on impulse and picked up the phone. Why she chose to do so, what inner prompting directed her action, Tess never knew.

Within half an hour Iain MacKenzie was outside her front door.

'I can't thank you enough,' she said, as she got into the passenger seat.

'I'm sure you'd do the same for me,' he said.

'I hope Flora didn't mind too much.'

On the subject of Flora's feelings, Iain remained silent. He concentrated on driving, and soon the smell of the river filled the car as they passed over the water, grey and shot through with neon light.

'Why don't you try to sleep?' Iain's voice sounded in the darkness. 'You never know what's going to happen during the next few days.'

Tess leant back and closed her eyes. 'I wonder,' she said, and stopped. Iain waited. 'I wonder if my father chose to be ill. Things have been so difficult.'

They reached the Kingston bypass, and Iain put his foot down. After a minute or two, he asked, 'How is your situation? Do you need any more help with pensions or with any of the red tape?'

Iain was the sort of person who used expressions like 'red tape'. There was a long pause, then Tess sighed. 'Everyone's fallen over themselves to be helpful. Only . . .'

He turned his head to look at her. 'Only . . . ?'

She put up a hand to her mouth and was surprised to feel it shaking, so she replaced it in her lap. 'Only,' she gave each word due weight, 'I appear to be pregnant – quite pregnant, actually – but I've managed not to tell anyone yet. I didn't want anyone to know. *I* didn't want to know.'

The situation struck Iain as odd. 'No one knows?'

'No.'

'Is it not rather wonderful?' he asked quietly.

'*No!*'

He was taken aback by the passionate quality of her rejection.

'I can't cope with a baby.'

The car sped on, rapier headlights stabbing through the darkness.

Eventually, Tess said, 'I hope you're not too shocked by my reaction.'

He reflected. 'I've learnt not to be shocked unless I know the story and I don't know yours.'

211

Tess shifted in the seat and the discomfort eased in her groin. In archaeology a distinction is drawn between methods used to establish absolute dating (the sequential placing of events in a fixed time-scale) and relative dating (the ordering of events by cross-referencing one to the other). Driving into the dawn towards her stricken parents, Tess placed a marker on the precise moment when she acknowledged and cross-referenced her pregnancy and, with it, her doubt, her guilt and the question as to whose baby it was.

'I don't want it,' she said. 'But I can't possibly get rid of it. I know I should be pleased, but women aren't necessarily pleased any longer to have babies.'

Iain glanced at his watch. Three fifty-five. 'Flora and I couldn't have any.'

He did not mean to administer a corrective, but he was tired and the subject was one that remained raw. In the dark, Tess flushed bright scarlet. 'I'm sorry,' she said, and added, 'Thank you for doing so much for me.'

Iain negotiated the slip-road off the motorway and cut the speed. 'George was my friend. And I hope you're also a friend.'

'Stupid, isn't it? Being pregnant and widowed.'

Tess's voice quivered, and Iain detected a touch of hysteria. He stamped on the brake, brought the car to a standstill, reached over and took Tess's hands in his own.

'Difficult, certainly. But not, I think, stupid.'

Weak, and fearful of what lay ahead, she said, 'I don't know. I don't know.'

After he had escorted her to the reception desk at the hospital, Iain said goodbye and drove back to London.

He was greeted by Flora sitting up in bed with a knitted bedjacket around her shoulders, drinking tea from a Thermos.

'I can think of better starts to a day.' She drank from the cup with one of her slurping noises. 'Is the Colonel all right?'

'I didn't ask, Flora.'

'We'd better watch that girl.' Flora unscrewed the flask and poured herself a refill. 'I reckon she'll use us, given half a chance.'

Iain towered above her. 'Do you think,' he asked coldly, 'I might have a cup?'

'Of course,' Flora was at her mildest and most gentle.

It was during her elevenses, when she was checking through the supermarket bill, that Flora recollected Iain's face as he had got into bed. For some reason, the memory made her uneasy.

At eight o'clock the next morning Tess and Mrs Frant drove back to a silent, shaken Appleford.

'The ambulance couldn't get into the village because of the traffic,' Mrs Frant told her daughter. 'There was . . .' she bit her lip '. . . a delay.'

'Yes,' said Tess.

As they drove by, Ron Davis was standing in the recreation ground surveying the litter, which was stuffed into hedges, up trees and dumped in heaps. A layer of broken glass flowed, glittering treacherously, over the grass where the dogs and children walked.

But in the Three Horns pub, Dave was bagging up his takings with a smile. Upstairs, his wife was bed-bound with three aspirins. Normally well attended, Betty's jump and pump keep-fit club had only one participant, Jeanne Rudge – she had adopted the French version of her name after working as a waitress in the Dordogne. The rest could not face it.

Ron Davis told Jimmy Plover that he doubted if the mess would ever be cleared up. As he was imparting this view, there was a shout from the other end of the recreation ground and Dan Preston waved frantically. Ron and Jimmy broke into a run.

'There's a body in the grass,' Dan informed them. 'Alive but out for the count on something.'

Looking neither to the right nor to the left, Mrs Frant drove on.

'We have to be thankful that Daddy died peacefully,' said Tess, as the car eased into the drive of the High House.

'Do we?' Mrs Frant felt as if the words were being dragged out of her.

By mutual consent, the two women hovered on the doorstep, reluctant to go in. It was as if they both sensed that, once they crossed the white stone into the hall, what had happened would acquire the status of truth.

Then Tess pushed open the door and stepped into a hard, painful future.

During the afternoon the marquees were struck and stowed. The foreman rang the front-door bell of the silent house, whose curtains had remained drawn, and stood, square and uninterested, on the doorstep.

'We're very sorry to hear of the death of the Colonel,' he said to Tess, who answered the door.

She murmured, 'Thank you.'

'You won't be wanting us next week, then. Not till the funeral's over.'

'No, we won't be wanting you again. I don't think.'

But the foreman had a timetable, which he produced. 'The hard-core is due for next week, for the permanent toilets and access to the car park.'

'You're joking. I had no idea.'

'Then there are the litter-bin facilities and the refreshment point.'

She stared at him. 'What do you mean?'

The foreman stared back and his expression suggested that he was not going to get involved but she ought to find out what was going on. 'Well,' Tess swallowed, 'my mother and I won't be pursuing the project.'

'I see,' said the foreman, and took his leave.

Metrobank were not pleased. The personnel officer, pompous, middle-aged and something of a bully, telephoned Tess to inform her that, of course, she must take compassionate leave. Again. But, he underlined the words, the bank could only see their way to giving her four days. Tess must, of course, take time off to help her mother with the funeral, he continued, but . . .

Four days after the funeral, Tess returned to the office and Bill put the situation into perspective. He sat Tess down by his desk and plied her with coffee she could no longer stomach. 'It's most unfortunate, Tess, but we can't keep covering for you. Clients are not interested in your personal affairs.'

'No.' Tess was perfectly ready to concede the point. She had opted to work in a world that rejected making time to grieve. Familiar with its laws, she accepted them.

Weary and apprehensive, she looked up at Bill. He cleared his throat and panic squeezed her stomach. It would be so easy for everything to fall apart. She summoned the reserves of her energy. 'What's been going on?'

'Good girl.'

She indicated the piles of papers and prospectuses on his desk. 'Looks like the nine layers of Troy. Why don't you give me some?' she said wryly, in a way that was becoming habitual. 'I can bone up on them between wrestling with probate and maddened villagers.'

Bill leafed through the top layer and pushed three thick documents towards her. 'I'd be glad of your views on these.' He got up from his chair and walked around the desk. A hand, impersonal and dutiful, dropped onto Tess's shoulder. 'I'm sorry,' he said, as the phone began to ring, 'I really am.'

At least, Tess reflected, I have a place. She smiled at Bill as he muttered into the phone, careful not to appear too grateful, and got to her feet, noting as she did so that a brochure for a business in the Caymans, which he had retained, had an air ticket secured to it with a paper-clip.

Freddie was away. GONE TO CRUISE THE CASBAH IN MOROCCO, said a large notice on his desk.

The others went out of their way to welcome Tess back, and then, as quickly, returned to their desks. They did not refer again to her father's death. Yet, for a second or two, they had stepped out of the circle drawn around their desks to make a verbal gesture and she was touched.

Back home in Appleford, the phone and the doorbell would be ringing. There was a structure for dealing with a death in the village and an unwritten rule that, however despised the deceased, it would be observed. It was a way of ensuring that one's own death was honoured.

Molly Preston had come round with one of her shepherd's pies. Jimmy Plover house-sat during the funeral as burglars were known to strike at such times. Ron Davis supervised the car parking. Eleanor Thrive organized the team of sandwich- and cake-makers. Jilly Cadogan made an ostentatious point of arranging the flowers in the church.

The Widow had insisted that she stayed for a couple of nights with Mrs Frant, just in case.

'Come and live with us,' Becky had urged Tess. 'Please. For a bit.'

But Tess, who had a shrewd idea of the limits of Becky's philanthropy, said no. Anyway, she preferred her isolation: the safety of the dust and silence of the unsold Pimlico flat where she could think.

George. Her father. The unborn baby.

Tess surveyed the office: the screens guarding their neon information and the figures of her colleagues.

'Since the heart of the capitalist system is profit, it is not surprising that the profits are a vital component of corporate valuation.' (From *How the City Works*, a manual to which Tess had referred frequently in the early days.)

That was a fact, and a simple one. But the edges of the fact were blurring, slipping, gathering doubt and ambiguity. What was profit? Clearly, it was not just a matter of deducting costs from revenue. There were also questions of depreciation to consider, of earnings per share, and much, much more. According to the Bible, it profited a man nothing if he had lost his soul, yet Juvenal, the Roman satirist, felt that all profit was sweet, whatever its source.

It could be argued that her father had lost his soul in search of profit, and it had profited him nothing.

Tess returned to a theme she had discussed with Becky. We are not entirely fashioned by our nurture. We choose to make ourselves.

'Of *course* we do. Of course,' Becky had insisted. But then she would, wouldn't she? 'You can,' she added. 'You must step outside the frame.'

Knowing this, and accepting it, but beset with doubt and fear, Tess was posed the question as to how she was to steer her pregnant barque around the sharks and barracudas cruising the City's water.

How was she going to wrestle and kill the monster that was feeding off her family? How was she going to interweave the moral, physical and spiritual, and profit from the deal that had been handed to her?

How?

She did not know.

'When I told Becky I was pregnant,' she wrote in her diary, 'she did not seem that interested. Sometimes I wonder why I love her. But I do.'

Chapter Eighteen

'I'm afraid that the news is not good,' said the smart, successful and ruinously expensive Rufus Metcalf to Tess, during a consultation after Colonel Frant's funeral.

Rufus had been recommended by Louis as a red-hot lawyer who would help her to grapple with her father's estate, which invoked the undying enmity of Colonel Frant's country solicitor with whom he had originally placed his affairs.

Tess could not afford a Rufus but, if she had lost a few illusions during her widowhood, she had acquired prudence. Prudence suggested that successful people tended to have successful people on their side and she had two priorities: to keep her job and to keep her mother afloat. Wily, foxy fighters were better on your own side.

On the fate of Appleford, she had less time to expend in speculation and subsided into a weary fatalism. Viz., what was happening to the village had been bound to happen anyway.

Of the baby she thought little. Except for the times when she wondered, twitchy and fearful, why she had not got rid of it while it had been possible.

Very often at great turning-points, men acquire new wives and women cut their hair. Tess had taken to putting hers up, piling it in a coil, shiny with pregnancy hormones, on top of her head. It suited her. Now, she leant forward over Rufus's desk.

'The bad news?'

'According to Mr Flee, your father's original solicitor, your father had not taken out estate insurance. And I'm afraid he had failed to renew his stop-loss insurance too. Probably he felt that he had no more funds to do so.'

'Meaning?' The question was superfluous.

'There is no insurance against the Lloyd's claims on your father's estate. At the moment there is a large cash call outstanding, with which your father was attempting to deal at the time of his death. Indeed, he is owed money from the Countrymen organization. But I must warn you that the likelihood is there is more owing.'

Organized and unmoved, he waited for her reaction. 'Oh, Dad,' she murmured.

Refus had seen this play before. A members' agent trawling through dinner parties, prowling Henley, the private views and cocktail parties, the Rotary Club dinners. A word slipped into a ready ear. The introduction to the Rota Committee. The acceptance. (And, of course, the payback to the member's agent.)

His own parentage of sufficient vagueness, he understood perfectly the allure of Lloyd's for the man and the woman in the terraced house or the modest colonel in the shires, who had made a little money. For, as much as its promised yield, Lloyd's seductiveness lay in its establishment dazzle and its exclusivity.

'How does that leave my mother and me?' Tess's hair slipped from its anchorage and she tucked it back into place without a hope of hearing anything positive.

Rufus glanced at the papers in front of him, which was unnecessary for he knew what they contained. 'There are additional problems. Your father signed a five-year lease for his fields with the Countrymen, which makes it difficult to sell your house for its proper value. Normally, it would be very valuable and I think the best advice is for your mother to stay there, for she will then have a roof over her head. You will, at least, have some income from the Countrymen.'

'Do we know about the planning permission for the showground?'

Rufus shrugged. 'Tricky but the Countrymen are experienced in this kind of operation. They know the loopholes in the Criminal Justice Act. They argue that they wish to be legal and above board and, indeed, that is exactly what they are. They also have access to the best legal advice. These events have to be held somewhere and they maintain they are the most responsible set-up to arrange them.'

Tess stood up. 'Dad must have been desperate to do this. But I didn't realize quite how desperate. Imagine that weight of worry crushing you. All the time.'

'He was certainly badly advised over Lloyd's and, it would seem, placed on some dubious syndicates. But your father could not have predicted the disasters. Nor is he the only one.'

'No, I suppose not.' Fearing the size of the bill, Tess terminated the interview.

'It is anticipated,' ran the opening lines of the Chairman's speech to the meeting of the Appleford Society, the first to be held after the rock gathering, 'that if the plans for the permanent showground go ahead, which seems likely, there will be an anticipated annual tally of traffic movement of approximately two hundred and fifty thousand vehicles. This will have considerable impact on village roads and streets and on the nearby B5032.'

It was Saturday morning and Tess was sitting with her mother in the High House reading the minutes of the meeting. On the table between them lay Colonel Frant's ties, which they had been trying to sort out. But, somehow, the pile for throwing away had become muddled with the one for keeping.

'I can't throw this away.' Mrs Frant had held up a tattered regimental tie. 'I can't.'

In the end the women had given up and sat staring at the melded heaps.

'Apparently,' Mrs Frant now stared at the calendar on the wall, 'there was uproar at the meeting. I got some hate telephone calls afterwards.'

'Oh, Mum.' These days, Tess found she was often inarticulate, words having been chased away by events and emotions that were too big.

Mrs Frant gave her odd laugh. 'Nigel Pavorde ... *Nigel Pavorde* cuts me dead, if you please.'

Tess read on. 'Seventy-five per cent of weekends between March and October could have one or both days affected by the planned activities, including three weekend music festivals a year.' She dropped the paper. 'They're probably exaggerating in order to have a better bargaining position.'

Her mother's hands twisted together. 'It doesn't make much difference, does it?' There was a desperate, anguished silence. 'I don't think your father understood quite what he had done. I don't think he would have countenanced living with this ...' she, too, searched for words '... this nonsense and noise. He intended only to have the rock gathering, make some money, pay the Lloyd's bill and then return to normal.' Another painful silence. 'I blame myself. He never talked to me about this sort of thing because I'm so bad at detail.'

Tess poked at the morning's post and extracted the letter from the Countrymen, which had arrived in it. It was polite but inexorable. Anticipating a favourable decision on Planning Application No. 12/341, the foreman and his lads would commence 'the erection of nine toilet blocks, three service buildings and some structures for formal shooting'.

The letterbox rattled but neither woman moved. Later Tess, passing through the hall, picked up a white envelope on the doormat whose contents were soft and heavy. As she did so, her nostrils wrinkled and her stomach heaved. Suppressing a desire to open the door and pitch the envelope outside, she went instead to fetch newspaper, Sellotope and a plastic bag.

I will be calm, she told herself, as she deposited the parcel in the dustbin. I will be calm for . . . and added, with a sense of extreme detachment . . . for the baby.

That evening Mrs Frant took her longer route around the garden but avoided the spoilt paddock and the meadow. From a deckchair on the terrace, Tess watched her, a less vigorous figure than of old marching the pathways of a life that had vanished in a garden blazing with orange and red. She resolved to make no mention of the envelope and its contents.

Her mother returned. 'I like to look at border when I'm particularly agitated,' said Mrs Frant, and pointed to the strip of lawn running beside it. 'You can see how worn it's become.'

Tess handed her a cup of tea and Mrs Frant settled herself in the deckchair. 'At least,' she drank thankfully, 'you've got George's baby.'

It was eight forty-five on Monday morning and Tess's phone rang on her desk at Metrobank.

'Dear,' said Mrs Mantle, 'how did the funeral go?'

Mrs Mantle was one of Tess's more idiosyncratic and favoured clients.

'As well as could be expected. Thank you.' Tess could hear Mrs Mantle's budgerigars shrieking in the background – Mrs Mantle had a passion for pedigree birds. This suggested that she was in the kitchen, probably surrounded by bills from the morning post which was why she had got on the phone.

'Now,' said Mrs Mantle. 'The tally, dear.'

Tess had already extracted the printout and was flipping through it. 'Fifty-three thousand, Mrs Mantle.'

'That's nice, dear. Now, I need a little something to help me out. I've been such a naughty girl.'

'How much?'

'Three and a half, dear.'

Good God, is that what one paid for a pedigree budgerigar? Tess assessed the figures on the Strip – Bid, Ask, Mid-Close, Vol, Sector. 'I was thinking of top-slicing your holding in Quaxocos. Will that do?'

'Fine, dear. Just send the cheque.'

Tess had bent over to shove the printout back into her desk drawer when the size of her stomach struck her. Then she knew she could not hide it for much longer. She looked up to see Freddie's raised eyebrows.

'Confess, darling.'

She sighed.

'It's so obvious, Tess. Everyone knows. They just don't say.'

'I . . .'

Freddie waggled a finger and spoke into his phone. 'Give us a price for size, then.'

Tess's phone rang again. It was a solicitor with whom she had struck up a friendship – always wise in her business.

'I've got a plum for you, Tess,' he said. 'Half gaga, I'm afraid, and living in squalor until his nephew returned from Canada and found a whole raft of stock hidden under the carpet. He's worth about three hundred grand and the nephew wants to set up a structure to put him in a decent home. Doesn't have to be too long-term. He's eighty-five and apparently, in his day, quite a famous cricketer.'

'Fine, Andrew. Send me the details. And, Andrew, thank you.'

'Location meeting.' Freddie chucked a file over to Tess. 'More, more of the same. The company view . . . who cares? Far East. Blah, blah. Bloody old Willis will drone on as the expert and, therefore, no one's allowed to contradict him.'

Freddie knew that Tess knew that he did not mean a word of it. 'Tess, darling. You've got to face up to it. Take it from one who's had to do the same.'

'OK, OK.'

They walked down the corridor, Freddie chattering *sotto*

voce. 'Now when's it due? George came back for the last weekend in April. You stopped being sick secretly in the loos July-ish. January, then. Ish.'

'How do you get to know everything, Freddie?' Tess was grateful for his bothering. A second elapsed. Then another. 'What am I going to do? They'll sack me.'

'So. Get another job. *Penses-toi à ton* brownie-point mountain, as they say. Our very own tragedy queen. Just think. Widow bravely bears dead hero's baby, he who gave his life for peace in Ireland. So touching. And Metrobank sacks her. *Not good copy.* I've a good mind to ring up the *Mail* and graciously grant them an exclusive.'

'I want my job, Freddie. I don't want a baby. I like my job and I'm just getting good at it.'

'Tough, my darling. You should have thought of that.'

She raised a pair of angry eyes to his. 'Biology is a bugger.'

'Now on *that*,' said Freddie, 'I am the expert.'

Tess stopped outside the ladies. 'You go ahead.'

When she arrived at the meeting room, they had begun without her. As she came in, the men stopped talking and Tess was terribly conscious suddenly of the tell-tale click-clack of her high-heeled shoes.

After the meeting Tess asked to see Bill and confessed to her pregnancy. Bill was not amused. 'Good God,' he expostulated. 'What next?'

He did not mean to be unkind or callous, but his priorities were different. Quite, quite different. As Director of UK Equities and Special Situations, he had a margin to achieve to justify the existence of his department. In what she hoped was a considered manner, Tess outlined her plans for maternity leave and childcare.

'I can give you eight weeks max,' said Bill. 'Then, Tess, you've really had your whack of compassion.'

When she returned to her desk, Tess consulted the *Estimate Directory* and studied the form for several companies she had marked. Employees of Metrobank could only deal on the market for themselves after their clients had been serviced. But Tess required capital. What was the point of being passively feminine and non-opportunistic with regard to herself if she was the opposite when it came to clients? What was to stop her making some money? Surely the risk entered into on behalf of another was the risk you also assumed for yourself.

Dear Iain [Tess wrote],

I hope you and Flora are well. Forgive me for bothering you yet again, but I wondered if I could ask you to check if there is any possibility of more money from the Army? My father left quite a few debts and I am exploring all avenues in an attempt to meet them.

'If you write back . . .' After she had read the letter, Flora spoke across the breakfast table in a very soft voice indeed, 'I shall think the less of you, Iain. She's just using you and taking advantage of your good nature.' Iain replied that afternoon, writing from the office.

Dear Tess,

I am sorry to hear of your difficulties. I have today made some enquiries about possible *ex gratia* payments but whether or not we can squeeze you into the correct category I don't know. I will get back to you.

Yours, Iain.

P.S. I am hoping to be made redundant in the first round of the Army cuts which are being threatened, and going to live up north.

His letter coincided with the one containing Rufus Metcalf's staggering bill. Fortunately, the estate agent phoned to say that, at last, there was a cash buyer for the Pimlico flat, provided that Mrs Mason vacated the premises within the month.

Before she closed the door for the last time, Tess stood in the tiny hallway and said goodbye to her dead husband.

The flat felt stale and unresponsive and, however hard she tried to call up something of George, an essence, a wisp of memory of the man who had once lounged in and out of its rooms, she failed. Only the taste of grief remained on her tongue.

She closed the door, deposited the key and drove over to Becky who was accompanying her down to Appleford.

'How are you feeling, Bec?'

'Ghastly. How are you feeling, Tess?'

'Ghastly.'

'Why are we in this jam?'

'Biology,' they mouthed at each other.

'The funny thing is,' said Tess, 'the bigger this baby grows, the less I think about it.'

'Liar,' said Becky.

Tess negotiated the car down the Kingston bypass. 'It seems that Dad increased his underwriting limit to three hundred thousand in 'eighty-five and four hundred thousand for 'eighty-six. The managing agent suggested it.'

Becky glanced at her. 'There could be some profits from the good syndicates, you know, if he was on any. You must sit tight and trade through.'

'I don't think he *was* put on any. Anyway, I've made a bit of money on the market. It's pitiably little, but it helps. The only trouble is, the rail fares from Appleford are going to slaughter me. Still, Mum will help look after the baby.'

As they drove into the High House, Becky had an uninterrupted view of the lavatories, basted in grey concrete and hooded in green corrugated iron. 'Oh, my Lord,' she exclaimed. 'They look awful.'

'I know,' said Tess miserably.

Becky pinched Tess's arm between two fingers. 'Listen, I promise not to fight with your mother.'

Tess smiled at Becky and felt better, for this declaration of a cessation of hostilities was a mark of profound affection.

Without doubt, Mrs Frant's trials and tribulations had weakened her support for the absolutes of good manners and of restraint. There is not much else to recommend them, but worry and fatigue can and frequently do provide a licence to be rude and Mrs Frant availed herself of it. The battle inside her was being waged, but it was not at all sure that her training would remain in place. Indeed, it would be true to say that, at the end of her life, Mrs Frant was not half as well-mannered as in her heyday when it would not have mattered. Nor was she as controlled. On occasion, and this frightened her daughter, she showed an open contempt for the world that had let her down.

Mrs Frant greeted Becky with barely concealed dislike and immediately switched the conversation to Jack, who was back in hospital with his stomach complaint.

'It was bad enough that he couldn't get back for the funeral,' said Mrs Frant, with longing. 'I was so hoping to see him. Still, Penelope,' she emphasized the name and stared at Becky to underline the point, 'is a very nice girl and keeps me fully in touch. It's so lovely how they are just like that.' She crossed her two forefingers. 'Like that.'

'I'm so glad,' said the leashed-in Becky.

'Really? I didn't imagine you would care one way or the other.' Mrs Frant was icy.

Lunch was eaten in a strained atmosphere and afterwards the two pregnant girls lumbered outside for fresh air.

It was busy in the main street and two large delivery vans were parked outside the stores, which had been outlined in scaffolding. A notice explained that, due to demand, the shop space was expanding and a tea-room was also opening.

Becky worked it out. 'This means that the planning permission for the showground has got the OK. You bet. Someone's leaked it. Or he's got a crony on the council.'

Tess knew that Becky was almost sure to be right.

In silence, they turned off and walked up the lane towards the fields. Gradually their figures lost their substance and became silhouettes: dark, distorted, fecund outlines against the grey goose-down winter sky. At the top, they paused and looked down on Appleford, whose lights were being strung, one by one, onto an electric necklace hung round the village. A Jaguar was being driven along East Lane and turned in at a house with the scrunch of tyre against gravel.

'That's probably Jilly Cadogan,' said Tess.

'I first met Louis here, do you remember?'

Tess touched Becky's arm. 'Yes, I do.'

Becky did not respond to the gesture. 'Charles badly wants a son.'

Tess had never been so conscious of her isolation. 'Does he?' she said, and moved ahead. Then she stopped. 'Do you ever think about Martha?' she asked.

Becky's answer came on the rebound. 'I can't afford to.'

Burdened and heavy, the silhouettes walked on and, like the sudden release of a blind, night descended over Appleford.

Chapter Nineteen

Becky's attempts to ignore her pregnancy were, Tess informed her, truly magnificent. She neither read a book on the subject nor attended a class, and demanded an elective Caesarean of her immensely expensive gynaecologist. 'If you don't give me one,' she informed his startled eminence, 'I won't pay the bill.'

'I don't want to huff and puff with the beard and sandals brigade,' she snapped at Charles, who had suggested, gently, that she should consult the National Childbirth Trust.

If only ... he caught himself thinking, forgetting that it was precisely Becky's unusual and unpredictable qualities that had attracted him to her in the first place ... if only she could be more like Martha. Gracious and feminine about the whole business. More accepting.

If only ... thought Becky in turn, if only I could see Louis. Then I think I could bear all this.

She knew she had taken the wrong path. Because she was honest and it wasted energy not to be clear, Becky acknowledged that the fault was hers and called on her still plentiful reserves of energy to get through. Being trapped was, after all, the fate of many. Becky's was an optimistic and opportunistic spirit not easily quenched and nor would she allow it to be so. The nature of nature was change, she lectured herself, and if she was pulled down by pregnancy's peculiar alchemy, which had changed a slim, fast-moving woman into a huge, curved, rooted bolus, then she must endure it and wait.

'Who was it who declared that pregnancy was God's joke on

women?' she asked Tess, after the latter had forced her to accompany her on a shopping expedition to Mothercare. They had taken a taxi back to the riverside flat.

Tess was sprawled on the primrose sofa. 'God knows,' she said wearily.

Becky shot her a look. 'How are you feeling?'

'Fat and boring. Apparently . . .' there was a tiny hesitation which Becky did not notice '. . . I'm big for my dates. How are you feeling?'

'In a state of suspended animation.'

'Why are we in this jam?'

'Biology.' By now they had perfected the timing of their chorus.

'Not long to go.'

'Not long to go. Christmas and then . . .'

Beached and exhausted, the women sighed in unison. Becky roused herself. 'What's the latest at the bank?'

Tess showed signs of coming to life. 'Quite good, actually. I've pulled in two more clients with lots of dough. An author who's just made a killing with a novel and yet another farmer. Farmers are rolling in it. How's Coates?'

'Quiet. But I'm doing a lot of chatting up. The rumour shop is operating at full tilt at Lloyd's. Lots of external Names talking to the press and big talk of a huge year-end deficit.'

They fell silent for the shop talk had lost some of its savour, but neither would ever admit it. Tess poked with her foot at one of the many shopping bags dropped onto the floor. It fell over, disgorging a pile of white terry Baby-gros. 'I can't quite believe what's happening to me.'

Another silence.

'Becky.'

'Um.'

'Are you sure you want a Caesarean? Isn't it a bit drastic unless you have to have one?'

'Quite sure. You should do the same.'

'You forget.' Tess was at her driest. 'I'm on the National Health.'

'So you are.'

'Becky, why are you having this baby?'

Becky turned a pair of tired eyes on her friend. 'I can't think. Charles, I suppose. I wasn't quick enough off the mark to hide it. Or do anything. I can honestly say it's the very last thing I wanted. Anyway, I owe him *something*.'

Tess balanced a Baby-gro on the end of her foot. 'In the end, there is reproduction.' She sounded grave. 'And we made the mistake of thinking we were cleverer. Unless, of course, you really wanted this baby.'

'Shut up, Tess.'

Tess retrieved the Baby-gro and stowed it away. Secret lives were so much more interesting than the surface life, the one by which others judged you, and could be compared in its relative truths and falsehoods to others and was plainly in view. But the true Tess, the real Tess, now operated under cover. That much, she had learnt.

She looked across to Becky, the friend whom she had betrayed. Becky operated secretly too, in the darkness, and the essential Becky was also hidden.

Soon after that Tess said goodbye for she craved, as she so often did now, the solitude of her flat.

There had been many jokes to endure at Coates about pregnant oil-and-energy experts. Ships in port. Lubricated working parts. Etc., etc. Becky put up with them good-naturedly, for their crudeness, sometimes vulgarity, indicated something important: that she was accepted. It was a relief, too, to be treated normally rather than as the china doll into which Charles apparently considered that she had turned.

'We've never had one of you before,' observed her boss, indicating Becky's bump. They were sitting in his office, decorated with hideous lumps of Christmas tinsel and the large, ostentatious cards with printed greetings that only firms can afford to send, discussing her maternity leave. 'The question is, can one insure the stable once the horse has bolted?'

'Very funny,' said Becky, who had established that kind of relationship with him.

He cleared his throat, a sign that he was on uneven ground. 'Are you sure about coming back?'

Half Lebanese, half English, he was a kindly man with three children of his own. 'It's a huge commitment and you're not taking much time off. You women can overdo things. It's not easy.'

Becky made to cross her legs and thought better of it. 'I've never been surer of anything in my life. Six weeks is my entitlement. I'll take it and I'll be back. David will handle my work and keep me up to date on anything urgent and I've invested in the latest technology I can lay my hands on so I can do some work at home.'

Her boss seemed thoughtful. 'You must think of the baby.'

Because she knew him to be just, Becky was prepared to overlook her boss's interference. 'But also of myself,' she said. 'And the firm.'

He then said something unexpected. 'Take care, Becky.'

On New Year's Day 1990, and without any warning at all, Lily arrived at the riverside flat clutching, among other things, an enormous shimmering blue patent-leather bag.

'Oh, no,' exclaimed Becky on opening the door, but stood aside to let her in. 'Is this a long or a short stay?'

'As long as it takes.' Lily dropped bags and baggage onto the floor, bracelets tinkling like the evening angelus. 'I've come to be a grandmother.'

'Good God.' Becky leant on the door for support. 'I have to hand it to you, Lily. Omit the mother bit and go straight to grandmother. Do you collect two hundred pounds when you pass GO?'

Lily looked all at sea: she had no idea what Becky was talking about. 'Ha, ha,' she said, tip-tipping in her white high heels into the sitting room. Her voice issued back into the hall where Becky was still rooted. 'Don't you Londoners go in for Christmas decorations? Or is it not smart?'

'You're a Londoner. You should know.'

'Not any more.'

'Did it ever occur to you,' Becky appeared in the doorway, one hand pressed into the small of her back, 'that I didn't invite you for a reason?'

Lily swivelled on her swollen feet. 'You didn't invite me, my girl, because you're not in the habit of having a mother.'

The humour that buoyed Becky through tricky encounters threatened to vanish, and she gritted her teeth.

After the long journey, Lily was in chatty form. 'Where's Charles?'

'Seeing his children.'

'Jean's God-botherers have been on to me. They wanted a contribution to the church hall. In memory of Jean. I imagine they need the money to fund the bribe to the council.'

Becky relived the sharp, intrusive memories and smells she carried as permanent luggage. The nose-pricking scent of mould, fetid urine and rotting food; kicking orange polystyrene hamburger boxes into the air (no autumn leaves in Paradise Flats); listening to the interchange of voices that never ceased. Angry. Hungry. Hungry for something . . . what? Alone.

'Did you give any?'

Lily looked evasive. 'I sent them a bob or two,' she said carefully. 'On condition they never bothered me again.'

Becky rubbed her back. 'Lily, I don't think I can cope with you so you can't stay long. I've got a maternity nurse coming as soon as the baby's born and that's scheduled in ten days' time.'

'*Scheduled*, is it?' Lily plonked herself down on the sofa. 'I had Jean,' she said. 'Cheaper than a nurse.'

Becky stood over her mother. 'You're unscrupulous and wicked.'

Lily darted a look at her daughter. 'Pots calling kettles black?'

'You can't stay for long.'

'That's a pity.' Thoroughly at home, Lily sat back among the cushions. 'I was planning to settle some money on the baby.'

Sometime during the night, Lily was aware of movement in the flat. Struggling with sleep and the embrace of one gin too many, she struggled out of bed.

The sight that greeted her in the hall was clearly not one that Becky would have built into her schedule. Her daughter was clinging to a door frame, weighed down by a suitcase and various bags, and Charles was fussing over her.

'Save us,' was Lily's dopey comment.

At the sound, Becky raised her head and sent Lily a look of pure hatred and fury. Trapped, my duck, thought Lily with a touch of malice. It gets you in the end. 'What happened to the famous schedule, then?' she asked, and beat a strategic retreat back into the nice dark womb of her bedroom.

'I don't ... like ... this,' Becky uttered, between whitened lips, as Charles drove at high speed into the hospital car park. 'I want to go home.'

'Well, you can't.' Charles jerked on the handbrake unnecessarily hard and leant awkwardly across Becky's bulge to unsnap the safety belt. 'It won't be too bad.'

'Only a man would say that.' But she clung to his hand for a second or two. Deeply moved by this unusual display of need, he stroked her hair. It was so unfair that the one time she was in trouble – and he had prayed for such an occasion – he could not help her at all.

As it turned out, Charles required all his wits. The baby was early and Becky's consultant was on a skiing holiday. Furthermore, at night only two theatres were operational and they were currently occupied with the remnants of a car crash that required putting back together.

On being told that she would have to go it alone, for the anaesthetists were also in theatre, Becky spat venom and sobbed. Then, as he dabbed at her face with a damp flannel, Charles saw her pull herself together and from then on conduct herself with . . . well, he felt it was courage.

The doubts that had plagued him lately melted away in admiration and he wielded the flannel with the fervour of the worshipper at the shrine. Whatever Becky decided to do, she did it well.

Eventually, Sister Liquorice, a large and beautiful Nigerian women, who giggled when she introduced herself as the midwife, commanded Becky to push.

'If you mean push off,' Becky's teeth had drawn blood on her lower lip and she was bathed in sweat, 'I am. To the Bahamas.'

'Push, lady. Push. Push your baby into the world.'

Sister Liquorice nudged Charles aside and took up her position at the business end of proceedings.

At the moment Becky gave birth, surrounded by Charles, nurses and the registrar – 'This is a flaming cocktail party,' she ground out, during one respite – the mobile phone in her overnight bag emitted a shriek for attention.

'Get it, will you?' gasped Becky.

'Don't be so stupid.' Charles dived towards it and snapped it off.

'Probably Australia.' Becky's face screwed up in anguish as Sister Liquorice told her to kneel. 'You should have answered it.'

At eight o'clock the following morning, Charles reeled out into the winter morning, the father of a daughter. The baby had taken a great deal of time and trouble to arrive but she was healthy and lusty, and Charles had wept – as he had wept three times previously – when she was placed in his arms.

My daughter, he thought, gazing on the little face that had not had time to unfold. My daughter. Slightly jaundiced, a little battered. My *fourth* daughter.

He must guard her, as he should guard her sisters, against the prowlers and the predators, sane and insane, who waited in the shadows. That was his absolute duty.

Later that afternoon, he returned to the hospital with Lily, whose bold slashes of red and green on a yellow background hit Becky between the eyes.

'Well.' She usurped the only chair in the room and her bracelets gave off their usual cacophony. 'Keeping the florists busy already, I see.'

Becky smiled with a touch of complacency for the bouquets had not stopped coming all morning.

'Where is she, then?'

Becky pointed somewhat wearily at the crib and Lily heaved herself to her feet. 'She's got her grandfather's eyes,' she pronounced.

'How do you know, you old fraud? They're shut.'

'So they are.' Lily sat down again. 'I could do with a cup of tea.'

The well-trained Charles went to find one.

After a second or two, Becky said, 'I'm not surprised you abandoned me.'

Lily's expression was a mixture of defiance and, yes, regret. 'In my day, there was less choice.'

'Do you want me to weep, Lily?'

From beneath the layers of fat, Lily's shrewd gaze raked her daughter. 'You look as though you've already been at it,' she remarked. 'Are you feeding her yourself?'

'No.'

Lily opened her large shimmery bag and produced a handkerchief. 'Nasty thing, feeding,' she remarked. 'I wouldn't do it.'

'Well, you didn't.'

Lily snapped the handbag shut.

'I must speak to Tess,' said Becky later, fretful and a little feverish. 'I want Tess.'

But the phone at Metrobank rang and rang and no one answered.

Earlier in the day, Tess had been talking on the phone to Louis, whom she had rung for advice. But first she told him Becky's news and then, somehow, because it was a subject they wished to discuss but felt inhibited in doing so, they found themselves discussing the implications of the plunge in the property market and the number of articles in the press about the City fat-cats.

'Of course, journos seize on telephone-number salaries and make lots of noise about takeovers. That's their game and good luck to them. But, at bottom, the business is safe and secular.'

Tess was puzzled. 'What do you mean, secular?'

'Long-term. Steady. As a society we're growing older and require pensions. That's why the funds dominate and they build in a self-adjusting mechanism.'

Tess was tempted to interject that it was a pity Lloyd's did not share this advantage.

'What is worrying,' she cast around for alternative topics, 'is the erosion of our manufacturing base.'

As they talked, Tess experienced the strangest sensation, almost as if her body had moved onto another plane.

Oh, baby, she addressed it directly for the first time, no one has thought about you.

'Do I gather,' said Louis, eventually, 'that you feel your father has been treated badly by Lloyd's?'

'I do.'

'But your father was aware of the risk he was taking.'

'No,' said Tess, 'I don't think he was.'

Before she put down the phone Louis asked, 'Becky is all right, isn't she?'

An hour or so later, Tess realized that she was in labour but continued to work, taking an obscure pleasure in denying it up to the last moment. When the contractions were fifteen minutes apart, she beckoned Freddie over.

He sized up the situation. 'Oh, my God, ball and string. Hot water.'

'Shut up, you idiot.'

'You can't have a baby in a merchant bank. It isn't done.'

'Unless you help me, I'll be setting a fashion.'

He was suddenly concerned. 'Isn't it early?'

'A bit,' she said reluctantly, and with sudden terror.

Within minutes Freddie had arranged the taxi and taken her to St Thomas's, where he kissed her heartily and said goodbye.

Alone and minus luggage, Tess was wheeled up to the labour ward.

It's not so terrible being alone, she decided, as she laboured through the afternoon and into the evening with strangers attending her. The body is too busy, too convulsed to worry much about other things. Like dying, birth is solitary.

She was surprised to discover, therefore, when David was placed in her arms that she had been wrong. Giving birth had ensured that she would never be alone again.

Two days and two fitful nights later, Becky pulled herself painfully upright in bed and reached for her earphones to listen in to the financial news. Poppy, as she was called, had spent the night in the nursery but Becky had been woken twice in the night by a kerfuffle in the corridor. Her stitches hurt: tightly knotted into her tender skin and she was filled with indignation that sacrifices of whole, sweet flesh should be so demanded of the female.

'No one tells you that you'll be mutilated as well as disfig-
ured,' she had informed Charles. 'No one tells the truth.'

Serviceable but not comfortable, the hospital pillows
bunched around Becky's hot body. No amount of money was
capable of replacing as new the bits of her body that had been
cut and sewn. No amount of money could restore to their
rightful place in Becky's psyche the bits that had been destroyed
when Lily had tossed a few things into a bag and left.

But it helped.

She rang the bell, asked for her bed to be remade with fresh
sheets and took a bath. She stepped on the scales: not bad, not
good. The mirror reflected a face plumped out by pregnancy
and a soft flab of torso and, to her extra-critical gaze, seemingly
enlarged shoulders. Only the eyes, with their marker eyebrows,
remained to remind her of the past.

Afterwards, she was left in peace to eat the breakfast she did
not want.

She toyed with the fruit juice and, as she did so, bewilderment and a fear she could not place clustered over her like
homing pigeons that had not flown far.

She gasped with shock and, in the compromised light of a
winter morning, wept. She sensed that the life she had fashioned
was in danger of slipping away, much as the good times were
slipping away with a decade that had been spectacularly careless.

As she wept, tears running over her sore mouth, Becky
retraced a wasteland of the solitary spirit, taught to her from the
first glimmer of consciousness.

Already she observed her daughter through a glass, darkly
and with detachment. Yes, evident were tiny feet and hands
tipped with shell. Yes, a body rearing in primitive reflex, a
tender stomach and tiny spine. There was, too, a suggestion of
intelligence behind the mostly shut blue eyes.

It was expected of her that she, the mother, would respond
to her baby in the approved manner. Then everyone could
relax. Yet, for Becky, the building of bridges to another human

being was something she regarded as impossible, even to a child.

'Bloody hell,' she said aloud, and her weeping stopped.

The nurses had remained impassive when Becky had informed them that she would not be breast-feeding, and gave her lessons in bottles and formula. Poppy struggled to take nourishment but it was a wearing business: although the baby fed and survived, the formula did not soothe and please her. She cried a lot. The nurses clucked over her and, more than once, bore her away for observation, leaving Becky quivering with relief and resentment.

Breathing space.

Yet Becky had to face the truth: there was no space left any more, and her sense of loss was profound.

She was flicking through *Tatler* when the door opened. 'Pouting lips and thighs that dazzle in Lycra, paint a chilly town a blazing scarlet in your own way . . .' She did not look up.

'May I come in?' asked Louis.

Pouting lips . . . thighs . . . blazing scarlet. Dazzled, but by electricity sending bolts through her body, Becky looked up. He reached for one of her hands, and sat down on the bed and, in the private, well-remembered gesture, ran his thumb gently over her dry fingers. 'Are you well?'

Again tears threatened and Becky choked them back. 'What do you think? I know now it's the second worst thing in the world to have a baby.'

'What's the first?'

'To repeat the experience.'

He laughed. 'And the baby?'

'She's fine.' Becky gestured towards the empty crib. 'Or so they tell me. They're doing something with her at the moment.'

Despite herself, despite everything, she grasped his fingers in hers. 'Louis . . . don't. Please don't ever leave me again.'

The door opened and the thin, tired wail of an unhappy

baby could be heard. Young and too plump, a junior nurse handed Poppy to Becky.

'Why is she crying?'

'She won't take enough of her feed. We thought perhaps you should have a go.'

'Oh.'

The nurse had no time to spare. She plonked the bottle on the side table and left the room.

'Why don't you feed her yourself?' Louis watched the struggles with the bottle.

'I don't want to.' Becky turned her now sparkling eyes on Louis. 'I have to get back to work.'

He observed the little face. 'It would be better for her.'

'Don't,' pleaded Becky. 'Not you too. Charles hasn't stopped on the subject.' She stroked Poppy's cheek in an experimental manner. 'It's for me to decide.'

Louis reflected. 'You needn't feed her for long. Just enough for her to know.'

'Babies don't know.'

'How do *you* know?'

'Louis, you're as guilty as the rest of them. When a woman has a baby everyone considers that her autonomy has vanished and she's public property. I've given birth, not lost part of my brain, and I've decided not to breast-feed.'

She spoke over a hunched shoulder but avoided Louis's gaze and he knew that it was not the whole truth.

'Point taken,' he said, reached over and pushed down the straps of her satin nightdress, to reveal swollen white flesh.

'This is the mother,' he said, running his hand down her body. 'You shouldn't ignore her.'

'I've had an injection to stop the milk.' Becky made no move to stop him. 'And don't go all Catholic on me.'

'Does that invalidate anything I might have to say?'

'You haven't listened to me.'

'Just concentrate, Becky.'

Scenting her mother, the baby turned her head towards the unused breast. Louis's presence had a hypnotic quality and Becky's skin goosefleshed. As she had banded the intricate patterns and cool beauty of her DNA on her daughter, his clean, hard elegance was burned into her make-up. So, too, was the knowledge that he understood the exact pathways of her greedy nature. There was no point in denial.

Then Louis said something very strange: 'You must build the bridge, Becky.'

Louis won and Poppy drank, then gorged on her mother's milk and he had watched, as tender and satisfied as he had ever been.

Was it possible that, after all, the grey stones, the incense and the calloused knees, the incomprehension of a small boy had had a point?

It was probably the drugs she had been given. Probably. But for an intense, vivid moment, Becky experienced the condition of complete femininity, acknowledged it, and moved on.

'I suppose you'll disappear now, won't you, and not come back?' she said to Louis.

'I don't know. If I have the strength.'

Perhaps, ran Tess's diary, which had been shoved carelessly among the bouquets that had been delivered to the High House and written in a deceptive state of euphoria, perhaps, I will be happy again. My son is perfect.

Chapter Twenty

If the world is arranged into noisy, aggressive tribes who wish to have nothing to do with each other, then it must also be acknowledged that its parts are interlocked. Unless we understand that, we understand nothing of the modern world . . .

It was six months later and Becky was making notes on her laptop for a lecture on insurance broking that she had been ordered to give by Coates to a girls' sixth form. She had noticed before that it was a job frequently allocated to the token female.

Tess was coming up to spend the day and Charles was preparing lunch in the kitchen.

. . . For example, if the American Congress had not passed the Comprehensive Response, Compensation and Liability Act in 1980, which required the clean-up of polluted sites retrospectively and irrespective of cost, a selection of Lloyd's Names, who live on the other side of the world, would not be facing enormous cash calls. This may seem strange or unfair to you and, in one sense, it is. But it is the reality of the world in 1990.

Like it or not, tribe is connected to tribe by a network of financial commitments, and disaster in one area links it with another.

Becky paused and stared at the screen. Since Piper Alpha, there have been enough disasters, she thought grimly, Hurricane Hugo, the Enchova oil-platform fire to name only two, to turn the world into one happy family . . .

Back in hospital that January and greeted by the sight of a milky, drowsy baby, Charles asked Becky, with a leap of his heart, what had made her change her mind.

Perhaps, he thought, it is possible we will pull together.

Becky was cross and suffering from the post-partum low that comes after experiencing strong emotion and did not bother to answer him properly. Charles satisfied himself instead by stroking his newest daughter's head with a gentle finger and tried not to worry about the question that bothered him not a little: how on earth was he going to afford to launch four daughters into the world?

Martha left it until June before ringing him at the flat to ask if the baby was doing well. Otherwise, apart from messages via the nanny when they exchanged the children, they had not communicated.

'How nice of you,' said Charles. 'Life was hell at the start, with a frightful old bat of a maternity nurse plus Becky's mother, but we got rid of them smartish and now it's a question of struggling with the nannies.'

'Oh dear,' said Martha at her end, hands trembling.

'Martha, we *are* friends, aren't we?'

'Are we?' Martha wanted to shriek that what she felt for her soon-to-be-ex-husband had nothing to do with friendship, but everything to do with outrage and violent longing to have the old happy days back.

'How are the children?'

'Oh, you've remembered them?'

Charles grimaced at the familiar note in Martha's voice. It spelt lecture with a capital L. With his free hand, he manoeuvred a file out of his briefcase and flipped it open. 'Is it really going to cost three hundred a term for Tiny's nursery?'

Martha sighed. 'I know it's a lot, Charles, but it's so convenient for Anthea's school and fits in with the run. More important, it's the best place for her.'

As usual, Martha had her arguments marshalled.

'That reminds me.' Charles recollected a previous conversation. 'Do you think Anthea should have some remedial help? Should I talk to the school?'

'Well . . . she's picking up a bit. Did you get her to read to you when you took her out on Sunday?'

Ranging over this and that, the trivia, but not trivial, aspects of a shared life and shared children, their conversation continued for another twenty minutes or so.

'I must go.' Charles disengaged himself reluctantly from this warm and cradling exchange. 'Becky's friend Tess is up for the day and I've got to finish the lunch. But it's so nice to think we can talk. It's good to be civilized about these things.'

By now, Martha had run her hand through her hair so often that it stood on end, and she had resorted to picking at the bobbly bits that always appeared on her leggings however she washed them.

'*Civilized!*' she exclaimed. 'My God, you do say the most stupid things sometimes, Charles.'

Charles was left to reflect uneasily that his grasp on the situation was less clear than he had supposed, which Martha, had she been consulted, would have pointed out in the first place.

As part of the paring-down procedure, Mrs Frant had sold her car. This left her reliant on Tess's, a somewhat tricky situation as their needs clashed. They had clashed today and, thus it was that with enormous difficulty – nappies, buggy, bottles, cuddly toys – Tess had brought David up to London on the train to have lunch with Becky, Charles and Poppy. The purpose was to celebrate the babies' first six months. The new decade babies – the 'deccies'.

'I never thought I would feel old,' Becky had said to Charles, in a rare confiding moment. 'It's a curious feeling. I'm so used to thinking of myself as a beginner.'

'I think I've always felt old,' replied Charles.

The outing threatened to exhaust Tess before she reached Becky: she had got up early to help her mother prepare the guests' breakfasts and dinner. The journey to London, which she had imagined would be fun, only served to underline her double life. During the week, she was free and successful, at weekends the reverse.

'I'm not a natural at motherhood,' Tess confided to her son, worried that she found it so difficult.

She looked down at him, wriggling in her lap. *You sleep when you want, cry when you want and you don't care about anything except your own needs. But I love you.*

'Tessy,' said Becky, as soon as Tess had disgorged herself and David into the hall of the flat, 'I must warn you that you can no longer smoke in this flat. Banned.'

'Oh? Yes, well, I suppose you're right.'

Later, Tess stood on the balcony and smoked defiantly and held a conversation through the door. 'Another letter came last week. The loss for 'eighty-seven was £217,985.'

Becky's voice sounded thin and disembodied through the glass door. 'I don't know how to help, Tessy.'

She exhaled. 'Just be there.'

Both women were aware that the difference between the onlooker on the bank and the swimmer in trouble is the one between death and life.

'Have some coffee.' Becky held up a cup and Tess tossed her cigarette into the street below and came to sit on the sofa. It was, she was glad to see with a prickle of malice, less pristine than of yore. David was grizzling in his portable chair and she picked him up, which meant that she had to perform one of those contortions, noticeable in new mothers, to ensure that the cup did not pass over his head.

Becky watched her, and her heart pinched with unfamiliar empathy. 'How's your mother?'

'She's incredible and she drives me dotty. Grandmother likes to think that she knows best. And yet, Bec, there she is getting up at dawn like one of those tough colonial ladies in Somerset Maugham, refusing to give up ... We're giving guests dinner now, you know. They're not quite as up-market as they used to be because of the showground. Less *fungi* and balsamic vinegar, more prawn cocktail.'

'Some income, though?'

'Yes. Without it ...' Tess tugged at the waistband of her full cotton skirt. It was still too tight and she had attempted a poor disguise with a T-shirt. 'Why are you so thin?' If anything, Becky post-Poppy was slimmer and smarter.

'You've been stuffing chocolate,' she accused Tess, accurately as it happened, knowing how the jibe would make her smart.

'You need energy to diet. The pundits never tell you that.'

Becky softened. 'You're gorgeous all the same, Tessy.'

They could hear Poppy wailing in her bedroom. Unfussed, Becky called out, 'Charles, get her, will you?' She looked at Tess, who wore a wooden expression. 'Is anything the matter, Tess?'

'No, nothing.'

Charles appeared with Poppy draped over his shoulder and placed her on Becky's lap. Poppy lay back and scrutinized her mother with the infant's urge to rediscover. Becky looked down and smiled. And, with a dazzling imitation of her mother, Poppy smiled back. Becky picked up a wooden toy, of the type favoured by parents and usually ignored by their children, and dangled it in front of her.

Tess took a deep breath and plucked up courage to look at Charles, an action, simple as it was, that was becoming more difficult as more time elapsed. As with many sins, it seemed worse the more it was brooded upon. 'How are your other daughters?'

He groaned. 'Expensive.'

After tea, Tess said that she must go and Charles got to his feet. 'I'll fetch the car from round the corner.'

In the car Charles looked straight ahead at the road and said, 'I understand your feelings, Tess, and we just have to get over this uncomfortable period as best we can. It will get easier, I'm sure.' He was handling Tess, whom he did not love, better than he ever handled Becky, whom he loved desperately, and managed to defuse the situation rather gracefully. 'I understand about the guilt and all that. And I've made up my mind to forget the incident completely.'

Craving release and the peace of post-confession, she almost said something about the troubled source of her guilt, but held back.

Not knowing.

But, if she did not forgive herself, Tess forgave Charles there and then. He handed her onto the train and efficiently stowed the mountain of equipment.

Charles's eyes rested on David for longer than necessary. *A son?* he thought, painfully and with longing.

'David's a lovely boy and the spitting image of George,' he said finally, and raised his eyes to Tess.

They looked at each other. He suspects, she thought, and was deeply moved by his effort to give her peace. How generous he was. In the split second between his remark and her reply, a layer of earth was brushed over a truth. Perhaps for excavation later. Perhaps not.

'Thank you,' she said.

Left alone with Poppy, Becky poured a final cup of coffee and put her feet up. Poppy sat silently in her bouncy chair on the floor.

On the rare occasions when she examined her life, Becky was aware that she flew close to the sun.

Aunt Jean imagery?

Yet, so far, her progress, an acquisitive, worldly pilgrim's progress, had been achieved with a mixture of luck, shrewdness and life-saving selfishness, the last being the most crucial. She was partnered, well funded, and, if the baby was a tie, she could throw money at the problem.

Lily was not so sure. 'Don't imagine you've got it sussed, my girl,' she informed Becky, before she left to go north after Poppy's birth. 'Money's no insurance. You can't buy order. You may fancy yourself rotten as the rich bitch but, at bottom, Becky Vitali, you're just the same as the rest of us.'

'Do you have to be so depressing? Or so smug?'

'Things have a way of not working out. Look at Jean. She set out to be a model housewife and mother – that's why I left you with her. And look what happened.'

What *did* happen to my pink-cardiganed, zealoty aunt? She had been forced by domesticity into being a saint, Becky concluded with a faint cadence of guilt, because that was the only way she could survive. For the first time ever, a lump ached in her throat as she recollected the years of Jean's impatient sacrifice – a reaction she put down to post-baby hormone displacement.

Wise Lily. She knew a thing or two about love, money and the whole damn thing. 'It pulls in two ways, you dozy mare,' she pronounced mysteriously.

'Meaning what?'

'Look at you,' her mother pointed out. 'Living with Charles and mentally shacked up with someone else with a poncey name.'

Becky wished that she had never confided to Lily the secret of Louis.

True, Louis loved her but he was married to Jilly and bound to Jilly by the strictures of a Church in which he no longer believed.

'It's called . . . I don't know what it's called but it's a situation that I can't alter. The trick is to get round it.'

'Will you ever call me Mum?'

'No, I don't think so.'

'It's lucky,' said Lily, 'that you weren't born when I was. You wouldn't have lasted a minute. It's easy now. One yelp from a so-called minority, the one-legged, single-parent lesbian, and the Queen sends you a telegram. It's all birth control and free market and whatever. And very wicked.' Lily looked as though she did not mind too much about the last. 'Suits you, though. All spend and top coat.'

'You're forgetting Aids and negative equity.' Becky could not help laughing. 'You're an old bat, Lily.'

'Mark my words.'

Fine, thought Becky, who minded Lily's mild criticisms more than she cared to admit. If the wicked grow and put on leaf like the green bay tree, so be it. Sodom and Gomorrah were much more interesting places than Eden.

However, every equation and every bargain has its tricky and often stubborn area.

'Becky,' said Charles, after he returned from depositing Tess on the train, 'I want us to get married as soon as possible. But I want to know that you mean to stick by it. And that you're married to me.'

'Ah,' Becky's answer darted towards him with the speed and accuracy of a snake's tongue, 'but would you be married to me or to Martha?'

It was, they both acknowledged, a fair question. Becky had made the discovery that, if you appropriate a person from someone else, the shadow of the latter remains. In their life together, Becky and Charles traced a Martha shape every day.

'Have you been seeing her?' Becky asked.

'No. But we've talked on the phone. I hope you don't mind.' Charles rather wanted Becky to mind very much.

'Oh, no,' said Becky, wishing that she could oblige. 'I do see that it's necessary.'

Buoyed up by his handling of Tess, Charles asserted himself.

'We must get married as soon as possible.' He allowed Becky a few seconds to digest this then added, 'And you can look after Poppy until bedtime because I have work to do.'

Becky regarded him blankly and he wondered if she was going to lose her temper. He should have known better because she rarely allowed herself to do so. Instead she threw back her head, exposing the delicious area at the base of her throat that drove Charles mad with desire, and laughed.

'You win,' she said, hefted Poppy onto her shoulder and headed out of the room to change the baby's nappy, adding over her shoulder, 'for the time being.'

He walked over to the balcony, where a drift of ash betrayed Tess's previous presence, and shoved his hands into his pockets. Sometimes Charles was driven to think that the only act that had given his life significance was to leave Martha.

He dated events mentally from before and after: before M., he had been an emotional innocent; after leaving M., he had turned into a bad father, an abandoner of wives, the seducer of friends and, lately, into the broker who had allowed his lover to sell him, professionally, down the river.

What astonished Charles to the depth of his soul was that he had never intended that any of this should happen. Yet it was done. Life crept up on you and leap-frogged over good resolutions. Because he took no comfort in solidarity, it made no difference to Charles that many others experienced the same.

At Coates business was booming. Its staff younger than Mawby's – the fruit of the human resources officer's forward thinking – Coates was attracting big international contracts.

Becky's team were rootless and excellent at their jobs. Coinciding perfectly with Becky's, their aims were to enjoy the business and their personal enrichment. Why not? They were required to survive and the world was shuddering with risk. After a while, opportunism becomes a state of mind and, if they cared to judge by the behaviour of financial, industrial and political leaders, the words 'fraud' and 'greedy' could be said to possess chameleon properties. Anyway, whichever way the business went at Lloyd's, the brokers earned their commission.

Becky put her finger neatly on the mood. 'The City likes short-term business. Quick profits. Quick cash. We lost our ability to think long-term with the Empire.'

'You mean men did,' said Tess. 'Women have housekeeping imprinted into their bones. Fruit-bottlers.'

'But they don't think big enough,' Becky replied. 'And they're lacking in the confidence department.'

Heigh-ho.

But they worked hard, these short-termists. They worked morning, noon and at night on corporate entertaining. Once, perhaps twice, a week Becky would phone Dominique, the French nanny – Poppy being destined to learn French with her formula – to tell her that she would not be back until late.

Unfortunately, Charles was often late, too, and they agreed to add a third to Dominique's wages, which was fine for the latter but left Poppy seriously depleted of parental attention.

One day in August, driven to it no doubt by the idea that the whole of her country was on holiday, Dominique decided to depart and did so that evening, with less than a day's notice.

Two days later, a grim Becky announced that Charles would have to look after Poppy for she had an all-day meeting and left him holding the baby. In desperation, he did the only thing possible and picked up the phone to Martha.

The situation remained dire. The nanny, who arrived on the Friday, was discovered with her head out of the window smoking and was dispatched back to the agency. Her replacement the following Tuesday announced that she had a rare blood virus and she was not sure if it was infectious or not. She, too, was dispatched smartly.

'This will not do,' said Charles, on the Wednesday night as, stupefied with tiredness from coxing and boxing Poppy, they undressed. 'We haven't seen her properly for days.'

He had just been in to check on the baby and had been transfixed by the skin drained to white wax by sleep, the closed half-moon crescents of her eyelids, and by his love for her.

'She'll survive.'

'I've been thinking. Martha . . . might . . . *possibly* help out.'

Becky slipped her lace knickers down her legs and reached for her nightdress. 'Did I hear correctly?'

'Yes.'

'*Martha!*'

Charles had not confessed that he had already used Martha. 'Martha could do it and we're in a big jam.'

'How do you know she could?'

Charles sighed and told the truth. 'She helped me out last week.'

The Martha-shaped space in Charles and Becky's relationship was, at that moment, more than usually noticeable. But Becky was a working mother and no one who is not quite understands the cocktail of desperation and ruthlessness that sweeps over a woman faced with the prospect of an all-day seminar with FEROC and no childcare.

For the next month, while the right nanny was recruited, Charles took to dropping by at Martha's once or twice a week when Becky was working late. Sometimes, he helped to bath Poppy with the other children before bearing her away to the riverside flat.

Mentioned casually by Becky, the arrangement took Tess's breath away. Yet, of all people, Tess should have been used to the idea that the surface of our everyday hides strange, subterranean accommodations and unexpected passing places.

The summer meeting of the Bollys was held at a restaurant near Fenchurch Street.

The weather hung over the City, a heavy, back-end-of-season mood that drained energy, and a perpetual wind whistled between high-rise blocks and buffeted plate-glass windows.

As chef was on extended holiday, the lunch was not good and the wine was too heavy. The talk was of syndicates racking up huge losses, the predicted Lloyd's deficit and a strange coincidence of disasters and the approaching millennium.

'It's a matter of adjustment,' Louis suggested. 'Of a new psychology.' His colleagues seemed only partly interested. 'Of accepting that events do not, necessarily, go all one way.'

'We know that,' said Dick Turner impatiently. 'But we over-expanded. And the press are on our backs.'

Louis raised his eyebrows. He turned to Nigel, who was writing. 'How are you?'

Nigel closed his notebook with a little snap. 'Having a bit of trouble,' he said. 'It's very odd but the skin between my toes has split and it's hell. It makes walking difficult. You've no idea.'

'No, I haven't,' said Louis.

'I'd never paid any attention to my toes before.'

'No, indeed.'

Louis stared at the waistcoated Nigel. Unlike the Munich Re, for example, which held massive reserves, Lloyd's had less to call on. The stock-market crash of 1987 had wiped millions off the value of investments, which formed part of the reserves, yet the level of underwriting had remained the same.

'Imbalance,' he said.

'What?' Nigel looked puzzled.

'Dietary imbalance,' explained Louis. 'Your toes.'

Waiting for Becky that evening, Louis was filled with a sense of loss. For a safe past. For his own mistakes. For the certainties that he should have re-examined and had neglected to do so. For the fact that he should have helped John Frant.

'What do you think?' he asked Becky. 'Apparently the resignation rate of Names is running at twenty per cent . . .'

Sleek in her favourite olive linen and in the knowledge that it was seven-thirty in the evening and she was not going home to deal with a tired baby, Becky wrinkled her nose. 'Keep your nerve.'

'And?' He waited for the answer that he knew was coming.

'Trade through.'

'Clever girl.'

'Story of my life.'

He piloted her into a taxi and they glided through the London streets. 'Remember the bomb?' he said.

She shivered. 'I never forget it.'

He moved close to her. 'Say it again.'

She closed her brilliant eyes. 'You'll have to make me.'

He touched her breast and she moved imperceptibly. Then he ran a gentle finger just behind her ear. She smiled, and Louis bent over to kiss her. Just before he did so, he allowed his lips to hover over hers. 'Trade through . . . darling.'

As he kissed her, his sense of loss grew unbearable, swelled to terrible proportions, and then, as Becky looked up and murmured that she loved him, vanished.

They dined at San Lorenzo, touching each other at intervals very discreetly but not, it transpired, discreetly enough. They emerged into Beauchamp Place followed by a journalist on a tabloid newspaper, who had also been dining in the restaurant. By random chance, the journalist was sniffing at the Lloyd's story and recognized El Medici. It did not take him two seconds to ascertain that Becky was not his wife.

Louis took the last train back to Appleford and arrived home well after midnight. He was surprised to find Jilly still awake.

She was wakeful because she was thinking. Lapped in pure cotton sheets and flounced nightdress, she had been reflecting on the knowledge that, once again, a third party had joined her marriage.

She did not mind. As her astrologer to whom she confided most things had pointed out, she had her own agenda. Anyway, Mars was in the ascendant and he was the god of war.

As with war, which she would now wage, acceptance was a skill, requiring the discipline of the *réligieuse* and, early on, Jilly had set about perfecting this art. Until now.

She looked up, and the pink shade from the bedside lamp threw a flattering light over her beautifully serviced face and skin. Not for the first time Louis was struck by how little he knew of the exact calculations and directional voices of his wife.

Abruptly she told him that some bills were outstanding and he apologized. He finished undressing and got into bed.

'Any news from the boys?'

'No.'

'Any interesting post?'

'No.'

Louis rolled over towards Jilly. 'Are you all right?'

'I'm getting old, Louis.'

He was amused. 'Is that all?'

'How like a man. Forty-eight is old.'

Louis sighed and rolled away. Jilly's periodic wrestling with the spectre of ageing required patience and, tonight, he had none.

I have journeyed from the land of lost content.

'I don't want wrinkles. I don't want to be a bore.'

Louis closed his eyes. 'Go to sleep.'

Jilly switched off the light. 'I think we should move. Thanks to the Frants, Appleford has changed and we should get out before the value of the house drops further. Anyway, with the boys gone, it's too big for us.'

'Talking of waste, I'd like a visit to France.'

'Oh.'

He knew very well that she disliked the beautiful shuttered villa in Provence, run at great expense and seldom visited. 'I don't want to move,' he said. 'Not yet.'

'But the village. It's going downhill.'
'Go to sleep, Jilly.'

Half an hour later, Louis got out of bed and went into the bathroom where he searched for his headache pills. Gasping slightly from the pain, for it was worse standing up, he shuffled back to bed and waited for the thudding to grow quiet and leave him in peace.

Chapter Twenty-one

By chance, Becky passed Louis on the escalator at Lloyd's as she had once before, before the adventure had begun. On that occasion, she had been coming down and Louis had been going up.

They exchanged a look, brief but complete.

A reporter from a tabloid newspaper rang Becky in her office.

'Am I speaking to Becky Vitali?'

'Yes.'

A brisk, young-sounding woman, she was doing a piece on Lloyd's and how it worked, and was interested to know how the pieces fitted together. She was also interested in women in the insurance business. Could she interview Becky?

Becky indicated she could give her five minutes on the phone.

After a quick gallop through the business, the reporter suddenly asked, 'Is there a degree of co-operation between the broker and underwriter where the relationship is in danger of passing the boundaries of what, business-wise, I mean, is acceptable?'

'No.'

'Not at all?'

'Of course, if you're particularly friendly with an underwriter it might be the case that an insurance broker uses them without properly assessing the rest of the market and without keeping the interests of his client uppermost.'

'Quite,' said the journalist.

'But I've never heard of it happening,' added Becky coolly.

'Does your employer, Coates, use one or two, possibly three underwriters to the exclusion of others?'

'It depends on the business.' With that Becky terminated the conversation.

The same reporter rang Jilly Cadogan.

Afterwards, Jilly rang Louis and said, 'I've had a reporter on the phone.'

'What?' His shock was uncharacteristic.

'Asking about you and ... this woman. An insurance broker. Apparently you've been in cahoots for some time. She wanted to know if I had any comments on this professional relationship.'

The silence that followed was frightening.

It was worse than anyone had imagined. It always is.

Louis read the paper on the train to London. Jilly read it over the breakfast table in the green-and-white breakfast area. Becky read it on the bus. Charles was the last to read it as he had been giving the nanny and Poppy a lift to the baby clinic and did not have time for newspapers until he reached work, and then wished he had not found time for them at all.

The piece was matter-of-fact and avoided direct allegations. Under the headline 'What Does Go On By the Lutine Bell?', it referred to the ongoing researches of the recent Finance, Trade and Industry Committees and pointed out that while many external Names were suffering ruin, working Names, by and large, had escaped. Names such as the dashing Louis Cadogan, nicknamed El Medici, a noted figure and hugely wealthy underwriter whose Midas touch made him a legend. He was, the report went, just the sort of figure that up-and-coming insurance brokers did well to cultivate. Brokers like the beautiful, ambitious Becky Vitali and, indeed, they had been spotted dining together only the other night in one of London's most fashionable restaurants.

Jilly stared at the white tablecloth and let her coffee grow cold. This, she thought, was not part of the bargain. Charles felt sick. Louis phoned Rufus Barker, and Becky ...? Becky shrugged and an old recklessness that had lain quiet in her for a long time was ignited. Battle lines were being drawn.

'All right,' said Jilly, when Louis returned that evening. She was sitting in the swagged, toile-de-Jouy drawing room. The french windows were open onto a serene autumn garden filled with roses and coryopteris. 'What have you been up to?' She was very angry. Naturally.

Louis sighed, and the memory taunted him of a distant, sunlit time when they had been innocent and young. 'I don't know what to say.'

'Well, that's a first.'

Jilly twisted on the sofa to reach for her gin and tonic. 'I suppose I have to congratulate you on being exposed as a liar and a cheat.'

He leant against the mantelpiece. 'I'm sorry.'

'You'd better tell me.' The gin was ice cold as she liked it. 'All of it. I gather the rise of this woman has been pretty spectacular.'

Louis looked straight at Jilly and told the truth, and with the confession arrived a sensation of release and relief and of walking out of the shadow.

'You understand I don't mind about the woman,' she said, for Jilly always played fair. 'I know your first loyalty is to me and the boys.'

That was true. The houses in Appleford and France, the bank account and the portfolio of shares. The solid wedge of capital, although she was never quite sure where Louis put all his assets, was the deal. Their bargain, struck when Jilly, deeply in love with a man with a failing veterinary practice in Essex, chose to marry Louis instead, was the stronger for being unarticulated.

'But,' she added, a tight, joyless look descending over the immaculate visage, 'it was unforgivable and careless of you to get into the press. How do you think I feel, knowing that everyone we know is discussing us over breakfast or sniggering into their gin?'

'I agree,' said Louis, impressed as always by the immutability of his wife. Jilly's instinct was for form rather than content, and in some ways it was admirable. You knew where you were. 'I'm sorry, Jilly.'

'Have you been up to tricks at Lloyd's?'

Louis considered the question, which was less simple than it appeared. 'Put it this way. There were opportunities and I have taken them. And I've been lucky and in the know. Those who have lost out have been none of those things, which is, perhaps, not fair. Their losses are not their fault, but they are a consequence of a decision. They need not have taken the risk in the first place. Anyway, quite a few insiders have lost money too. The press never prints that.'

Jilly was growing bored. She held out her glass for yet another refill and Louis obliged. 'If the John Frants of this world elect to take on unlimited liability and not enquire as to what it means and where their risk is being placed, then there is a case for saying they're foolish. If they don't cover themselves they're foolish.' He paused. 'Wherever you go, whenever you go, there are always insiders. Sometimes journalists can make very stupid assumptions.'

Jilly's mind, however, was ranging over a variety of options. She never encouraged Louis to talk about his work, and never listened when he did. Except, of course, for its proceeds, Lloyd's did not interest her. She searched for an opening to make the best of her advantage.

'I've known about all your women, Louis, over the years.'

'I imagined that you did and I hope I never overstepped the mark.'

'Until now.'

He ignored her interjection. 'In return, I never enquired into your activities.'

'No,' said Jilly, thoughtfully. 'You didn't.' They both knew – or, at least, Louis thought he knew – that Jilly's activities had been more to do with spending his money than in taking lovers and he had been careful to pay her the compliment of never referring to what might be construed as a wounding lack of candidates.

The gin required more ice and she got up to replenish it. 'Is she *much* younger than me?'

Tall and elegant as ever (Jilly often thought that Louis would have that tailored English look on his deathbed), he walked over to the french windows and stood looking out. 'She has courage.' And humour and a carefully controlled recklessness that made his heart turn over in his breast. 'And she's tall.'

'Oh. Not like me.' Jilly crossed her thin, bird-boned ankles.

'No, not like you.'

Behind his back, and to her surprise, Jilly winced with pain.

That night, Charles did not return home and Poppy had whimpered a long time for her father before she went to sleep.

The next morning the other tabloids had jumped on the wagon. Louis and Becky figured in two diary pieces and in a scurrilous little article tracing Becky's career from Streatham to Lime Street in which she managed the no mean feat of being portrayed as both a bimbo and a ruthlessly ambitious career woman. The piece also conveyed the suggestion that insiders such as she and Louis made a fortune out of fleecing poor witless Names, who had been reduced to begging on the streets.

'Congratulations.'

She looked up from rereading the worst bits to see an unshaven Charles in the kitchen doorway.

Becky knew then that an episode was at an end. The battle had been fought, and it was time to sew the jewellery into the hem of her skirt and depart with the retreating army. A voice in her head sang a song. Whether it was of liberty or lament she was not sure, but she lifted her hands, palms up, in a gesture of penance for she owed something to Charles. 'I'm sorry, Charles. Truly.'

'When I think . . . Becky . . .'

'When I think,' she supplied the rest of the text, 'what I gave up for you. Is that what you're going to say? Am I right? If it was so precious what you gave up, darling Charles, why did you do it? You didn't have to leave Martha.'

'But I did.'

Becky regarded him out of her impossible eyes and Charles was very much afraid that he saw contempt in their depths. 'This is not a moment to debate free will, but you did have the power to choose.'

'It seems I chose wrong,' said Charles, grinding his foot into a newspaper that had slid to the floor. 'And I will pay for it.'

'You've certainly done that.' Becky thought of the huge sums that departed Charles's bank account each month for Martha's.

In the grip of the strongest emotion he had ever experienced, Charles struggled to speak. 'You tempted me, Becky. And you've betrayed me and made me look a fool.'

She studied him with incredulity. 'Charles, darling,' she said at last, 'you must grow up.'

'Yes.' Charles picked up one of the other newspapers and gazed at the front page without seeing it. 'At thirty-six, that's something I'll have to do.'

The telephone rang and Becky got up to answer it. It was Tess.

'If you need a home, you can come and live at the High House,' she said, and Becky found herself fighting back tears.

Very quickly, Becky discovered that public morality, in contrast to what went on in private, came decorated with teeth. Scenting copy, the press proceeded to cast her, unequivocally, in the role of the scarlet woman, the articles by other women being the most vitriolic. Louis's dash and cash, however, appealed to readers who, apparently, cherished in their collective memory the icons of Sir Walter Ralegh and Sir Francis Drake. In the press, at least, Louis was forgiven for philandering. Press and readers alike enjoyed that aspect but there was more to milk.

'Was it expertise or lust that caused El Medici to underwrite a bad risk in Nigeria,' asked the journalist, 'which contributed to the spectacular losses? Judging by his superlative track record, it had to be the latter. The question must then be posed, "Given livelihoods are dependent on it, is lust the correct fuel to run Lloyd's?"'

On reading this article, Louis experienced a degree and intensity of anger that he could not remember ever having felt before – a common reaction when an uncomfortable truth is being aired.

'Bad or what?' expostulated Nigel, when he read it – free, for once, from the envy of the big boys that had accompanied his working life.

Yet penance was necessary. The scene in which Louis, on the advice of Rufus, stood on the front step of his home with Jilly at his side and read a statement, checked by Rufus, to the assembled rat pack would remain a scar on Louis's memory. Their marriage was solid, he told them, very much the establishment figure in his pin-striped suit. His wife, immaculate in Escada, was supporting him.

More painful was the scene with Becky.

'Even now,' said Becky, when they met secretly after work in a pub in darkest Fulham, 'you're not going to leave her?'

'I can't,' said Louis. 'You know that.'

'So we go on as before?'

'Yes.'

'I just don't understand,' said Becky, her courage and stamina for once on the ebb, 'how a posse of men in frocks and a theology that went out with the ark can exert such a strange hold over you.'

'You have to take my word for it,' said Louis. 'It's too difficult to describe. Unless you know.'

Feeling bitterly excluded, she looked away. 'How can you be such an ogre at work and something quite different in your private life? An earthshaker in the office, a mouse at home. How can you reconcile such different visions?'

'I can't explain it,' said Louis. 'I wish I could. But it's me and bred into me. I have to abide by it.'

'But you have the morals of a polecat. And I'm an expert so I know.'

'Becky.'

'Is it my background, Louis? Streatham and all that?'

'If I told you, Becky, that your transformation is one of the best I've ever seen, then you must take it as a compliment.'

The implications were not what she wished to hear. 'Thank you for putting me in my place. You've just ratified an outdated class system. But,' her venom was watery, 'that makes sense to you.'

'No,' he contradicted, more sorry than he could say. 'That's gone. It's what you make of yourself.'

'Tell me about Louis.'

'Becky . . .'

'If you know the right people, of course.'

He leant forward and took both her hands in his. 'If I also tell you that I love you more than anything or anyone ever in my life, would you believe me?'

Becky's face was running with tears. 'You've done this to me once too often, Louis,' she said, 'and I believed you. As I've believed no one else.'

'The first thing we have to learn, Becky, is that nothing is straightforward. I can't let go of what I believe to be right.'

'You don't, really, and it's outdated nonsense.' She wiped away her tears with the back of her hand, an inelegant gesture that conveyed to Louis the depth of her grief. She waited for a moment longer, granting him the benefit of the doubt. Hoping. 'Louis, I've made up my mind. This time, I'm going for good.'

The drums sound and the Army departs, sweeping up with it its baggage and women.

He released her hands, sat back and, with that gesture, Louis let Becky go.

Charles had to be dealt with.

'I can't understand why you behaved as you did,' he said. 'You owed loyalty to me. We were happy, weren't we? Or did I calculate it all wrong?'

They were in the bedroom of the flat and Poppy could be heard wailing in the background.

'Nobody,' said Becky, beginning to pack, 'is owed loyalty. You earn it.'

'And didn't I?' Her quiet, dispassionate tone had made Charles livid.

All trace of the ease and unquestioning good humour that had once distinguished him were erased from his expression – and Becky, with an uncharacteristic genuflection to the part she had played in it, accepted that it was her fault. She favoured him with a long look. 'Up to a point.'

Jane, the latest in the line of nannies, appeared at the door holding in her arms a pacified Poppy dressed in a red sleepsuit. 'I'm going now,' she said nervously, eyeing the heaps of Becky's clothes on the bed and chairs. 'She's all bathed and fed.'

'Oh, you're going out?' said Becky, startled.

'Yes, it's my evening off and Mr Hayter said I could.' Jane held out the baby to Becky who, after a second or two, took her. Hair all mussed and fluffy from the bath, lips as red as the flower she was named after, Poppy snuggled into her mother's shoulder and her thumb found its way into her mouth. Despite herself, Becky allowed her hand to curve around the infant skull and cup it.

Charles's gaze sought and found a picture on the wall, which he had insisted on buying. A chic little oil of an autumnal landscape, its creator had given full rein to a series of clichés. There were apples laden on trees, hips in the hedge and a glorious spectrum of orange and gold in the painted trees. Then his gaze transferred to the white sanctuary of the bedroom he had shared with Becky, where only a hint of colour was permitted.

Ripeness had eluded him, and he was ashamed.

Poppy was in bed by the time Becky had packed, her underwear and suits folded as she preferred. On top of the open suitcases lay a couple of fat jewellery rolls. In a move that was to haunt him for years, Charles snatched them up.

'You can't have those.'

'No?'

He knew of old the raised eyebrows and half smile that Becky adopted when he behaved badly, and flinched. It was an expression he hated and, at that moment, Charles was aware that he had touched rock bottom.

'Naked I came and naked I went. Is that it?'

'I gave you every single piece.'

Becky put her head to one side and stepped back. 'Fine. Take them. I don't mind.'

On reflection, *that* was the cruellest thing she had ever said for Charles had chosen the watch from Kutchinsky, the pearls from Mikimoto, the Tiffany ring, and the earrings from Van Petersen – those sparkling milestones that Becky had flaunted – with passionate love and passionate care.

With a sound that could have been a sob, or a muffled groan, Charles turned on his heels and, still clutching the jewellery, left the room.

Before she fastened the suitcases, Becky assembled her

papers, her Filofax with its contact addresses, the joint building-society account book and, finally, she helped herself to the blue enamel cufflinks she had given Charles.

She fastened the suitcases and zipped up the small bag. Then she unzipped it, extracted the box containing the cufflinks and laid it on the pillow on his side of the bed.

They would do more damage there than anywhere else.

The suitcases were heavy and she slid them experimentally onto the floor. In the event, they proved too much for her to carry and she called to Charles for help. There was no answer and thus it was that Becky found herself pushing two large suitcases with difficulty down the passage to the front door while Charles sat and watched her from the white drawing room.

'Welcome to the club,' said Lily, when Becky rang from the hotel in which she had taken a room. Becky could hear her bracelets at the other end of the line. 'Chip off the old block.'

'Looks like it,' said Becky. 'But it's for the best. Charles is a much better father than I am a mother. Still . . .'

'Do you want to come up here?' Lily interrupted. 'You can, you know.'

'No,' said Becky, but she was pleased. 'Thank you.'

'You'll see her. You have your rights. The lawyer will make sure of that.'

Becky hesitated and then plunged in. 'What was it like, Lily? The missing-the-baby part, I mean. Did it bother you a lot? *Did* you miss me?'

'You get over it,' said Lily, who preferred not to explore memory. 'I wouldn't worry about that.'

'You're an old liar, Lily,' said her daughter, shrewdly.

'Yup. That's me, chuck.'

Loneliness, Becky repeated fiercely, after she had put down the phone, was the condition of being human. *Never* forget it. As a nostrum it had served her well over the years when she was learning to grasp at the tempting fruit on the tree. (Charles's painting must have affected her more than she had realized.) But a tree drives roots into the earth somewhere, lets loose a scented whirl of blossom into the storm, ripens its seeds and, when it dies, leaves something behind.

Becky stared at the notice on the wall, which stated that patrons were requested to leave the room as they found it.

She had left her baby behind.

Coates Brothers did not like scandal of any sort. Young-based and go-ahead they might be, but the firm, nevertheless, relied on a reputation for probity.

'You made a mistake in getting found out,' said her boss. 'And I'm afraid I've had one or two comments from some of our clients. None of whom bear too much examination themselves. But the markets, you know, they're not what they were. The Lloyd's fall-out being only part of the problem. There's nothing to stop the big multi-nationals bypassing London and going elsewhere. The Munich Re, the Swiss Allianz. You know . . .'

'I see,' said Becky. 'So it's garden leave, is it? Till things die down? How long?'

'No,' said her boss. 'It's not garden leave. It's the sack.'

Becky looked down at her lap and back up again. 'Have none of you erred and strayed?'

'None of us got into the newspapers.'

Becky got to her feet. 'That's life and the going was good while it lasted. You win some and you lose some.'

Her boss heaved an inward sigh of relief. You never knew, these days, with women. Sometimes, in situations like this, they got uppity and took you to court. Becky favoured him with her most dazzling smile, and left him reflecting that it was unfair that she should be so penalized. Then, after an hour or so, he forgot about her.

She spent the next two days on the phone in an attempt to

get another job, and realized rapidly that discretion was going to be the better part of valour. Publicity-wise, she was red hot and to touch her was to risk being burnt.

Time wasted, she told herself, was time gone. A spent echo, that left her a little older, a little more brittle. That it was unfair that she was losing the job she loved, and furthermore, did with brilliance, was not to be thought of, for Time, she told herself, was greedy and she would *not* waste it.

Thus, seething with stratagems, some grand some not, Becky made her plans and worked out the debt and credit of her pecuniary loss.

Her family, such as it was, she did not consider at all.

On the Friday after Becky had left Charles, Tess and she travelled down together to Appleford on the evening train, Becky burdened with her suitcases and Tess spilling papers out of her increasingly battered briefcase. At the station, Tess got into the car and drove it gingerly into the village.

'I hate driving,' she said. 'I hate it. We must pick up David first from the baby-sitter we use when Mum's busy. I must warn you, the High House is not like it used to be.'

'You know what they say about beggars.'

Tess was offended. 'I hope you don't feel quite like that.'

Becky touched Tess on the arm. 'O doubting one,' she said, 'I meant only that we're all beggars these days.'

'Don't let my mother hear you say that.'

The village had changed, even in the comparatively short time since Tess and Becky had waddled pregnantly up to the rise. Building was going on in two fields, and a third had been turned into a permanent car park. A pastiche period house had filled the gap between two rows of houses. The butcher had packed up – couldn't compete with Sainsbury's, Tess explained. The road down to the mini-supermarket had been widened, and an antique shop now proclaimed itself opposite the new tea-room. The air of the village was busy, preoccupied and unafraid of profit.

However, several of the larger houses were up for sale and there was talk that one would be made into a conference centre.

'Reilly's pigs went completely off their heads,' Molly Preston had informed Tess, not entirely innocent of wishing to make a point. 'The noise, you know. He's had to sell up.'

Tess had taken the point.

Mrs Frant was out playing bridge, and Becky sensed a strategic feint. The house had decayed – well, no, she thought, not so much decayed as given up. It was no longer a well-kept, well-ordered home. It was a place for a through-put of people, hedged on each side by parked cars and buildings.

After a drink, Tess scooped David into a pushchair and they went out to inspect the showground.

'I think I told you that Dad only signed a lease for five years. The Countrymen were covering their back in case there was new legislation or the appeals were thrown out. They're anxious to be seen to be law-abiding because in the eighties they ran into trouble when they tried to organize rock-festivals all over the country.'

Eeyore's Paddock, scene of the Widow's protest dance, was ruined, only an escaped comma of soft virgin grass here and there to remind them of what it had once been. Becky shaded her eyes and looked up and out over the route where she and Jack had once walked.

A long time ago.

'What happens this weekend?'

'I have an awful feeling it's an historic battle. At dawn a whole load of fanatics in Civil War dress will be turning up to re-enact Naseby or something. Actually, they're not too bad. Apart from the shouting and the gunpowder, the noise is moderate. Watch out for the camp followers, though.'

Becky dropped her hand. 'Louis doesn't know I'm here, Tess. I'll have to be very careful.'

'Is this really it? No more Louis?'

'That's it.'

'What do you feel?'

'I feel like one of those leaf skeletons, if you must know.' Tess gave a little exclamation of grief for her – she understood so well what Becky was feeling. Becky added, 'But leaf skeletons travel and they survive.'

'Well, you're only here for a week or two. Just until you sort something out. And Mum could do with some help.'

Now I know I've sinned, thought Becky.

Chapter Twenty-two

'Have a tissue.' Wilbur poked a box across his surgery desk, which was littered with drugs manuals and oddly shaped rubber tubes. The room smelt of the insides of old pill bottles.

Tess cried harder.

'It's perfectly natural to feel up and down for some time after having a baby.'

'As long as nine months?' Tess sobbed harder. 'I can't look at anything with suffering in it. Or read it. I cry over the *Evening Standard* in the tube, and I cry if I see a beggar in the street. I cry if I see an advert for Dr Barnardo's. Or children starving on the *News at Ten*. I can't go on. I can't work like that. Apart from anything else, it's exhausting.'

A recent arrival to the village, Dr Wilbur had acquired the reputation, discussed in low tones, of an earnest but thoroughly up-to-date psyche picker. (He had been known to ask his more elderly patients about the contents of their dreams.)

He leant forward. 'You're still grieving, you know, Mrs Mason. But, I wonder, is anything else troubling you that you would like to tell me about?'

'No.' Tess felt as if the denial had been snatched from her lips by a superior force. *That* option was no option. It was finished and final. Or was it? Tess was honest enough to know that, in a curious way, she had come to like her secret, for it gave her power, to tell or not to tell, with which she played.

In other words, she had become a subversive.

'No, nothing else is bothering me,' she replied. 'I mean, yes, there is one thing. When am I going to get thin? That's what's really bothering me, Dr Wilbur, and I've got to the stage when I'd eat a raw egg if I thought the stomach upset would get me to lose weight.'

Faced with this peculiar female logic, Dr Wilbur retreated into textbook-ology. 'In the majority of cases, the mother's figure snaps back to normal within eight weeks or so. But it *can* take a little longer.'

'If you really believe that's how women's bodies behave,' said Tess, 'then you're a tile short of a roof, Dr Wilbur.' She smiled to show that she bore him no ill will.

'I'll give you a tonic,' said the somewhat flushed Dr Wilbur. 'It might soften you up.'

Tess emerged from the surgery. I can't go on crying, she told herself. I have to stop it.

She wondered if she might be going mad.

These days, there were not many private places left at the High House except for Colonel Frant's study. Here Mrs Frant struggled with the correspondence and kept her photographs of Jack and Penelope. The latest, framed in cheap wood, was taken after Jack had left hospital in the summer. If do-gooding could be stamped on an expression like a flag, Penelope had hoisted hers aloft. Jack, thin and pale, was less certain and more tortured.

Often, on her way to and from her bedroom, Becky caught sight of bits of the photograph – Jack's chin, his leg, Penelope's bright and definite smile. Finally, she had ventured into the room to look at it properly and, after studying it, concluded that Jack had not stood a chance of escaping his wife.

On Sunday evenings, mother and daughter sat in the study and made up the accounts. They tended to speak softly for they felt that another presence shared the room. Banished from the rest of his house, Tess's father seemed almost palpable among his books and papers.

'You'll ring Nigel Pavorde in the morning?'

Nowadays, Mrs Frant's voice held a permanently anxious note. Tess looked up from puzzling over the figures in the account books and noticed that her mother's embroidery basket, with an unfinished tapestry folded into it, had been shoved into the corner and clearly had not been touched for weeks.

'Mum, darling. I've done so several times. The answer is always the same. They won't release the deposit because of the open years. That is, as I explained before, they can't close the accounts until they know every claim is in.'

Her mother sighed heavily. Looking at her, Tess grew frightened. It seemed to her that her mother's bones were eroding internally and that her height and solidity were melting. She was no longer invested with the maternal authority that had kept Tess rooted in childhood. A vital essence of Mrs Frant was being leached – as water, whittling out scoops and hollows, harvests soft limestone.

You can't go too, she thought. Not yet.

George and their marriage, and what had taken place and what she had learnt of him and herself, had never seemed so remote.

'I can't *bear* not knowing.' Her mother's face puckered with feeling. 'And I don't see why, at my stage of life, I have to put up with it. I dream of those men ... laughing at my predicament, asking for more. Of letters ...'

'Mummy.' Tess was appalled. 'Perhaps you ought to see the doctor.'

An expression, which could only be described as cunning, flitted across Mrs Frant's face. 'Perhaps I should.' She brushed back some hair from her forehead and looked away.

'Oh, Mum,' Tess said, and drew her close.

Undermined by her daughter's sympathy, Mrs Frant allowed her fear to gush over. 'Your father *never* meant to do this to us. Did he? He was not a bad person. Only trying to do his best.'

Death usually brings revisionism of one sort or another.

Grieving and requiring reassurance that her husband had indeed been the man she had thought him, Mrs Frant's voice ran up and down the register of bewilderment and anguish.

Downstairs David cried and Tess released her mother, for she knew that it was unlikely that Becky would go to his aid. Looking round for help, she retrieved the unfinished tapestry from the basket, banged it gently to remove the dust and unfolded it on her mother's lap.

'One more hellebore to go, Mum.'

Alone, Mrs Frant picked up the canvas and jabbed a needle into a hole. She pulled the purple thread through with a savage motion.

'Morning.' The Director of Marketing and Investment Trusts addressed the eight-thirty Location meeting. 'I want to focus on two long-term issues. One, the prospect of a Labour government. Two, what are your views on biotechnology and should we be doing more with it?'

'Doing more with it' translated roughly into 'making money from it'.

'Labour won't get in.' Kit sounded definite. Freddie shook his head in disagreement.

'No, they won't.' Tess was with Kit. 'However strongly the electorate feels about the muck-up in health and education they'll resist more taxation.' She was conscious that a steel band had taken up residence around her forehead. Five o'clock. At *five o'clock* she had been up with a fractious baby.

'OK,' said Fergus. 'Let's assume they do get in. We're struggling with recession and it has hit the City and our manufacturing base. At the same time, the government has been forced into more market-oriented policies ... privatization, contracting-out and deregulation. Labour wouldn't be able to halt the process, however much they would like to, because the pressure on government finances would be just too great.'

Unobtrusively, Tess pressed her head into her hands and wondered whether, if she located the precise spot, she could kill the nerve that was torturing her.

'Tess,' interjected Fergus, 'are you with us?' He emphasized the word 'with'. 'Would you like to add anything else?'

Just then, Tess had no views whatsoever. Paracetamol, she thought desperately, *where did I put them?*

'Just to reiterate, I don't think high taxation will be acceptable during a recession.'

'I think that's been agreed,' said Fergus.

Kit studied his agenda and Freddie stared raptly at the floor. Bill drank his coffee with little slurps. No one looked at Tess and, suddenly, she understood that a new agenda had been set. It explained every tiny lapse in her concentration or effectiveness in terms of her biology: working mother.

She was damned if that was going to happen and set about retrieving the situation. 'Can we move on to biotechnology and the related area of nano-technology, which is still terribly new and experimental but which we should bear in mind?' The men waited. 'Like Japan and micro-technology, biotechnology is worth looking at. Companies run on low overheads, they have highly motivated staff, they operate as the discovery arm for the pharmaceutical industry where they are highly cost-effective. Granted, they cannot be seen as blue chip but the pay-off is their nimbleness . . .'

Tess was now fluent in this language. Yet running under the surface was a seam of other words from another language. Nappies. Weight percentiles. Formula. Teething. Safety gates. Mummy.

Mummy.

Freddie took over. He pushed a paper covered in tabulations across the table towards Fergus. 'We've done some research . . .'

Freddie was being nice. It had been less of the 'we' and more of the 'I'.

The meeting continued. As it broke up, Fergus said, 'By the way, I want you all in the boardroom at six thirty. There's a presentation scheduled for a new venture in insurance partnership. No ducking out.'

Tess's head beat out its protest in waves of pain. A tom-tom banging a message of despair. Six thirty. Six thirty.

At home, David will be needing me.

Mrs Frant was not disposed to make Becky feel welcome at the High House, and did not do so. Becky's presence diluted the pure air that Mrs Frant so prized.

Why should she welcome this cuckoo? she asked herself. She disliked and distrusted Becky and, despite the years, the hostility had not abated. The physicality of dislike now struck Mrs Frant, for it was akin to stretching after sleep or eating when hungry and gave a piquant pleasure. Since many pleasures were now denied her, Mrs Frant had no intention of exercising restraint.

At times, and secretly, Mrs Frant thought of herself as already dead – a shade, winging though layers of time that had been folded back on themselves, searching for John. (Mrs Frant had been reading the latest theories in the science section of the *Sunday Times* and rather fancied herself as a post-modernist ghost outwitting relativities.)

In her stronger moments, panic and fear temporarily capped, she decided that hatred was useful: it was one way of confirming that she *was* still attached to the world. And, as the woman born and bred to manners but who was losing the habit, she was also amazed to discover that she was comfortable with hatred.

'This telephoning business.' She accosted Becky in the hall as the latter was finishing a long session on the telephone. 'You have to pay for it, you know.'

'Of course.'

'I've decided to put in ... well ... a payphone.' Mrs Frant

had difficulty articulating the word 'payphone' and, for a second, Becky felt pity for her.

She took the bull by the horns. 'Mrs Frant,' – 'Angela' was, of course, out of the question – 'I know Tess had to persuade you to let me stay here but I am grateful.'

Like many women, Mrs Frant operated elliptically. But, faced with the girl she had demonized, she felt an upsurge of power. Glancing through to the drawing room in which sat two interested guests (why could these people not get on with their lives?) she shovelled Becky into the kitchen.

Stock bones boiled on the cooker and the now shabby kitchen was impregnated with a moist, gelatine-flavoured atmosphere. A crate of milk sat on the table with three cartons of cut-price margarine. A catering tin of cheap instant coffee and two kettles took up one sideboard. The window over the sink, which looked out onto Eeyore's Paddock, now provided an excellent frame for the row of concrete lavatories.

Mrs Frant took up a battle position by the table. 'I didn't – I don't – want you at the High House but Tess does. Because you're in trouble and because she wishes it, I'll do my best to put up with you. But I insist that you pay your way.'

'Of course,' Becky repeated.

The riposte was sharp. 'There's no "of course" about it. We both know that.'

Becky's polite smile did not falter. Indeed, it held a hint of mutual understanding. 'Do you dislike me because of Jack?'

Jack?

Strange. These days, these terrible days, Mrs Frant barely missed him. But, in its way, that was worse than missing.

'Yes. And no. Jack would probably have gone and half killed himself running around with refugees without you dumping him.'

'Because . . . because I left my own baby?'

Leaving a baby was too ghastly a subject to tackle. Mrs Frant turned to poke ineffectually at the boiling bones with a wooden spoon. 'I hated you long before that,' she said. 'And I hate all this business,' she said angrily. 'Cooking. Stock and margarine. Thinking about every penny. Widowhood. I wasn't brought up to expect that things can go wrong, you know. I don't have the resources to cope.' The spoon banged against the edge of the saucepan: the clack and clamour of an unquiet woman. 'I admire Jack, though. And I admire Tess.'

Once embarked, Becky was not going to give up. 'Why *do* you dislike me?'

Wooden spoon held like a sword, Mrs Frant swivelled to face Becky. 'I dislike you, Rebecca,' she pronounced her verdict, 'because you have insufficient heart.'

With a clumsy movement, Becky turned away and her hair flew around her cheeks. As surely as if a bullet had drilled a hole in Becky's beautiful breast, Mrs Frant had inflicted a wound.

After lunch, a humbled Becky offered to look after David and take him for a walk. While she was gone, Tess rang up.

'I've spoken to Nigel, who's been negotiating with the managing agents. It's just possible they can release the deposit but nobody can be sure. If they do, it will cost us.'

'How much?' Mrs Frant laid a hand on the region of her heart.

'About ten thousand.'

'Robbers.'

'They have to keep back a reserve, just in case.'

'At this rate, I won't have any money to live on.'

'Listen, Mum, I'm doing my best and playing the market a bit. It's difficult and the market is bumpy but I should make enough to pay some bills. Till things are sorted out.'

Mrs Frant removed her hand from her chest. 'Did that idiot have anything else to say?'

'No. But I thought I'd talk to Louis Cadogan again.'

When Tess managed to track him down, Louis listened with courtesy and attentively, and she became conscious of the difference in their age and experience.

'It's an impossible situation,' she said. 'Daddy's estate has been wiped out by the cash calls. My mother needs capital to live on. She can't sell the house. Or she could but for practically nothing and, anyway, the money would be whipped away. And Lloyd's won't release the deposit because of the lapsed estate insurance.'

Louis listened and then said, finally, 'It was a pity that your father didn't renew.' Tess bristled. 'It's a great pity that Nigel and the rest didn't do a bit of housekeeping which, after all, they're paid to do.' She felt treacherous tears gathering and fought to get the words out first. 'Daddy was ill and frightened and there was no one prepared to help or advise, or to take responsibility.'

'Tess.' Louis sounded weary and he was. '"Help" and "responsibility" are not applicable words for insurance, which is a matter of rules and regulations. I must point out that, in your father's case, these have been followed to the letter.'

Tess's fury routed her tears. 'And in *your* case?'

He was silent.

'I do hope,' Tess was dry and bitter, 'that if you are ever in a situation which requires help that no one suggests that responsibility and help are abstracts that do not apply to you.'

'Dear Tess,' went the letter the secretary tossed into her in-tray at Metrobank, 'I hope you are well and the problems have sorted themselves out.' Tess, who had been crying again in the ladies' and frantically endeavouring to hide the traces, blew her nose.

A voice cried in the wilderness.

She was going mad.

'As I think I mentioned to you, I was hoping to come out of

281

the Army and it looks as though that is going to happen. We are very pleased and hope to move north to Scotland ... After so many years in the Army, I hope I can adapt. We are looking forward to it very much ...' Clearly Iain was neither a stylist, nor a poet.

In fact, the drama had unfolded a little differently from the harmonious arrangement his letter suggested ...

When she watched him come through the front door on a Friday evening, Flora MacKenzie had known, and she beat at her ungenerous bosom with a (practised) little fluttering gesture, a sure indicator that she was angry.

'You've put in for redundancy?'

Iain chucked his briefcase onto the floor where it landed with a thud. 'A free man, Flo. Mind you, it took some persuading.' Leaving her frozen, he stuck his hands in his pockets and went in search of the drinks tray.

Flora pursued hotly, 'Are you telling me that you had to beg them to let you opt for redundancy?'

'Affirmative.'

She sat down hard on a chair, whose stretch covers were plain and severely practical. 'Iain, have you *any* idea of what's happening out there? Or are you like one of those things that live buried in the sea bed?'

'We'll find out.'

She closed her eyes and her hand continued its tattoo against the green Marks and Spencer lambswool. 'I thought you were joking about Scotland,' she almost screamed.

'I would love to meet up with you again before it all happens,' Iain terminated his letter to Tess, 'because, I imagine, we will lose touch when we move. I was going through some of my things the other day and came across some photos of George in the early days. You might like to see them.'

The telephone rang. It was the bright and bushy-tailed reporter from the tabloid newspaper. She was searching for

Becky to do a follow-up piece and had heard that Tess might be able to help. Could she tell her where she might contact Becky?

'No, I bloody could not.' Tess put down the phone and regarded it for a moment. 'Bugger,' she said aloud.

Freddie looked up. 'That's better, sweetie. *Much* more life. Like the old Tess. Professional widder-wimmin can be a tad dreary.'

'Shut up, you heathen.' The blood was back in Tess's cheek.

Again the phone rang. It was the agency broker. 'Tess, that order you placed for the Epigram shares. We've had a spot of trouble with the registering. Can you enlighten?'

Tess shuffled through the print-out. 'Half the stock is held in Guernsey and half here. OK?'

Two seconds later, the phone rang again. 'Tess,' said Bill, 'I've got a little project for you in darkest Humberside. A local landowner who's made some money selling off land for a supermarket. It means an overnight stay.'

She felt her hands clench. 'Is that necessary?'

'Afraid so. I want this one netted in. Best bib and tucker.'

Oh, God, oh, God.

No, don't call on Him. He isn't there. Clearly.

What does my son look like these days? How many teeth has he? When did he first smile? When did he crawl?

Do I care?

Is the face of well-to-do England changing? [ran one of the think pieces, entitled 'The Wages of Greed', in a quality Sunday paper, as the winter of 1990 laid its chilly finger on the land.]University professors are quietly removing their children from fee-paying schools, the cricket greens are deteriorating in picture-postcard villages. There is a rash of FOR SALE signs in the stockbroker heartlands.

Why?

Quite a lot of it is to do with the crisis at Lloyd's. Some

call it 'The Lime Street Factor'. Others who find themselves struggling with impossible cash calls call it 'legalized' theft by Lloyd's insiders, who regarded the external Names as so many sheep to be fleeced.

But if the villages of Middle England are having the stuffing knocked out of them and the sheep are being sheared to the bone, it must be pointed out that the Lime Street Factor extends a bony finger around the world. In Canada and Australia, too, there are those reeling from cash calls and very vocal about it.

Clearly, with the recent revelations and a new militant mobilization of burnt Names, the reputation of Lloyd's has taken a nose dive that will affect future business as other insurance markets around the world leap into the breach . . .

It was decided that the Bollys' Christmas lunch should be austere: they would forgo one course and give its cost to charity. There was much discussion as to whether the smoked salmon or the flambéed crêpes in brandy should constitute the sacrifice.

Nigel Pavorde read the article during the cheese course. 'Bad or what?' His notebook lay in his pocket. 'Stomach uneasy. Bowel movement 7.30.' Unsure of what his response should be, he looked to the others for the lead. What should he think? His business was to tie a small knot on a parcel.

He was not sure but he thought, maybe, his guts were on the move again.

'What do you think, Matt?' Chris Beame was flushed with wine.

Matt seemed troubled and more than usually conspiratorial but he was safe in the knowledge that it was not he who would suffer. 'The publicity will do damage, but we must remember that the core business is sound.'

'We are guilty,' said Louis, who had grown thinner and more lined, which rather suited him, 'of sins of omission.'

It struck him again that, whatever he did, wherever he was, it would be impossible to fillet the Catholic theology out of his blood and bone.

'What are you talking about?' Nigel was thoroughly bewildered.

In revenge, Louis gave a lecture. 'Decline and fall is quite usual. Predictable, even. You know that, Chris, from history.'

'Is it?' said Nigel.

'But so is resurgence. We must reinvent ourselves. There are ways . . . Offer limited liability. Shares in the business, etcetera.'

The port was circulated, and Matt lit up a cigar. 'We'd better get on with it.'

'You're sitting on the port,' said Chris Beame.

Chapter Twenty-three

'We ought to invite Angela onto the committee.' Eleanor Thrive operated on the assumption that her charitable impulses made up for her hopeless inefficiency, with the result that no one took her seriously, of which she remained in blissful ignorance.

The members of Appleford's Christmas co-ordinating committee were drinking coffee in the Cadogans' dining room. The table was spread with a rug, which was covered in bits of paper.

'No,' said Jilly Cadogan. 'I think not.'

Today the Widow's trembling was obvious, and the more obvious it became the more it was ignored. From politeness – and from terror. 'Won't it hurt her?' she said, recollecting the slights that had come her way.

'Angela is no longer one of us,' said Jilly. 'I feel sorry for her.'

'Yes,' said the Widow, greatly daring and with the recklessness of the worm who had turned. 'Of course, you would understand. The publicity and gossip and all that . . .'

Jilly flushed a deep, angry scarlet and set her mouth in a thin line.

'Well,' Margery Whittingstall decided to pitch her tent in Jilly's camp, 'I think that after all that's been done to Appleford there's no way we should invite her to help with the Christmas flowers. Or the party either.'

'Oh,' said Eleanor Thrive faintly, and gave one of her silly laughs. 'We *are* sending her to Coventry, then.'

*

Becky was not versed in the classics but she understood the role of fortune in history. One had only to think of Queen Victoria's luck in marrying a man who was interested in drains and Christmas trees. But Becky also knew that fortune must be wooed and – another vital requirement – it was best to be in its path when it came along. In other words, she was not going to give up. Somewhere in the busy, greedy structures that supported Lloyd's, there would be a job that fortune was keeping open.

Stubbornly she worked through her contacts. Was there anything in the brokers'? The underwriting agencies? The syndicates?

'Oh, yeah, oh, yeah,' jeered one of her more macho ex-colleagues. 'Think again.'

'Your name's too hot, baby,' said another, a cocaine-snorting high flyer, currently occupying a senior position in one of the top brokers. 'Just a bit awkward right now.'

Others, more sober, were tactful. Their message, interpreted collectively, ran thus: the situation was difficult and a lot of mud was being slung about. It was whispered that the 1989 year of account looked as though it would be disastrous and heads might roll. External Names were rattling sabres and the press was prowling.

Sorry.

The headhunters who had heard tell of Becky were sorry too. Jobs, they said, were not quite as plentiful as they had been. There were no longer stories to relate of whole teams being poached, hardly any of apocryphal golden hallos or goodbyes or sweeteners to rack up in the tally of City folklore. They told Becky other tales. Something had happened to confidence. The mood had changed. The ecology of the bedrock had altered, and the easy provender had vanished. When a tide recedes, they implied, the creatures who have been too slow, too old, too disadvantaged are beached. In 1990 – and we should have seen it – the death toll had climbed, leaving victims bloated with a decade's glut gasping on the sand.

If rebellion seethed in Becky, she hid it. Patience was an art and she was greatly practised in it. Energy was finite and she would not waste more than a second or two in analysing the anomaly that it was she who had lost her job, not Louis.

'You know I've never been into isms,' she told Tess, 'and I refuse to interpret what has happened to me from a feminist perspective. It's what happens, that's all.'

'We're different,' she said, on another occasion when they had been discussing the subject of the modern woman. 'We don't sit and look out of windows any more. We've let ourselves out by the front door and we do things. We cannot be expected to be treated differently from the others out there.'

Tess, struggling with guilt and weeping, wanted to cry out; You've forgotten the wretched biology we always talked about, but realized that that did not really apply to Becky.

This, I believe, is true, Becky told herself. I am the new woman taking on an old world. Let's see what happens.

'No use crying for the moon,' said Lily who, on hearing the news, had winched herself into a new frock and white high heels, grabbed her shimmery patent-leather bag and got herself down to London on the coach. Once there, she had demanded that Becky join her for a night out in a wine bar in Victoria.

'I'm not. That's the way it works.' For once Becky had allowed herself a glass of wine. Louis liked wine. Good wine. 'Never waste your palate on indifferent stuff,' he had said (the one with the money), and he had looked at Becky. 'Only the best. The finest.'

Dozy mare.

'That's it, chuck.' Lily was on her second gin and French. 'Tell you what, Bec, let's drink to that.'

'From Paradise Flats to a penthouse in Battersea to where? From no money to plenty to none . . . Well, I was paid off.'

Lily looked shrewd. 'Keep it safe.'

Becky leant back on the leatherette bench. 'You'll have to

be careful, Lily. You're beginning to take your duties seriously as a parent.'

'Ho hum, as Jean would say.'

Both women laughed.

Lily got drunk. Becky did not: she supported her mother back to the hotel in Kensington and put her gently to bed.

'Mum,' she said, looking down at the recumbent figure. The word was foreign on her tongue.

Poppy took a minute or two to recognize her mother. When she had run through the images in her mental filing cabinet and made the connection, her smile illuminated her face.

Becky took her in her arms and felt the small body fit against hers. A smell of baby invaded her nostrils and she buried her lips in the light, curling wisps of hair. She knew then, irrevocably, that it was impossible to travel through life without some luggage, even if it was only a memory.

Charles was not speaking to Becky. As soon as she arrived, he left the flat, leaving her with Poppy and the long-suffering Jane.

'I'm sorry,' said Becky, to the girl. 'This is all very difficult for you.'

'Not at all,' said Jane, sturdy and sensible-looking. 'All my families have been split up.'

'How many have you worked for?'

'Five,' said Jane. 'Do you want me to make Poppy's lunch before I go out?'

While she was in the flat, Becky took the opportunity to read through Charles's papers, pushing aside the personal stuff to concentrate on work documents.

Nothing big appeared to be going on, just a few whispers of a deal in Brunei. But, then, everybody has whispers in Brunei, it was part of mythology. Plus, they were erratic about paying. A trip was planned to America and another to an Alaskan oilfield.

Charles's work diary for the coming week had three lunch engagements with a couple of well-known underwriters with whom he used to do business at Mawby's. Becky smiled. Charles was working the floor.

In a rare, unbent moment when out walking David, caught between the polite *froideur* of the present and the last hostility, Mrs Frant had shown Becky the mark left by a horse-chestnut leaf on the twig. 'See,' Mrs Frant had said, 'look at the tiny nails in the horseshoe-shaped scar. You can see exactly which bit belongs to the other.'

When she said goodbye to Poppy, Becky remembered that image.

Back at the High House, she and Mrs Frant preserved a more or less civilized front, Mrs Frant because she loved her daughter and Becky because she loved her friend and because it suited her position to behave well. If the High House physically dominated the rise at the end of the village, it also contained two women intent on occupying the moral high ground.

That Christmas, the air seemed polluted and there were no log fires and soaring Christmas trees. No spice, no crackers and, to be truthful, no hope.

During the days after Tess had left, David kept the two women endlessly occupied. So did the guests. Becky worked hard. Her cuticles grew rough from washing-up and her hair less smooth and curbed. Sometimes she imagined that her clothes smelt of baby, and she was forcibly reintroduced to plastic toys and other joys, such as plastic bibs in which bits of food lay festering, which she had imagined that she had left behind – in that other life. She was also reacquainted with the snobberies, many and various, dispensed by those spending money to those providing the services. Being Becky, she laughed at this manifestation of human behaviour in a way that Mrs Frant, sliced to her aching heart by her predicament, never would or could.

Estranged from Appleford (Mrs Frant had taken note of the

Christmas rejection), she resigned from rotas, councils and committees. Considering what she had given over the years, the silence was unforgivable. But there had been too much bad feeling, and too many wounds inflicted over the business of the showground for Mrs Frant to be a welcome presence, even among her friends. Especially among her friends, for friendship depends on a commonality of interest. But if she mourned the finish of an old life, if she missed its fabric, if the isolation was not good for her, she said nothing. Fed by grief and something worse, impotence – for it is imperative to our sanity that we can control our affairs – her hatred, rich, black and festering, grew.

What, then, did Mrs Frant have left?

Courage? A determination to see things as they were? Perhaps. Yet it was odd that Mrs Frant, that most maternal of women who might have been expected to fall into the doting-grandparent category, appeared curiously unmoved by her grandson, so smooth of cheek and so deliciously silky-haired. But, thought Becky, who had no energy to waste on regret for her own position and certainly none for Mrs Frant's, she had always been odd.

Only two factors could possibly be said to unite the women: their dislike of each other and their fear of the post – Becky's because it yielded nothing, Mrs Frant's because she lived in daily dread. Sometimes, when the postman's tread sounded on the gravel outside, Mrs Frant shook with anticipation. Sometimes, she fled into her depleted garden and marched and remarched her routes until she could face whatever lay on the table in the hall.

'I am sorry,' Becky ventured one morning, when Mrs Frant finished reading a letter. The older woman had turned chalk white. 'I wish I could help.'

'You have *no* idea,' said Mrs Frant, 'no idea – of what it is like to live in limbo. I expect,' she turned her drained features towards the kitchen window and the ruined paddock beyond, 'it amuses you to see your victims close up.'

291

'Victims?'

'The ones that suffer for the mistakes made by others. The sheep that you fleeced.'

'Some of them are suffering with you,' said Becky, battling with her patience. 'There are ruined insiders as well as outsiders at Lloyd's, you know. Less fuss is made about them in the press.'

'Good,' said Mrs Frant. 'If I'm down to my last penny, it is fitting that they should be too.'

Mrs Frant's world view, united with the draconian cast of her outrage and her rigid sense of fitness, was remarkably similar to Aunt Jean's. Maybe, thought Becky, it has something to do with being an older generation. For a second or two, she envied Mrs Frant the beliefs built on such a bedrock, for flexibility was tiring and held a quotient of risk.

'At least,' murmured Mrs Frant, casting aside the latest letter from her lawyer, 'I have my life insurance.'

She shot a speculative, secretive look at Becky but the latter, busy assessing the odds for the future, did not notice.

She remembered, early on in their marriage, remarking to John that it was comforting to think that one could grow old with a plant. She had meant the hellebore, whose hidden aspects she so admired. A gardening reference book had yielded up the knowledge that the word hellebore stemmed from the Greek verb 'to kill' and that the *Hellebore niger*, 'the black hellebore', was so-called for its black root. (This discovery had coincided with Mrs Frant's second, and more important, discovery that the guarding of private areas in a marriage were vital to its success.)

In the twilit tundra in which her life was now conducted, Mrs Frant concentrated on the idea of the black, fibrous taproot anchoring the hellebore. As an image, it lent her strength.

The Black Root was the code name she now gave to her preparations.

*

Did Becky think about him? Did her shallow, disloyal soul crave his forgiveness? Did she regret his absence from her life? Did she regret her daughter?

Unvarnished truth is plain and heavy. Sometimes, it is bitter. Unvarnished truth teaches us that some people are forgettable – who as soon as the door is shut or the coffin lid fastened on them are as if they had never been.

Left in the clinical white flat (which would have to go on the market), Charles sensed that he had left no impression on Becky, and a terrible desolation swept over him. Outside the windows, the Thames failed to sparkle, and each morning Charles regarded the dull sludge movement of the water and reflected on the ills in his life that had now accrued emotional compound interest.

In her area of the flat, Jane attended to Poppy, moving through the days with practised routine skills. But in the evenings when he managed to get home Charles took Poppy from Jane and put her to bed himself.

Frequently, he felt ill. Nothing he could lay his finger on. A vague sore throat. An ache in a joint. As the winter drew down, he felt even iller and drained of resources.

Martha was ironing and listening to *Woman's Hour* when the doorbell went. Switching off the iron and the radio in one practised movement, she hefted Tiny onto her hip and, sighing a little, opened the door.

'Charles . . .'

He was a sorry sight. Pale, unshaven, crumpled, swaying just a little.

She smelt the stale drink on him and got the picture. 'Heavens,' said Martha, her kinder impulses blunted by the lengthy attrition of grief and anger. 'You again.'

He tried to say something but failed.

'What on earth . . . ?'

Once upon a time, a long time ago, before the story had taken an unexpected twist, had spiralled like the LMX, Martha

ELIZABETH BUCHAN

would have leapt forward and drawn him in, absorbed him into
the circle that contained her love and nurture. Instead, an
unfamiliar, defensive woman was staring at Charles as he occupied the doorstep like a vagrant. With an awful heightening of
additional guilt, he realized that part of the punishment for his
actions was the destruction of the old Martha and the emerg-
ence of this stranger.

'Martha . . .'

She stood still, reading the signs, absorbing the terror in his
blue eyes and suddenly, with an inner prompt, understood that
her patience had been rewarded. Nevertheless, she made no
move.

'I'd gathered she'd left you.'

'It wasn't quite like that.'

'Well, whatever—'

'Please, Martha. Let me come in.'

'Why should I?'

'Please.'

Tiny wriggled with pleasure in Martha's arms, banging down
on her mother's hip. Looking away, for a hidden smile was
playing around her mouth, Martha stood aside and Charles
walked back into his home. In the hall, he slumped against the
wall and asked for a glass of water. Martha put out a hand and
touched his forehead.

'You're ill, Charles. I hope you haven't got a bug which
you'll give to the children. If you have, you'd better go. I can't
cope with anything more right now.'

'No, I don't think it's a bug. Where are Anthea and Pammy?'

Martha sighed. 'At school, Charles.'

With an effort, Charles pulled himself upright. In the dim
hall, Martha appeared to have grown so thin that she was in
danger of vanishing. Disappearing into the essence of abandoned wife. Then he noticed, with an observance of detail that,
until now, had not been a habit with him that her hair had also
grown sparse and dry.

'Oh, Martha. How do I say I'm sorry for everything that's happened?'

'In the normal way,' she replied, and kicked the door shut. 'But it would be better if you didn't say anything.' She seemed unmoved by his outburst and the obvious release that flooded through Charles, and bent down to put Tiny on the floor. 'There, sweetie pie. You're too heavy for Mummy.'

Immediately Tiny metamorphosed into a limpet on Charles's right leg. He made as if to touch his daughter but his dizziness made him stagger.

Martha unpicked Tiny from her father. 'You'd better come and lie down.'

While he lay and shivered, Martha made him a cup of tea and brought him a couple of aspirins. Charles groaned and pressed his head back into the pillows of the bed that had once been so familiar and drifted in and out of a doze.

Could a clock be made to turn back? And which one? For some reason he was lying on Martha's side of the bed, and he swivelled his eyes to the left. The patterns on the wallpaper responded by fusing into a grotesque and nightmarish tracery, so he closed his eyes and watched sparks float behind his lids. Then he fell asleep.

In the kitchen, Martha traced with her fingertips the dates on her calendar, which was pinned onto the noticeboard, but in the end she had spent too many weeks as the abandoned wife to tally them and she gave up.

When Charles woke, Martha was sitting on the edge of the bed with a second cup of tea. 'You must go,' she said. 'It's getting late.'

Charles tried to raise his head and muttered in a thick-sounding voice, 'May I stay?'

'No,' she replied, and got up. 'Drink your tea before you go.'

He struggled upright and did as he was told. Martha busied herself in stowing the ironing in the chest of drawers. Vests and knickers that required replacing. Once upon a time, there was a busy, innocent and virginal girl. Along came a prince and promised to lay the riches of his love at her feet and the girl had believed him . . .

'Martha?' Charles interrupted the story and she lost the ending. She hesitated, a hand on the drawer, then closed it. Charles pushed back the duvet and manoeuvred himself to his feet. Then he walked three steps across the bedroom and fell against the chest of drawers where she stood, whether from penitence or as a result of flu he never knew.

'Take me back,' he whispered. 'Please.'

Martha's thin knuckles tightened and her bones sprouted beneath the white skin. Take him back? Every nerve end throbbed with outrage at Charles's presumption – and yet, and yet, this was a moment of triumph.

But forgiveness?

In a well-remembered gesture, she reached out and placed her hand on Charles's cheek, testing the texture of the hot skin under her fingers. Then slowly, and with infinite care, she moved her hand down his body, encircling his wrist, running the length of his hot fingers with her cool, possessive ones.

He submitted, and while Martha read him as she would read a book, he felt the past soak away.

'Go back to bed, Charles.'

She manhandled him to his feet and together they collapsed in a heap on the pillows. With a groan that wrung pity from her deepest soul, Charles rolled over and buried his face – awkwardly and rather painfully – in Martha's breast.

And there they lay, bound together, by their shared years, circumstance, habit, their children, and by Martha's frail, unbeautiful arms.

After a minute or two, Martha stirred. 'We must get Poppy.'

*

If Charles was in the process of obliterating the past, Iain and Flora were facing a future that, apparently, did not include each other.

Flora was very, very sorry but she could not relocate north. She cried as she said the words, which was unusual in itself, and Iain was moved to try to take her in his arms but she shrugged him off.

'You can't let me down now,' he said. 'We agreed.'

She twisted a handkerchief around her capable fingers and he noticed that the velvet on her hairband had frayed slightly. 'I've changed my mind. I can't live up there. It isn't me. I don't want to live among strangers. I belong down here. So do you.' Her voice was low and soft. 'You don't have the right to tear me away from my roots.' She considered her husband. 'The male menopause does odd things, you know.'

Furious and speechless, Iain had slammed out of the house and driven for miles through the night. When he returned, Flora was asleep and he woke her. 'Do you still mean what you said? About not coming?'

Half awake and neat, even in sleep, she seemed much younger and more the girl with whom he had fallen in love and sworn to cherish.

'Yes,' she said.

'You married me for better or worse.'

'Not for the unspeakable, not for exile,' she flashed, and, for the only time he could recollect, her voice sounded loud and harsh.

'That's that, then,' he said, expecting to be contradicted.

By now, Iain should have known that life specializes in surprise.

The look Flora gave him was one that had chilled him in the past, and it chilled him now. She sat up in bed and she looked her age. It was then that she told Iain she was not sure if she wished to remain married to him anyway, and this mad scheme of his had forced the issue. The years of Army life had taken their toll, she had lost heart packing up house after house and he had never appreciated her sacrifice and her discomfort. Of course, if they had had children, it would have been different.

Iain sat on the edge of the bed and dropped his head into his hands. 'If you really feel like that,' he said, 'then there's no future. I'll give you a divorce.'

Seconds fled, never to be compensated for.

'Iain ... listen ... maybe ... perhaps ...' For once, Flora seemed lost for words.

But he cut off any possible reversal. He stood up and, with a rush of relief, acknowledged something that he had suppressed for years: he thoroughly disliked his wife. 'We've said enough, I think. I'll make up the bed in the spare bedroom.'

Within seconds of climbing into it, he fell into a deep and refreshing sleep.

Chapter Twenty-four

Louis should have known that it was rare for Jilly to give up. 'You know,' she said, while they waited for Thuk to put the last touches to the Sunday roast, 'there are lots of houses for sale in Appleford. The Barfords are going. They say they can't stand the place any longer. It's quite spoilt. We really should think of moving out.' She paused. 'You owe it to me, Louis.'

Jilly was exacting the price for the publicity, which did not surprise her husband. 'The Barfords have lost money,' he said. 'That's why they're selling up.'

'Oh.' Jilly's expensive forehead wrinkled a fraction. 'They didn't say anything.'

'Would you? By the way, have you seen Angela Frant lately?'

'No,' said Jilly, flatly.

The phone rang and, for some reason, Jilly went to answer it in the hall. Louis could hear traces of a conversation conducted in a low voice. It did not interest him in the least.

The temperature had crept slowly downwards and he had not noticed. By and large, the autumn had not impinged on his attention and neither had the winter. He had not been aware of the gold and red taking over from the dying green of the trees, the brittleness creeping over Jilly's garden and the transformation of his roses from lax bushes into stark sculptures.

What Louis had noticed was the change in himself; what he could only conclude was a seepage of optimism and energy.

It came as a shock to realize that he was grieving. For all manner of things. Not necessarily his youth, which he perceived as nothing special and he strove always to see through the commonplace. Besides, he had not enjoyed being young. No, Louis was mourning something more significant: the years to whose passage he had not paid enough attention.

He grieved, too, for Becky, with a curious grief that was almost physical. Sometimes it sat, large and hot, in his chest, very often in the old place in his head, or, like dry rot stealthily colonizing the hidden infrastructure of a building, spread through his spirits.

Louis had arrived, and he knew the place well, at the intersection of an affair when the absent lover still makes free with the mind and absorbs the desires.

(Louis was not aware, and Becky took good care that he was not aware, that he had only to walk to the other end of Appleford and ascend the rise to see her.)

The question he asked himself was: What now? A decade had run its course, and a shift was taking place in his life, and he had little doubt that the easy times had vanished. He had talked of reinvention, that rabbit-out-of-the-hat trick, which he, as yet, had still to work on himself.

It was an open secret that the total losses at Lloyd's for 1988 were likely to be enormous.

'Will we be affected?' were Jilly's first words when Louis mentioned it.

'To a degree. But it's containable. I've ring-fenced and there are funds.' He had not specified what or where. 'I'm afraid others will suffer. The wretched Nigel has taken a hit or two.'

Jilly had considered the issue. 'I wouldn't want to miss skiing.'

'No,' said Louis, 'of course not.'

The telephone conversation in the hall was now punctuated with long silences and, then, a burst of rapid sentences. At last Jilly hung up and came back into the drawing room. She had, Louis noticed, a heightened colour.

'You don't look very well, Louis,' she commented. 'Aren't

you? Which reminds me. Since you're sleeping so badly why don't you move into the spare room?'

'As you like.' Louis seemed indifferent and Jilly got up to instruct Thuk to make up the bed and they went in to lunch.

If she was truthful, Jilly enjoyed having the bedroom to herself after all these years. No little mutterings, no snores, no heaving body beside her. Just silence and the comforting (i.e. flattering) pink glow of her bedside lamp.

In the spare room, it was a different story. Jilly was correct: Louis was not sleeping. Tired and fractious, his mind continued to run through strategies and to wrestle with problems. An underwriter with syndicate losses running into millions had shot himself and his death, a violent and particular circumstance, fixed in Louis's mind in a way that alarmed him.

His headache, which hovered all day, grew worse and he got up to do something about it. Gratefully, and greedily, he swallowed the pills.

Later the headache turned crushing, then malevolent, and he began to moan with pain.

A voice said distinctly in his ear: You must save your skin. And he heard himself answering, I can't. It's too big. Too final.

He fell asleep once more, a twitching, anxious sleep. Then, as the demons prowling in his subconscious rose from their depths, the weakened blood vessel, situated near the surface of his skull, burst.

Some time later, he was conscious of a conversation being conducted over his body. There was a high, anxious-sounding voice. Jilly? Then the slower, deeper tones he recognized as his eldest son's. Then the speakers went away. Or was it Louis who went away?

Later, there was another conversation, a slower exchange between two people when he caught the words 'not too serious' and 'lucky'.

Am I, indeed? Louis tried to summon a response but was too tired. He endeavoured to move but found it impossible, indeed painful, for he appeared to be anchored by ties to a hospital bed. An immense weight held him down, heavier than anything he had ever lifted. Ever imagined. He set about locating a mental image to find the one that fitted him. Ah. That was it. Fixed to the bed with tubes. A Gulliver of the intensive care ward, for he had worked out that that was where he was.

But how odd that his mind should feel so liberated. Extraordinary how it seized the day with a wild, joyous abandon to perform all kinds of tricks. At one point, he chose to glide above his body and look down. At another, he sank through endless dark air towards . . . he was not sure. The huge debt? The final reckoning?

Perhaps I'm about to meet God, he thought, and a warning darkened his exhilaration, the tocsin sounded, and he was back in the grey stone church.

'Louis?'

No, he was not meeting God but Jilly. Pale and preoccupied, she bent over him as he forced open his eyelids.

'Thank goodness,' she said and, finding a spare space between the tubes, touched his shoulder. Even that hurt, and Louis winced, for it would appear that each nerve ending in his body had forced its way to the surface of his skin.

He made a supreme effort to look normal and was rewarded for Jilly's face cleared.

'You did keep the insurance updated, didn't you?' she asked, her fingers burning into his skin. 'You did, didn't you, Louis?'

Returning was a more difficult process than might be supposed. First of all, it was frightening. Every breath was a conscious one. Every thud of his heart a herald of possible trouble. Every dawn the last. Every step hedged with qualifications. Every word spoken qualified by a question mark.

He had suffered a minor stroke, which had affected his left side. In future, he would not have to bother to reinvent himself: that had been done for him. No butter. No wine. No stress. No this, that or the other if he was to recover: the consultant painted a picture that filled Louis with boredom and despair. As it happened, the consultant warned with a downward inflection, the situation was retrievable but it must be looked on as an alarm bell to which he must listen.

Alone, sweating, clammy and without a prop, Louis contemplated a future that had changed.

After two days, he was moved into a private room, away from intensive care and the activity centred on the prone forms, whose silence exuded an intense, threatening quality. His sons came, unable to look him fully in the eye, and went away again. Jilly came and went. Outside in the corridor, the nurses and other mysterious figures of authority and knowledge passed to and fro in a practised hurry. Ladies bearing books and magazines put their heads round the door. Meals arrived, to be contemplated and then removed. Louis was being sucked into a panoply of medicine and illness, falling into routines, needing them even while the world outside became pale and remote.

He slept often and dreamt strange, vivid dreams, one dream in particular.

The door opened.

'Good God,' said Becky in his dream. 'You look awful.'

So did she, in dark glasses and headscarf patterned with horses. 'Disguise,' she announced, throwing them off onto a chair. 'I said I was your sister.'

Worry had drained the colour from her face and he knew that she had suffered. She sat down on the bed, light, insubstantial, leant towards him and smiled her smile, full of humour and wickedness. Louis's overburdened heart and circulatory system throbbed with love. 'Let me ask you something. Are your insurances rock solid?'

Louis felt the dark lift from his spirit. Risking the pain, he laughed and the weight of tubes and the prognosis became feather light. His hand inched over the starched counterpane towards Becky's. Their fingers touched and held. Louis felt tears run down his cheeks.

Her face touched his and Louis knew that she was crying, too. 'Oh, Louis. You fool. You might have left me.'

A smell of medication, illness and his fear filled the room. On his tongue, Becky's tears tasted salty and normal while his were thin and ungenerous.

In his dream, Louis moaned.

Still holding his hand in hers, she leant back, the thick arresting eyebrows raised above the fabulous eyes. Ironic and utterly compelling, doubly so now that he was ill.

'You're not a good proposition, Louis. Any longer. But . . .'

The 'but' hung over him. There was, he wanted to tell her, no safety in human relationships. No love, really, except of the self and sometimes not even that. No security. No insurance. Except for the 'but'. . . and on that hung everything.

'Kiss me, Louis,' she ordered.

On that small, dreamt word – 'but' – Louis began to heal.

'Two down,' said Matt, poking his conspiratorial face above another terrible tie into the bunch of hothouse flowers on the dressing table. 'You and Nigel, who's having his piles seen to. By special dispensation, lunch has been set back a month or so, so you can make it.'

Matt had made the journey at some inconvenience to Appleford where Louis was now convalescing, and Louis was touched. 'Fine,' he said. 'Tell me what's happening.'

'General mayhem.' Matt's face lost its geniality. 'A body called the Outhwaite Action Group is suing.' He did not seem concerned. 'Nothing squeals as long and hard as a man or a woman who thinks they've been defrauded. But if they win, a nasty legal precedent will have been established that members' agencies can be held liable for the failures of a managing agent. We shall see.'

'The Name bites back.'

'Quite a few suicides, one way or another. Pareham got a letter the other day from one of his lot enclosing a death threat.'

Louis shifted in the bed and turned his aching mind to business, from which he had been detached. 'If the bad publicity continues we'll lose capacity. You can see their point of view.'

'Yup.' Matt sat down and looked hard at his friend. 'You all right? Really all right?'

Before Louis could answer, Jilly came in bearing a coffee tray. 'So good of you, Matt. Louis has been a bit down and needs cheering.' Louis recognized the tone that she had used to address the children when they were young and uncontrollable.

'Thank you, darling.' He restrained the urge to bare his teeth at his wife. He watched Matt drink his coffee, and lusted after its strong dark fragrance. 'In the future we'll have to think corporate. Woo in their funds somehow.'

'You're supposed to be ill . . .' Matt put down his cup.

The two men continued their conversation until exhaustion hit Louis, a hammer appearing out of nowhere, and Matt said goodbye. Louis watched him go, and listened to the car draw out of the drive.

A business on the brink of a crisis was already finding ways to adapt and mutate. That was the way it happened, he concluded, as Matt's engine faded into the distance. The idea of those schemes fabricated to turn disadvantage around, as ever, intrigued him.

Take the days one at a time. Slowly. Carefully. Eating, washing, walking, talking required thinking about, and energy had to be hoarded.

The left side was scheduled for re-education. And what would he teach it?

On the bad days, when he experienced the double assault of hurting body and depressed spirit, Louis's bedroom was a place of torture, which was inflicted with an indifference that he, used to control, found shocking. A fever of impatience and despair seized him, sending his thoughts swooping and dipping into the dark. His illness, his unreliable vein, were, he supposed, the encounter with the very devil who had been promised by the priests of his youth. *Lucifer was there. He was there. Like God, he never went away.* Louis had imagined that he had discarded such fatalism. But no. The devil, it seemed, had merely bided his time.

Jilly made some attempt to understand, but her ability to enter Louis's hushed arena was limited. After the initial shock had faded, it was clear that her impatience was held in check. Just. However, she exhorted Louis frequently to get out of bed and do his exercises. Illness frightened her, and she wished it banished from her house for it carried with it a spectre of her own decay.

He thought back on the marriage they had shared. In the early days, he had loved Jilly and she had loved her penniless Essex vet. After a while, Louis had stopped loving Jilly. And Jilly? Louis did not know what Jilly felt, and in his lack of curiosity lay indictment.

That was the way it had worked.

Jilly kept herself busy. The phone rang often and Louis could hear conversations accompanied by gusting laughter, or low-voiced, urgent exchanges. She went out: massages, facials, hair, some committee work, she explained, groomed and perfumed in contrast to the unkempt quality imposed by illness and of which Louis was conscious. But the house was always immaculate, the sheets fresh, the fridge full, the garden a delight and the flowers perfect. Jilly kept her side of the bargain.

'Becky,' Louis addressed the dream Becky, 'I am frightened of my own body.'

'Nonsense. You're merely renegotiating its limits.'

He laughed, as he always did when he talked to her, and felt its healing quality trickle through him.

'All the same, you'd better tell me.'

He sighed with pleasure. Becky listened to the list of physical changes: the long journey between bedroom and the adjoining bathroom, the effort required to take a bath, the hard thump of his heart inside his chest, the nagging headache that descended in the afternoons, his hunger at being deprived of butter, cream and coffee. And wine. Of course, wine.

'Tough,' said Becky, who did not care either way if she had these things or not.

At last he said, 'Tell me about you.' But that part of the dream went blank for Louis did not know where Becky was or what she was doing. All she could say was: 'I'll manage. I always do.'

Yes, she would, he thought, his heart overwhelmed by a tenderness that constantly took him by surprise.

Before Christmas, he was surprised by a visit from Tess who brought from Mrs Frant's garden a carefully culled bunch of witch hazel, which had come into bloom. Its light, sweet scent floated through the drawing room to where Louis had now progressed. Jilly had given up making coffee and Tess was presented with a glass of sherry while Louis received yet another carafe of water.

'You're privileged.' Tess pointed to the witch hazel. 'My mother doesn't yield up her precious plants easily.'

She was lying: Mrs Frant had not wished to yield up anything, but Tess had insisted.

She looked round the room, which was decorated with Jilly's customary flair. Louis imagined that Tess found it a little too dressy for her taste as he himself now did – these days, he found himself longing to strip clean, white and bare all the rooms in the house. 'Louis, I must apologize for being so rude to you. It's on my conscience.'

'Don't even think about it.'

'But I must,' she said, pressing the point, not entirely disingenuously. Nowadays Tess did not mind what Louis thought.

'How is your mother?'

'Hanging on. Just.' One of the advantages of being hit by tragedy, and there were not many, was that if you did not feel like it there was no need to put a brave face on things. 'She has been put in an intolerable situation.'

'I'm truly sorry.'

Tess saw that he was. 'I wish I could help her but it's beyond help. I need a miracle. Trouble is, God doesn't provide them these days.' She looked straight at Louis, her thick hair tumbling down from its loose knot. 'It's strange, isn't it? All his life my father was so careful with money. But when it came to Lloyd's, and Nigel's blandishments, he developed a blind spot.' She stared at her fingers clasped round the glass. 'He simply developed a blind spot.'

'It was a business proposition, Tess. And it went wrong.'

'A blind spot,' she repeated wearily.

There was no adequate answer and Louis did not presume to make any. After a few seconds, he asked, 'Did she send you?'

Tess knew perfectly well to whom the 'she' referred. 'No, she didn't.'

'But she knows I've been ill?'

'Oh, yes.'

'Is she well and where is she?'

'She's fine but looking for a job and I'm not answering the second part of your question.'

'I'll see what I can do about the job bit but, given the circumstances, it will be awkward.'

Rarely had Louis been so conscious of failure: the failure of his wretched body, of commitment and courage. He looked at the girl sitting opposite him in the affluent room: drawn and a little too plump. She, too, was struggling.

Worse than his failures, perhaps, his beliefs were threatening to prove inadequate. In maintaining loyalty to the structures taught him by his faith, imperfectly held, imperfectly enacted,

Louis had seen the only way possible to manage. He had not reckoned on the contrariness of feeling and impulse that made his decisions seem meaningless.

The trick was: hang on whatever.

Trade through, Louis.

He pulled himself together. 'How are you, Tess? And, of course, the baby.'

'He's fine.'

He was conscious of a slight detachment on her behalf. 'Sleeping through the night?'

Her '*No*, unfortunately' gave Louis the answer. Tess added drily, 'Metrobank's hours were not constructed with the working mother in mind. In fact, I think there's a plan to make it as difficult as possible. But I've rumbled them and it's a fight to the death.'

'I hope not,' said Louis, and because it had been forced to his attention, 'you must look after your health.' Tess made a gesture with her hands that suggested she did not have any choice in the matter and Louis added, 'I've never really told you how sorry I am about George. It was cruel.'

The new bold Tess told him the truth. 'I'll survive without him.'

'More sherry?' Jilly appeared in the doorway.

God tapped on Louis's shoulder quite a few times during the stuffy, wakeful nights that he endured as he got better. What have you done with your life? he asked.

I accrued money, Louis answered. On political risk. Someone has to.

Indeed, said God. And was it enjoyable?

Very.

And is it difficult to let it go?

Very. Neither do I wish to.

And your duties and responsibilities? What about those?

Don't ask me, said Louis, involuntarily. Those, I fear, are on the debit side.

Quite, said God. And there is always a reckoning. Would you not say?

Chapter Twenty-five

Not all old habits become otiose and some are useful, indeed necessary. Unlike the habits of a failed marriage, which from the instant of dissolution are redundant. A case in point – Iain's vocabulary would, perhaps, never shed its Army embellishments – was the habit of thinking out even the smallest of manoeuvres in strategic terms. As an ex-Army officer, and one trained to be congenitally opposed to waste, Iain had made a thorough reconnaissance of his feelings, identified his objectives and targeted his mission. Now he must wait until he had healed a little, and the shock of Flora's departure – and his relief – had subsided. Until he was able to admit freely that he was relieved. This was not automatic. He did not care for the idea that his marriage had been so lacking in adhesion and rootedness that it had been as easy to end as pulling a weed from the earth after spring rain.

Yet, for all the thoroughness of his emotional investigations, Iain was unable to see the blind spot (how could he?), or even admit to myopia, when it came to the subject of Tess, a condition that had shaped the downward course of his marriage, and which the sharper-eyed Flora had spotted. On sitting the examination on the subject of ourselves, it is impossible to gain full marks. Iain scored higher than most but, nurturing a passion that was beginning to astonish and delight him, not quite high enough.

Christmas and New Year came and went before he made his move. Why should I not? he asked himself, a little more frequently than was perhaps consistent with someone who had carefully calculated the odds. Risk-taking did not end when you quit the streets of Belfast. *If I don't, then ... well ...* Iain had never been an articulate man and, at times of powerful emotion, words came in second place.

'You great lump,' as Flora would say, unaware of the ardour that sat in her husband's sometimes too silent breast. If she had not been, the future would have been different.

The train from Oban sped southwards, through the Highland defiles clenched by winter: dark, snowy and swathed in silence.

At Edinburgh, which was swarming with people after the Christmas break, Iain changed onto the Intercity for London and sat in second-class listening to the muffled beat of Walkmans and the conversations of mobile *phonistes.* He looked out of the window. Already the contours and signposts of the North were changing, reknitting into lighter colours and Midlands' plains. Even the air looked different.

The young man opposite was again wielding his phone. 'Tell Bev to make sure the respray job's done ...'

The showmanship amused Iain. Along with the extra bills and never being out of reach, the owner acquired an auxiliary set of behavioural rules.

When things change, they change quickly. Obviously, he and Flora had agreed that the marriage was over but the speed with which it disintegrated had appalled Iain. One minute Flora was there, the next she had moved out, got herself a job as chief administrator in a private hospital and, her hair newly highlighted with blonde streaks, dispensed authority and clutched clipboards as content as he had ever seen her.

Iain had packed his bags and left the South for a decaying manse situated on the Sound of Mull from whose windows he could observe his fish farm, bought from a couple who had had enough.

Now, he was coming south, leaving behind a bare refrigerator, an unmade bed and an infestation of sea lice on his salmon.

Why were his fish infested?

The profit for this, his first year in the business, would be nil.

Sea lice.

Mobile phones.

Flora with blonde highlights.

At King's Cross, he indulged in a taxi. The capital folded around him: choked with cars and now alien, whose surface anarchy concealed a profounder one. At Covent Garden, he got out, paid the taxi and walked into the restaurant where he sat and waited until Tess arrived, rushed and breathless, a mass of papers stuffed into her briefcase. She was dressed in an unflattering dark suit, chosen to suggest just how serious she was about her work.

Iain seemed both taller and thinner than Tess remembered him, browner, too, and rather too conventionally dressed. Halfway through the main course, he put down his knife and fork.

'Don't you like it?' Tess was eating her (theoretically slimming) sole enthusiastically.

'Food can get in the way,' said Iain, 'and I don't want it to just now.'

Tess felt her body miss a beat. A second of change, of reassessment, or realignment into a new position. 'Well, I shan't waste a mouthful.'

They talked fish farms, Scottish politics and Scottish money, much as once, long ago, she had talked Irish politics with George, until she put down her knife and fork and said, 'Iain, I never really understood what George was up to in Ireland. Are you allowed to tell me?'

He considered. 'Put it like this—'

She interrupted, 'Put it straight, Iain. That's all.'

'Over there, the Army operates its own unit for intelligence-gathering. George was part of it. He would have been trained in surveillance and countersurveillance. He would have been out on the streets or whatever, doing just that.'

'He never said.'

'It wasn't, isn't, something to talk about. For obvious reasons. The players know all the tricks of the sneaky-beakies. Sometimes it's stalemate. Sometimes we're cleverer than they are. Sometimes the players are cleverer than us. When George died it was the latter.'

With a weary gesture, Tess pushed back her hair. 'You're all the same. It would have been a lot easier for me if I'd known.'

'Of course.'

'I suppose I should have thought harder, asked more questions.'

'There was no need.'

She looked across the table at him, sharp and defensive, but there was no trace of patronage in Iain's expression. Neither was he going to continue the conversation.

'Coffee, Tess?'

Tess ate all the petit fours and eyed the adjacent table's quota with longing. Iain laughed, which she considered suited his face, and ordered a second plate. 'Don't they feed you at Metrobank?'

'I'm on a diet, so most of the time I'm famished. Anyway, with things at home as they are, every penny counts.' Tess rummaged in her bag and produced a packet of cigarettes. 'I know I shouldn't but it's a way of subduing the body. Otherwise I think of nothing but food. It's unfair,' she held up the lit cigarette and a youthful resilience illuminated her face, 'but I was born in bondage to my appetites. So there's no escape. Sometimes I can't wait to be old when it won't matter any more if you can't see me for chins.'

Tess might have added that she was famished for colour, music, passion and some kind of form, the things that she craved, while she grieved for her father and her husband,

314

struggled to put things in order for her mother and to love and cherish her son. Struggled to make work work.

'Tell me about David.'

She took a breath. 'David? He's . . .'

Midway through describing him, Tess wondered if Iain sensed her ambivalence. 'I love him, oh, I love him to bits,' she assured the listener, 'with feelings I didn't know were possible until I had him. But it's difficult. I don't think motherhood is a natural condition.'

Psychiatrists are familiar with the syndrome of burying a fact in the subconscious, of willing it into the never-had-been. But Tess's secret was proving protean and quicksilver, as tenacious in its hold as the bindweed that was beginning to creep through the garden of the High House. Was David George's or Charles's? Perhaps that, as much as anything, shaped her view of her son.

Forced back onto old hunting grounds, and to the diary, Tess nagged at the old question. How can you reconcile the longing for faith without belief? Would faith make it possible to keep and carry her secret and her anxiety? To hold the ambiguity steady between her cupped hands. Faith would confer a measure of absolution because it held out the promise of forgiveness. Faith would give her strength to get through.

'Are we,' she wrote, 'victims of our age? Willing but rudderless, longing for the infinite but educated into scepticism. Children of science and privatization.'

The concept of the lost generation rather pleased her.

Suddenly, Iain leant forward and took one of her hands. Taken by surprise, Tess blushed a deep red.

'Tess, I've loved you for a long time, longer than I realized, and I want you to come and live with me in Scotland.'

No one ever sheds risk . . .

'You know nothing about me.'

'I've astonished you.'

'Yes, you have.' She added, unaware (unforgivable, she

315

reflected later) of the hurt it would inflict, 'You're not like George, after all.'

Iain closed his eyes for a second. 'I want to rescue you.'

'Good Lord,' said Tess, who had never suspected that he was a romantic. She stared at him with wide eyes and retrieved the situation. 'No, you're not a bit like George and I was stupid not to see it.'

She heard Becky's voice in her ears.

Take it, take it, you fool. March with the Army.

The next morning at the High House, Tess got up at five thirty and crept into Becky's room where she lay, a restless mixture of limbs and quick breathing. Tess snapped on the bedside light and bent over her. 'Bec.'

In the light, Tess's face was clearly sleepless, and lines had arrived around her eyes. Fine lines that traced their own history. Becky's face was better preserved: its smooth skin suggested the survivor, a high-octane energy that maintained its taut, lubricated look. It was the face of less reflection and sharper-focused ambition.

Becky stirred, flung out an arm and said something incomprehensible. Then she opened her eyes and shut them again. 'You're only waking me up because you want me to deal with David. Am I right, or am I right?'

'Right.'

Becky sat up. 'Or is it Mr Right we should be talking about?'

'I need to think and I can't do it here. I'm going for a walk.'

Becky shivered in the cold bedroom. 'Only for you . . .'

Tess sat down on the bed. 'I don't know what I would have done without you.'

Instead of saying, 'Nonsense,' or the equivalent, Becky just said: 'No.'

'But what would you have done without me?'

'Sleep.'

When Tess left, Becky lay and thought. She hated being awake at this hour for she was at her most vulnerable. She turned over and pulled the thinning sheets over her shoulder – the good ones were used for the guests – and tried to doze.

She heard Aunt Jean singing one of her hymns, a thumping, jolly number, and at odds with the careworn face and body. 'I expect,' she muttered to her dead aunt, 'that Up There they're begging you to shut up.'

Becky ran a hand over her thin haunch. She wanted her job back. She craved the adrenaline rush, the whiffs of fear and exhilaration, the precise calculations, the beat of business in the Room, its faint suggestion of old socks and men's changing rooms. Insurance was a world to itself, and its idiom was the background mutter in her brain – reinsurance, settlements, renewals – words arranged like inviting canapés at a party.

Strange how she never thought of Charles. Or, much, of Poppy. The horse-chestnut-leaf scar was fading. She was free again, free to operate and to move where she wished. To make money. The jewellery was, indeed, sewn figuratively into Becky's hem and who knew what was coming next?

But she thought of Louis.

She pictured his broken head. The blood pumped by the stricken heart.

Louis.

Tess took the car and drove out of Appleford up towards the trigonometrical point and parked in the field below. It was dark, and cold, and her breath plumed out around her. Dawn was trying hard to make itself apparent, but the weight of the winter night was almost too heavy to lift. In the distance, Appleford was shrouded in ghostlike livery and, as she watched, a few lights stole on in upper storeys.

As a child, Tess had run through fields such as this one, arms wheeling, breath heaving. Innocent and free of knowledge.

ELIZABETH BUCHAN

Now she was walking with maturity on her shoulders, and all
that came with it.

۰ Up, and further up. The walk of a woman chased by devils
and goblins, accompanied by the crack of ice and frosty silence.

What have you done, Tess?

She had learnt to strive, to compete, to do business. To
outwit the sharp, predatory life in a medium where it flourished
and fed. The dip of an index and its climb upwards, and she
could move. The quiver of a rumour and she was there. The
suggestion in a tone of voice, and she could repackage it in
financial terms. Yes, there was no doubt that she had not done
badly. Unlike her mother, Tess was fluent in the language of a
non-domestic arena. Both she and Becky had abandoned the
view from the kitchen window and chosen to go out through
the front door.

Yet it was not enough. No, it was not *enough*.

She stubbed her foot and stumbled. Toe stinging, she looked
down and dimly made out the stone's white surface threaded
through with a seam of crystal.

It was the metaphor that she sought. Around the stone
flowed the rushing impulses of the spirit. Restless, hungry rivers
of feeling and yearning, pushing over the hard lump of work
and motherhood. And in the stone, the crystal that she longed
to extract.

She moved on, the grass crisp round her chilled feet. She
was no longer a girl but a woman, who woke, dressed, made
breakfast, changed her son's nappies, commuted, worked and
occasionally remained awake to watch *News at Ten*.

A fish farm in Scotland. A second marriage to be built on
the residue of the old, as Troy was rebuilt each time on its
previous destruction. A marriage to be conducted in the shadow
of the mountains and ruddy glens, in the wind and the rain of
the north. And this for Tess, who had been bred in the good-
mannered landscape of the south?

A breeze got up and smacked the tree branches against

318

others. Its ice stung Tess's cheek and sent the blood diving away from the surface of her skin.

She raised a hand and brushed her wet eyes where the skin felt pulled and taut with fatigue. Slowly she turned and made her way, feet crunching slightly on the long grass, back to the car. Behind her, a silence closed over her path and returned the landscape to the winter.

Ambiguity, the not knowing, was the condition of living.

When she let herself back into the High House David was shrieking. For once, there were no weekend guests, and Mrs Frant, who had been ordered by Tess to rest as much as possible, was still in her room. Dressed in leggings and a jumper, Becky was dashing around the kitchen endeavouring to mix hot-oat cereal. Tess peeled off her outdoor things and dropped them in a heap on the floor.

'Pick 'em up,' said Becky.

'Later.' Tess sat down and began spooning cereal into David's mouth. 'You should be doing this yourself, my boy,' she informed her son, who ignored her.

Becky subsided thankfully with a cup of coffee. 'Better now, are we?' Her tone was more sympathetic than the words. 'Walked it off?'

'Sort of.'

Becky shrugged. 'There's a chance of a job,' she announced.

'*Becky*. Where?'

'Abroad. Swiss Securité. Dennis Badge rang, but it's very iffy so I won't say anything.'

'Oh, Bec.'

After breakfast, Tess sat with David on the sofa in the now unfamiliar drawing room and read him a story. It felt cold, for they did not light the fire unless there were guests. In the old days, at her father's insistence, a fire had roared throughout the winter.

David laughed and wriggled, stabbing his finger on the pages emphatically and with huge enjoyment. After Tess had put him down for his morning nap, she took a cup of coffee up to her mother.

Mrs Frant was sitting on her bed in her underwear, staring out of the window, caught midway through dressing by the more urgent desire to look at her garden. Beside her was a large envelope that Tess knew contained her will. Its flap was open. In reminding yourself of your mortality, did the idea become more acceptable or less? On balance, Tess concluded, it was worse. She kissed her mother and gave her the coffee and Mrs Frant announced, in something of her old manner, that she would be down for lunch.

'Mum,' Tess sat down on the bed and put her arm round her mother, 'if you had a chance would you like to leave Appleford and start afresh somewhere else?'

Mrs Frant did not ask why Tess had introduced the subject. She did not look at her and the silence was charged with the old, heavy imperatives that Mrs Frant's love and passionate will had laid on her daughter over the years. Then the older woman shook off Tess's arm, sat down at her dressing table and picked up the silver-backed brush that Colonel Frant had given her as a wedding present. 'Don't be silly, Tess. We can't leave this house.' She banged the brush on her head so hard that Tess heard a crack.

'*Mum!* Do be careful.'

There, thought Mrs Frant with satisfaction. Now my head hurts and I can think about that. For a second, Tess struggled to understand what was going on. 'If it would make you feel better.'

'I'm not going to Africa.'

'Did I say that?'

'No.' Mrs Frant made an effort, visibly reassembling the pieces of the calm, capable maternal figure that she had been.

A force that, once, had almost smothered her children. No longer, Tess vowed, in a split second of revelation between her mother banging down her hairbrush and the moment of impact. But it hurt her to watch.

'Sorry, darling.' Mrs Frant turned to face Tess. 'I'm not quite myself these days. Sometimes I don't feel quite real, sometimes all too real.'

'Mum, I wish I could help.'

Mrs Frant stroked her daughter's thick fair hair. 'You're doing your best.'

They got through the weekend.

On Monday morning, Tess left the house as usual. Becky fielded David and waited for Mrs Frant to come downstairs. She failed to do so and, after a suitable interval, Becky laid a breakfast tray and took it upstairs. She knocked on the bedroom door and pushed it open.

'Tess asked me to bring you up breakfast.'

It was dark and absolutely still in the bedroom. Becky took in the flowered curtains, the old-fashioned furniture and a large photo of the Colonel on the dressing table, now slicked with a film of dust. There was a smell of toothpaste and of damp towel, and the wastepaper basket needed emptying.

Mrs Frant raised herself on one elbow and inspected the tray. Then she heaved herself upright, pulled the sheets straight and smoothed back her hair. The persona she presented to Becky clicked back into place.

'Are you all right, Mrs Frant?'

'How much longer are you going to stay here, Rebecca?'

With the cruelty of which at times she was capable, Becky observed the heavy furrows engraved into the face below her. Absent hormones and age had long ago banished the feminine. Becky took note. Age obliterated gender.

'I won't be here much longer. But I hope I've repaid you by helping out.' Becky produced her smile.

White and shivery as she was, Mrs Frant was proof against

Becky. Even so, as she pulled a knitted woollen bedjacket around her shoulders, her hands were trembling. Becky placed the tray over Mrs Frant's knees and a hand shot out and trapped her wrist.

'You've always taken advantage of Tess's good nature and generosity.'

Becky calmly removed the hand. 'Why don't you stay in bed today, Mrs Frant? You need the rest. I can cope downstairs.'

The two women looked at each other. I've had enough, said Mrs Frant silently. I want to go. Because you are indifferent and heartless, you will help me. Not understanding, Becky stared back. You awful old woman, she thought.

Mrs Frant gave a nod, so slight that afterwards Becky thought she had imagined it.

Something made her say, 'You wouldn't do anything foolish would you, Mrs Frant?' The stuffiness in the room was over-powering and Becky quivered to escape.

'Oh, no, I always think of my children,' said Mrs Frant, feeling the beat of her love for them. Inside her head the door was flung wide open but no onlooker could possibly have known. 'And you must allow me to judge what is foolish or not. My husband is dead, leaving me to cope. My son . . . well. I miss my home, for the High House is no longer mine.' Mrs Frant's hands locked together. 'I miss my life and I can't have it back. Simple enough to understand but not to accept.'

You're mad and awful, thought Becky, and I won't have you putting a hex on me. But Becky also knew that she must protect Tess, whom she did love. For her sake she said, 'Would you like a bath, Mrs Frant? Shall I run one?'

'Don't be mis-led,' said Mrs Frant. 'The obvious is not necessarily the best solution.' A spark of animation suddenly smouldered in the drawn face.

The chaos theory. A butterfly flaps its wing, and an earth-quake shakes China. Where did this drama begin? With a letter? No, further back with Colonel Frant's desire to make his capital work twice. No, with the mining of asbestos, with the seeping of oil over sweet land, with the whirling of hurricanes, the rip of escaped gas, with the desire of the first human to step out of Eden.

'A bath, Mrs Frant? I really think you should have one.'

Mrs Frant's hands wandered over the tray and lighted on a piece of toast. 'Will you stop bothering, please,' she said. 'I resent it and it isn't necessary.'

Becky stepped back. 'That's more like it,' she said, with satisfaction. 'I'd better go and see to David. But,' she turned at the door, 'I will be watching and, if necessary, I will summon the entire might of the social services to ensure that Tess isn't overburdened.'

Left to herself, Mrs Frant was quite calm and cool. Death, she thought, gazing through the door to the other side, and a very good thing too. Until now, she had not understood that an integral ingredient of a good death was the taking control of it, as her life, her middle-class, unambitious life, had not been, in the end, controlled.

There was joy to be had in sloughing off the armour, in tearing through the layers of what had been taught as appropriate behaviour, in the sacrifice – the pelican tearing out her own bloody, painful breast to feed the young.

Let it finish.

Cut the Black Root.

Chapter Twenty-six

'Louis.' Jilly Cadogan addressed her husband in the draped, immaculate drawing room. It was just before dinner and Thuk could be heard banging saucepans in the kitchen. 'Louis.'

'Yes.'

Louis was aware that, behind the cover of her excellent care, Jilly had been watching him during the weeks of his illness and slow, oh, so slow, recovery. The soft-hard scrutiny of the big cat.

'I don't know how to put this ... In fact, I don't know how to begin.' Jilly's smooth segue into the next sentence suggested exactly the opposite. 'I think your time is up, Louis. I mean our time. We've come to the end.'

There were no guests for dinner but Jilly was in full fig: dressed in cashmere and silk, made up, scented and bejewelled. Louis's thoughts ricocheted wildly and came to rest on one: how like Jilly to go into battle, for he had no doubt that this was battle, daubed so skilfully in her war paint.

'Oh?' He had been considering the impact of an out-of-sorts body on the mind. He was sweaty from the effort of walking from room to room, depressed that it should be so difficult. Depressed that re-education meant precisely that.

Jilly went over to the drinks tray on the table – under the portrait of Louis's grandfather in the red hunting coat – and poured herself a sherry, her manicured hands tipped with varnish moving gracefully among the bottles and glasses. Louis had no such recourse. Alcohol was still off limits: one more thing, one more subtraction (those luscious wines, fruity and flinty, he had drunk in the past).

Glass in hand, Jilly swivelled. 'I want a divorce, Louis.' Oddly enough, her announcement added nothing to the inner darkness that now filled Louis. His first thought was: I'm in no state to move. His second was: Why now? His tired response was instinctive: No.

Jilly sat down opposite Louis and crossed her legs. Then she got up to corral into safety a glass poised too close to the edge of the drinks table and sat down again. She pulled gently at the pearls at her neck and straightened her shoulders. From one foot dangled an expensive high-heeled shoe, and that carelessly appended shoe did more than anything else to rouse Louis.

'You choose your moments, Jilly.'

She favoured him with a look which, after the first, kinder years of their marriage, Louis had come to know and understand.

'You know what I mean,' she said, and Louis knew that his days as a cheque-book husband were over. 'I've enjoyed being married to you, particularly in . . .' Jilly's expensive and precarious top teeth bit her carmined bottom lip '. . . the early days. I've stuck by you, yes?'

'Was that *such* a hardship? It didn't appear to be, if I remember correctly.'

Jilly, however, had a case written in her head and there is nothing so immutable as the middle-aged woman who, having hovered on the stepping stone by the shore, decides to move to the next one. 'I've done what was expected. The children have grown up, yes?'

'Yes.'

'So . . .' Jilly's slenderized shoulders lifted under the cashmere and silk. 'It's at an end.' She did not add, You are at an end, sick, finished. He added it silently for her. But, because illness had thrown him back on the senses and had killed logic and deduction, Louis was not prepared for what came next.

'I want to marry someone else.' Jilly's shoe fell off onto the carpet with a soft sound.

Shaken by extreme surprise, Louis could only manage, 'Who?'

Jilly told him and Louis said, 'Why don't you put your shoe back on?'

'Oh, really, Louis.' Jilly shook her head angrily, and contained in that exchange were the reasons why, in the end, they had failed to love one another.

The man in question, Gerald, was one of Louis's colleagues: rich and successful and in the process of divorcing. If life held out the ever-present threat of dissolution – explained in terms of the guilt, sin and retribution – one element had remained predictable and, curiously, consolatory. Jilly had always been both honest and consistent in her approach to the management of her desires. Now she was taking out further reinsurance. In that moment frozen between unwelcome news breaking and the nerves activating, Louis admired her.

'How long has this been going on?'

Jilly put her head on one side and considered her answer. 'As long as you have been involved with that woman.'

Louis was surprised for, adept in deception, he had flattered himself that he could read the signs.

'I didn't think ...' Louis struggled to his feet before he finished the sentence '. . . you would be quite this cold-blooded.'

'Ah,' she bit out, 'but I didn't imagine I would be put through so many hoops.' She shuddered at the memory of the newspaper articles and the gossip that had hummed and circulated – and the Widow's revenge. 'Anything but that.'

Suddenly, Louis understood Jilly's humiliation and saw how her life in Appleford had been placed by the publicity on another footing, how her hard-won equilibrium and status had been shaken, roughly and without mercy. 'I owe you an apology.'

'Thank you.'

'Will you pass me my stick?'

He caught a glimpse of tears as she got up to do so and, his own weakness making him extra sensitive, did not take advantage of that exposed flank. He leant heavily on the stick and felt the handle bite into his flesh.

'What do you want to do, Jilly? Tell me and we'll work it out peaceably.'

Her eyes widened in surprise for, lacking empathy with his weakness, she had been expecting Louis, the buccaneer, to fight. Her tears disappeared. 'You're pleased, really, aren't you? You've been planning to go off with that woman.'

He sighed. 'How little you know me, Jilly, even after all these years.'

'How little you know me, Louis.'

He summoned energy. 'But I accept that is partly my fault. You must know that I won't divorce you, and I had intended for us to stick it out together.'

'Don't worry.' Jilly got up and placed her glass on the table. Her heels moved over the edge of the carpet onto the parquet and gave a hollow little tap. 'I reckoned you would come up with the Catholic nonsense, so I'm divorcing you. And you can't stop me.'

Tap. Tap.

'Soon, actually. Gerald would like us to get married as quickly as we can. He's doing up a villa in the South of France and wants me to help.'

'France!'

'Yes. I think we'll live there for a couple of months a year.' Complacent and triumphant, Jilly again tugged at her pearls, buoyed by the red blood of conquest, proof that her femininity retained its power. 'Don't you have anything to say, Louis?'

In a flash, he perceived that Jilly, like the maiden who craved her token flaunted at the joust, craved him and Gerald to wage combat. He was almost prepared to oblige her but, stick in hand, left arm and foot unre-educated, he would make a poor champion.

'What is there to say? Except shall we have supper?'

Jilly remained where she stood by the drinks tray. She looked at her feet. She looked at her hands, with their sparkling rings, spread out in front of her. 'You always were detached.'

'That's not true.'

'You wouldn't know what truth was if it sat in your lap.'

His blood thundering in his ears, Louis concentrated on lifting his left foot in front of the right. Good. It worked. Then the right was placed in front of the left and Louis shuffled, a limping cavalry, towards the dining room, yearning for peace, for resolution and for an easy path through what lay ahead.

None of those comforts would be granted – indeed, are ever granted. Louis was feeling . . . what? It had been best described as 'the weight of life', a phrase, so Becky had once told him, that Tess had read in a book on Eskimos. They used it to describe the important emotions.

'Of course,' Jilly said, over Thuk's leek and potato soup, 'I was going to wait until you were better. It looks rather bad but Gerald wants . . .' She left the rest unsaid.

Louis remained silent.

Eventually Jilly put down her soup spoon. 'What about the money?'

'What about it?'

'I warn you I shall be employing a good lawyer. Gerald's, actually.'

Louis felt sweat break out over his skin. 'Why bother, Jilly? They cost money and cause trouble.'

Jilly dismissed the idea with a contemptuous little *moue*. 'Even if you don't, I need someone to advise me. Which is, perhaps, the point.' She flicked her gaze over the Meissen in the cabinet, the silver on the sideboard, and her eyes darkened. 'Suggesting that I don't need advice is a cheap trick, Louis, which might prove expensive. And, by the way, I won't under any circumstances take the dog.' He saw that she was pleased with the way in which she had ranged her defences, and it saddened him to think that they had reached that stage.

'Lawyers are divisive because it's their business.' He, too, pushed aside his food. 'I repeat, Jilly, I am not divorcing you. I won't for the reasons you know perfectly well and I did not, do not, seek it.'

'You certainly did nothing to ensure it didn't happen.'

'What we had worked,' said Louis.

Later, sleepless between the sheets, he concluded that he had neglected to look. I had stopped observing. I had failed to read the signs.

I did not change. Why? For change is the condition of a successful life.

Mea culpa.

Inside Louis the darkness deepened. Oh, Becky, he thought. How like Jilly you are. The difference being that Louis loved Becky down to her last disgraceful fibre.

It rapidly became clear why Jilly had insisted on lawyers, for she intended to go for the jugular. She wanted to be bought out of the house, and she wanted a lump sum.

The amount she named was staggering. 'You can't have that much,' Louis informed her, via the solicitor although they were still living in the same house.

'Yes I will,' she said, via hers.

'I will give you half of that.'

'Three-quarters.'

'Done.'

'You see?' she snapped at him as they passed in the hallway, several thousand pounds the poorer in extracted legal fees. 'We did need a lawyer.'

The news of their impending divorce trickled through the village. In itself, a divorce was not sufficiently startling or remarkable to take precedence over other village matters. The proposed bypass to accommodate the extra traffic generated by the showground and, in some quarters, the evolving spectre of a future Labour government were inciting far stronger passions than a mere marital breakdown. A stream of people was moving out of the village, a corresponding stream moving in, and in the flux small matters were lost.

Nevertheless, the Cadogans' break-up, a source of distress to a few friends, gave good theatre to some watchers. And, as it is with these issues, sympathies that had lain with Jilly, the wronged wife, did an abrupt turn. She, it was said, was a woman who was planning to abandon her sick husband.

Her swan song in Appleford was a soup and champagne rally for the Conservatives, which, Louis said, rousing himself from apathy, summed up the straddle that the party was being forced to make to win supporters. In preparation, Jilly packed her clothes in neat, tissued layers and went round the house fixing labels on furniture and objects. Red for her. Blue for Louis. She wanted to be quite sure that there was no mix-up by the furniture removers, and the house began to resemble a French nationalist fête.

'Don't you trust me?' Louis asked, watching the precise way in which she divided the spoils.

Jilly's answer was swift and unhesitating. 'No.'

On the day of her departure, Louis woke early, convinced that someone was moving around downstairs. There goes Jilly's furniture, he thought with a spark of malice, for burglars had been operating in the area.

He pulled himself together. His leg and arm were more co-operative now so he hauled himself out of bed and searched for a likely weapon. There was none. Then, as noiselessly as his disobedient body would permit, he crept downstairs and stood in the open door to the drawing room. Scissors in hand, Jilly was on her knees by the Regency card table over which they had argued and which Louis had insisted on keeping.

'For Christ's sake, Jilly, what are you doing?'

She started, guiltily, and he caught a glimpse of her set, determined face – and a transparent plastic bag containing five or six blue labels that she had removed from his furniture and replaced with her own. Red stained her face to match the labels.

In that moment, Louis knew he had now experienced the best and the worst, as he was capable of the best and the worst. Why should he have expected differently? For he was as greedy and duplicitous as his wife.

Sweat dampened his striped pyjamas. Viewed by his inner eye, which had been so blind, the structure and beliefs of Louis's life appeared to dismantle and reassemble in wholly unfamiliar configuration. Jilly's action provided both his salvation and a glimpse of the abyss, as dangerous and terrifying as any encountered on the course of his illness.

'You devil,' he said quietly.

Jilly leapt to her feet. 'And if I am,' she said, 'what can you do about it?'

The blood beat and roared in his ears. A tide swept through Louis's unresisting body, bearing him along strange pathways. With a groan he stepped forward, swayed, lifted his face to the light, tried to say something and slid to the floor.

At the other end of Appleford, Becky heard the ambulance siren in the distance and turned over in bed.

Then she heard Tess get up and go into the bathroom, followed by the sound of taps running. David stirred in his cot. Small movements, intimate and reassuring. Not that Becky required reassurance. She had taken stock and it was time to move on: unencumbered and free. For this she was grateful. Becky's gaze could be as fierce and focused as she wished. She was not required to look either side, or to stretch out a hand to hold up a child, or to think of anyone else. (By spring, scars on chestnut twigs have healed.) Lily may have been no mother, but when she reappeared in her old age, she had had the good manners and good sense not to bother Becky. In the end, they understood each other well.

If she thought of Louis, she only permitted herself a second or two of recollection, a mental cameo of him sleeping at the other end of the village. Having taken too much of her, he was now finished and gone.

The front door opened and shut. The gravel scrunched as Tess wheeled her new bicycle down the drive. Then there was a brief moment of peace.

The mewing, snuffling sound from David's room grew louder. Becky swung her legs over the bed and scrutinized them. Still glossy and lightly muscled. Still long, no shrinkage there.

Good.

She glanced at the mirror. Suddenly, she stuck out her tongue at her image and grinned. She would require all the assets that had tumbled randomly out of the gene pool into her face, and she must – she must – move on.

Clothes neatly to hand on the chair, Becky got dressed, intent on her plans.

Guests were due that evening and, as usual, Mrs Frant had made the preparations, but she was not seated in her customary place in the kitchen. Becky peered briefly into the empty drawing room, and got on with feeding David. Apart from the baby's noises and the clink of Becky's tea-cup and plate, the house was silent.

After breakfast, Becky wheeled David to the child-minder and left him, weaving unsteadily but happily among the other toddlers. When she returned to the High House, the silence still held sway. There was a mark on the wooden floor, a crack had sprouted on the wall and there was a stain on the plaster under the stairs. This was a house brought to its knees by a poverty of energy.

The door to Mrs Frant's bedroom was shut. Sensing trouble, Becky paused in front of it then knocked.

No answer.

She knocked again and pushed open the door. Inside, the silence was clamorous and the room smelt of cheap talcum powder, dust and an unquantifiable something. Age? Despair? Neglect? Mrs Frant lay on her bed, motionless.

Drawing closer, Becky looked down. Stockings neatly pulled up over her strong legs, tweed skirt brushed down over her knees, lambswool cardigan shielding a floral blouse, Mrs Frant was fully clothed and decently assembled except for her mouth, which was wide open. At long intervals her breath soughed in and out of it.

Lying there, she seemed inexpressibly lonely, an embodiment of muted grief and of the many things that had been left unsaid.

On the bedside table was a letter in one of the cheap envelopes that Mrs Frant so hated using. To Becky's surprise, it was addressed to her.

You won't have resisted reading this. I know you too well,
Rebecca. But no one else is as selfish and uncaring as you
are, so I know I can rely on you to do nothing.
    Do not revive me. I have had enough of life. This is my
wish. You will see me out, Rebecca, you will see me out.
Get rid of this before anyone gets there.
    If you care for Tess, you will do this. It is for her and
Jack's sake.

An unpleasant sound escaped the dying woman, and Becky flinched.

The obvious thing was to return the letter to the envelope,

to leave the room and to walk out of the house. To wash her hands of this act.

The obvious thing was to pick up the telephone, call the emergency services and wrench Mrs Frant back into the life she had arranged to leave.

More publicity, more branding in the tabloids, another awkward reputation sullying her job prospects ... 'Broker in death pact ...' Talk, gossip, speculation, Tess's wrath and bewilderment. The probable results of Mrs Frant's act inched their way through Becky's brain which, for once, was refusing to work.

She looked again at the letter. The cheap envelope nagged at Becky, for it symbolized the fall of Mrs Frant, a hard, bitter and, apparently, endless fall.

Mrs Frant stirred, her eyes fluttered, opened and stared at Becky for a second, admitting Becky to her Gethsemane, and then closed. During that second of exchange, Becky was forced, once again, by Mrs Frant to look into the shallows of an insufficient heart.

Sew the jewellery into the hem, and march with the Army.

An empty pill bottle on the table and a drained glass. That would be Mrs Frant's last courageous march.

Outside, in her empty garden, the sun was dim and unsure of itself, but the light peculiar to spring, papery and the perfect foil for yellow spring flowers, was shining over the land busy with growth and over the new roads, the new houses, the new shops.

Frozen to the spot, Becky's mind drifted.

The master rig line slip. Rate on line. Excess-of-loss.

Excess-of-loss.

In front of her lay a suffering, dying woman. As surely as she stood there in the stuffy room, Becky was being punished for her deficiencies and her knack of survival. A punishment set all those years before, when Mrs Frant had first cast her eye over Becky and decided that she would not do for her son.

Mrs Frant's breathing was noisier now, but less predictable. And each strained inhalation and exhalation tore at the watcher. Becky was repulsed, terrified and, yet, curiously exhilarated by the power Mrs Frant had granted her.

She undid her watch and placed it on the bedside table beside the empty pill bottle and the letter. Then she sat down on the side of the bed, as she had not done for her aunt Jean, sought and found Mrs Frant's hand, the strong, capable hand with its surprisingly artistic fingers, and held it. With a tenderness that was new to her, she stroked the aged skin, sprinkled liberally with its flowers of death, the age spots. The flesh was cool and slightly damp. Becky visualized the chill, like a sheet of ice, spreading up from the fingers, through the palm, moving steadily through the arm towards the heart, its target.

Struggling with terror and threatening nausea, Becky forced herself to keep stroking the hand. No one deserved to go out of life unattended, without anyone to pretend to care.

Oh, Aunt Jean. At least, you knew your God was waiting.

And Becky, loving Tess better than she had imagined, owed it to her to usher Tess's mother – if not lovingly, then as politely as Mrs Frant had endeavoured to live – out of the final exit. For a brief moment, that fractional pulse of the butterfly's wing, and with a compassion that she was not aware flowed within her, Becky did just that.

After half an hour, Becky got up, smoothed the dent she had made on the bed, picked up the watch and the letter and went downstairs towards the phone.

Her explanations were even, measured and convincing. After Mrs Frant had been loaded into the ambulance, Becky gave an account to the policeman that timed her arrival back at the house five minutes later than it had been and her entry into Mrs Frant's bedroom twenty-five minutes after that.

Sergeant Franks and Dr Wilbur both admitted that it was

deeply regrettable, and the latter signed the certificate and let slip that, of course, he had been prescribing tranquillizers and sleeping pills. It was possible that Mrs Frant had been confused as to the dosage but . . . he did not think so.

'Ah, well,' said Sergeant Franks, who had witnessed similar scenes, even in Appleford, 'ah, well.'

Of Tess, Becky did not like to think. But as she waited in the High House to greet her, unaware that silence and their secrets were to be the element that bound each of them to the other for ever, Becky vowed that her silence would last the rest of her life.

Tess was remarkably calm. She insisted on remaining at work, taking no days off.

'They'll sack me if I do so let's not discuss it. You can cope.' When questioned by Becky about the funeral, she said, 'Just use Dad's. Same hymns. Same service. Same grave. It's all there. Same sandwiches.'

The only time she broke down was after the funeral when Jack, who had flown back, and she were sitting in the dusty drawing room. The mourners had gone and Jack, whiplash thin and tanned, was drinking whisky. Tess and Becky had hit the wine.

'Do you know the worst thing?' said Tess.

'No.' Even Jack's voice now seemed sun-baked.

'It's funny,' said his sister. 'Awfully, awfully funny . . .'

'Tess,' said Becky, and put her arm around her. Easy.'

'Mum did this for us, you know.' She swivelled to look at her brother. 'But you wouldn't, of course, because you're never here. Too busy bloody helping the world. Mum killed herself because she thought that the life insurance would give us capital to pay off Lloyd's.'

'Oh, my God,' said Becky.

Tess raised her red-rimmed eyes and clenched her fists.

'Mum could never read the small print, could she? She just didn't have it in her. Between her and Daddy—'

'You mustn't think,' said Becky. 'Don't say any more.'

'Mum killed herself for no reason. The insurance companies won't pay up for suicides.'

Chapter Twenty-seven

Fortunately, David took to the journey on the train. Very fortunately, for it was punctuated by delays and, finally, at Doncaster, engine failure. Along with the other passengers, Tess and her son waited on the platform for an hour until an alternative engine could be located.

The wait was tedious and Tess had grown tired of pointing out features of the station to the restless child by the time they climbed back into the carriage. David settled to sleep and Tess watched as the land began to throw up lumps of folded rock and hill and outcrops of stone grey slate – a fitting backdrop to the harsher world through which she now passed, having left behind a sunlit childhood.

Becky had accompanied Tess to the hospital to identify Mrs Frant's body and she had slipped her hand under Tess's elbow. Strangely enough, after the first outpourings of shock and horror, Tess was not as angry and guilty as most relatives are of a suicide. The thing was too big and, in deciding to remove herself from its path, Mrs Frant had acted logically. Her peaceful dead face had given away nothing to her daughter.

'But I didn't think that anything else could happen,' cried Tess.

Becky's hand was comforting and Tess felt the faint suggestion of relief, of having been released.

Yet having certainties so decisively dismantled sapped strength, as did grief and bereavement. Tess had experienced both, and quite early. Now there was only one thing of which she was certain: suffering did not ennoble. Whether or not she would retrieve her energy she had no idea.

Jack's certainties were of a different order. He had returned to Africa, to the patient Penelope and his African children. 'I'm doing what I wish,' he told his sister. 'You cannot ask for more.'

Freddie had said she was a damn fool.

In the train David slept on; her ruffled, radiant son who, save for the push-pull of his strong appetites, was unmarked. Looking down at him, Tess smiled. Then, as sleep was a subject of abiding concern, she thought, I'll have hell getting him to bed tonight.

At Glasgow, they left the train and went to spend a night in a hotel. Iain had offered to drive down and collect them but Tess, feeling that this was a journey that she and David should make alone, declined the offer.

But the next morning Iain was not at Oban station, and Tess's heart gave an unreasonable thump of disappointment. Holding hands, she and David stood at the station entrance, shivering in the sharp, clean air. Essence of fish and brine filtered through the other smells and, in the sky above, gulls tore past in noisy formations.

Eventually, Tess spotted Iain walking up the station approach. He lifted his hand and waved, and she was rooted to the spot by an overwhelming fear.

'I'm so sorry,' he said, panting slightly. 'The fan-belt on the van snapped and I had to leave it at the garage.'

He seemed paler than before. Nerves.

They drank tea and ate sandwiches in an adjacent café. By now, David was over-tired and over-excited but he was a convenient focus for attention while the ice was being broken.

Once or twice, Iain directed a look at Tess, considering and speculative, and she became aware of a hunger to *get things sorted*.

Oh, George.

Finally, they bundled into the van – it, too, smelt of fish –

took the ferry across the strait to the Morven peninsula and drove along a silent, twisting but gloriously open road, fringed by the Highland glens and mountainous outcrops.

The solitude settled over Tess, much as a piece of clothing settles over the body.

'You'll never do it, sweetie-pie,' Freddie had said. 'You can't leave the real world for some toy fish farm.'

Can't I?

'*Think*, darling. Think red veins in the cheeks. Horny hands from toiling. The broad beam from stuffing yourself with plum duff and doorstep sandwiches. The utter, utter loneliness of never wearing a decent rag.'

The utter loneliness of a brain on permanent hold.

Will I be running away?

She had consulted Becky, and Becky had replied, 'It depends what you're leaving and what you're going to.'

Quite right.

I certainly haven't found God in the marketplace. So I might as well go and look for Him elsewhere.

'But the marketplace,' said an acerbic Becky, 'is precisely where you should be searching.'

'Even so,' said Tess, realizing at that point with a wrench of her gut that, if she left, she would be saying goodbye to Becky too, 'I should go and look at what Iain is offering.'

'I hope you're not expecting too much,' said Iain at last, signalling left. The van snaked up a single track road, breasted a rise and then dropped down towards the edge of the Firth where, sailing mistily through the water, was the coast of Mull. Iain pulled up in front of the manse, a house with many windows. He got out, walked round to the passenger side of the van and held out his hand to Tess.

'Welcome.'

The silence struck Tess: a rounded, uninvaded, complete silence.

Inside the house, courtesy of the generous windows, it was

surprisingly light and sunny. On the Sound of Mull side, there was no garden to speak of, only turf, a rough wooden bridge over a spring and the water beyond. Behind the house, the moorland stretched into the distance. The view was breathtaking, for the house had been positioned to take advantage of the point where there was a gap in the mountain range. The composition of water, house and highland suggested to Tess's southern-acclimatized vision both marvels and space, and also terror of the unknown.

Iain led Tess through the house and up to the spare bedroom. Dust – the dust that she and her mother had fought unsuccessfully at the High House – was evident here, too, dredged over window-sills and furniture. A curtain ring had sprung loose from the rail over the big window on the landing. In the kitchen, a clock ticked on the wall, ten minutes slow, and a half-empty tin of baked beans occupied the fridge.

In the evening, after Tess had put David to bed – he was a little apprehensive in the strange, beautifully proportioned room with a large single bed – they sat down to a bottle of wine.

'Is this crazy?' Tess folded her hands around her glass, a gesture that was calmer than she felt.

Iain stared into his. 'I don't think so. I've loved you for a long time.'

'I'm sorry about Flora.'

He sighed. 'So am I.'

'Why did you decide to come here?'

He shrugged. 'Family and things. Anyway, I didn't think it would be easy. But whether that's a fault or an advantage, I don't know.' He grinned. 'Do I sound like a masochist?'

'The winters?'

'Are pretty dreadful, or can be,' he finished. 'I'm not going to pretend that anything is better than it is.'

'You're very kind, Iain.'

She shifted round in the seat to look out across the darkening water. 'I should like to tell you . . .' She paused. She wanted to warn Iain that if he took her on, he would be taking on someone whose first marriage had been difficult and whose search for a faith had yielded nothing so far, but she thought better of it. Perhaps these topics would never get aired and perhaps it would not, in the end, matter. 'I'd like to tell you many things, but I think I have to take it slowly.'

Iain gestured to the still, shrouded landscape. 'It'll be peaceful.'

She got up, went over to the window and listened to the sound of the water on the beach. 'Yes. And very beautiful.'

Iain was silent.

'Funnily enough,' Tess breathed on the glass and wrote a + and a − in the misted patch, 'I don't think I'll miss the bank, all that tension, drama and excitement.'

'You won't find those here.' Iain came to join her by the window. 'You do realize that, Tess?'

She was conscious that she had hurt him and turned to face him. 'But that's the point, Iain.'

'I don't propose to hijack you. Only to live with you.'

Contrite, she turned towards him. 'How indifferent I must seem, after your kindness. I'm sorry. I think grief makes you selfish. Forgive me.'

'Over there,' he said, pointing to a house whose lights made patterns in the gloom, 'are the Knights. He was a merchant banker who made a fortune, and she's an artist. I must introduce you. Further up the valley in the big house are Wendy and Martin. *They* used to live in Birmingham – he was a personnel manager, I think. He's now a prawn fisherman.'

'Is he surviving?'

Iain gave a short laugh. 'Only just.'

She remained by the window. 'Tell me about the fish, Iain.' She held out her glass for a refill. 'I tried to read up on the topic before I came, but I didn't get very far.'

The next morning, they drove back to Lochaline to do some shopping, Iain having had no idea of Tess and David's requirements, where she searched in the shop for David's currently favoured cereal and yoghurt. At the check-out, she looked at the women with carrier bags and thick coats. A tough breed, she supposed, but not necessarily. Perhaps their battle with wind, weather, land and water was as profound and prolonged as, should she stay, hers would be.

In the afternoon, Iain took them out in the boat to inspect the fish farm. There was not much to see, he explained, only the platform, the electric light and a dim view of threshing forms.

She balanced David in the crook of her arm. 'Do you use a lot of chemicals?'

''Fraid so. Disease is a big problem.' Iain leant over and cupped some water in his hand. 'Sea lice are the biggest. With salmon, at any rate. But I've heard tell of a light someone's developing that attracts the lice off the fish which, if they can get it off the ground, would be better.'

Ecologically acceptable? Non-polluting? What was the fish farm's value in the market?

'And the downside to fish farming?'

Iain laughed and touched Tess's hand briefly. 'We speak another language here. This isn't the stock market.'

'Sorry.' She flushed and then, recollecting her wits, adjusted the balance. 'But it is, was, my language, Iain.'

He gave her a long look. 'All right. Well, a fish farm doesn't hold the answer to over-fishing and chemical pollution. We are forced to use chemicals. The fish catch diseases, which are passed on to the other fish. The sea bed becomes polluted with the chemicals and also fish faeces. So, you see, it isn't simple. But it's the best I can do.'

Far out to the west – seawards – the weather gathered in ominous-looking clouds.

'Do you miss things from your other life?' Tess fought with a piece of hair whipping across her face.

He searched for the words. 'I've been amazed at how quickly

you forget what you imagined was engraved into you. I grew up with the Army, breathed it, worked it. And yet, the moment I stepped out from under it, I forgot. It left me.'

Tess could not quite agree, for his language and bearing proclaimed his former profession, but she said nothing.

Again – David blissfully asleep on a cocktail of fresh air and unaccustomed exercise – they shared a bottle of good wine for supper at the kitchen table.

'The year begins,' Iain said, and she listened attentively, for in the recital of a timetable she could learn about him, 'when the sheep and pregnant ewes are brought down from the hills.'

Sleepy and lazy, Tess pictured the ewes, back legs bandy with their burden, picking their way down the paths, accompanied by the dogs. An expectant progress towards the lambing sheds, the bitter night and the exhausted aftermath of birth.

The hinds are still being culled then, too, Iain told her, before the real winter descends. In February the Highland Cattle Society holds its bull sale. In March they burn the heather to improve the grazing.

As he talked, the pattern of the year was picked out, as ancient and recognizable as the pictures in a Book of Hours. April saw lambs back in the fields and, since the grass was young and sweet, it was the best month for heifers to have their calves. In May, the hunt for vermin on the moors begins and the ferrets are let loose on the hill fox. June is shearing time and the moment to make repairs to the land and house.

'Don't tell me,' said Tess, 'August is grouse-shooting, followed by pheasant and stag season. Slaughter.'

'Not if you weigh it up fairly. It involves skill, too.'

'Yes.' Tess pushed back her hair impatiently.

She turned, as was becoming a habit, to look out over the water.

'A fair fight, Tess.'

She shrugged, but smiled at him all the same.

On their last day, Iain was up early. Tess found him in the

kitchen making sandwiches. 'I thought we'd go and take a look at the deer.'

'Can you spare the time?'

'Johnny McAndrew has agreed to stand in for me today. He sometimes does.'

They drove up the glen and took a road winding up the hillside. Down below them, the water was grey and white and the fish farm grew small and insignificant. Near the summit, Iain parked the van and picked up David in his arms. 'Come on.'

With Tess bringing up the rear, they scrambled up the heather and over the rock, David sometimes held by one or other, sometimes held between them.

'He's doing well,' said Iain. 'A trouper.'

'Yes,' said Tess, the shade of George crossing her mind. Then she remembered Charles and was silent.

If I come and live here, she thought, no one will ever have the chance to guess about David.

Before reaching the top, they sat down to rest. A wind whipped around their faces and the air was as clean as starched sheets, scented with heather and the rain that had fallen during the night. Iain got out his binoculars and swept the hill behind.

'This will probably be impossible with David,' he said, 'but never mind. We need extreme stealth. If you disturb the sheep or grouse it'll alert the deer and it'll be hours before they settle.'

Tess gathered her son into her arms and hugged him. 'We're going to be very quiet, Mousy, otherwise we'll frighten the deer.'

Iain wriggled further up and peered over the ridge. He stiffened, then wriggled noiselessly down.

'They're up,' he whispered. 'Go and take a look. I'll hold David.'

Tess took the binoculars and inched, rump up, towards the vantage point. It took her some time to get the deer into her view but, eventually, she was rewarded by the sight of a couple of hinds grazing on the opposite slope. Large, warm-looking, liquid-eyed animals enjoying a leisured graze. Undoubtedly an ancient sight, full of pleasures and interest, but it did not stir Tess in the way figures on a print-out did. After all, it was only deer on a hillside.

Her lack of response depressed her.

She turned to signal to Iain and David. As she did so, she dislodged a flurry of small stones. Immediately, the hinds' heads shot up, their laziness vanished in a second. Together, they scented the wind and vanished.

'Sorry," said Tess, slithering down. 'That was stupid.'

His arm firmly around a contented-looking David, Iain said, 'It takes years of practice.'

They exchanged a look. 'Yes,' said Tess. 'Yes, I see that.'

Tess looked around the drawing room at the High House. 'I never thought I'd leave this house without a backward thought.'

'Oh, good,' said Becky, 'you're growing up.'

'*Thank* you.'

'While we're at it,' said Becky, 'growing up, I mean, don't you think you should give up the fags?'

'Nope,' said Tess. 'I must have one vice.'

Becky wrinkled her nose. 'As you like. Do you want to go for a walk?'

'My hair will go frizzy in the drizzle.'

'You'll go Afro in Scotland.'

And so, for the last time, the two walked through a changed and transmogrified Appleford, and along the old Roman way. The lane followed an ancient route and skirted an equally ancient field, now laid out as a golf course and car park. For a moment, they watched its flag beat against the club house, and the stream of cars rolling in through the gates, then continued upwards.

'Have you met the tenants?' Becky loped easily up the rise.

'No. But Rufus says they're fine.'

'Don't you think it would be better to sell it?'

Tess held out her hand for Becky to pull her along. 'No. It would never achieve its real value. Anyway, it's an insurance for the future.'

'Ah,' said Becky.

'I want to thank you, Bec. You helped me a lot.'

'Sure,' she replied, aware as Tess was aware that their friendship would alter, subtly but irrevocably. From now on, their lives would no longer match one another's, and their tastes and needs would differ. With no more daily exchange, no chance of intimacy, there would be no necessity for each other and the immediate pulse connecting them would weaken.

Ah, well, thought Becky, it's best to travel alone. She turned her head towards Tess and said, 'You never did tell me what made you decide.'

'I'm forty-five, you know,' Iain had said, after they had washed up and drunk their coffee on Tess's last night.

'What are you trying to say?'

'Only that.'

'I bring problems. A son and debt. Or, at least, resolving it might be a long-term problem.' Abruptly, she turned away. 'You never know where that can lead you. My mother killed herself as a result of debt. And that was the very last thing I would ever have imagined.'

If Mrs Frant had been listening to her daughter, and it was probable she was, she might well have given one of her snorting, anarchic laughs.

'I want to help.'

She glanced up at him. 'You always have done, Iain. You are the perfect gentle knight.'

He was amused. 'Thank you.'

347

She touched his cheek. 'Do you think I can tough it out here? I don't like the north very much.'

('God, Tess,' said Becky, and raised her eyes to the sky. 'You do sail close to the wind, sometimes.')

'I don't want to hurt you, Iain, I don't want to let you down.'

He stared at the woman he had loved for so long. 'I don't know the outcome,' he said, 'but the battleplan looks good.'

'Once a soldier,' said Becky, 'always a soldier. But you could do worse.'

Tess got undressed in the spare room, tossing her skirt and jumper at the chair, which she missed. They fell in a soft lump to the floor. For a second or two, she stood and stretched her naked body, feeling the cold air tease her skin into a thousand bumps.

She knew how hard it was to live with someone else and her marriage to George had not supplied her with a map for the road she had chosen.

The water ran, soft and reddy brown, into the basin; she splashed her face and neck then the rest of her. She towelled herself dry, observing a faint pink creep up her arms and legs as she did so. She had placed a foot on the chair and bent over to dry it when the knock sounded on the door.

Tess straightened up. I can, of course, she thought, tell him to go away. A second passed. Two seconds. She was struck by his courage, for Iain had no idea what he was taking on, what secrets she bore and would protect him against. Nor did she know his.

She glanced down at her bare limbs. 'Come in,' she said at last, and turned towards him as he stood, tense and unsure of her reply, in the doorway.

At dawn, she heard David cry out and Tess drew away from Iain's tenderly proffered, but overly protective, arm and slid out of bed. It was freezing cold and it took a few seconds to locate her jumper on the floor. By the time she reached David he was wailing heartily.

Half an hour later, when she had given him a drink, which he had demanded, and cuddled him back to sleep, every muscle was stiff with cold, and the skin between her fingers felt cracked with it. She thought she would never be warm again.

That would be the life here.

And yet. And yet. On an impulse, she bent and stroked her son's hair.

She had proved she could flourish in easier territory, but it was time to take on the tough. Out of it she would fashion a life. Out of her lessons in subversion, she would fashion a transparency and a structure.

If she moved her head, Tess could see, or rather sense, through the gap in the ill-fitting curtain the mountain, and trace its huge, uneven outline. She pictured herself toiling up it, carrying her griefs like a stone. The desire to reach the top pushing her onwards, the hard-won breath, the slight, very slight disappointment once the summit is reached. Leaving the stone on the top.

After she laid David back in the bed and tucked him in, she bent over him, breathing in his innocent child's smell. Then she went over to the window and drew back the curtain, just a little. On the horizon to the east, the black was invaded by violet, rose and opal, and land and water met in a clash and fusion of light and shape.

God was in his heaven?

She would never know. *That* was the basis of existence: ambiguous, ambivalent, fluid.

Tess slipped to her knees and rested her chin on her arms on the sill. The cold crept relentlessly through her body and her teeth began to chatter. But, as she watched, the light redefined.

Ah, yes, she thought. Yes.

'Yes?' said Becky, handing Tess a tissue.

'Yes,' said Tess.

Chapter Twenty-eight

In the end, the job in Switzerland came to nothing. Perhaps, the potential employers had not liked what they had heard.

No matter.

Becky's money was running out and (Tess was very apologetic) she was required to quit the High House within the month before the new tenants – he had made a fortune in designing software packages – moved in.

Becky craved London. She craved the terrible red city brick, and its softer greyish-yellow companion. In her bones, she knew the strip of acid soil in front gardens, the back yards, window-boxes slipping off cracked sills, the wild and beautiful patterns of dry rot, the spreading damp and litter deposits. She knew London's smells – rich, unpleasant, historic and peopled – its reach and its depravities. The city gave her a purpose.

As nimble as ever, her mind sorted out the possibilities and weighed them against the probabilities. Hair in a French plait, linen suit pressed, she took the train up to London and made her way to Mawby's who, after sacking Charles, had decided he was too valuable and had re-employed him at a vastly better salary. Becky demanded to see him.

When she was led through the open-plan area, she sensed a ripple of recognition, unease, even, and felt regret. But for a few miscalculations, Becky might be sitting in the senior office directing operations.

Was it a case of becoming institutionalized by a career? There were other avenues Becky could have sought out that would not have meant approaching her ex-lover and the father of her child.

Had Becky flung off the chains of Streatham only to become a prisoner of the workplace? She knew from experience that the most successful and brilliant of business strategists can possess the most impoverished of imaginations, visualizing no further than life in office. She need not have worried. By birth and circumstances she was a realist, by temperament one who seeks out the glitter of gold in order to spend it. She knew that the good, clever, foxy broker makes money. Masses of it. Given this potential, it was unlikely that Becky would busy herself with running a tea-shop or, equally, become dull. And dullness was the worst crime of all.

'Blood is a funny thing,' Lily had said. 'You're just like me. Big ambitions.'

Becky was not quite sure about that, but she let it pass.

Carole, the secretary, recognized her and rushed forward. 'Hallo,' she said. 'How are you?'

'Fine.' Becky glanced at the banks of computer terminals attended to – mostly – by young men in shirtsleeves and braces, talking their private language. 'The techies are still in control.'

As one of life's non-techies, Carole did not understand. In the office light, she looked a little sallow and disappointed. She led Becky towards Charles's office.

'Come in,' said Charles, cradling a phone with his head, and continued his conversation.

Becky sat down. He was dressed in his uniform of striped shirt and loud braces and looked no different from the moment she had first seen him.

'How are you?' she asked, when he put down the phone.

Suspicion clouded his face and he glanced uneasily between her and the computer terminal. Then he reached out a hand and turned it off.

'No need to worry.' Becky was amused.

'Is this a social call?'

'Not exactly,' said Becky, 'but I wanted to know how you and the admirable Martha are.' There was a silence. 'And Poppy.'

Intense wariness crept over Charles's face. 'She's fine. We're all fine. In fact, thriving. She's looking forward to seeing you next weekend.'

Becky crossed her legs and sat back in the chair. 'I rather thought it was time Poppy came and lived with me. When I'm settled, of course.'

Charles's flinch was genuine and his reaction spontaneous. 'No. She can't. We agreed, Becky. Poppy lives with us and her sisters and she's happy and settled. Martha loves her.'

Becky raised her eyebrows. 'Surely her place is with her mother.'

'She hardly knows what you look like.'

'Really?' Becky's tone was neutral which, from of old, he knew was a warning.

'I mean, she thinks of you as a sort of aunt.'

Charles shifted in the chair and walked his fingers up and down the dialling buttons of the telephone. Walking up and down the memories. Suddenly he understood. 'What do you want, Becky?'

'All right,' she said, and turned the full force of her eyes on him. 'I'll tell you. Poppy in return for a job.'

'I see.' He swivelled in the chair so that Becky was presented with his profile. 'That's not so easy.'

'Sorry, Charles.' The trace of a smile hovered on Becky's lips. 'But a girl has to live.'

He ran through the options and likely scenarios. 'They wouldn't give you Poppy.'

'Want to bet? In court, mothers tend to be flavour of the month. You *can't* bet on it, Charles, and you might end up burnt.'

'I have been burnt,' burst from Charles, with the force of pent-up pain and regret. 'Badly.'

'Come on. We had a good time, good fun, at one point. Now

it's over. And don't pretend that your heart wasn't with Martha a good deal of the time because it was.'

Every line and curve of Becky stirred memories of mysterious elements of sex, and of cruelty, to which Charles had responded so powerfully but with which it had been impossible to live.

Oh, silky-fleshed, scented, *hard* Becky, who had so teased and blinded him. He looked down at the pad on his desk and then at the pile of papers in his in-tray. 'You wouldn't dare take Poppy away.'

'Look,' said Becky, who, of course, could not appreciate the exact irony of what she was saying, 'you're not exactly a paragon and the issue is not clear cut. A mother is a mother, you know.'

Quick as a flash, he fought back, 'How would you know?'

She shrugged and smiled and said, in her disarming way, 'It's true I took time to learn, but I didn't have much of a start. There you go.'

Carole bobbed her head round the door. 'Coffee, Mr Hayter?'

Charles was never sure, never quite sure, if Tess had kept her word about *that* episode. It was in his memory, an excess liability, and he wished it was not. And, because he did not reflect on it unless driven to, he had no notion that it had been that unthinking coupling, as much as Becky, which had driven the good nature from his heart and outlook.

'If you get me a job, a good job, I'll undertake never to try to take Poppy off you. Simple.'

'You are *extraordinary*.' Like most cowards, Charles was only rude when he thought he had the upper hand. 'I don't believe you're real.'

'Needs must.'

'But can I trust you?'

Becky picked up her handbag and got to her feet.

'OK,' he said quickly, 'it's a deal.'

Becky surprised Charles by blowing him a kiss. 'You'd better not let admirable Martha know.'

'Blimey!' Becky was provoked into the exclamation when the phone rang at the High House and Jilly Cadogan invited her to lunch in London.

'You'll have to pay,' she said.

'That's the idea,' said Jilly.

The restaurant was expensive and fashionable, and Jilly, in short navy blue skirt and jacket with a silk body underneath, swept into it on a cloud of Giorgio, wearing the faint smile designed to accentuate her teeth.

At the sight, Becky gritted hers and redoubled her determination. 'How did you know I was at the High House?'

'You were spotted some time ago.'

'Is Louis better?'

'I'm divorcing him, you know.'

'No, I didn't.'

'You haven't been listening to Appleford's gossip, then.'

Out of Jilly's soft, pampered mouth issued hard truths. 'He's not the man he was, you know.' She took a tiny mouthful of poached salmon and washed it down with mineral water. 'Poor Louis. I've probably cleaned him out. I stood my ground and got, more or less, what I wanted.'

Becky was curious. 'What do you want from me?'

'I'm giving Louis to you. And I just wanted to be sure that you'd be nice to him.'

'Is he aware of your touching concern?'

'No.' Jilly took another miniscule mouthful of steamed spinach. 'Where is he?'

'In hospital having a rest. He had a bit of a setback and they wanted to keep an eye on him. They're giving him a rigorous dose of physiotherapy. All knee-bends and parallel bars, poor thing.' She shrugged. 'The insurance pays, you know, so why not? The problem will be when he comes out of hospital next week.'

Becky had given up the pretence of eating. There the two women sat, surrounded by crystal, silver, the swags and loops of expensive décor, the French wallpaper and Irish linen napkins, and by the half-eaten remnants of exquisite food that would be thrown out.

'That's your problem,' said Becky.

'Men are so self-indulgent,' said Jilly, avoiding Becky's eye. She fumbled in her Chanel handbag, produced a silver box, opened it and popped a pill into her mouth. 'They think we are, but the truth is quite the opposite.' She pursed her glossed lips and smiled. 'You're welcome to him.' She thought for a moment and added, 'And you get the dog.'

Becky smiled back. 'But I don't want Louis any more.'

'If the techies get to rule the world what will happen to the non-techies?' Becky was on the phone to Tess in Scotland. 'Those who can't cope with computers. There's plenty of them.'

'Frankenstein lives again,' said Tess, who was watching a couple of fishing boats from the drawing-room window of the Manse. 'No, I'm wrong. Frankenstein was capable of love. Computers aren't.' She waved at Iain coming up from the beach with David. '*Why* have we got onto this subject?'

'Oh, I don't know,' said Becky. 'We ought to keep an eye on the future. By the way, I've been offered a job by Osbrooks. Director. So I'm in business.'

'*Osbrooks!* Goodness.'

'I've had the house cleaned and I'll hand over the keys on Saturday.'

'You've got somewhere to stay, Bec?'

'Well, sort of,' she said. 'Don't worry about it. Tess.'

'Yes.'

'You know you've opted out. Lost the battle for wimmin?'

'If you like.'

There was a silence.

At her end, Tess stirred. 'Bec. Will you do something for me?'

'Of course.'

'Will you go and look at the graves from time to time? Just to keep them tidy. I wouldn't like to think that they were left. Please.'

As ever, Becky packed quickly and neatly in a quiet, abandoned house, discarding anything she considered superfluous.

Tick-tock.

She was disposing of papers when the doorbell rang, a sharp, questing sound. Holding a sheaf in one hand, she opened the door.

The man on the doorstep was in ambulance uniform and behind him in the drive was the ambulance. As Becky stared, the driver got out of the cab, went round to the back and opened the doors. 'Wrong house,' she said, and tried to close the door.

'Nah,' said the chap, a big, brawny fellow you could trust to haul you out of a car smash. 'He said here.'

'He?'

The man consulted his clipboard. 'Mr Cadogan.'

The colour fled from Becky's face. 'No. You've made a mistake.'

'I don't think so. It's been arranged.'

Becky pushed past him towards the ambulance and jumped up the steps between the open doors. 'No,' she said. 'I'm not looking after you.'

Louis looked up from the wheelchair in which he was confined. 'Yes, you are.'

'You never even asked.'

Thin, pale, but still elegant, he spread his hands in an old gesture. 'You don't ask for a last chance, you take it.'

357

Becky swivelled. 'Take him away,' she said furiously. 'He doesn't belong here.'

The driver did not much care either way. 'If you would make up your mind, sir.'

Louis lifted up his re-educated left hand and held it out to her. 'It's not as bad as it looks, Becky. Truly.'

She looked out through the ambulance's doors, which provided a frame for the ruined paddock. 'I've just got everything organized. I don't want you. I don't want *anybody*.'

A burden. A slobbery, needy, disintegrating, energy-consuming burden.

Wasn't that just like a man? At the bottom of the pond lies a mud-slick of sentimentality and a conviction that, in the end, people will act for the best.

'What makes you think that after all we've been through I'm going to drop everything to nanny you?'

'It's precisely because we've been through, as you put it, everything.'

Passion and sorrow. Did these bind a man and woman? She supposed they did.

'How can I be sure?'

Louis took his time to answer. 'There is no insurance,' he said. 'Ever.'

'Well, tough,' said Becky, and she had never looked so beautiful. Tall and lustrous-eyed. 'I've done enough lately to fill the book of saints. So, Louis, I'm sorry, I think not.'

A sound made Becky turn her head. Louis had put up his good hand to his face, and she knew without being told that behind it he was hiding tears. Another sound escaped from him and, this time, he turned away his head.

The ambulancemen were embarrassed and became angry. 'Can't we get on?' asked one aggressively.

'I'm sorry,' said Becky, letting herself down into the drive, filled with a sudden wild grief and a light-headed sensation. 'I can't afford you any more, Louis.'

What was it that Jilly had said? Becky fought the anguish that was threatening to swamp her and the memories. That she had cleaned Louis out. He hardly had a bean left (even allowing for a bean, in Jilly's terms, being relative).

But Louis was also a fighter, and a veteran one.

His eyes sought and found Becky's. 'There's the bank account in Switzerland,' he said. 'I thought we'd go over and arrange things. Possibly live there.'

'*What* did you say?'

'Money in Switzerland,' said Louis. 'It was in transit when Jilly's lawyers were asking questions. So you see . . .'

Slowly, Becky positioned her foot back on the ambulance step and hauled herself up. Then she stood over Louis, her wretched heart beating like a hunted animal, and placed a hand on his shoulder.

Louis waited.

Then she bent over and kissed him.

The Bollys welcomed Louis back. No. It would be more precise to say that it was as if he had never been away. The meal, in the Lloyd's Club, was up to scratch. A frost had come down over the country but, in London, its clean, astringent dazzle was routed by the orange neon and press of traffic.

All in all, the mango mousse was voted a success.

Less satisfying was the comparison made in the press that day between Lloyd's and the Munich Re. The article was written in a pessimistic vein. Who could judge whether, after all the recent disasters and Names' revolts, if Lloyd's could pay out sufficient compensation? Would it not be better, as an insurer, to go somewhere else where the equity was not tied up in hundreds of what, after all, were only modest houses in the Shires and Home Counties?

Nigel's waistcoats had grown more outrageous. In the note-book lying in his breast pocket, the timetable of his digestion had been duly noted. 'Wind, 10.32. Bowel movement, 10.35.' The wine had made him sleepy and he was not paying attention.

Matt, greyer and more gaunt but just as sharp, was discussing with Louis the welcome development of corporate underwriting. A little sunburnt from sitting in the mountain café (while Becky skied the morning away) surrounded by the rich who had descended on Gstaad ('Euro-trash,' said Becky, 'I love 'em'), Louis was jotting down notes.

'You know, Matt,' he said, 'I think we might have trouble in store with the problem of organo-phosphates. I think we should look into them.'

As he left the restaurant, his mobile phone (which Becky had insisted he carried) shrilled.

'OK, darling,' she said. 'I want you to be a very good boy and just put your stamp on . . .'

That night, in the flat in Knightsbridge, Louis twitched in his sleep and groaned. Then he woke up properly. 'Hold me, Becky.'

Painfully, for she was very tired, she inched her way across the large double bed and held him until he was quiet.

And thus it was, in her way and, yes, with love, Becky paid her dues, for little by little, understanding had crept into her insufficient heart.

In its chrysalis, the butterfly dreaming of a past life when it soared, light and powder blue, into the sunlight, twitched its embryonic wings and was quiet.

I wonder what I have done?, ran the entry in Tess's diary. *What have I done?*

Meanwhile, the frost stole over the two graves in Appleford's churchyard and transformed the shared headstone into a tablet of ice.